Tales of Love, Lies, and Expectations

"The hardest thing in the world is to simplify your life. It's so easy to make it complex."

– Yvon Chouinard

This is a work of fiction. Similarities to real people, places, or events are entirely coincidental.

THE SHIFTING BALANCE

First edition. November 26, 2024.

Copyright © 2024 Hugo Raymond.

ISBN: 979-8230319832

Written by Hugo Raymond.

Table of Contents

The Shifting Balance 1
Chapter 1: The Fragile Foundation 2
Chapter 2: Silent Battles 62
Chapter 3: A House Divided 72
Chapter 4: Unraveling Truths 103
Chapter 5: The Burden of Choices 124
Chapter 6: In the Shadow of Lies 165
Chapter 7: The Breaking Point 244
Chapter 8: A New Beginning 257
Chapter 9: Crossroads 269
Chapter 10: The Shifting Balance 354

The Shifting Balance

Chapter 1: The Fragile Foundation

1. The Weight of Expectations

Sophia Collins stood by the window, her eyes scanning the bustling city outside. The glass was cold to the touch, but it didn't seem to matter. She had been staring at it for what felt like hours, lost in her thoughts. The weight of expectations hung heavily on her shoulders, a burden that had been there for as long as she could remember.

It wasn't just the pressure of her career, though that alone was enough to make anyone feel suffocated. No, it was the quiet, insistent pressure from every corner of her life. From the moment she had gotten married, there had been an unspoken expectation that she would balance it all—the career, the family, the image of a perfect life. Her husband, James, had always been supportive, but there was a constant undertone in his words. "Do you have time for us?" he'd ask, though always with a soft tone, never demanding. It was as if he didn't want to disrupt the fragile balance they had created, but she could hear it, all the same—the quiet resentment that came from feeling neglected.

And then there were the children. Isabella, or Izzy as she liked to be called, was now a teenager, full of opinions and dreams that were often at odds with Sophia's own. It was hard to reconcile the idea of being both a mother and a woman with her own aspirations. She had tried, so many times, to convince herself that she could be everything—everything everyone expected her to be. But deep down, she knew the truth: she was failing. She could never be perfect, and the world seemed to be growing more and more unforgiving with every passing day.

"How do I keep up?" she thought, her fingers lightly pressing against the glass. The city below was alive, vibrant, and full of possibility. Yet here she was, trapped in a cycle of trying to meet expectations that no one could truly define. They were vague, elusive, yet they weighed on her like an anchor pulling her deeper into the sea. Every decision, every choice, seemed to be measured against a standard she could never quite grasp.

Her thoughts drifted back to her childhood, to the lessons her parents had instilled in her. They had always told her that success came with sacrifice. "You can have it all, but it will cost you," her mother had said one evening, over dinner, her voice a mixture of weariness and pride. Sophia had believed that. She had embraced the idea of balancing everything, knowing it would be hard, but that was the price to pay for a good life, right?

But as the years had passed, Sophia began to feel something she hadn't anticipated—a deep, gnawing emptiness. No matter how much she accomplished at work, no matter how perfect the family seemed from the outside, there was always this quiet voice inside her that questioned whether it was worth it. Was the success truly fulfilling if it meant losing connection with the people she loved? Was her career worth the hollow feeling she got when she looked at her children and realized she wasn't fully present for them?

"How much longer can I keep pretending?" The thought crossed her mind, unbidden, and she felt a wave of sadness wash over her. It was easier to ignore it, to bury it beneath a mask of efficiency and composure. But it wasn't gone, not really. It was like a weight that pressed on her chest, a constant reminder that she was failing, even if no one else could see it.

Sophia turned away from the window and glanced at her reflection in the mirror across the room. She barely recognized the woman staring back at her. She had always been proud of her ability to juggle everything, to keep the balance intact. But now, as she saw the lines beneath her eyes and the faint tension in her jaw, she realized how fragile that balance had become.

She wasn't sure what to do next. The weight of expectations was suffocating, and for the first time, she questioned if she had ever truly chosen the path she was on, or if it had simply been laid out for her by others—by society, by her parents, by the people who expected so much from her.

Was it too late to make a change? Would anyone understand if she said she was tired of being everything to everyone?

Sophia took a deep breath and forced herself to focus. For now, there was no time to dwell on the questions. She had work to do, a family to take care of, and expectations to meet. But deep down, she knew one thing: the weight of those expectations could not be carried forever.

Sophia's fingers gripped the edge of the desk, her mind racing as she scanned the reports before her. The numbers blurred into one another, a mass of figures and percentages that felt increasingly irrelevant. She should have been focused, her sharp mind applying itself to the problem at hand, but all she could think about was the gnawing emptiness she felt inside. It was as though every success, every achievement, was hollowed out the moment it was reached, like trying to fill a cup with water that always slipped through the cracks.

Her phone buzzed, snapping her out of her thoughts. It was a message from James: *"Are you coming home early tonight? Izzy has an event at school, and I know she'd love for you to be there."*

Sophia stared at the message, a wave of guilt washing over her. How many times had she missed these events? How many times had she told herself that she was doing this for them, that the late nights, the long hours, were sacrifices she had to make? Yet, here she was, once again choosing work over her family.

She quickly typed a response, her fingers moving mechanically: *"I'll try. Can't promise, but I'll make it."*

Her heart sank as she hit send. She hated this. The constant tug-of-war between her professional life and her personal life. Each side demanding more, each side making her feel like she was failing in some way.

James had always been understanding, but she could see the quiet frustration building in his eyes. She'd seen it when they'd had dinner together just last week, when he'd asked, with an edge to his voice, "When was the last time we just sat down as a family, without distractions?" He didn't say it outright, but she knew what he meant. He was tired of the distance growing between them, tired of being with someone who was always just out of reach.

Her thoughts were interrupted by the sound of the office door opening. She looked up to see her assistant, Clara, standing in the doorway, her expression unsure.

"Ms. Collins, there's a call for you on line two. It's urgent," Clara said, her voice hesitant, as if she sensed something was off.

Sophia nodded absently and stood, already feeling the familiar weight of the phone call pressing on her. Work always found its way to her, no matter what she tried to focus on. It was the price of success, she reminded herself, though it did little to soothe the growing anxiety.

Taking the call, she settled back into her chair, trying to push aside the heaviness in her chest. The conversation lasted longer than she expected, filled with the usual back-and-forth of negotiations and deadlines. By the time it ended, Sophia felt drained, as though her energy had been siphoned away, leaving her hollow and exhausted.

She glanced at the clock. 6:30 p.m.

Izzy's event started in thirty minutes.

With a heavy sigh, Sophia closed her laptop, grabbed her purse, and headed for the door. She'd have to rush if she wanted to make it in time. But as she walked down the hall, she found herself slowing, her footsteps faltering. She had done this so many times before—dashed from work to make it to some family event, only to arrive late and disconnected. Always apologizing, always trying to make up for lost time with empty promises of being better next time.

Was there even a "next time"? She wasn't sure anymore.

When she finally stepped into the car, the weight of her decision hit her. She had chosen to leave work unfinished again. She had chosen to show up, even if she wasn't sure she could give her daughter the attention she deserved. And yet, a small voice inside her whispered that maybe this was the first step—choosing family over everything else, even if it was just for one night.

By the time she arrived at the school, the event was already in full swing. She could see Izzy from across the room, her daughter standing in a crowd of students, laughing with her friends. For a moment, Sophia just stood there, watching her, feeling a strange mix of pride and sadness. Izzy was growing up so quickly. She was becoming a person in her own right, and Sophia realized she had barely been there for her.

When Izzy spotted her, a smile spread across her face, and she made her way over. The moment their eyes met, Sophia felt a weight lift from her shoulders, just for a moment. This was why she had made the choice. This was why she had fought so hard against the tides of expectations.

"Mom!" Izzy exclaimed, her voice bright with excitement. "I'm so glad you came."

Sophia bent down, giving her daughter a hug. "I wouldn't miss it for the world," she whispered.

But inside, the question still lingered: *Was it too little, too late?*

Sophia stood there for a moment, enveloped in Izzy's embrace, feeling the warmth of her daughter's enthusiasm seep through her. It was a fleeting comfort, like a gentle reminder of everything that had been lost in the years of chasing success. As they pulled apart, Izzy's eyes sparkled with pride, her excitement palpable. For a second, Sophia allowed herself to bask in the feeling of being seen—really seen—as more than just the woman who provided, but as the mother she longed to be.

"I was hoping you'd be here," Izzy said, her voice softening, but with an edge of quiet expectation that only mothers could recognize. It wasn't just about showing up; it was about being present. Truly present. Sophia nodded, fighting the lump in her throat.

"I'm here now. That's what matters," she replied, her voice betraying none of the conflict swirling inside her.

They joined the group of parents and children gathered by the stage, listening to the speeches and the music. As the evening wore on, Sophia found herself half-listening to the chatter, her mind drifting back to her career, to the things she had left behind at the office. The pull to go back was like a distant hum, always there in the background, a constant reminder that there was always more to be done. But for the first time in a long time, the voice urging her to leave seemed quieter, almost drowned out by the sound of her daughter's laughter and the warmth of the moment.

Izzy had taken the stage to speak, her voice bright and full of confidence as she shared a story about her experiences over the past year. Sophia's heart swelled with pride, but also with a pang of regret. How many moments had she missed? How many milestones had she let slip by while she focused on everything but this?

As the event came to an end, Sophia pulled Izzy aside, wanting to spend a few more moments with her before they had to leave. "You were amazing up there," she said, ruffling her daughter's hair. Izzy's cheeks flushed with pride.

"Thanks, Mom. It means a lot that you came."

Sophia smiled, though the weight in her chest remained, unspoken and heavy. "I'll always come, Izzy. No matter what." The words felt like a promise, but deep down, she wasn't sure how much she could keep that promise. Life had a way of pulling her in a thousand directions, and she wasn't sure how much longer she could balance everything without losing herself completely.

As they drove home, the silence in the car was comfortable but thick. Izzy sat in the passenger seat, absorbed in her phone, while Sophia navigated the roads with practiced ease, her hands gripping the wheel.

"I know I haven't been around as much," Sophia finally said, her voice quiet, almost tentative. "But I'm trying. I really am."

Izzy looked up from her phone, her expression thoughtful. "I know, Mom. You're just... really busy." She hesitated before continuing, her voice softer now. "But I want you to be happy, too. Not just busy."

Sophia's heart ached at her daughter's words. It wasn't the first time Izzy had said something like that, but hearing it now, after everything, hit harder than she expected. *I want you to be happy, too.* The weight of those words, coming from someone so young, was almost unbearable. How had she missed the signs? How had she let her own happiness slip away in the pursuit of a life she thought she was supposed to want?

"I am happy, Izzy," she said, forcing a smile. "Just... sometimes it's hard to balance everything."

Izzy nodded, but there was a quiet understanding in her gaze, as though she knew more than Sophia had ever given her credit for.

When they arrived home, the house felt empty in a way that made Sophia's chest tighten. The house was the same as it had always been, but it no longer felt like the haven it once did. It was as though she had been living in a place, not a home, a space filled with things but lacking the warmth she once cherished.

She dropped her keys onto the kitchen counter and leaned against it, taking a deep breath. The weight of the past few years, the weight of her choices, was bearing down on her all at once. She had built a life that looked perfect from the outside, but inside, it was crumbling—held together by fragile threads of duty and expectation.

Her phone buzzed again, snapping her back to the present. This time, it was a message from James. *"We need to talk."*

The three words sent a chill down her spine. She had seen that message too many times, and each time, it was a harbinger of something that needed to be addressed. Something important. Something that couldn't be ignored any longer.

Sophia stood up straighter, setting her jaw as she walked toward the living room. She didn't know what this conversation would bring, but she knew one thing for sure: something had to change. And it had to start with her.

Sophia sat down on the edge of the couch, her phone still in her hand, the message from James flashing on the screen in front of her. The weight of it pressed on her chest, heavier than anything else in the room. She stared at it for a long moment before unlocking her phone and typing a response: *"What's going on?"*

The reply came almost immediately: *"Can we talk when you're ready? It's important."*

Sophia's mind raced. She knew that tone. It wasn't just a simple conversation; it was a turning point. Something had shifted between them recently. They hadn't been in sync for months, maybe longer, and this felt like the moment where the distance between them would finally become impossible to ignore.

She took a deep breath, trying to steady herself. The house was still, quiet except for the soft hum of the refrigerator in the kitchen. It felt like time itself was holding its breath, waiting for her to take the next step. She had been running on autopilot for so long, keeping everything together, but now, everything seemed to be unraveling at the edges. It wasn't just her relationship with James that felt fragile—it was everything. Her career. Her family. Her sense of self.

Sophia stood up, her fingers still clutched around her phone, and walked to the window. She looked out at the street below, watching the cars pass by, each one carrying someone, some unknown story, some unseen burden.

How did I get here? she wondered. How had she let herself slip so far from the woman she had once been? The woman who dreamed of a life filled with love and laughter, not schedules and sacrifices. She had allowed the weight of expectations—her own and others'—to define her. And in doing so, she had lost sight of the things that truly mattered.

Her thoughts were interrupted by a soft knock on the door. She knew it was James. No one else would come knocking at this hour.

She opened the door, and there he was, standing in the hallway, his face as familiar as the back of her hand, but somehow, it felt like a stranger's face now. The smile he gave her was strained, not quite reaching his eyes, and his posture was rigid, as if bracing himself for something.

"Hi," he said quietly, stepping inside without waiting for her to invite him in. His presence filled the space between them, but there was a noticeable distance in his gaze, a space that had never been there before.

"James," Sophia said, forcing herself to meet his eyes. "You wanted to talk."

He nodded, his expression unreadable. "Yeah. I think it's time we had a serious conversation about where we're headed."

The words stung more than she expected. *Where we're headed.* As though they were no longer a couple, no longer partners, but two separate entities drifting in different directions. She had known this day would come, but it didn't make it any easier.

"I've been thinking a lot," James continued, his voice lower now. "About everything. About us. And I don't know if we're... if we're still on the same page."

Sophia swallowed hard. *On the same page?* They hadn't been on the same page for so long, it felt like a distant memory.

"I don't know, either," she said softly, her voice betraying the weight of her emotions. "I've been trying, James. I've been trying to keep everything together. But... it feels like we're falling apart."

He ran a hand through his hair, looking at the floor as if he couldn't bear to look at her. "I've noticed, Soph. And I've tried, too. But it feels like no matter what I do, I'm just... I'm just here. I'm not the priority. And that hurts."

The words hit her like a punch to the gut. She had never intended for James to feel like that, but somewhere along the way, she had become so consumed by her own struggles that she had lost sight of him. Of *them*.

"I never wanted you to feel that way," she said, her voice cracking as she took a step closer to him. "I never wanted to make you feel invisible. But... I've been so caught up in everything, and I don't know how to balance it all anymore. I thought I could, but it's like... I'm drowning."

James met her eyes then, his expression softening slightly, though the hurt was still there, lingering in his gaze. "I can't keep doing this, Soph. I don't want to live in this constant state of uncertainty. It's not fair to either of us."

The words hung in the air, heavy with finality. Sophia's heart pounded in her chest, a painful truth settling inside her. She had known, deep down, that they were teetering on the edge, but hearing it spoken out loud made it all the more real.

She closed her eyes for a moment, taking a shaky breath. "I don't want to lose you, James. I don't want this to be the end."

He stepped forward, his hand gently touching her arm, his voice soft but firm. "Then something has to change. We both need to decide if we're willing to fight for this, or if we're just holding on because we're too afraid to let go."

The words echoed in her mind, louder than any of her doubts or fears. *Are we willing to fight for this?* Or were they already too far gone?

"I don't know if I can," Sophia whispered. "I don't know how much more I can give."

James nodded slowly, his expression a mixture of sorrow and understanding. "I get it. But we can't keep pretending everything is fine when it's not."

For a long moment, they stood in silence, both lost in their own thoughts, the weight of their conversation hanging between them like a storm cloud ready to break.

Finally, Sophia spoke, her voice barely above a whisper. "What do we do now?"

James looked at her, his eyes filled with something between resignation and hope. "We figure it out. Together. Or apart. But we can't keep pretending."

And just like that, everything shifted. The weight of expectations had become too much to bear, and now, they were left to decide if they could rebuild—or if the damage was irreparable.

Sophia's thoughts churned as she stood there, rooted to the spot. James's words echoed in her mind, reverberating like a distant drumbeat. *Together or apart.* The choice was no longer something they could ignore. It had come to this: a decision, a turning point that neither of them could avoid.

She glanced up at him, studying the way his shoulders sagged, the subtle tension in his jaw. He was still the man she had loved, the one who held her hand through tough times, the one who shared her dreams. But now, there was a wall between them. A wall built from years of unspoken words, miscommunications, and the slow erosion of trust.

"What if we can't fix it?" she asked quietly, the fear rising in her chest like a tidal wave. "What if we've already fallen too far apart to come back from this?"

James shook his head, a small sigh escaping his lips. "I don't want to believe that. I don't want to think we've reached the point of no return. But I can't keep pretending either. I don't think we're doing each other any good by holding on when we're both barely hanging on."

The truth stung. It was so simple, so painfully clear. They weren't the same people they had once been. They had changed, drifted, and while they could try to rekindle what they had, it wasn't guaranteed. They could try to rebuild, but that didn't erase the cracks that had already formed.

Sophia crossed her arms over her chest, not because she wanted to shield herself, but because she needed something to hold onto. She needed to feel something—anything—in this moment of uncertainty.

"I'm scared, James," she confessed, the vulnerability slipping out of her before she could stop it. "I'm scared of losing you, but I'm also scared of what comes after. What if we don't know how to be without each other? What if we destroy everything we've built?"

He looked at her, his gaze softening with understanding, though there was a sadness there, too. "I know you're scared. I am too. But we've been pretending for so long that everything's fine. The truth is, we're both lost, Soph. We're not the same people we were when we started. We've both changed, and maybe... maybe we need to find ourselves before we can figure out how to move forward."

She met his eyes, seeing the honesty in them, the rawness that matched her own heart. *He's right,* she thought, her chest tightening. *We've both changed.*

There was a long pause as they both stood in the quiet, neither one willing to speak the words that could fracture the fragile moment they were in. Neither one wanting to admit that they were at a crossroads.

Finally, Sophia spoke again, her voice softer now. "Maybe we've been trying to fit into roles we never really wanted in the first place. I've been trying so hard to be everything for everyone—wife, daughter, employee, friend—that I forgot who I really am. And I think... I think you've been doing the same."

James took a slow breath, nodding. "I've been so focused on keeping up appearances, on making sure everyone else thinks I've got it all together, that I forgot what really matters. And what really matters, Soph, is *us*. Not what we're supposed to be. Not what people expect us to be. But who we are, right now."

Her heart squeezed painfully in her chest. The realization hit her like a wave. It wasn't about fitting into some ideal of perfection or keeping up with the pressures of the world. It was about finding themselves again, together or apart, and allowing the space to be who they truly were without all the expectations.

Sophia let out a shaky breath, wiping away the single tear that had fallen down her cheek. "I've been so afraid of what this means," she said, her voice trembling. "Afraid of losing you. But I think... I think I've also been afraid of losing myself."

James reached out, his hand brushing against hers, a small but powerful gesture. "You're not going to lose yourself, Soph. We can figure this out. But we can't keep pretending we're okay if we're not. We have to face what's in front of us, no matter how hard it is."

The silence that followed was heavy but not entirely oppressive. For the first time in months, they weren't pretending. They weren't trying to fill roles or play parts. They were simply two people, standing in front of each other, raw and vulnerable, facing the truth of their situation.

"I don't know what's next for us," Sophia said quietly, her eyes meeting his. "But I want to figure it out. I don't want to let go without trying. I don't want to give up without knowing we've both given everything."

James nodded, a faint smile tugging at the corner of his lips. "We'll figure it out. Together. One step at a time."

Sophia took a deep breath, feeling the weight in her chest begin to ease. The uncertainty wasn't gone, but the heavy burden of pretending was lifting. They were at a crossroads, but for the first time in a long while, she felt like they were facing it as equals. They weren't perfect, but they were real. And maybe, that was enough.

The weight of expectations was still there, but it no longer felt suffocating. It was just a reminder that they had to decide what truly mattered in their lives—what they were willing to fight for.

And maybe, just maybe, they could find their way back to each other.

Sophia's heart felt lighter, though the uncertainty lingered like a shadow, ever-present and just out of reach. She couldn't deny that there was a sense of relief in acknowledging the truth. They weren't perfect, but neither was the world they lived in. It wasn't about achieving some unattainable standard. It was about being honest with each other—and themselves.

James's hand remained on hers, warm and reassuring, a simple gesture that held so much meaning. Their fingers intertwined, the connection grounding them in the midst of all the chaos they'd experienced.

"Do you think we've already decided what comes next?" Sophia asked, her voice barely above a whisper. She wasn't sure if she was asking James or herself. The decision seemed so monumental, yet in this moment, it felt like a fragile thread, something that could break with just a touch.

"I think we've already started making the choice," he replied, his voice steady but tinged with emotion. "We're facing it. That's the first step. The rest will come."

She nodded slowly, letting the words settle inside her. *The rest will come.* She wasn't sure if she believed it yet, but somehow, hearing him say it gave her hope. They didn't have to figure everything out in one day, one moment. They just had to start moving forward—together, or apart.

The quiet stretched between them, comfortable now, filled with the understanding that neither of them was alone in their uncertainty. It was no longer about pretending to be something they weren't, about meeting the world's expectations. It was about finding their way back to who they were, to what they needed from each other—and what they needed for themselves.

Sophia squeezed James's hand, a silent promise that she wasn't ready to give up just yet. They still had time. Time to heal, time to grow, time to rebuild. But it wasn't about forcing something that wasn't meant to be. It was about being honest with each other, even if that honesty was uncomfortable and raw.

As the minutes passed, the weight of expectations didn't feel quite as heavy. She could almost breathe again, feeling the pressure of always being "enough" slowly release its grip. She didn't have to be the perfect wife, the perfect daughter, the perfect woman. She just had to be herself.

James took a deep breath, his eyes meeting hers. "Whatever happens, I want you to know, I never stopped loving you. I never stopped wanting this—wanting us."

Her heart swelled at his words, and she smiled softly. "I know. I never stopped loving you either. But love is more than just words, James. It's actions. It's making choices, even when it's hard."

He nodded in agreement, his gaze unwavering. "Then let's make the right choice. Let's not let fear dictate our future."

Sophia's chest tightened, not with anxiety but with the realization that they were in this together, truly and fully. She had spent so much time fighting the pressure, fighting the expectation of what they should be, but now she could see it more clearly: it wasn't about living up to some ideal. It was about building something that was their own, something that wasn't defined by the world around them, but by their shared experiences, their shared love, and their willingness to face whatever came next.

She leaned in, brushing her lips against his, a gentle reminder that even in the uncertainty, there was still something worth fighting for. Something worth holding onto.

The kiss was soft, tentative at first, but it grew deeper, more sure, as they both gave into the moment—the moment that wasn't about expectations or perfection, but about love, real and raw.

When they finally pulled away, the world outside still loomed large, full of unknowns, but inside that room, inside this moment, they were just two people who had made a decision. They had chosen to face the weight of their lives, their expectations, and their love, with honesty.

Together.

And that, in itself, was a choice worth making.

The room, once filled with the silence of unspoken fears, now seemed to hum with a quiet kind of resolution. Sophia could feel the shift within her, something that had been lying dormant for so long, waiting for this exact moment to awaken. She wasn't sure what the future held, or how they would navigate the challenges that still loomed ahead, but she knew one thing for certain: the weight of expectations was no longer a force that controlled her every move. It was something she could carry with more strength, even with its weight still present.

James shifted next to her, his fingers lightly brushing against hers once more, bringing her back to the present. His eyes held a depth of understanding, as though he could feel the transformation happening between them, even without a word being spoken.

"I've been thinking," he began, his voice steady but soft, "about everything we've been through. About how hard it's been to live up to what others expect, what we expect of ourselves. I think that's been part of the problem all along."

Sophia turned to him, her expression thoughtful. "We've been so focused on what everyone else wants from us, that we forgot to ask ourselves what we truly need. What we really want. I'm not even sure I've ever fully allowed myself to think about that."

James gave a small, almost self-deprecating laugh. "Same here. I've been so busy trying to be what I thought you wanted, what I thought society expected, that I lost sight of the things that matter most."

She could hear the sincerity in his voice, and for the first time in a long while, it didn't feel like he was speaking out of obligation or guilt. It felt like a true moment of clarity for both of them. It was as if they had both shed layers of who they thought they should be, and were finally standing before each other as who they truly were.

Sophia smiled softly, feeling a warmth spread through her chest. "Maybe this is what we needed all along. Not to meet anyone else's expectations, but to find our own. Together."

James nodded, his face relaxed in a way she hadn't seen in a long time. "Exactly. We've been living in a world of 'shoulds' for too long. What if we just started living for ourselves, for each other, and stopped worrying about the rest?"

The simplicity of the idea struck her. It wasn't about grand gestures or monumental changes. It was about choosing each day to prioritize their relationship, their needs, over the noise of external pressure. It was about rediscovering their connection on their own terms, without the weight of everyone else's opinions suffocating them.

"I think we can do that," she whispered, more to herself than to him. But when she looked up at James, she saw a glimmer of something new in his eyes—hope, maybe, or perhaps something deeper.

"We can," he agreed firmly. "And no matter how hard it gets, we'll face it together. We'll find our way."

For a moment, they both sat in silence, the future ahead of them still uncertain but somehow lighter. The road they would travel wouldn't be easy, but it was theirs to walk. They had reclaimed their right to choose, to decide what their life, their love, would look like—without apologies, without the weight of expectations.

The kiss they shared after that moment was different from the first. It wasn't tentative or unsure; it was confident, filled with a promise of what was to come. It was a kiss that acknowledged the struggles they'd faced and the ones they still might face—but also one that spoke to their shared resolve to build something that would withstand it all.

As they pulled away, their foreheads resting together, the words "We're in this together" hung between them like a sacred vow, a silent understanding that no matter what challenges came next, they would face them as one.

The world outside hadn't changed. The weight of society's expectations still pressed down on them. But for the first time in a long while, Sophia felt free. Free to live, to love, and to define herself not by others' standards but by her own.

And, maybe for the first time, James felt it too. The freedom to be who they were, together, without fear of falling short.

They didn't need perfection. They just needed each other.

The days that followed felt different, as though the weight of expectations had dissolved into something more manageable. It was as if, by acknowledging the truth between them, they had unlocked a new chapter in their relationship—one where the constant pressure to conform, to fit into the mold of what was expected, was no longer the driving force.

They began to redefine what love meant, not as a duty to meet standards but as a shared commitment to understanding and growth. There were moments of hesitation, moments where the old fears crept back in, but they faced them together, side by side, no longer in silence but in honest conversation.

One evening, as they sat together on the porch, watching the sun set in a fiery blaze of colors, Sophia spoke again, the words coming to her almost instinctively. "James, do you ever wonder if we're truly enough? Just as we are, without trying to meet anyone's expectations?"

James glanced over at her, the weight of her question settling between them. He'd thought about it often, but hearing her voice it made the reality of their situation more palpable.

"I think," he began slowly, choosing his words carefully, "that for a long time, I believed we weren't enough. I believed that love—real love—had to be earned, that it required proving ourselves worthy over and over again. But now, with you, I'm starting to see that maybe we are enough. Maybe we've always been enough."

Sophia turned to look at him fully, searching his face for the sincerity she knew he was capable of. What she saw there wasn't just a man willing to work through the tough moments; it was a man who had come to accept that love, in its truest form, didn't demand perfection. It only demanded honesty and effort.

"I think so too," she whispered, her hand reaching for his. "I think we've spent too much time trying to measure up to some idea of what we should be. But maybe being enough is about accepting each other's flaws and loving each other in spite of them."

His hand wrapped around hers, and he squeezed it gently, as though offering her an unspoken promise that he would never stop choosing her.

"Maybe it's about loving ourselves, too," he added quietly. "Not just each other."

Sophia let the words sink in, realizing that he was right. They had spent so much time trying to meet external expectations, trying to mold themselves into something they weren't, that they had forgotten to love themselves. To appreciate who they were, as individuals, and not just as a couple.

She leaned her head against his shoulder, feeling a sense of peace settle over her. There was still a long road ahead, but for the first time in ages, the road didn't feel so daunting. It wasn't about perfection, or about being the right version of themselves—it was about embracing the journey, with all its messiness and its beauty.

"I think we're finally starting to get it, James," she said, her voice light, as though a burden had been lifted from her chest.

He nodded, his gaze fixed on the horizon. "I think so too. It's not about finding the perfect love. It's about finding the love that's real. That's enough."

And in that moment, as the world around them faded into the golden light of the evening, they understood that their love was not about meeting expectations or living up to ideals. It was about learning to be enough for each other, and most importantly, for themselves.

The road ahead would still be challenging, but now it didn't feel impossible. They were stronger together, not because they were perfect, but because they had chosen to love each other, flaws and all.

And for the first time, Sophia realized that the greatest gift of all was not in trying to meet the world's expectations, but in accepting that they were enough, just as they were.

As the weeks passed, the quiet moments of connection between Sophia and James began to weave a fabric of trust that felt stronger than any pressure from the outside world. They no longer worried about the roles they were supposed to play, or the standards they were expected to meet. Instead, they focused on what was real—their shared dreams, their mutual respect, and the simple, profound act of being present for each other, no matter what.

Their conversations, once strained by unspoken fears, became deeper and more vulnerable. The more they opened up to each other, the more they discovered not just new facets of each other, but of themselves. The weight of expectations had once suffocated them, but now, they were learning to breathe again, together.

One evening, as the first chill of autumn set in, they took a walk through the park, their hands intertwined. The crisp air seemed to sharpen their senses, and for a moment, the world around them felt perfectly still.

Sophia glanced up at the sky, her breath forming small clouds in the cool evening air. "Do you ever wonder," she asked softly, her voice barely above a whisper, "how we ever got caught up in all those expectations? How we let them control us for so long?"

James looked ahead, his expression contemplative. "I think it's easy to get lost in them. The world is constantly telling us who we should be, what we should want, how we should live. It's hard to see beyond it, to find our own truth."

Sophia nodded, feeling the weight of his words. "I've spent so much of my life trying to be what everyone else wanted me to be. I thought I had to be perfect—perfect in my career, in my relationships, in every part of my life. But the more I tried, the more I lost myself."

James stopped walking and turned to face her, his hands resting on her shoulders. "I've been there too. We've both been there, trying to fit into these boxes that we didn't even choose. But I think we've started to find a new way, haven't we?"

Her eyes met his, and for the first time in what felt like forever, she felt completely understood. "We have," she agreed, her voice steady now. "We're not perfect, and that's okay. We don't have to be."

James smiled, a slow, knowing smile that made her heart skip a beat. "You know, I think that's what makes us perfect for each other. We're imperfect, but we're real. We're learning to be who we truly are, and that's all I ever wanted."

Sophia felt a warmth spread through her chest, a feeling of belonging that she hadn't known in a long time. "I never thought I'd hear someone say that and actually mean it."

He chuckled softly. "Well, maybe that's the thing. We've been so busy trying to be something we're not, that we never realized who we already are is enough. It always has been."

The words hung in the air between them, a revelation that felt almost like a quiet epiphany. Sophia let out a breath she hadn't realized she'd been holding. It was as though something had shifted in her, some heavy, unseen burden had been lifted, and for the first time in a long time, she felt truly free.

"I think you're right," she said softly. "We don't need to be anyone else. We just need to be ourselves. Together."

James nodded, his expression warm and assured. "Exactly."

And with that, they continued walking, side by side, not in search of anything else but the simple pleasure of each other's company. The world around them seemed to fade into the background, as if it no longer mattered. The weight of external expectations, once so consuming, no longer had the power to dictate the course of their lives.

Their future was still uncertain, but it no longer felt daunting. It felt like a journey worth taking, one step at a time, on their own terms.

The freedom they had found in each other was enough to carry them forward, and that was all they needed.

As autumn deepened, the world around them transformed. The leaves turned to shades of amber and gold, the air grew colder, and the nights longer. Yet, inside their home, a warmth seemed to radiate, not from the hearth but from the bond they were quietly building.

In the days that followed, they began to build new routines, ones that didn't hinge on meeting anyone's expectations, but rather on creating a space where they could both thrive. Sophia found herself waking up early to walk in the park before work, something she had always wanted to do but had never allowed herself. James started picking up new hobbies, things he had once dismissed as frivolous, but which now seemed like a way to reconnect with the parts of himself he had neglected. Together, they made time for the things that truly mattered—long dinners with no rush, walks in the rain, mornings spent lingering over coffee.

Their conversations took on a new depth. It wasn't just about their hopes and dreams anymore; it was about their fears, their regrets, and the places where they still felt broken. They spoke of their childhoods, of the ways they had been shaped by their families, their expectations, and their own internalized ideals of what it meant to be successful, loved, or worthy.

"Sometimes I feel like I'm still trying to prove myself," Sophia confessed one evening, her voice soft but clear, as they sat on the couch together, a blanket draped over their laps.

James didn't respond right away, as if weighing her words. "Prove yourself to who?" he asked finally, his tone gentle but insistent.

She took a deep breath. "I don't even know anymore. To everyone? To myself? I guess I've spent so much time trying to be someone other people could admire, that I forgot to ask myself what I really want."

James turned to face her, his gaze steady. "And what do you want, Sophia?"

The question hung between them, unspoken for a moment, as if it required more than just words to answer. She thought about it, then slowly, almost hesitantly, she spoke.

"I want peace. I want to feel like I'm enough as I am. Without the pressure, without pretending to be something I'm not."

James reached for her hand, his touch warm, grounding. "You are enough, Sophia. You always have been."

Her eyes filled with tears, not of sorrow, but of release, as if the simple act of being seen, truly seen for who she was, allowed her to let go of years of unspoken burdens.

"I don't know what it was that kept me from believing that," she whispered, squeezing his hand back. "But I think I'm starting to."

James smiled softly, a sense of quiet contentment settling in his chest. "And I'm here, no matter what. You don't need to prove anything to me."

They sat in silence for a while, the weight of the conversation settling, but this time, it wasn't heavy. It was freeing. They were both learning to shed the need for validation, learning to embrace who they truly were, flaws and all.

Over time, the changes they had made in their relationship began to ripple out into other areas of their lives. James started saying no to things that drained him, things he had once done out of obligation. He realized he didn't need to please everyone, and that his own peace of mind was just as important as the expectations others had for him.

Sophia, too, began to set boundaries with her family, with her career, and even with herself. She realized that she couldn't continue to live for others, not when doing so left her feeling exhausted and disconnected from her true self. It wasn't about being selfish; it was about being self-aware enough to know when something wasn't serving her well-being.

And, as the holidays approached, they found themselves planning the first Thanksgiving they would spend without the usual pressures of family expectations. It was a quiet affair, just the two of them, cooking together in the kitchen, laughing over burned biscuits and enjoying the simplicity of being in each other's company without the need to impress or perform.

That evening, as they sat down to dinner, James raised his glass to her. "To us. To being enough. To finding peace, finally."

Sophia smiled, the warmth of the moment filling her heart. "To us," she echoed. "To being real."

They clinked their glasses, the sound echoing softly in the quiet room. It wasn't about grand gestures or achieving some ideal. It was about finding each other in the messiness of life, accepting themselves and each other, and realizing that they didn't need to measure up to anyone else's standards but their own.

In that moment, Sophia knew that whatever came next, they were ready. They had each other, and they had the freedom to be who they truly were.

And for the first time, she felt like she could truly breathe.

As the year drew to a close, the weight of expectations, which had once dominated their lives, felt almost foreign. Sophia and James had crafted something that was their own—a quiet, but powerful existence built on understanding, freedom, and mutual respect. They had not solved all their problems, nor had they erased all their insecurities, but they had created a foundation of trust that allowed them to navigate the complexities of life with more ease.

They no longer feared failure, nor did they chase after the perfection they once thought was necessary. They embraced each day as it came, and with each passing moment, their bond deepened.

One cold December evening, after a long day, they found themselves wrapped in blankets on the couch, a fire crackling in the hearth. It was the kind of evening where the world outside seemed distant, and the warmth inside cocooned them in a sense of safety and contentment.

James leaned back, staring at the flames, lost in thought. "You know," he said after a long silence, "I never thought I'd find peace. Not like this."

Sophia looked up from the book she had been reading, her eyes soft. "What do you mean?"

He glanced at her, a small smile tugging at the corners of his lips. "I thought peace was something you earned. Something you had to work for. But now, I'm realizing it's something you create, with the right people, in the right moments."

Sophia nodded slowly, letting his words sink in. "I used to think peace meant everything falling into place, like some kind of perfect picture. But now, I think it's more about acceptance. Accepting who we are, where we are, and where we're headed."

"Exactly," James agreed. "It's about being content with the journey, not just the destination. And sharing that journey with someone who gets it."

She smiled, feeling a warmth spread through her chest. "I never thought it would be this simple, but it really is."

There was a long pause, filled only with the soft crackling of the fire. For once, it wasn't uncomfortable. It was a quiet acknowledgment of how far they had come, and how much they had grown, both individually and as a couple.

"Do you ever think about the future?" Sophia asked quietly, breaking the silence.

James turned to her, meeting her gaze with an intensity that spoke volumes. "All the time. But now, it feels different. I don't feel like I have to control it anymore. I just want to take it one day at a time, with you by my side."

Sophia felt a flutter in her chest, the kind of feeling that came when you knew, deep down, that you had found something worth holding on to. "I feel the same," she whispered. "The future feels uncertain, but for the first time, I'm not scared of it."

James reached for her hand, intertwining their fingers. "We'll face it together, whatever comes. And we'll keep creating the peace we've found, no matter what happens."

Sophia squeezed his hand, feeling a sense of peace wash over her. It was a peace that didn't depend on external factors, but one that came from within. From the trust they had built, the love they shared, and the understanding that they didn't need to conform to anyone's expectations but their own.

The world outside might be chaotic, unpredictable, and filled with its own pressures, but inside this space they had created, there was nothing but calm.

As they sat together, the fire slowly dying down, they knew that whatever challenges lay ahead, they were ready to face them—together, with open hearts and minds.

They had learned to release the weight of expectations, and in doing so, had found the kind of freedom and peace that only comes when you allow yourself to be truly seen and loved for who you are.

And in that quiet room, amidst the fading light of the fire, they both realized that this—what they had built, what they had discovered—was enough.

It always had been.

As the new year began, the world outside had shifted once again. The weight of the past seemed lighter now, like a distant echo, fading as each day brought a new beginning. Yet, for all the changes, one thing remained constant: their shared commitment to a future built on understanding, trust, and authenticity.

Sophia and James had learned not just to accept each other's flaws but to embrace them as part of the whole. They no longer sought to change the other into something they weren't. Instead, they had learned the art of compromise, the beauty of silence shared, and the peace that came from not constantly striving for perfection.

One crisp January morning, the couple woke early to catch the sunrise. They stood side by side, their breath misting in the cold air, watching as the first light of the day slowly painted the sky in shades of pink and orange. The quiet of the morning wrapped around them like a soft blanket, and for a few moments, they simply stood in each other's presence, allowing the beauty of the moment to sink in.

Sophia, her hand resting gently on James's arm, finally spoke. "Do you ever think about how much we've changed?"

James turned toward her, a small, contented smile on his lips. "Every day," he said softly. "But it doesn't scare me anymore. I think change is just part of it—part of us. We've both grown in ways I didn't expect."

Sophia nodded. "Me too. I used to feel like I was always running from something, always trying to outrun my mistakes or my fears. But now... now I feel like I'm walking with them. And somehow, that makes it easier."

James squeezed her hand. "That's the peace we've been searching for. The moment you stop fighting everything, the moment you stop pretending, that's when everything starts to fall into place. And even the mistakes, the fears—they're part of it. Part of us."

She smiled, her heart swelling with affection for him. It wasn't about getting everything right. It wasn't about being flawless or achieving a perfect life. It was about walking the path together, with open eyes and hearts that were willing to accept the beauty and the pain of the journey.

As they stood there, watching the sun rise higher into the sky, something shifted within Sophia. She realized that, for the first time in her life, she wasn't afraid to be herself. She wasn't afraid to be imperfect, to be a work in progress. She wasn't afraid of failure, because she knew now that failure wasn't the end—it was simply another step in the process of becoming.

James looked at her, his gaze thoughtful, then added, "I think we've finally learned what it means to live without the weight of others' expectations. We've given ourselves the freedom to be."

Sophia's heart fluttered with the truth of his words. They had come so far, not just from where they had started but from the versions of themselves they had once been, bound by old fears and dreams that weren't their own.

She squeezed his hand in return, then turned to face the horizon, her voice steady and full of promise. "And we'll keep living that way. For us. For who we truly are."

James nodded, his eyes following hers to the edge of the world where the sky and earth met. It felt like a new chapter was unfolding before them, a chapter where the weight of expectations would no longer dictate the pace or direction of their lives.

They had discovered that love wasn't about meeting someone's ideal, but about embracing the reality of who they were together—their shared moments, their quiet victories, their laughter, their struggles, their imperfections. They had found the peace they had been searching for, not in the distant future, but in the present, in each other, in the simple, beautiful act of being real.

As they turned to leave the hilltop, walking back to the warmth of their home, the world around them felt full of possibilities. Whatever the future held, they knew they would face it together, no longer bound by the weight of expectations, but free to live their truth, side by side.

The journey wasn't over, but it no longer felt daunting. It felt like a new beginning.

And for the first time, they were both ready to embrace whatever came next.

2. Behind Closed Doors

THE HOUSE WAS SILENT, save for the soft hum of the refrigerator in the kitchen and the occasional rustle of paper as James flipped through his work files in the study. Outside, the world continued, oblivious to the quiet storms brewing behind the closed doors of the Collins family home. Inside, there were no loud arguments or dramatic confrontations—only the subtle, almost invisible tensions that had taken root over the years. The walls, decorated with carefully chosen family portraits and framed memories, hid the unspoken truths that neither Sophia nor James dared to confront.

Sophia sat in the living room, her gaze fixed on the window, watching as the last light of day slowly faded into dusk. The house, a symbol of their years together, felt colder now, even though it had once been a place of warmth and laughter. It wasn't just the fading light or the crisp evening air; it was the absence of connection, the distance that had slowly crept between her and James. Once, they had been partners in everything, sharing dreams and challenges. Now, the silence between them spoke volumes—each unspoken word, each unfinished conversation, built a barrier that neither knew how to break.

She had tried, many times, to bridge the gap. But it always seemed like there was something more important, something urgent pulling James away from her. The constant demands of his job, the endless meetings and deadlines, had consumed him. And in the rare moments when he was home, he was always distant, wrapped in his thoughts, his mind far away from the family he had once been so present for. She missed the man he had been—the one who would smile at her across the dinner table, the one who would pull her close after a long day, the one who would laugh with her until the world felt lighter. But that man had disappeared, and in his place was a shadow—someone who seemed to exist only to fulfill his role, to meet expectations, to keep up appearances.

Sophia's heart ached as she thought of the distance between them. She had tried to talk to him about it, tried to open up about her fears, her frustrations, but the words always got stuck in her throat. There was no room for vulnerability in their relationship anymore. The door had closed on that part of their lives, and they had both quietly accepted it, unwilling to confront the painful reality that they had drifted so far apart.

In the kitchen, James poured himself a glass of wine, his movements mechanical, almost absent. He hadn't noticed Sophia's absence from the dinner table. He hadn't noticed much of anything lately. His mind was consumed by work, by the endless pressure to perform, to succeed. It was easier that way, to lose himself in the demands of the outside world than to face the uncomfortable truths at home. The weight of his own guilt pressed on him, but he pushed it aside, burying it under layers of denial. It was easier than admitting that something was wrong, that his marriage, his family, was unraveling at the seams.

He took a long sip of the wine, letting it coat his mouth, the bitterness a reminder of how far things had fallen. He had no answers, no solutions. Just a quiet, growing awareness that the life he had built, the life he had always dreamed of, was slipping through his fingers. But what could he do? What could he say? The doors between him and Sophia had closed long ago, and he didn't know how to open them again.

Outside, the night deepened, the stars shining in the sky like distant promises. Inside, the house remained still, a silent witness to the unraveling of a once-beautiful life. Behind closed doors, Sophia and James were both searching for something they had lost, both longing for a connection they couldn't quite reach. And though they sat in the same house, shared the same space, their hearts were miles apart.

3. The Illusion of Perfection

SOPHIA STOOD AT THE edge of the room, her fingers lightly grazing the sleek surface of the polished dining table. The house was immaculate, every corner carefully curated, the air tinged with the scent of freshly cleaned hardwood. It was a picture of tranquility, a display of everything she had worked so tirelessly to create. And yet, beneath the surface, something felt off—something she couldn't quite name, but that lingered like a shadow in the corners of her mind.

The walls, adorned with family portraits and soft hues, told a story of success and happiness. To the outside world, the Collins family was the epitome of balance—she and James, the ideal couple; their children, bright and ambitious. Yet in the quiet moments, when no one was watching, the cracks began to show.

Sophia couldn't remember the last time she and James had truly spoken—beyond the logistics of daily life, the endless stream of tasks, the planning. They had become skilled at pretending, at creating an image of harmony. They smiled at each other over dinner, exchanged polite pleasantries, but their eyes no longer met with the warmth they once held. The love that had once been so vibrant now felt distant, like an old photograph fading with time.

She often wondered if it had been her ambition that had done this—her need to climb higher, to prove herself not just as a mother and wife, but as someone capable of more. The promotions, the recognition at work, the accolades—all had come at a cost. The time she spent in meetings, the late nights in front of the computer screen, the constant juggling of responsibilities had chipped away at something that was once solid, once meaningful. She had been so focused on achieving perfection in the external world, she hadn't realized how much she was losing inside her own home.

James, too, had changed. He had always been the steady one, the anchor. But now, he seemed more distant, more resigned to the roles he had to play. It was as if he had retreated into a shell, his emotions buried beneath a facade of duty. They had both become experts at maintaining appearances, keeping up with the expectations of others, while quietly wondering if they had traded their happiness for an image that didn't truly fit them.

And then there were the children—Izzy, who had always been so full of promise and potential, now seemingly distant, her own expectations of life shifting as she grappled with the pressure of being the perfect child in a perfect family. And Ethan, the youngest, so often lost in his thoughts, as though he were watching the world around him and wondering where he fit in it all.

It was easy, almost comforting, to pretend that everything was fine. The illusion of perfection was a shield they all held up, protecting themselves from the vulnerabilities that lay beneath. But the longer they lived within the walls of their own creation, the more it became clear: perfection wasn't the answer. It never had been.

Sophia could feel it now, that tension—like a taut string about to snap. She had built this life, but at what cost? She looked at the faces around her, the ones she loved most, and realized that they had all been living for an image, not for each other. And that image, no matter how carefully crafted, was nothing more than an illusion. The real work, the real connection, was something they had all neglected in the pursuit of perfection.

For a moment, she allowed herself to stop pretending, to feel the weight of the truth. The house, the family, the life—they were all just pieces of a puzzle she had tried to fit together. But no matter how perfect the pieces seemed on their own, they never truly belonged together. The illusion had been shattered, and now, the question was: could they rebuild something real, something imperfect but true?

Sophia didn't have the answer yet, but she knew one thing for certain: it was time to stop pretending.

Sophia stood there for a long moment, the weight of her thoughts heavy in the stillness. Her mind raced, yet she could barely hold onto any single thought. The room, so perfectly arranged, seemed to mock her, a constant reminder of the walls she had built, both literally and metaphorically. The weight of expectations—society's, her own—had pressed down on her for so long that she had forgotten what it felt like to breathe without them.

She turned slowly toward the kitchen, where the soft hum of the refrigerator was the only sound. It had become a refuge for her lately, a place where she could retreat, even if only for a few minutes, and gather her thoughts. But today, it felt different. The clinking of the glass as she poured herself a drink, the slight chill of the counter under her hands—it all felt so real, so raw in a way that the rest of her life had not been for years.

Her reflection in the window was clearer now, and she saw it all—the lines on her face that had been painted over with makeup for years, the eyes that had once sparkled with excitement now dull with fatigue. She had let this happen, let the illusion of perfection take hold. She had convinced herself that if everything looked right on the outside, maybe it would all be okay on the inside too. But now she understood—nothing could be more untrue.

As she sipped the cool drink, she thought back to the early days with James. The way they had talked for hours without the need for interruptions, their plans for the future feeling endless, the laughter shared in the small moments. But somewhere along the way, they had started filling the gaps with work, with schedules, with obligations. The promises made between them had slowly turned into routines. They had become like actors, playing roles rather than living authentically.

James had once been her partner in everything. Now, he seemed like a stranger who shared the same space, but not the same life. She wondered if he too had felt the weight of the unspoken truth between them, but had been too afraid to address it. Perhaps he was waiting for her to speak first, just as she had waited for him. But both of them were locked in a silent standoff, each afraid that breaking the illusion would mean breaking everything else.

Her phone buzzed on the counter, a text from James: *"Dinner at 7? I'll be home late."*

It was a simple message, one that spoke volumes in its emptiness. Dinner at 7. As though they were simply two people, meeting for a meal, not a couple struggling to reconnect. She stared at the message for a moment, her finger hovering over the screen, unsure of what to say. What could she say that would change anything?

She had no answers. The illusion of perfection had promised that they would always find their way, that love would prevail, that everything would fall into place. But now, she realized, it was the very thing that had kept them apart, trapped in a world of appearances and expectations.

As the evening sun began to set outside, casting long shadows across the room, Sophia finally understood. Perfection wasn't about how things looked—it was about how they felt. And right now, everything felt wrong.

There was no simple way to fix it. No easy answer. But maybe, just maybe, the first step was acknowledging the truth. The truth that things were broken, but that was okay. Maybe it was time to stop pretending.

Sophia took a deep breath, setting the phone down. She wasn't sure what tomorrow would bring, but she knew one thing: she wasn't going to hide behind the illusion anymore.

It was time to face the mess. To start rebuilding.

Later that evening, as Sophia set the table for one, she couldn't help but think about the masks they all wore—hers, James's, the children's. Everyone had their roles to play, each of them trying to live up to an image of who they were supposed to be. But the cracks were becoming more evident, and no matter how much they polished their lives, the foundation was crumbling.

She caught herself in the reflection of the kitchen window, setting the last place setting—a silent dinner that had become far too familiar over the past few months. A sad realization hit her: the perfect dinner, the perfect home, the perfect family—it was all a lie. A lie they had convinced themselves was the truth because it was easier to live in denial than to confront the reality of their dissatisfaction.

The door creaked open just as she was placing the final fork on the table. James entered, his tie still slightly askew from the long day. He glanced at the table, his eyes scanning the empty chair across from him, and for a brief moment, there was a flicker of something in his gaze—regret, maybe. Or resignation.

"You're home late," Sophia said softly, though her tone betrayed the weight of unspoken words.

James gave a small nod, removing his coat and hanging it on the hook. "Yeah, I know. I had a last-minute meeting. You know how it goes."

He didn't look at her, didn't ask how her day had gone, didn't offer anything that hinted at the connection they once had. It wasn't even the lack of affection that stung—it was the indifference, the quiet distance that had settled between them like a thick fog.

She swallowed the bitter taste in her mouth and sat down. "I know how it goes," she said quietly, her voice barely audible over the clink of silverware as she began to serve the meal.

The silence stretched on between them as they ate, the sounds of chewing and utensils clattering on plates the only noise. It was as if they were both waiting for something—waiting for an acknowledgment, a gesture, some sign that they were still capable of breaking through the walls they had built around themselves. But neither of them spoke. Neither of them made the first move.

When the meal was finished, James pushed his plate away and sighed deeply. "Sophia, I—" He hesitated. There was something in his voice, an edge to it, something raw that she hadn't heard in months. "I don't know what's happening to us anymore."

Sophia's heart skipped a beat. Was he finally ready to confront the truth, to speak the words she had been silently yearning to hear? Or was this just another empty attempt to pretend they could fix something that had already been broken?

She looked at him, her gaze softening. "I don't know either," she admitted. "But I think we've been pretending for too long. I can't keep up the act, James. I can't keep pretending that everything's fine when it's not."

James looked down at his hands, his fingers twisting nervously around the edge of his glass. "I don't know what's happened to us. We used to be... different. We used to talk, laugh, share things. And now... now it's just routine. We've fallen into this pattern, and I don't know how to get out of it."

Sophia felt a pang of sorrow for him, for them. She had spent so much time focusing on maintaining the illusion, on keeping everything looking perfect for the outside world, that she had failed to notice the disconnection growing between them. It wasn't just the lack of intimacy—it was the lack of communication, the absence of understanding.

"I don't know how to get out of it either," she whispered, the weight of the admission heavy in her chest. "But we have to try. I don't want to keep living like this. It's exhausting."

James didn't respond right away, but after a moment, he met her eyes. "So what do we do now?"

Sophia paused, the question hanging in the air like a fragile thread. She wasn't sure if there was an easy answer, if there was even a way back to what they had once been. But she knew that they couldn't go on pretending. The illusion had been shattered, and now it was up to them to decide whether they could rebuild what had been lost, or whether it was time to let go.

"I think we start by being honest with each other," she said softly, her voice trembling with the uncertainty of what that might mean. "No more pretending, no more hiding behind the image of who we're supposed to be. Just... us. The way we are."

James took a deep breath, and for the first time in what felt like forever, a small, genuine smile tugged at the corners of his mouth. "I think I can do that," he said.

It wasn't a promise. Not yet. But it was a beginning.

As they cleared the table in silence, the weight of the evening seemed to lift, if only a little. There was still so much work to be done, so much pain to confront. But for the first time in a long time, Sophia felt a flicker of hope. The illusion of perfection had been stripped away, and in its place, there was something raw, something real.

And maybe, just maybe, that was enough to start over.

4. The First Crack

SOPHIA STOOD IN THE kitchen, the hum of the refrigerator the only sound breaking the quiet. The morning light filtered through the blinds, casting long shadows across the counter. She had become accustomed to the solitude of these moments, the calm before the storm of the day's responsibilities. The children were at school, and James was already at work. The house felt like a shell, empty yet suffocating, as if it were holding its breath, waiting for something—anything—to break the monotony.

She stirred her coffee absentmindedly, watching the steam curl up, wondering how much longer she could maintain the facade of a perfect life. The image she had carefully crafted over the years was starting to crack at the edges. The once-clear lines of her ambition and her marriage were beginning to blur, leaving her to wonder if it was all worth it.

For years, Sophia had strived to be everything to everyone. The perfect wife, the perfect mother, the perfect professional. But somewhere along the way, she had lost sight of herself. She had become a reflection of what others expected her to be, trapped in a role that no longer fit. Her career had soared, but at what cost? Her relationship with James, once full of shared dreams and quiet understanding, had shifted. They no longer spoke the same language. They had become strangers, living side by side, but not truly living together.

James had always been the steady one, the rock. He was the one who kept the world from spinning off its axis when things got tough. But even he, with all his strength, had begun to show signs of wear. He was distant, withdrawn, a shadow of the man she once knew. Was it the years of sacrifice, the pressure to provide, or something deeper, something unspoken that had driven them apart?

Sophia's thoughts were interrupted by the sound of the doorbell. She startled, then sighed, already knowing who it was. It was Izzy, their daughter, home earlier than usual.

"Mom?" Izzy's voice drifted in from the entryway, tense and uncertain.

Sophia put down her coffee cup, her heart sinking. She hadn't been prepared for this. She had hoped for a moment of peace, a break from the mounting tension that had settled over their family. But there was no escaping it now. The crack that had formed between her and James had grown wider, and now it seemed like Izzy had noticed, too.

Sophia stood up, smoothing the front of her blouse, and walked toward the door. Izzy was standing in the hallway, her arms crossed, her face a mask of concern. It wasn't the first time that Sophia had seen that expression on her daughter's face, but it had never felt so heavy before.

"Mom, we need to talk," Izzy said, her voice small but firm.

Sophia nodded slowly, her stomach tightening. She had a sinking feeling that this conversation would be the beginning of something much bigger than either of them could handle. The first crack had appeared, and there was no telling how deep it would go.

As they sat down together, the silence between them stretched, heavy with unspoken truths. Sophia could feel the weight of the years bearing down on her. She had been so focused on holding everything together, on keeping up the appearances, that she had forgotten the most important part of the equation—her family.

"Mom, I know things haven't been right between you and Dad," Izzy began, her voice breaking the silence like the first raindrop before a storm. "I don't know what's going on, but it's affecting all of us."

Sophia's throat tightened. She had hoped that her children were too young to notice the growing distance between her and James, but Izzy was perceptive, just like her father. She had always been the one to pick up on the smallest details, the quiet shifts in the air. And now, it seemed that she had finally connected the dots.

"Izzy, it's not what you think," Sophia started, but the words felt hollow, empty.

"I'm not stupid, Mom," Izzy interrupted, her voice sharper than Sophia had ever heard it before. "I see the way you and Dad avoid each other, the way you both act like everything's fine when it's not. It's like you're both pretending."

Sophia's heart clenched. The truth was out, and it stung more than she had anticipated. She had tried to shield her children from the cracks in their marriage, but it seemed the damage was already visible.

"I'm sorry, Izzy," she whispered, her voice barely audible. "I never wanted you to see this."

Izzy's expression softened for a moment, but the hurt was still there. "I just want things to be normal again, Mom. I want you and Dad to be happy. I don't want to feel like I have to choose between you."

The words hit Sophia like a punch to the gut. Her daughter was right. She had become so absorbed in her own struggles that she had failed to see how it was affecting her family. How long had Izzy been carrying this burden? How long had she felt torn between two people who couldn't seem to hold it together?

The silence between them stretched again, this time filled with a weight of regret and unspoken fears. Sophia knew that things couldn't stay the way they were. The cracks were deepening, and the only way to stop the fracture from spreading was to face the truth—no matter how painful it might be.

It wasn't just about her anymore. It wasn't just about her career or her marriage. It was about the family that had been built on love, and the love that was now slipping through her fingers.

Sophia took a deep breath, looking at her daughter with a new understanding. The first crack had appeared, and now it was up to her to decide whether to repair it or let it break wide open.

Sophia sat in the silence that followed, the weight of her daughter's words hanging in the air like a thick fog. She wanted to reassure Izzy, to tell her that everything would be fine, that this was just a phase, but deep down, she knew it wasn't that simple. The cracks in their family had been growing for months, if not years. She had ignored them, hoping they would heal on their own, but the truth was, they had only spread.

Her mind flashed to the early days of her relationship with James, when everything had seemed so effortless. They had been a team, partners in life and love, navigating the world together with the same shared vision. But over time, the world had changed, and so had they. Their ambitions had pulled them in different directions. The connection they once had seemed to fade, replaced by routine, then silence, and finally, the void that now stretched between them.

"Mom?" Izzy's voice cut through her thoughts. Sophia turned to see her daughter's concerned face, her brow furrowed in worry.

"I'm sorry, Izzy," Sophia said again, her voice thick with emotion. "I didn't mean for you to feel this way. I didn't want you to have to carry this burden."

Izzy shook her head, her eyes softening. "It's not your fault, Mom. It's just... hard. I don't want to lose you both. I don't want things to stay like this."

Sophia nodded slowly. She didn't want that either. She didn't want her daughter to grow up with the same sense of dread, the same undercurrent of tension that had begun to plague their home. But she also didn't know how to fix it. How do you repair something that has been broken for so long, something that felt too fragile to hold together?

"I don't know what's happening between your dad and me, but I'm going to try," Sophia said, her voice filled with a quiet determination. "I promise, I'll try to figure this out. I won't let it destroy us."

Izzy didn't respond immediately. She seemed to study her mother, as if searching for any hint of doubt in her words. Then, after a long pause, she finally nodded. "I just want to see you both happy again, Mom. I don't want us to be a family of strangers."

The simplicity of her daughter's words hit Sophia harder than anything else. They weren't asking for perfection. They were asking for connection. For love. For the kind of family that didn't hide behind masks, behind false smiles and pretenses.

Sophia stood up slowly, brushing a stray lock of hair from her face. She felt exhausted, both physically and emotionally, but there was a new clarity within her. For too long, she had been so focused on appearances, on maintaining the perfect family portrait that she had neglected the heart of it. The truth was, the cracks weren't just in her marriage—they were in the very foundation of her life.

"Izzy, thank you," Sophia said, her voice steady now. "You're right. We need to fix this. And I'm going to make sure we do."

As Sophia walked over to the window, looking out at the world beyond, she couldn't help but feel a strange sense of hope. Maybe this crack wasn't the end. Maybe it was the beginning of something else—something that would force them all to confront the truth, to rebuild not just their relationship, but their family.

James, too, would need to face what had been left unsaid for so long. He couldn't keep pretending everything was fine. They both had to stop hiding behind their roles and expectations. Only then could they start to heal.

But for now, Sophia had to take the first step. She had to find the courage to look at her own reflection, to face what had been broken—and to make a decision about whether she was ready to repair it.

Sophia sat back down at the kitchen table, the weight of her thoughts pressing against her chest. The house felt too quiet now, as if it had been holding its breath along with her. The laughter and chaos that had once filled these rooms—children's voices, the hum of a busy life—seemed a distant memory. Now, there was just the quiet echo of what used to be.

Her phone buzzed in her pocket, a reminder that life outside her small bubble continued on. She reached for it and saw a message from James. She hadn't spoken to him much over the past few days. It wasn't out of anger, necessarily, but more from exhaustion. There were so many things left unsaid between them, and each word felt like it might be too much.

Can we talk tonight? I'm sorry about everything, Sophia.

Her fingers hovered over the screen as she read the words again, the simple apology feeling like both a relief and a heavy burden. She hadn't expected him to reach out. Not like this. Not so openly.

James had always been more reserved, more guarded in his emotions. It was part of what had attracted her to him in the beginning—his quiet strength, his ability to remain calm when everything around him seemed to be falling apart. But now, that very trait seemed like a wall between them, one that she couldn't break down no matter how hard she tried.

We'll talk. Later tonight, okay? she typed back. She didn't know what they would talk about, but there was no avoiding it now. There was too much left unsaid, too many cracks in the walls they had built around themselves.

She dropped the phone back onto the table and sighed. It wasn't just about the marriage anymore. It was about everything—their life, their future, and what they were willing to sacrifice to keep it together. Could they rebuild? Or had they both already moved on in ways they hadn't fully realized?

Izzy's words lingered in her mind: *I don't want us to be a family of strangers.* What did that mean, exactly? Were they strangers now? Was that the inevitable result of years of putting up walls, of pretending that everything was fine when it wasn't?

Sophia pushed herself up from the table and walked over to the counter, absently reaching for the coffee mug that had long gone cold. She stared out the window again, as if the world beyond could provide some kind of answer. But the sky was as uncertain as her thoughts, the clouds heavy with the threat of a storm that hadn't yet broken.

She had spent so much time avoiding the inevitable conversation with James. She had hoped that if she kept quiet, if she kept pretending, it would all resolve itself. But the cracks were too wide now. She couldn't ignore them any longer.

The truth was, she had been afraid—afraid of what the conversation might lead to. Afraid of what they might uncover about themselves, about each other. But she couldn't live like this anymore. Not with the constant weight of uncertainty hanging over her head.

As the minutes stretched on, Sophia could feel the tension building in her chest. She had to prepare herself, not just for the conversation with James, but for the reality of what that conversation might mean. What if they couldn't fix this? What if the cracks were too deep?

But even in the midst of that fear, a small part of her still clung to the hope that it wasn't too late. That somewhere beneath the surface of their complicated lives, there was a path back to each other. It wouldn't be easy. It wouldn't be quick. But if they could face the truth, together, maybe they could find a way forward.

The hours passed slowly. When James finally arrived home that evening, it was as if the house itself had held its breath, waiting for the moment to come. The tension in the air was palpable, and neither of them knew quite how to begin.

James set his briefcase down at the door and took a deep breath. "Sophia," he started, his voice hesitant, but steady. "I know I've been distant. I've been... avoiding things. But I can't keep pretending like everything's fine. It's not fine, and I know you know that too."

Sophia felt a pang of recognition in his words. He wasn't pretending anymore. Neither of them could. They were both exhausted from the silence, from the distance that had crept into their marriage.

"I've been thinking about it," she said, her voice a little softer than she intended. "About what you said. And about what Izzy said earlier. I don't want to keep pretending, either. We can't fix this if we don't face it."

James nodded, his expression both resigned and hopeful. "So, what do we do now?"

Sophia paused, considering his question. She didn't have all the answers. But maybe they didn't need all the answers just yet. Maybe they just needed to start by talking—by being honest with each other, for once. And that, perhaps, was the first real step toward healing.

Sophia took a deep breath, feeling the weight of the moment settle between them. For so long, the space between her and James had been filled with silence—unspoken words, unresolved tension, things that neither of them had wanted to confront. But now, with the first real conversation in what felt like years, everything seemed to come rushing forward, ready to spill out.

"I think we've been avoiding this for too long," she said, her voice steady but laden with emotion. "We've been living parallel lives, James, and I don't even know when it started. I don't want to keep pretending that everything is okay. I need you to hear me."

James stepped closer, his expression softening. "I hear you, Sophia. I really do. I've just been so wrapped up in my own head, in everything that's going on with work and... other things. I didn't even see how far apart we'd drifted. And now, I don't know how to fix it."

Sophia looked at him, seeing the familiar trace of vulnerability in his eyes. It was something she hadn't seen in a long time—perhaps not since their early years together. The walls he had built around himself had always been a defense mechanism, but now they seemed to crumble under the weight of their shared realization. They had both been pretending, in their own ways.

"We need to start by being honest with each other," she said quietly. "I know we've both been holding onto things. I've been angry, James. And I don't even know where that anger comes from anymore. But it's there. And I can't keep carrying it alone."

James nodded slowly, his hand instinctively reaching for hers. "I've been angry too, Sophia. At myself. At everything. But I've been so afraid of what admitting it might mean. Afraid of what it might mean for us."

"Maybe it means we have to rebuild," she said, the words tumbling out before she had fully processed them. "Maybe it means we start over in some way. We can't keep pretending that everything's okay when it's not. We owe it to ourselves, and to Izzy, to try."

The realization settled between them with a weight that neither of them could ignore. This was not going to be easy. There was no quick fix for what had been broken. But for the first time in a long time, they both seemed willing to face the truth, no matter how uncomfortable it was.

"I don't know how to do this," James admitted, his voice low. "But I want to try. I want to figure it out. I don't want to lose you, Sophia."

She felt a tightness in her chest, but it wasn't as heavy as it had been before. There was a shift, a small but significant one. They were finally acknowledging what had been missing, what they had both ignored for far too long.

"We'll figure it out," she said, her voice stronger now. "One step at a time."

They stood there for a moment, just looking at each other, the silence between them no longer filled with distance but with the quiet understanding of what needed to be done. They had a long road ahead of them, but this was the first step—a step toward healing, toward rebuilding what had been lost.

Sophia didn't know what the future held, or whether things would ever go back to the way they once were. But she knew one thing for certain: they couldn't keep moving forward in the dark. They had to face the truth, together, no matter how painful it might be.

And maybe, just maybe, that would be enough.

The following days felt like a blur to Sophia. The conversation with James had been a small spark, but she knew that it wasn't enough to heal the years of distance between them. Still, it was a start. It was the first time in a long time that they had truly connected—spoken honestly without the weight of pretense hanging over them.

James was trying. She could see it in the small gestures, the way he made an effort to be more present, to listen more carefully when she spoke. But the cracks between them were deep, and she knew that simply talking wasn't enough to mend them. It would take time, and maybe more than time—maybe it would require something deeper. Trust. Vulnerability. The kind of honesty that demanded more than words.

For now, though, Sophia was trying to take things one step at a time. She didn't want to rush. She didn't want to force an outcome that wasn't ready to happen.

It was late one evening when the next conversation began to unfold. The house was quiet, the kids had gone to bed, and the soft hum of the refrigerator was the only sound that filled the kitchen. Sophia was washing dishes, lost in thought, when James walked in, his footsteps soft on the tile.

"Can we talk?" he asked, his voice steady but carrying the weight of something unspoken.

Sophia set the dish she was washing into the sink and turned to face him. "Of course," she said. She had no idea what he was about to say, but she was ready. She had to be.

James hesitated for a moment, then stepped closer. "I've been thinking a lot about what you said, about how we've been living parallel lives. I can see now how much I've been shutting you out, Sophia. I've been trying to protect myself, but in doing so, I've pushed you away. And I'm sorry for that. I know I can't just expect you to forgive me overnight, but I want you to know that I'm willing to do whatever it takes to make this right."

Sophia's breath caught in her chest. She had always known that James had a hard time expressing himself. He wasn't the type to wear his heart on his sleeve, and yet, here he was—vulnerable, open in a way she hadn't seen before. It was raw, and it was terrifying.

"I don't know if I can forgive you overnight," she said quietly, her voice betraying the fear she'd been holding inside. "But I want to. I don't want to keep living like this. We've been stuck in this rut for so long, and I'm tired of pretending that everything's fine when it's not."

"I'm not asking for you to forgive me right away," he replied, his tone soft but earnest. "I just want you to know that I'm committed to trying. I know that it won't be easy, and I know it won't happen all at once. But I need you to believe me when I say I'm here, and I'm ready to do the work."

Sophia felt the weight of his words sink into her. There was sincerity there. She could see it in his eyes, in the way he was standing before her, vulnerable and open. For the first time in a long time, she allowed herself to believe in the possibility that things could be different.

"You're right," she said after a pause. "It won't be easy. But I'm willing to try, too. I don't want to lose us."

James stepped closer, reaching out to gently take her hand. "We're not going to lose us. Not if we don't let go."

The simple truth of that statement hung in the air between them, a truth that felt both fragile and strong. They didn't know what the future held, but they knew this much: they weren't giving up. Not yet. Not when they still had a chance.

The next few weeks were a mixture of small victories and moments of doubt. There were days when Sophia felt as if the distance between them was too wide to bridge, and nights when she couldn't sleep, wondering if they had made the right choice. But there were also days when the connection between her and James felt stronger—when they laughed together, when they talked about things that mattered, when they found comfort in the simple act of being present with each other.

There were still moments of silence, of hesitation, but they were learning to navigate them. James was still working on breaking down the walls he had built around himself, and Sophia was trying to let go of the anger that had kept her distant for so long. It wasn't easy, but it was progress.

As time went on, their conversations became more open, more honest. They started talking about things that had been buried deep inside them for years—the fears, the insecurities, the things they had never said. It was hard, painful even, but in a way, it was freeing. For the first time in a long time, they were truly seeing each other.

Sophia didn't know where this journey would take them. She didn't know if they would come out of it stronger, or if they would find themselves at a crossroads, unable to go any further. But she did know one thing: they weren't alone anymore. They had both chosen to fight for something worth saving.

And that, she realized, was a victory in itself.

The next few months brought their fair share of challenges. Life wasn't magically fixed, and the old habits didn't fade away overnight. But there was something different now—an unspoken understanding that they were in this together, for better or for worse.

Sophia found herself, little by little, letting go of the walls she had built. They were still there, in some places, but they weren't as high or as thick as before. She found herself looking at James differently—seeing him as more than just the person she had been angry at, more than just the man who had once been distant. She saw him now as someone who was trying, someone who had his own struggles and fears, just like she did.

THE SHIFTING BALANCE

There were still moments of tension, still times when the old wounds flared up. They fought, of course. It wasn't a perfect reconciliation. But they had learned something invaluable: how to communicate, how to be honest without fear of rejection. And with that came a deeper connection.

James, too, had his moments of doubt. At times, he wondered if he was truly capable of being the man Sophia needed, the man who could provide stability and security in their relationship. There were nights when he lay awake, feeling the weight of everything on his shoulders. But then, he would remember their conversations—their long talks where they had shared things that hadn't been said in years—and he would remind himself that they were both in this together. They were a team, and as long as they kept communicating, they could figure things out.

One evening, as they sat together on the couch after the kids had gone to bed, Sophia turned to James, her expression thoughtful. The air between them was calm, the kind of quiet that felt comfortable, like a promise.

"I've been thinking," she began, her voice soft. "About everything we've been through. I don't know if we'll ever completely go back to the way things were before, but I think we're building something stronger, something real."

James nodded, his hand finding hers in the dim light. "I agree. I don't think we'll ever be the same, but I don't want us to be. I want to be better, for both of us. And for Izzy."

There was a tenderness in his voice that Sophia hadn't heard in a long time. It was as if he was saying everything he hadn't said before, all the things he had kept hidden behind his defenses. And for the first time, she truly believed him.

They sat in silence for a while, just holding hands, the weight of their shared commitment hanging in the air between them. It wasn't a declaration of perfection. It wasn't a promise that everything would be easy from here on out. But it was something they both needed—a moment of peace in the middle of the storm, a moment of reassurance that they had made it this far, and that they were still fighting.

Sophia leaned her head on James's shoulder, feeling the warmth of his presence beside her. It wasn't the resolution of everything, but it was a start. A new beginning.

"I'm glad we're doing this," she said softly, her eyes closing as she let herself relax in the comfort of his embrace.

"Me too," he replied, his voice steady, filled with quiet determination. "Me too."

The days ahead would undoubtedly present more challenges, more moments of doubt and struggle. But Sophia felt something different now—a sense of hope, something she hadn't allowed herself to feel in a long time. She didn't know what the future held, or if their relationship would continue to evolve into something stronger, but for the first time in a long while, she was willing to find out.

And that, perhaps, was the greatest shift of all—the willingness to believe in each other again.

The weeks following their quiet moment on the couch passed in a gentle rhythm. The challenges didn't disappear, but they felt more manageable now. Sophia and James both knew that they were facing something real—a journey of rediscovery, not just of each other, but of themselves. And though there were still days of uncertainty, the foundation they were building felt stronger, like the first cracks in a wall being carefully smoothed over with time and effort.

There were moments when the old patterns threatened to resurface—when the frustration of their past would bubble up, or when the pressure of their day-to-day lives would create a strain in the air. But each time, they found themselves navigating through it with more patience, more understanding. They didn't always have the answers, but they were learning how to ask the right questions.

One evening, as they sat together at the dinner table, the conversation shifted to something unexpected: their dreams.

Sophia had always been the practical one. She had put her own ambitions on hold, focusing on the family, keeping everything running smoothly, and making sure everyone else's needs came first. But as she listened to James talk about his work, his hopes for the future, something stirred within her. It wasn't jealousy. It was something deeper—an awakening.

"I've been thinking a lot about my own goals," she admitted, looking down at her plate for a moment. "About what I want, beyond just... everything we've been dealing with."

James looked up, surprised, his fork hovering mid-air. "You've always been so focused on us. What do you mean?"

Sophia hesitated before answering, unsure if she was ready to voice the thoughts she had kept hidden for so long. "I've spent so much time building our life that I forgot about the things I want for myself. I used to have dreams, James. I used to want more than just this. I still do."

James put down his fork, his gaze softening. "Sophia... I never wanted you to lose sight of who you are. You're not just a mother, a wife, a caretaker. You're more than that. If there's something you want, something you need to pursue, we'll figure it out. We'll make it work."

The words settled around her like a weight lifting off her shoulders. She hadn't realized how much she had needed to hear that until now. She had buried so much of herself beneath the layers of responsibility, but James was offering her the space to rediscover who she was, to reclaim the parts of herself she had abandoned.

For the first time in a long time, she allowed herself to believe that she could have both—a family and her own dreams.

"I've always wanted to write," she said quietly, a hint of excitement in her voice. "But I've never had the time, or the energy, or the courage to actually try. Maybe it's silly. Maybe it's too late."

James reached across the table, taking her hand in his. "It's never too late. You should do it. Write your stories. Whatever it takes. I'll support you. We'll make it work."

Tears welled up in Sophia's eyes, but they weren't tears of sadness. They were tears of gratitude, of realization. She didn't have to give up on her own dreams to be a good mother or a good wife. She could be both.

That night, after the kids had gone to bed and the house was quiet, Sophia sat at her desk, her laptop in front of her. The cursor blinked in a blank document, daring her to write. She hesitated, unsure of where to start, but then something clicked. She began typing, slowly at first, but then with more confidence as the words began to flow.

It wasn't perfect. It wasn't even close to being finished. But for the first time in a long while, Sophia felt like she was doing something just for herself. Something that mattered.

James came into the room, his steps light on the carpet. "How's it going?" he asked, peering over her shoulder.

Sophia smiled, glancing at him. "It's a start," she said, her voice steady, filled with quiet hope.

"You're doing great," he said softly, pressing a kiss to the top of her head. "I'm proud of you."

In that moment, Sophia realized something important. The path forward wasn't going to be easy. There would be challenges, moments of doubt, and times when they would both feel overwhelmed. But they were no longer alone in it. They had each other, and they were learning to support one another in ways they had never done before.

For the first time in a long time, Sophia was excited about the future. Not just because of the potential of her relationship with James, but because she was starting to believe in herself again. She was no longer just a woman defined by her roles as a wife and mother. She was Sophia—the woman with her own dreams, her own ambitions, and a future that was hers to shape.

And that, more than anything, was the beginning of something new.

The days following Sophia's leap into her writing journey marked a subtle yet significant transformation in their household. Her decision to carve out time for herself was met with mixed reactions from the family. Izzy, in her innocent curiosity, would often wander into the room where Sophia wrote, asking about the stories she was working on. It brought a smile to Sophia's face, even if it interrupted her flow.

James, true to his word, stepped up in ways Sophia hadn't expected. He started handling bedtime routines with more regularity and took on extra chores around the house, creating pockets of time for her to focus. Though his efforts were not always seamless—he burned dinner once and forgot to pick up Izzy from a playdate—Sophia appreciated his intent. They were small gestures, but they meant the world to her.

One evening, as Sophia sat in the living room with her laptop, the sound of laughter drifted in from the kitchen. James and Izzy were baking cookies, a rare occurrence that Sophia couldn't help but document with a quick photo. The sight warmed her heart. These moments of lightness, of shared joy, were what she had been longing for.

But not everything was smooth. Sophia's newfound independence created tension at times. There were moments when James seemed to struggle with the shift in their dynamic, moments when he would retreat into silence or distract himself with work.

She noticed it but chose not to push him, understanding that they were both adjusting to the changes.

One particularly challenging weekend tested the balance they were trying to maintain. Sophia had a writing deadline she had set for herself, a personal goal to finish a chapter by Sunday evening. The kids, however, seemed determined to derail her progress. Izzy had a meltdown over a missing stuffed animal, and their son, Noah, who had been unusually quiet lately, chose that weekend to rebel against every household rule.

James tried his best to handle the chaos, but his patience wore thin. By Sunday afternoon, the frustration between him and Sophia bubbled over into a heated argument.

"I can't do this alone!" James snapped, pacing the living room. "I'm trying, Sophia, but it feels like I'm failing. You're always busy now, and I'm just—drowning."

Sophia closed her laptop, the words she had been typing vanishing from her mind. "I'm not abandoning you, James," she said, her voice tight with a mix of guilt and exasperation. "I'm just... trying to find myself again. Can't you see that?"

Their voices softened as the weight of their emotions settled between them. They both knew the argument wasn't about the chores or the kids—it was about their fears, their insecurities, and the uncharted territory they were navigating together.

"I know," James finally said, sitting down on the couch. "I know you're not leaving. It's just hard. I'm used to being the one with goals, with ambitions, and now... it's different. I'm trying to adjust, but it's not easy."

Sophia sat beside him, her hand finding his. "We're both learning, James. And it's okay to feel like this. But we're a team. We can figure it out."

In the quiet that followed, they found solace in each other's presence. It wasn't a perfect resolution, but it was enough for now.

The weeks that followed were marked by subtle but meaningful shifts. They began scheduling weekly check-ins, time to talk about their feelings, their struggles, and their wins. These conversations became a cornerstone of their rebuilding process, creating a space where they could be honest without fear of judgment.

Sophia's writing continued to grow, not just as a personal passion but as a bridge to others. She joined a local writer's group, where she found a supportive community that encouraged her to push boundaries and share her voice. For the first time in years, she felt seen—not just as a wife or a mother, but as a creative individual.

James, too, began exploring his own interests outside of work. He reconnected with old friends, joined a local soccer league, and even started volunteering at a community center. These activities brought a new energy to their relationship, giving them both fresh perspectives and experiences to share.

One evening, as they sat together on the back porch, watching the sun dip below the horizon, James turned to Sophia, his expression thoughtful.

"You know," he said, his voice soft, "I think this is the happiest I've felt in a long time."

Sophia smiled, her hand resting on his. "Me too."

It wasn't about perfection or having all the answers. It was about the small victories—the moments of connection, the shared laughter, the quiet understanding that they were growing together.

The cracks in their foundation hadn't disappeared, but they had been filled with something stronger: hope, resilience, and a commitment to each other that could weather any storm.

And for the first time in a long while, the future felt bright.

The healing process was not linear. There were days when old habits crept back in—when James's frustration with work or Sophia's preoccupation with her writing caused tension to resurface. But something had shifted fundamentally. They both had learned to recognize these moments as opportunities for growth rather than failures.

One rainy afternoon, Sophia found herself reflecting on how far they had come. The house was unusually quiet; the kids were at a neighbor's, and James was at his soccer match. She sat at the dining table, her laptop open, but her focus wandered to the raindrops trailing down the window.

Her thoughts drifted to the woman she had been a year ago—overwhelmed, lost, and yearning for something she couldn't name. The journey to rediscover herself hadn't been easy, but it had been worth every step. She realized that the cracks in their lives, the struggles they had faced, weren't something to fear. They were reminders of their humanity, their resilience.

Later that evening, when James returned home drenched from the rain but grinning from ear to ear, Sophia couldn't help but smile.

"You look like you just won the World Cup," she teased, handing him a towel.

"Not quite," he laughed, shaking his hair like a dog and sending droplets flying. "But it was a good game. And I scored, so there's that."

As they settled into the living room, James stretched out on the couch while Sophia curled up with her laptop. The sound of the rain outside created a soothing backdrop, a reminder of the storms they had weathered together.

"I was thinking today," Sophia began, her fingers tracing patterns on the laptop's surface. "About us. About how different everything feels now."

James looked over at her, his brow furrowing slightly. "Different in a good way, I hope?"

"Very good," she assured him. "I just... I feel like we're finally living our lives, not just going through the motions. It's messy and complicated, but it's real."

He nodded, his expression softening. "I feel that too. And honestly, I think those cracks we talked about—they've made us stronger. Like that Japanese art, you know? The one where they fill broken pottery with gold?"

"Kintsugi," Sophia supplied, her smile widening. "Yes, exactly. I like that."

James reached for her hand, their fingers intertwining. "We're not perfect, Soph. But we don't need to be. I think... I think we're finally figuring out how to be us."

That night, as they lay in bed, Sophia felt a deep sense of peace. It wasn't the kind of happiness that came from external success or fleeting moments of joy. It was the quiet contentment of knowing that, despite everything, they had chosen each other every single day.

She whispered into the darkness, her voice steady and sure, "Thank you, James."

He turned toward her, his hand finding hers beneath the covers. "For what?"

"For staying. For trying. For us."

James squeezed her hand gently, his voice warm with emotion. "Always, Soph. Always."

The journey they had embarked on was far from over, but they no longer feared the unknown. They had learned to embrace the cracks, to see them not as flaws but as a testament to their strength and love. And as they drifted off to sleep, the rain outside began to ease, leaving behind a world cleansed and ready for whatever came next.

Chapter 2: Silent Battles

1. Unspoken Words

The evening sunlight filtered through the half-closed blinds, casting slanted, golden lines across the dining table. It was a picturesque setting—plates carefully arranged, glasses sparkling with condensation, and the faint aroma of roasted herbs wafting through the room. Yet, the silence between Sophia and James was anything but serene.

Sophia moved with deliberate precision, placing a serving spoon beside the dish of vegetables. Her movements were an effort to mask the storm of thoughts raging inside her. James sat at the far end of the table, scrolling through his phone, his brows furrowed in concentration—or perhaps avoidance.

The silence was heavy, dense with unspoken words. It wasn't the comfortable quiet of shared understanding but the kind that gnawed at the edges of peace. Sophia wanted to speak, to confront the distance that had grown between them like an invisible wall. But every time she opened her mouth, her courage faltered, swallowed by the fear of what his response might be.

James glanced up briefly, as if sensing her unease, then returned to his screen. He wasn't blind to the tension either, but words had never been his strong suit. He prided himself on being a man of action, someone who provided and solved problems. Yet here, in the heart of his own home, he felt powerless.

Sophia's fork clinked against her plate, startling them both. She looked up, her eyes meeting his for a fleeting second before he looked away.

"Is everything okay?" James finally asked, his voice low and cautious.

THE SHIFTING BALANCE

The question hung in the air, both an invitation and a challenge. Sophia hesitated, the weight of a thousand small grievances pressing against her chest. The late nights he spent at work, the way he barely noticed her anymore, the growing void that no amount of forced smiles or polite exchanges could bridge.

"It's fine," she replied, her tone betraying the lie.

James knew it wasn't fine. He recognized the tightness in her voice, the way her hands clenched around her napkin. But instead of pressing, he nodded and returned to his plate. It was easier that way—easier than peeling back the layers of disappointment and resentment that had silently built over time.

Sophia wanted to scream. She wanted to demand why he hadn't noticed the changes in her, in them. She wanted to tell him about the dreams she had put on hold, the loneliness she felt even when he was in the room. But the words refused to form, stuck behind the barrier of her own doubt.

Across the table, James wrestled with his own thoughts. He had noticed—how could he not? But every attempt to address it felt like stepping into a minefield. He feared saying the wrong thing, feared making things worse. So, he chose silence, hoping that time would smooth the rough edges of their discontent.

As the meal went on, the only sounds were the clinking of cutlery and the occasional scrape of a chair against the floor. The room, filled with sunlight and the warmth of home, felt colder than ever.

When dinner was over, James stood and began clearing the table. Sophia watched him, her heart aching with the weight of everything left unsaid. She wanted to reach out, to break the silence, but the fear of rejection held her back.

"Thanks for dinner," James said softly, his eyes lingering on her for a moment longer than usual.

"You're welcome," she replied, her voice almost a whisper.

And just like that, another evening passed, their words unspoken, their hearts heavier for it.

2. A Life Divided

THE HOUSE WAS QUIET in a way that didn't feel peaceful but rather fragmented, like the aftermath of an argument left unresolved. Sophia sat at the kitchen table, her laptop open to a spreadsheet that blurred before her tired eyes. The soft hum of the dishwasher was the only sound, filling the silence with a kind of monotony she found unbearable. She glanced at the clock—7:45 p.m. James would be home soon, though she wasn't sure if she was ready for the tension his presence would inevitably bring.

Their lives, once intertwined with the ease of a shared rhythm, now felt like two separate tracks running parallel, close enough to see but never to touch. Sophia's days were consumed by work—meetings, deadlines, and the constant pressure to prove herself in a world that still hesitated to take her seriously. James, on the other hand, had thrown himself into his career as an architect, finding solace in the predictability of blueprints and the logic of design. The problem wasn't that they didn't care about each other. It was that their priorities no longer aligned, and neither could admit it aloud.

Upstairs, Isabella slammed her bedroom door with the force only a teenager could muster, while Ethan's soft voice filtered down the hallway as he talked to his action figures. The contrast between their children was a constant reminder of the divide within their family. Isabella was sharp and rebellious, her words often laced with a bitterness that Sophia didn't know how to address. Ethan, on the other hand, was gentle and introspective, his quiet nature often overshadowed by his sister's louder presence.

Sophia closed her laptop and rubbed her temples. She had planned to make dinner but got lost in a string of emails that led to nowhere. Another night of takeout, she thought with a pang of guilt. Just as she reached for her phone to place the order, the front door creaked open, and James stepped inside, his face drawn with the exhaustion of the day.

"Hey," he said, his voice neutral, almost detached.

"Hi," Sophia replied, trying to sound upbeat but falling short. "How was work?"

"Fine," he answered, setting his bag by the door. The one-word reply hung between them, a wall neither seemed willing to climb over.

They used to fill these moments with stories about their day, laughter over the little absurdities of life, or plans for the weekend. Now, their conversations felt like exchanges of necessity rather than genuine connection. James headed to the kitchen, opening the fridge with the practiced motion of someone who already knew it would disappoint him. He sighed and closed it, turning to Sophia.

"Takeout again?"

"I didn't have time to cook," she said, her tone defensive though she hadn't meant it to be.

James shrugged. "It's fine. I'll eat whatever."

It wasn't fine, and they both knew it. But neither had the energy to say what they were really thinking. Sophia wanted to tell him how overwhelmed she felt, how she couldn't keep balancing everything without breaking. James wanted to tell her that he missed her, that he felt like they were living two separate lives under the same roof. But the words remained unspoken, buried under layers of pride, fear, and exhaustion.

Upstairs, Isabella's music blared through the walls, a pounding rhythm that seemed to echo the tension downstairs. Ethan padded into the living room, holding one of his action figures and looking between his parents with a kind of quiet wisdom that made Sophia's heart ache.

"Can we watch something together?" Ethan asked, his voice hopeful.

James glanced at Sophia, and for a moment, their eyes met. In that brief exchange, there was a flicker of understanding, a shared guilt over how far they'd drifted from the family they once were.

"Sure, buddy," James said, his voice softening. He turned on the TV, and Ethan climbed onto the couch, his small body curling into James's side.

Sophia hesitated, then joined them, sitting on the opposite end of the couch. The show was something silly and light, the kind of background noise that didn't require attention. Yet, for the first time in weeks, the room felt less like a battleground and more like a refuge, however fragile.

As the credits rolled, Ethan had already drifted off to sleep, his head resting on James's arm. Sophia reached out to adjust the blanket over her son, her hand brushing against James's. They froze for a moment, neither pulling away nor acknowledging the touch.

A life divided, Sophia thought. But maybe, just maybe, there was still a way to build a bridge across the chasm.

3. The Price of Ambition

THE MORNING SUNLIGHT filtered through the high-rise windows of Sophia's office, casting elongated shadows on the polished mahogany desk. The view was breathtaking—an endless sprawl of city life pulsating with ambition, energy, and relentless pursuit. It was a world Sophia Collins had fought her way into, clawing up every rung of the corporate ladder with determination. But the silence in the room, heavy and pressing, reminded her of the price she had paid for her success.

The calendar on her desk was packed with meetings, deadlines, and endless obligations. Her assistant had highlighted an important presentation scheduled for the afternoon, but her thoughts were far from spreadsheets and projections. She glanced at her phone, where the screen lit up with a text from James: **"Ethan's recital tonight. Don't forget."**

Sophia stared at the message, her fingers hovering over the keyboard. The recital. She had promised Ethan she would be there, watching as he performed the piece he'd practiced for weeks. But the presentation today was crucial, a once-in-a-lifetime opportunity to pitch her ideas to the board. She thought of Ethan's hopeful eyes, the excitement in his voice when he'd told her about the event.

"This is the balance I wanted," she told herself, a mantra that had become less reassuring with each repetition. Work was her passion, her escape from the monotony of suburbia, the proof that she could be more than just a mother or a wife. Yet, every missed birthday, every forgotten recital, felt like a withdrawal from a bank of love that was dangerously close to being overdrawn.

James, always steady and patient, had been her rock in those moments. But lately, even he seemed distant. His support had turned into quiet resignation, his once vibrant conversations reduced to monosyllabic exchanges. She could feel the strain in his voice when he mentioned the recital that morning over breakfast.

"Do you even know what piece he's playing?" he had asked.

Sophia had deflected with a weak smile and a vague nod, hoping he wouldn't press further. But his disappointment had been palpable, a weight she carried into the elevator and through the revolving doors of her office building.

Her phone buzzed again, this time a reminder from her assistant. It was time to head to the conference room. Sophia gathered her notes and rose, smoothing her blazer. She took one last look at Ethan's text, the guilt gnawing at the edges of her focus. **"This is for them, too,"** she whispered, convincing herself as she walked out the door.

Hours later, the presentation was over, and Sophia stood outside the building, the late evening air crisp and biting. The exhilaration of her success was overshadowed by a hollow ache. She checked the time—6:45 p.m. The recital had started fifteen minutes ago.

Her driver pulled up, but instead of getting in, she hesitated. She thought of Ethan on that stage, scanning the audience for her face. She could almost hear James's voice in her head, a mixture of frustration and sadness: **"It's not about being there for every moment, Sophia. It's about being there for the moments that matter."**

Sophia turned abruptly. "Change of plans," she told the driver, her voice steady.

By the time she reached the school auditorium, the parking lot was nearly full. She sprinted inside, her heels clicking sharply against the tiled floors. The recital was in progress, the melodic strains of a violin filling the space. She slipped into the back row, scanning the stage until she saw him—Ethan, his small frame poised with concentration, bow moving fluidly across the strings.

Sophia's chest tightened as she watched him. For a moment, the noise of her world faded, leaving only the sound of her son's music and the realization of what she had been missing.

When the applause erupted, she joined in, clapping so hard her palms stung. Ethan caught sight of her, his eyes widening in surprise before breaking into a grin. Sophia waved, a lump forming in her throat.

Later that evening, as they sat together at the kitchen table eating leftover pizza, Ethan recounted every detail of his performance. James leaned against the counter, arms crossed, watching her with a mix of relief and hope.

"You made it," he said softly when Ethan dashed off to retrieve his sheet music.

Sophia nodded. "**I don't want to miss these moments anymore, James.**"

He didn't respond immediately, but the faint smile tugging at his lips said enough.

That night, as she lay in bed staring at the ceiling, Sophia resolved to find a way—some way—to balance her ambitions with the life she was slowly letting slip away. But deep down, she knew that balance would come with its own set of sacrifices. The question was, which price was she truly willing to pay?

4. Lost Connections

THE DAYS IN THE CARTER household had begun to blur into a monotonous routine, where conversations were brief and largely functional. The hum of the coffee machine in the morning and the faint clatter of dishes in the sink late at night were the only constants. James and Sophia had once shared everything—from dreams to petty arguments about the right way to fold laundry. Now, their exchanges were reduced to logistics: who would pick up Ethan from soccer practice or whether Izzy's tuition payments had been processed.

Sophia often found herself staring at her phone during her lunch breaks at work, scrolling aimlessly through social media. Pictures of smiling families at picnics, heartfelt anniversary posts, and milestones celebrated together filled her screen. She couldn't help but wonder when her own family had stopped creating such moments. The distance between her and James had grown not from one catastrophic event but from countless missed opportunities to connect.

For James, the silence was heavier in the evenings. After long days at the office, he'd come home to a house where his wife seemed absorbed in her own world, and his children were either too busy or too disinterested to engage. Izzy, now 16, had taken to retreating to her room, headphones clamped firmly over her ears. Ethan, though only 10, had begun spending more time with his video games than with his father. James couldn't remember the last time they'd tossed a ball around in the backyard or laughed over a silly joke during dinner.

One night, as Sophia sat on the couch flipping through a work presentation on her laptop, James lowered himself into the chair opposite her.

"Do you remember when we used to plan vacations together?" he asked, his voice hesitant, as if testing unfamiliar waters.

Sophia looked up, startled. The question was unexpected, as was the softness in his tone. "Yeah," she replied, though her voice carried more hesitation than nostalgia. "But things are different now, aren't they?"

"Different doesn't mean worse," James countered. "Or at least it doesn't have to."

Their conversation was interrupted by the sound of Ethan shouting from his room, frustrated by some game. Sophia closed her laptop with a sigh, standing up to attend to him. James watched her walk away, the moment slipping through his fingers like sand.

Meanwhile, Izzy had noticed the shift in her parents, though she never mentioned it out loud. She kept a diary tucked beneath her mattress where she scribbled her thoughts: "Mom and Dad are like strangers passing in the hall. They talk, but it's like they're speaking different languages."

Izzy had her own battles to fight—friends who felt more like adversaries, a growing pressure to excel academically, and questions about her place in the world. She often felt invisible, her struggles drowned out by the tension between her parents. Ethan, on the other hand, hadn't yet learned to articulate what he felt, but he understood one thing: the warmth that used to fill their home was missing.

Over time, the small fractures in their relationships began to deepen. Dinners became silent affairs, each family member retreating into their thoughts. The shared laughter and casual intimacy that once defined their family seemed like a distant memory.

But beneath the silence, there was a yearning—an unspoken hope that the threads connecting them could still be mended. For James, it was a longing to rediscover the bond with his wife and children. For Sophia, it was the guilt of losing herself in her ambitions and the fear of becoming irrelevant in her family's life. And for Izzy and Ethan, it was the silent wish for their parents to notice them again, not as responsibilities but as the unique individuals they were growing into.

The connections weren't lost entirely, but they were frayed, waiting for someone to take the first step toward repairing them.

Chapter 3: A House Divided

1. The Echo of Unsaid Things

The house was never silent, but the noise never seemed to carry meaning. The hum of appliances, the shuffle of feet, the occasional clink of dishes—each sound filled the air like static, masking what no one dared to say. Sophia sat at the kitchen table, her hands clasped around a mug of tea that had long since gone cold. Across from her, James read the newspaper, the rustling pages creating a fragile barrier between them.

It wasn't that they didn't talk. They exchanged words, plenty of them: schedules, grocery lists, updates about the kids. But the conversations never strayed into the territory where feelings resided. There were too many emotions tucked away, too many fears and resentments carefully packed into the corners of their lives.

Sophia glanced up from her untouched tea, watching James. His face, half-obscured by the paper, looked tired, the lines on his forehead deeper than she remembered. She opened her mouth to speak, to ask him if he was happy—if he was still happy with her. But the question stuck in her throat, its weight too heavy to lift.

"Did you see Ethan's report card?" James asked, lowering the newspaper just enough to meet her gaze. His tone was casual, as if he hadn't noticed the pause before her answer.

"Yes," she said, grateful for the interruption. "He's doing well in math, but his teacher mentioned he's been distracted in class."

James nodded, his brow furrowing slightly. "I'll talk to him. Maybe he just needs a little encouragement."

Sophia nodded too, the conversation slipping back into safe, shallow waters. But her thoughts lingered on Ethan. He was only twelve, but she could see the same patterns in him that had taken root in their marriage—unspoken thoughts, quiet frustrations. It terrified her to think that her son might one day grow into a man who didn't know how to say what he felt.

Upstairs, Ethan sat on the edge of his bed, headphones around his neck. He stared at his phone, scrolling through messages from his friends, his thumb pausing over a text he wanted to send but couldn't bring himself to type out. *Why didn't you invite me?* he thought, the question gnawing at him. But instead, he typed, *Cool, have fun,* and pressed send, the hollow words sitting like stones in his chest.

Isabella, in the next room, was no better. At seventeen, she was an expert at crafting the perfect façade. Her Instagram feed was a parade of smiles and sunsets, each post meticulously curated to convey a life of effortless happiness. But in reality, she felt adrift, unsure of who she was or what she wanted. The pressure to be perfect—to meet her parents' expectations and maintain her own image—left little room for vulnerability.

In the living room, James put down the newspaper and looked toward the kitchen. He could feel Sophia's presence even without seeing her. He knew she was there, knew she had something on her mind. But he didn't ask. He hadn't asked in years, and now the silence between them felt like a wall too high to scale.

Sophia rose from her seat, carrying her mug to the sink. She stood there for a moment, staring out the window at the fading light. The question was still there, lodged in her throat. She thought about Ethan, about Isabella, about all the ways their family seemed to be unraveling while they all pretended everything was fine.

"James," she said finally, her voice barely above a whisper.

He looked up, surprised by the break in the routine. "Yes?"

Her heart pounded as she searched for the right words. But as always, they eluded her. "Nothing," she said, shaking her head. "Never mind."

He nodded, relieved, and returned to his paper.

And so the echoes of unsaid things filled the house once more, their weight pressing down on every room, every heart, and every fleeting moment of connection they let slip away.

2. Breaking the Silence

THE MORNING LIGHT STREAMED through the half-drawn curtains, casting long shadows across the living room floor. Sophia sat in her usual spot on the worn beige couch, her fingers tracing absent circles on the armrest. The quiet was almost oppressive, punctuated only by the faint hum of the refrigerator in the adjoining kitchen. It wasn't the peaceful silence of a content home but the heavy, loaded kind, where unspoken words lingered like ghosts in the air.

James was across the room, leaning against the doorframe with his arms crossed. He had been there for nearly five minutes, watching her, waiting for the courage to form the words he had been carrying for weeks. His throat felt tight, and every attempt to speak felt like walking into a storm he wasn't ready to weather. Yet, he knew this moment had been building, and avoiding it any longer would only deepen the rift between them.

"Sophia," he finally began, his voice low, tentative.

She flinched slightly at the sound of her name, as if startled that he had spoken at all. Turning her head, she met his gaze, her eyes betraying a mixture of surprise and weariness.

"What is it, James?" she replied, her tone neutral but guarded.

He shifted uncomfortably, pushing off the doorframe and taking a few hesitant steps toward her. "I think we need to talk."

Her lips pressed into a thin line. "About what?"

James ran a hand through his hair, a nervous habit Sophia had grown to recognize over their years together. "About us. About how we've been...living. Or not living, I guess."

Sophia's eyes narrowed slightly, but she didn't interrupt. Instead, she tilted her head, inviting him to continue.

"I feel like we're just... coexisting," James said, his voice growing steadier. "We don't talk anymore. Not really. We go through the motions—work, dinner, the kids—but it's like we're strangers living in the same house."

Sophia let out a small, bitter laugh, leaning back into the couch. "And whose fault is that, James?"

The sharpness in her tone stung, but he refused to back down. "I'm not saying it's all on you, Sophia. I know I've pulled away too. But don't pretend you don't feel it."

She looked away, her gaze fixed on the floor. The truth of his words was undeniable, but acknowledging it felt like opening a wound she'd worked hard to ignore. "And what do you want me to say?" she murmured, her voice barely above a whisper.

"I want you to say what's on your mind," he said, taking a seat in the armchair across from her. "Tell me what you're thinking, what you're feeling. Anything. Just... don't shut me out."

For a moment, the room was filled with an unbearable tension. Sophia's chest tightened as she wrestled with the words she had buried for months. Finally, she drew in a shaky breath and spoke.

"I'm tired, James. I'm tired of pretending everything is fine when it's not. I'm tired of carrying the weight of this family alone while you bury yourself in work. And I'm tired of feeling like no matter what I do, it's never enough."

Her voice cracked on the last word, and she quickly wiped at her eyes, refusing to let herself cry. James sat silently, her words hitting him like a physical blow. He had known she was unhappy, but hearing it laid bare was something else entirely.

"I didn't realize..." he began, but she cut him off.

"No, you didn't," she said, her tone laced with both sadness and frustration. "Because you never asked. And I was too afraid to tell you."

James swallowed hard, guilt and regret coiling tightly in his chest. "I'm sorry, Sophia. For not seeing it sooner. For not being there when you needed me."

She looked at him then, really looked at him, and for the first time in a long while, she saw something that resembled vulnerability in his expression. It was a small crack in the wall he had built around himself, but it was enough.

"I don't know if we can fix this," she admitted, her voice soft. "But I want to try. For the kids, if nothing else."

"For the kids," he echoed, though deep down, he hoped it could be for them too.

The silence that followed was no longer heavy but tentative, like the first steps on unsteady ground. It wasn't a resolution, but it was a beginning. And for now, that was enough.

3. Fading Bonds

THE DINNER TABLE WAS set, the clinking of plates echoing softly through the house. Yet the silence between the family was deafening. Sophia looked up from her untouched plate, glancing at James, who seemed lost in thought, his fork absently tracing patterns in the mashed potatoes. Across the table, Izzy scrolled on her phone, her face illuminated by its soft glow, while Ethan pushed peas around his plate without eating.

This used to be the time they all connected—their sacred hour. Conversations would flow, laughter would bounce off the walls, and even the arguments had a warmth to them. But now, the bonds that once held them together felt frayed, slipping through their fingers like sand.

Sophia cleared her throat, forcing a smile. "How was school, Ethan?"

He shrugged, eyes fixed on his plate. "Fine."

"And you, Izzy?" Sophia pressed, her voice strained with forced cheerfulness.

"Same as always," Izzy replied without looking up, her tone clipped.

Sophia bit the inside of her cheek, glancing at James for support, but he remained silent. His jaw tightened, his eyes glued to the plate as though avoiding the tension in the room. She felt the sting of isolation, a creeping sense that she no longer knew her family. They were like strangers orbiting the same house, their connections eroded by time, distance, and unspoken grievances.

Later that evening, Sophia found herself standing in the dimly lit living room, gazing at a framed photo from years ago. In it, the four of them were at the beach, smiling so broadly their cheeks must have hurt. She traced her finger over the glass, her heart heavy with longing for those days.

"What happened to us?" she whispered to no one.

"It's not just you," James said from behind her. His voice startled her, but it lacked the warmth it once held. "We're all... slipping away."

Sophia turned to face him. "And you're okay with that? Pretending everything's fine when it's clearly not?"

James sighed, rubbing the back of his neck. "It's not that simple, Sophia. Everyone's busy with their own stuff. Izzy's got her friends, Ethan's growing up, and you—" He stopped, as though saying more would open a wound he wasn't ready to confront.

"And me what?" she demanded, her voice rising. "Say it."

"You've been so caught up in your work, trying to prove something to yourself—or the world—that you've left the rest of us behind," James said, his tone bitter but his eyes filled with hurt.

Her breath caught. She wanted to defend herself, to argue that she was doing everything for them, but deep down, she knew there was truth in his words.

"Maybe," she admitted quietly. "But you've been distant too, James. You come home, but you're not here. You bury yourself in work or zone out like you're somewhere else. It's not just me."

The silence between them was heavy, laden with years of unspoken frustrations. In the distance, the sound of a door slamming echoed—likely Izzy retreating to her room. Ethan's voice, muffled by the walls, carried a melancholic tune from his guitar. Each sound was a reminder of how far apart they had drifted.

Sophia sighed, sinking onto the couch. "How did we get here?"

James joined her, his shoulders slumping. "Life happened, I guess. And we forgot how to keep holding on to each other."

Sophia rested her head in her hands, the weight of his words settling over her like a heavy fog. She thought of all the times she had chosen deadlines over family movie nights, the weekends spent glued to her laptop instead of joining Ethan at his soccer games or listening to Izzy's endless chatter about school drama. Somewhere along the way, she had convinced herself it was all for the greater good—working hard now so they could enjoy a better future. But what was the point of a future if the present was falling apart?

James spoke again, his voice softer this time. "You remember that camping trip we took? When Izzy was ten and Ethan was still afraid of the dark?"

Sophia smiled faintly despite herself. "How could I forget? Izzy spent the whole time complaining about mosquitoes, and Ethan wouldn't let go of that flashlight."

"Yeah," James chuckled, a flicker of warmth returning to his tone. "But do you remember how, on the last night, we all sat by the fire? Izzy fell asleep on your lap, and Ethan finally put the flashlight down. It was just... quiet. And it felt right."

Sophia nodded, her throat tightening. "We used to have so many moments like that. Now it's like we're just... surviving. Coexisting."

James leaned back, his gaze fixed on the ceiling. "Maybe we need to stop blaming time or circumstances and start making an effort. All of us."

"But how?" Sophia asked, her voice almost pleading. "It feels like we're too far gone."

"We're not," James said firmly. "Not yet."

His words hung in the air, a fragile thread of hope in a sea of doubt. Sophia wanted to believe him, but she knew it wouldn't be easy. Rebuilding something that had slowly crumbled over years required more than just good intentions. It required action, consistency, and a willingness to face the pain they had avoided for so long.

The next morning, Sophia woke up with a sense of determination she hadn't felt in months. She decided to take a small step—something tangible. While James left for work and the kids were still asleep, she rummaged through the cluttered closet in the hallway. At the back, buried under old holiday decorations, she found the family photo album. Its spine was worn, the pages filled with memories of better times.

When Izzy finally emerged from her room, her hair a messy tangle and her phone glued to her hand, Sophia called her over. "Sit with me for a minute."

Izzy hesitated, glancing toward the kitchen as if searching for an excuse. "I'm kind of busy, Mom."

"It'll just take a second," Sophia insisted, patting the spot next to her.

Reluctantly, Izzy sat down, her legs tucked beneath her. Sophia opened the album, flipping to a photo of a much younger Izzy, her face smeared with chocolate cake at her fifth birthday party. "Remember this?"

Izzy rolled her eyes, but a small smile tugged at her lips. "Ugh, I looked ridiculous."

"You looked happy," Sophia said, her voice soft. "We all did."

Ethan joined them soon after, drawn by the sound of their laughter as Sophia pointed out another embarrassing photo. By the time James returned home, the album was sprawled across the coffee table, and the three of them were laughing like they hadn't in months.

James raised an eyebrow as he stepped through the door. "What's going on here?"

"Just... remembering," Sophia said, looking up at him with a tentative smile.

It wasn't a solution, but it was a start. And sometimes, all it took was one small moment to remind them of what they were fighting for.

4. Strangers Under One Roof

THE HOUSE, ONCE FILLED with laughter and warmth, had become a quiet battleground, a place where the walls seemed to echo the unspoken words that lingered in the air. Sophia sat at the kitchen table, staring at the cup of coffee in front of her, the steam rising in delicate curls, but her mind was miles away. The silence was oppressive, a stark contrast to the chaos of emotions churning inside her.

She had always prided herself on being the glue that held the family together, the one who managed the home, the children, and, somehow, her own dreams, all in the same breath. But lately, she felt more like a ghost drifting through the rooms, unseen, unheard, and increasingly irrelevant.

James, her husband, was in the living room, his eyes fixed on the television screen, but he wasn't really watching. She knew that. He had stopped watching anything with real interest months ago, distracted by work, by the weight of the responsibilities that always seemed to pile higher and higher. It was as if he were trapped in his own world, one where she and the children were just silent, moving figures, rather than the family he had promised to cherish.

Isabella, their eldest, had long since withdrawn into her own world. She was rarely home now, and when she was, her presence was as cold and distant as her mother's had become. The spark of rebellion in her eyes told a story of frustration and unmet expectations, of a girl who had once looked up to her parents but now saw them as nothing more than strangers. And Ethan, their youngest, seemed to be slipping through the cracks entirely. His boyish charm and laughter no longer filled the halls, replaced by long hours spent in his room, a constant state of unease hanging over him.

They were all there, under one roof, but each person was somewhere else. Their lives had become a collection of separate spaces, linked only by the physical proximity of their shared address. Dinner time, once a sacred ritual, had turned into a mechanical affair—everyone seated at the table, but no one truly present. The conversations had become fragmented, awkward, as if they were all speaking different languages, unable to understand each other's unspoken needs and desires.

Sophia had tried to reach out, to bridge the distance. She had suggested family outings, casual talks over coffee, even attempts at heartfelt apologies for her absence. But the words never seemed to land right, always lost in the shuffle of busy lives and emotional walls. She could feel herself retreating even further, not out of choice, but because she had been left with no other option. The weight of being both the caregiver and the one who had to apologize for her own absence was too much to bear.

She had loved them all so fiercely, once. But love, she had learned, was not always enough to hold things together. The reality of their lives—his career, her dreams, their children's independence—had fractured the connections that once seemed so solid. Each day was a reminder that the distance between them had become something far more than emotional. It had become physical. She wondered, with a deep sense of sadness, if they would ever find their way back to each other, or if they were doomed to remain strangers in a house that no longer felt like home.

James' voice broke through her thoughts. "Sophia, do you hear me?" His tone was sharp, his irritation clear. She looked up, startled, as if waking from a dream.

"I heard you," she replied quietly, her voice barely above a whisper.

For a moment, neither of them said anything. The silence crept back in, heavier than before. James' eyes returned to the screen, but this time, she could sense his restlessness, the way his fingers tapped nervously on the armrest. He was frustrated, but at what, exactly? At her? At himself? She wasn't sure anymore.

It had been so long since they had truly talked, really talked about anything that mattered. Their conversations were now just routines—about bills, about the kids, about work—but never about them. Never about what had happened to their marriage, to the love they had once shared.

Sophia stood up, the chair scraping against the floor with a harsh sound that broke the silence. She needed air. Space. A moment to think, to breathe. As she walked toward the door, she caught a glimpse of Isabella through the hallway, her back turned, her shoulders slumped as she sat in her room. It was like a punch to the gut. The realization that her daughter was no longer the little girl who once looked to her for guidance and affection.

Sophia stepped outside, closing the door softly behind her. The cool evening air hit her face, the chill sharp against her skin. She stood there for a long moment, letting the quiet surround her, the world outside offering her a temporary reprieve from the emotional chaos inside the house.

But even in the stillness, there was no escaping the truth. They were all strangers now. She didn't know how they had gotten here, but the distance between them was too wide, too deep. And though she stood outside, away from the tension, she knew that the moment she walked back through that door, she would still feel just as alone as she did every other day.

The question was no longer whether they could find their way back—it was whether they even wanted to. And she wasn't sure anymore if she had the strength to try.

Sophia stood there, her breath coming in shallow bursts, the weight of her thoughts pressing down on her chest. The quiet of the evening seemed to mock her, reminding her of all the things she hadn't said, all the things she didn't know how to say. She had spent so many years trying to keep the peace, to manage the chaos that was their lives, that she had forgotten what it meant to ask for help. Or perhaps she was afraid to admit that they had drifted so far apart that help might no longer be enough.

In the distance, she could hear the faint sound of traffic, but it felt distant, like another world entirely. She longed for a simple connection, a moment of clarity in the midst of the confusion. What had happened to the warmth, to the intimacy they had once shared? Had it been replaced by routine and obligation, by the mundane tasks of daily life?

Turning back toward the house, she hesitated for a moment before stepping inside. The door creaked as she pushed it open, a sound that seemed louder than usual in the stillness of the house. Her footsteps were tentative, almost hesitant, as she made her way back to the kitchen. James was still sitting on the couch, his eyes glued to the screen, his body tense with the unspoken frustrations that had been simmering for months.

Isabella's room was quiet. Sophia knew she was there, but the door was closed, the silence heavy with the unspoken tension between them. She could feel the walls that had been built around her daughter, the same walls she herself had started to construct over the years. They had both retreated into their own corners, away from the emotional turbulence that had come to define their lives.

Ethan was the only one who still sought her out, but even his presence felt fleeting these days. He would come to her with questions, with small requests, but he was becoming more and more distant, lost in his own world. Sophia could sense that he, too, was starting to feel the weight of the separation, the cracks forming in the foundation of their once-solid family.

Sitting at the kitchen table again, Sophia let out a deep sigh. It was clear now: they were all drifting, like pieces of a puzzle that no longer fit together. The love they had once shared had been eclipsed by their own personal struggles, by their inability to communicate, to reach across the emotional chasm that had grown between them.

"Do you want to talk?" James finally asked, his voice quieter now, tinged with something she couldn't quite place. There was a softness there, but it was buried under layers of frustration and hurt.

Sophia hesitated, unsure of how to answer. She wanted to say yes, to pour out all the feelings she had kept bottled up for so long, but the words caught in her throat. How could they talk when they no longer understood each other? When their conversations had become mere exchanges of pleasantries, avoiding the deep-seated issues that had been left unaddressed for far too long?

"I don't know, James," she said softly, her voice barely above a whisper. "I don't know what's left to say."

The words hung in the air, heavy and thick, like an anchor weighing her down. She wanted to believe that there was still hope, that they could fix this, that the connection they had once shared was not lost forever. But deep down, she was afraid that the distance had already become too great, that they were both too far gone to find their way back.

James sighed and turned off the TV, the room now filled with an unsettling silence. He looked at her, his eyes searching, but there was a distance there too, a void that seemed just as insurmountable as the one between her and Isabella, between her and Ethan.

"Maybe we've both been running," he said, his voice cracking slightly. "Maybe we've both been too afraid to face the truth of what we've become."

Sophia nodded slowly, the tears welling up in her eyes. She had been running, in her own way. Running from the pain, from the fear that she wasn't enough, from the overwhelming sense that she was losing everything she had fought so hard to hold onto.

But the truth was that they had been running together, side by side, only they hadn't seen it. They had been too focused on surviving, on getting through each day, to notice the small ways they were drifting apart.

The realization hit her with a sharp clarity. They weren't just strangers under one roof—they were strangers to each other, to the people they had once been, to the dreams they had once shared. They had become so caught up in their individual battles that they had forgotten how to fight for each other.

As the evening stretched on, the house remained silent, the weight of their unspoken words hanging heavy in the air. There was no easy solution, no magic phrase that could undo the years of distance, of hurt, of unmet expectations. But for the first time in a long while, Sophia felt something stir inside her—a flicker of hope, however small, that maybe, just maybe, they could still find their way back.

The journey would not be easy, and it would require more than just words. It would take time, patience, and a willingness to confront the truth of who they had become. But perhaps, in the end, it was worth fighting for.

Sophia stared at the dim light coming from the kitchen window, casting long shadows across the table. She felt the weight of the moment pressing down on her, but there was something else there, something unfamiliar—a quiet resolve, like a small spark in the darkness, waiting to be nurtured.

James was still in the living room, his face hidden in the soft glow of the dimmed television, but she could sense that he wasn't really watching. His thoughts seemed to be far away, as hers had often been. She had once believed that silence was a sanctuary, a place where they could both find peace. But tonight, the silence felt like a barrier. It was a wall built of years of unmet needs, unspoken resentments, and unacknowledged fears. It had kept them from really seeing each other, from truly being present.

"Do you think we're too far gone?" Sophia's voice was barely above a whisper, the question slipping out before she could stop it. She hadn't meant to ask it, hadn't even meant to voice the fear that had been gnawing at her. But now that it was out there, it hung between them like a specter.

James shifted on the couch, his gaze not meeting hers. "I don't know," he replied, his voice low, almost tired. "Sometimes it feels like we're just going through the motions. But then I think about the way we used to be, the way we used to look at each other, and I wonder if that version of us is still somewhere inside."

Sophia let his words sink in. That version of them—young, hopeful, full of possibility—felt like a distant memory, like a dream she once had but couldn't fully recall anymore. She wanted to believe it was still there, that they could rediscover it, but she didn't know where to begin.

"Maybe we need to start over," she said, her voice more certain now. "Not as strangers, but as people who are willing to really look at each other, to hear each other again."

The thought sounded almost absurd, but the more she considered it, the more it felt like the only way forward. They had both been living as though they were alone in this house, as though they were disconnected from the lives they had once shared. Maybe it was time to change that. Maybe they needed to strip away everything they thought they knew and rebuild from the ground up.

James finally turned to face her, his eyes weary but with something soft in them, something vulnerable. "Do you think we can do that?" His voice was tentative, as if he were testing the possibility, trying to gauge if there was still hope to hold onto.

Sophia didn't know the answer, but she felt something stir within her, something she hadn't felt in a long time—hope, but also fear. The fear of opening herself up, of confronting the mess they had become. But she knew, deep down, that it was the only way to move forward. They couldn't keep pretending.

"I don't know," she admitted, "but I think we owe it to ourselves to try."

The next few moments passed in quiet contemplation. Outside, the world continued on, oblivious to the turmoil unfolding inside the house. The night was still, the air thick with the weight of unresolved questions and shifting emotions.

Sophia stood up and walked over to the window, staring out into the dark night. It was as though the world outside mirrored the uncertainty inside, yet there was something oddly comforting in the stillness. Maybe it was the reminder that things could change, that the night could always give way to a new day. The question was, would they be ready for it?

James joined her by the window, standing close but not touching. They didn't need to. The silence between them felt different now. It wasn't an absence, but a quiet understanding, as if they had both acknowledged the distance between them and yet chosen not to ignore it.

"We're still here," he said softly. "That's something, right?"

Sophia turned to him, her eyes meeting his. She didn't know if they could ever be who they once were, but in this moment, she realized something important. They were still trying, still willing to face the truth, no matter how painful it might be.

"Yeah," she whispered. "That's something."

And for the first time in a long while, she felt a glimmer of hope—not because everything was perfect, but because they were both still willing to fight for it. To fight for them.

The silence in the room grew comfortable, almost peaceful, as the two of them stood side by side by the window. The world outside was still, the night unchanging, as if time itself had paused for just a moment. But inside the house, something had shifted. There was an unspoken agreement between them now—an understanding that whatever had happened in the past, whatever mistakes they had made, it was still possible to begin again.

Sophia's hand brushed against James's, a small, tentative gesture, but it spoke volumes. He didn't pull away. Instead, he let his fingers linger for a moment, as though testing the waters of connection again, unsure but willing to try.

"I used to think I knew everything about you," she said, her voice barely audible in the stillness. "The way you laugh, the way you think. I thought I had it all figured out. But now..." She paused, searching for the right words. "Now, it feels like I'm looking at a stranger, someone I don't understand anymore."

James exhaled slowly, his hand tightening ever so slightly around hers. "I get that. It's like we've become strangers under one roof. We've spent so much time building walls, putting on masks, that we lost who we were. Who we are."

The words hit her harder than she expected. Strangers under one roof. It was a simple phrase, but it captured everything that had gone wrong, everything that had led them here. They had lived in the same house, shared the same space, but somewhere along the way, they had stopped being a family, stopped being partners. They had become two people, each alone in their own way, trapped by their own fears, their own regrets.

"I don't want to be strangers anymore," Sophia whispered, her voice thick with emotion. "I don't want to live like this."

James turned to face her fully now, his eyes searching hers. "Then what do we do? How do we fix this?"

She swallowed hard, the question heavy in the air between them. There was no easy answer, no quick fix. They couldn't undo the years of silence, the years of avoidance, in one conversation. But maybe—just maybe—they could start with this, with the truth. With admitting that they didn't have all the answers, but they were willing to try to find them together.

"We start by being honest," she said softly. "With ourselves. With each other."

James nodded slowly, a look of resolve settling on his face. "And no more pretending? No more hiding?"

Sophia smiled faintly. "No more pretending."

They stood there for a long moment, the quiet of the house wrapping around them like a blanket. It was a fragile beginning, one that could easily unravel if they weren't careful. But in that silence, in that shared moment of understanding, there was something powerful. A promise, perhaps—a commitment to rebuild, even if they didn't know how.

The sound of a door creaking open broke the stillness. It was Emily, standing at the doorway, her expression uncertain as she peered into the room. She had been listening, no doubt, though neither Sophia nor James had noticed her approach. She was older now, no longer the child who had once run to them with open arms, but a young woman on the brink of understanding the complexities of their world.

"Are you two okay?" she asked cautiously, her voice softer than usual. There was a hint of worry in her eyes, a flicker of concern that had been missing for too long.

Sophia met her gaze and nodded, offering her daughter a reassuring smile, though it was tinged with sadness. "We're... trying," she said, her voice thick with emotion.

Emily stepped into the room, closing the door behind her. She looked from Sophia to James, and for a brief moment, there was a deep, almost painful silence, as though the weight of everything that had been said hung between them. But then Emily spoke again, her voice steady, but not without a trace of vulnerability.

"I think you're both doing better than you realize," she said quietly. "Maybe it doesn't feel like it right now, but at least you're talking again."

Sophia felt a lump form in her throat, her heart swelling with a mixture of relief and sorrow. Emily was right. It wasn't perfect, far from it. But they were talking, and that was more than they had done in months. It was a start—a small one, but a start nonetheless.

"We'll get there," James said, his voice thick with emotion. "It's going to take time, but we'll get there. Together."

Sophia nodded, feeling a tear slip down her cheek. It wasn't sadness, not entirely. It was the weight of the journey ahead, the uncertainty, but also the hope. Hope that maybe—just maybe—they could rebuild the connections that had been broken. Hope that they could start anew, not as strangers, but as a family.

And for the first time in what felt like years, Sophia allowed herself to believe in that possibility. Because in the end, maybe that was all they really needed. To believe. To try.

The house was quieter now, the hum of the refrigerator in the kitchen the only sound that filled the air. Emily had returned to her room, leaving Sophia and James standing together in the stillness, each of them deep in thought. The conversation, though brief, had cracked open something that had been tightly sealed for far too long. There was no turning back now—not because they couldn't, but because something had shifted, something had been set into motion that could not be undone.

Sophia took a deep breath, the weight of the moment sinking in. She felt a strange mixture of fear and relief. Fear because she knew the road ahead wouldn't be easy, and relief because, for the first time in a long time, they had actually said the words that mattered. They had finally acknowledged the distance between them, the quiet decay of their relationship, and now, for better or worse, they were faced with the possibility of healing it.

"I think we need to talk about everything," James said suddenly, his voice low and deliberate. "Not just the surface stuff, but the things we've been avoiding—the things we've been pretending aren't there."

Sophia looked at him, startled by the intensity in his voice. She had been bracing herself for a slow unraveling, but this felt different. He was ready. He was ready to confront the truth, no matter how ugly it might be.

"Yeah," she replied quietly, her voice barely above a whisper. "I think that's the only way we'll ever get through this."

They sat down at the kitchen table, the cold, empty space around them contrasting with the storm that raged in their hearts.

Each of them had built walls around themselves, carefully constructed over the years to protect them from the hurt, from the pain of confronting what they had become. But now those walls were crumbling, brick by brick, and they were left exposed, vulnerable.

Sophia's eyes met James's, and for a moment, the world seemed to fall away. The noise of the outside world, the hum of daily life, all of it faded into the background, leaving only the two of them. The space between them felt vast, but also charged with the possibility of something real, something raw.

"Where do we even start?" Sophia asked, her voice trembling slightly. "There's so much we've buried, so much we've ignored."

James leaned forward, his elbows resting on the table, his hands clasped together as though he were trying to gather his thoughts. "Maybe we start with the hardest part," he said quietly. "With what we've been too afraid to say to each other."

Sophia's heart skipped a beat. She knew what he meant. There had been too many moments when they had stayed silent, when they had let things fester, let resentment build. It had been easier to pretend, to hope that the problems would somehow fix themselves. But they hadn't. And now, they had no choice but to face them.

"I think we both know what it is," she said softly, her voice shaking with emotion. "We stopped seeing each other. We stopped really being there for each other."

James nodded, his face etched with the same sadness she felt in her chest. "I thought if I just kept going, kept doing everything right, everything would work out. But it didn't. I didn't see you anymore, Sophia. Not the way I should have."

The words were a blow, but they were also a relief. For so long, she had carried the weight of their unspoken distance, convinced that it was her fault. She had thought that maybe if she had tried harder, been more patient, more understanding, things would have been different. But hearing him admit it—hearing him take responsibility—was like a weight lifting off her shoulders. She wasn't alone in this.

"I didn't see you either," she admitted, her voice barely above a whisper. "I shut you out. I didn't want to deal with the fact that we were falling apart. It was easier to ignore it, to pretend everything was fine."

There was a long silence between them, a moment that felt as though the world was holding its breath, waiting for the next step. Sophia could feel the tears welling in her eyes, but she fought them back. This wasn't about tears. It was about truth. And maybe, just maybe, they were on the brink of finding it.

"I want to fix this," she said, her voice filled with determination. "I want to try, James. I don't want to give up on us."

He reached across the table, his hand brushing hers in a quiet gesture of solidarity. His touch was warm, familiar, but there was an intensity in it now, a silent promise.

"We'll fix it," he said, his voice steady. "But it's going to take time. It's going to take patience. And it's going to take both of us."

Sophia nodded, her heart swelling with a mixture of fear and hope. She didn't know what the future held, didn't know if they could ever truly go back to what they once had, but she did know this: they were both willing to try. And for the first time in a long time, that felt like enough.

The days that followed were both agonizing and hopeful. The house, once filled with the hum of daily routines and unspoken tension, now seemed quieter, more expectant. Each time Sophia and James crossed paths, there was an unspoken understanding between them—an acknowledgment of the journey they were beginning, but also of the difficult work ahead.

Emily, ever observant, had noticed the subtle shift between her parents. She had heard the murmurs late into the night, the faint sounds of their voices carried through the walls, words too low for her to catch but clear enough to know that something had changed. She didn't know exactly what, but she could sense it—there was a crack in the armor they had built around themselves.

For Emily, this change stirred a complicated mix of emotions. On the one hand, she had longed for this moment, when her parents would finally face the reality of their fractured relationship. But on the other, she felt the weight of being caught in the middle of it all, like an innocent bystander watching a storm roll in. She didn't want to be the reason they stayed together, and yet, she couldn't help but wonder if she would somehow be the reason they fell apart.

Sophia, too, found herself caught between two worlds. She had always wanted the best for Emily, but she had never realized how much her own unhappiness had been affecting her daughter. Emily had always been perceptive, but now, the distance between them seemed more pronounced. Sophia had so many questions—so many things she wanted to say to Emily—but she wasn't sure how to begin.

One evening, as the sun began to set and the soft golden light poured through the kitchen window, Sophia found herself standing at the counter, chopping vegetables for dinner. The familiar rhythm of the task was calming, and for a moment, she allowed herself to just exist in the quiet of it all. It wasn't until she felt a presence behind her that she turned to find Emily standing there, her arms crossed over her chest.

"Are you okay, Mom?" Emily asked, her voice gentle but laced with concern.

Sophia hesitated, the question catching her off guard. She had been so focused on her own struggles with James that she hadn't stopped to think about how this all was affecting Emily.

"I'm... I'm getting there," Sophia replied, her voice soft but firm. "I'm trying, Emily. But it's going to take time."

Emily nodded, her expression unreadable. For a moment, the two of them stood there, a silent understanding passing between them.

"You don't have to fix everything for me," Emily said quietly. "I know you want to, but you don't have to."

Sophia's heart tightened at the words. She had always felt that she had to protect Emily, that she had to shield her from the pain of their crumbling relationship. But hearing those words now made her realize just how much Emily had grown, how much she had already carried on her own.

"I know," Sophia said softly, wiping her hands on a towel before turning to face her daughter. "But I still want to. I want to make things better—for both of us."

Emily met her gaze, and in that moment, Sophia saw something in her daughter's eyes—a depth of understanding and maturity that she hadn't fully appreciated before.

"I know, Mom," Emily said again, her voice softer now, almost tender. "I just want you to be happy."

Sophia's heart swelled with emotion at those words. It was a simple statement, but it carried so much weight. She had spent so much time worrying about everyone else—about James, about the house, about keeping up appearances—that she had forgotten the one thing that mattered most. Happiness. Real, honest happiness. The kind that didn't require pretending or holding back.

"I'll get there," Sophia whispered, her voice thick with emotion. "I promise you."

As the days turned into weeks, the tension in the house slowly began to ease. James and Sophia had begun to have more honest conversations, small steps toward rebuilding trust. It wasn't perfect—there were moments of doubt, of frustration, of silence—but there were also moments of connection, moments when they remembered who they were before the distance crept in.

Emily, too, seemed to find a tentative peace in the changes. She had always been the quiet observer, the one who kept her feelings locked away, but now, there was a sense of openness that had begun to blossom between her and her parents. It wasn't easy, and there were still moments when the weight of their past seemed too much to bear, but there was progress. And progress, in its own quiet way, was enough.

Sophia often found herself reflecting on the path they had taken to get here. There had been so many times when it seemed easier to walk away, to give up on the idea of happiness and acceptance. But now, in the midst of all the uncertainty, there was a glimmer of something worth fighting for. She didn't know where the road would take her, or what the future held, but she was starting to believe that maybe, just maybe, it was possible to find her way back to something real. Something that had always been there—hidden beneath the surface, waiting to be discovered.

As the weeks unfolded, Sophia and James grew more accustomed to the silence that now filled their home. It wasn't an uncomfortable silence, nor was it one of avoidance. It was a quiet that gave them space to breathe, to think, and to realize how much they had let their lives drift apart. The change wasn't sudden, but gradual—a shift that began with simple moments of understanding and quiet moments of vulnerability.

James, who had always been the stoic one, found himself opening up in ways he hadn't in years. The anger, the frustration that had built up between him and Sophia for so long, began to slowly ebb away. It wasn't because they had solved everything, but because they were finally facing the issues, instead of ignoring them.

One evening, after a particularly hard conversation about their past, James sat down at the dining table with Sophia. The soft light from the overhead lamp bathed the room in warmth. It was a stark contrast to the coldness that had once settled between them, but now there was a sense of tentative hope.

"Do you remember when we first met?" James asked suddenly, his voice low but carrying the weight of unspoken thoughts.

Sophia looked up from the cup of tea she had been absently stirring. It was a question that seemed so simple, yet it held so much meaning. She smiled faintly, lost in the memory.

"Of course," she said quietly. "How could I forget? You were so full of energy, always making me laugh."

James chuckled, the sound soft and sincere. "I don't know if I can say the same about myself now. But you were always the one who understood me. I think I took that for granted."

Sophia's heart ached at his words. She had always known that James struggled to express himself, that his emotions were locked behind a wall he had carefully constructed. But now, hearing him speak with such honesty, it was a sign that perhaps they were moving forward.

"I took a lot for granted, too," Sophia admitted, her voice barely above a whisper. "We both did."

They sat in silence for a while, not needing to say anything more. It was a kind of peace, not born from perfect understanding, but from acceptance. It wasn't that the past had been erased—it never could be—but that they were starting to learn how to move forward with it, instead of letting it weigh them down.

For Emily, the shift was both relieving and unsettling. She had spent most of her life pretending everything was fine, convincing herself that the undercurrent of tension in the house was just a phase. But now, as she watched her parents struggle to rebuild their connection, she couldn't help but feel both hope and fear. She hoped for their happiness, but at the same time, she feared what it might mean for her own place in this changing dynamic.

It was a Tuesday afternoon when Emily and Sophia finally had a conversation that would change the course of their relationship. Sophia had been out in the garden, tending to the flowers she had always loved but never had the time for. Emily found her there, kneeling in the soft dirt, her fingers stained with earth. There was a quiet beauty to the scene, a sense of calm that Emily hadn't expected.

"I've been thinking a lot about you lately," Emily said, her voice unsteady as she approached.

Sophia paused, looking up from the flowers, her expression softening when she saw her daughter. "What's on your mind, Emily?"

"I just... I feel like everything is changing, and I'm not sure where I fit into it all anymore." Emily's words tumbled out before she could stop them. "I want things to get better, I do. But sometimes, I feel like I'm losing both of you in the process."

Sophia stood slowly, brushing the dirt from her hands before reaching out to gently touch Emily's arm. "I don't want you to feel that way. We're not going anywhere, I promise. We're just trying to figure things out... and I know it's not easy. It's not easy for any of us."

Emily blinked back tears, suddenly overwhelmed by the raw honesty in her mother's voice. She had always carried the weight of her parents' unhappiness, convinced it was her job to make things right. But now, Sophia's words were like a lifeline, a reminder that she didn't have to carry this burden alone.

"I know," Emily said, her voice thick with emotion. "I just want you to be happy, Mom."

Sophia smiled softly, her heart swelling with love for her daughter. "I'm trying, sweetheart. And I think, maybe, we're starting to get there."

The weeks continued to pass, each day bringing new challenges but also new moments of connection. Sophia, James, and Emily each navigated their personal growth and healing in their own way, but they did so with a newfound understanding of one another.

The house, once a place of tension, slowly transformed into a home again. The walls that had been silent witnesses to so many years of unspoken words and unacknowledged pain began to hum with the quiet promise of new beginnings. It wasn't perfect, and it would never be, but the cracks in the foundation had allowed something new to grow—something stronger than before.

And perhaps, in time, the distance that had once felt insurmountable would continue to shrink, until they were all standing together, no longer strangers under one roof, but a family, learning to love each other once more.

The days turned into months, and with every passing week, the subtle changes in their family dynamics became more noticeable. The house, which had once felt like a battleground, now hummed with a quieter energy—one of tentative understanding, of people who were trying, not to perfect the impossible, but to make something better out of what they had left. It was messy, awkward at times, but there was something undeniably human about it.

Sophia found herself spending more time alone in the mornings, sitting on the porch with a cup of coffee, watching the early sunlight filter through the trees. It had become her time to reflect, to gather herself before the demands of the day took over. There were still moments when the weight of the past crept into her thoughts—regrets about the things left unsaid, decisions made hastily, love that had been taken for granted—but there was a growing sense of peace as she let go of the burden of perfection.

One morning, as she sat lost in thought, James joined her on the porch. He was quieter now, his usual bravado replaced with a kind of gentleness that surprised her. He had never been one for deep conversations, but these days, he seemed to want to talk more. Not about grand things, but about small things—about the way the sun felt on his skin, about the silence that had become more comforting than it had ever been before.

He took a seat beside her, the creak of the wooden chair breaking the quiet.

"I've been thinking," he started, his voice low but steady. "About how we got here. And how far we've come... and how far we still need to go."

Sophia glanced at him, her gaze softening. "It's a journey, James. We can't rush it."

He nodded slowly, his eyes fixed on the horizon. "I know. It's just... it feels different now. Like, we're not pretending anymore. We're just... here."

There was something in his voice that caught her attention, something that wasn't quite sadness, but a kind of acknowledgment. A recognition of how much time had passed, of how much they had lost, but also how much they still had.

Sophia reached out, her fingers brushing against his. "We're here," she echoed quietly, "and that's enough."

For the first time in a long while, they sat in silence, but it wasn't uncomfortable. It wasn't the silence of avoidance or fear—it was the silence of two people who had learned to simply be with each other, without expectations, without the need to fix everything at once. It was enough, for now.

Emily, too, was slowly learning to navigate her place in this new reality. She had always been the bridge between her parents, trying to hold the pieces together when it felt like they were about to fall apart. But now, as their relationship shifted and healed, she found herself asking questions she had never dared to ask before.

One afternoon, as she was sitting in the living room, reading a book, Sophia came in with a smile. It was the kind of smile that reached her eyes, one that hadn't been there in a long time. It was a smile of contentment, of peace, of someone who was learning to trust again.

"Can we talk?" Sophia asked, her voice gentle.

Emily looked up, setting the book aside. "Of course."

Sophia sat down beside her, her eyes thoughtful. "I've been thinking a lot about us. About how much I've missed you, and how much I've let slip through the cracks. I want to be better, Emily. I want to be the mom you deserve."

Emily felt a lump rise in her throat. It wasn't that she had expected perfection from her mother, but to hear her speak those words—words that were filled with raw honesty—was more than she could have asked for.

"I've missed you too," Emily admitted softly. "I didn't realize how much until now."

They sat together in the quiet, the air between them filled with things they hadn't said, but also with things they now knew. Things they would continue to say, little by little, as they learned how to be together again.

James and Sophia's relationship, too, continued to evolve. They found themselves talking about things they had never discussed before—their fears, their dreams, their regrets. But they also talked about their future, about what they wanted the next chapter of their lives to look like. It wasn't easy. It never would be. But for the first time in years, there was a glimmer of hope, a belief that maybe they could make it work.

There was no magic solution, no instant fix. But they had something more important now: the willingness to try, and the courage to face whatever came next. Together.

One evening, as they sat down for dinner, Emily looked around the table at her parents. It was a simple moment—no grand gestures, no perfect speeches. But it was enough. For the first time in a long time, the family sat together, not as strangers under one roof, but as people who had been through the storm and were beginning to find their way back to each other.

And in that moment, Emily realized that love wasn't about perfection. It wasn't about getting everything right. It was about learning to forgive, learning to grow, and most importantly, learning to be there for each other, even when it felt impossible.

As the evening wore on, they talked and laughed, and for a while, the past didn't seem so heavy. It was a beginning, a new chapter for their family, one that was still being written.

And for the first time in years, there was no fear of what the future might hold. Because for the first time in a long time, they were all finally starting to believe that they could face it—together.

Chapter 4: Unraveling Truths

1. Secrets Beneath the Surface

The house felt too quiet. It always did after the kids had gone to bed, leaving behind the echoes of their footsteps and the soft hum of the refrigerator. Sophia sat on the edge of their bed, the evening light fading through the curtains, casting long shadows across the room. Her eyes wandered to the framed photograph on the nightstand, a picture from their anniversary last year. They looked happy, smiling as if nothing could break the facade they had so carefully built over the years.

But beneath the surface, everything was far from perfect.

Her mind replayed the conversation from earlier. James had said nothing as she had spoken, his gaze distant, as if he were somewhere else. He had always been like that—silent when it mattered the most. The silence between them had grown louder over the years, filling the spaces that once buzzed with laughter and love. She had tried, oh how she had tried, to get through to him, but each attempt felt like hitting a wall. And now, the weight of their unspoken words seemed too heavy to bear.

Sophia ran her fingers through her hair, feeling the tension in her neck. She had always been the one to hold everything together, managing the house, the children, and her growing career. But the more she gave, the more she felt herself slipping away. What had happened to the woman who once believed that love could conquer all? What happened to their promises, to the dreams they had once shared?

Across the room, James lay in bed, staring at the ceiling, his face expressionless. He had retreated into himself long ago, burying his feelings under layers of work and routine. His love for her, once so passionate, had faded into something unrecognizable. He had become a stranger in his own home, an unfamiliar presence whose silence spoke louder than any words.

It wasn't just their marriage that was at stake; it was everything. The children—Izzy, Ethan—they were growing up, and she could see the cracks in their little worlds as well. Izzy had started pulling away, seeking refuge in her books and the safety of her own thoughts, while Ethan struggled to find his place in a family where no one seemed to understand him. Sophia had always hoped they would turn out differently, that they would learn from her mistakes, but now she realized she had been too busy trying to fix everything to notice when things started falling apart.

Her thoughts were interrupted by the sound of James shifting in bed. She turned to him, her heart pounding. "James," she whispered, "are we really this far apart? Is there anything left?"

He didn't answer at first, and for a moment, she wondered if he had even heard her. Then, slowly, he turned his head, his eyes meeting hers in the dim light. There was a flicker of something in them—regret, maybe, or just the weight of years spent ignoring the truth. But in that moment, she realized that they both knew. They both understood that something had been lost. And now, the question was whether they could ever find it again.

James sighed deeply, his hand resting on his forehead as if the weight of the world was pressing down on him. The silence stretched between them, thick and suffocating, until Sophia couldn't stand it any longer. "Why do you always do this?" she asked, her voice barely above a whisper. "Why do you always pull away when things get hard?"

James closed his eyes for a moment, his jaw tightening. "I don't know," he muttered, almost to himself. "I don't know how to make it right. I don't know how to fix this."

Sophia felt the sting of his words, not because of the truth in them, but because of how long they had lingered unsaid. How many times had she asked herself the same question? Why had they let things go this far? Why hadn't they fought harder to keep their love alive?

"I feel like I'm losing you," she said quietly, a tear slipping down her cheek. "And I don't know how to stop it."

James reached out, his hand hesitating before it touched hers. The gesture was tentative, unsure. He was trying, but it felt like a hollow attempt—too little, too late. The space between them was so vast now, it seemed impossible to bridge.

"I don't want to lose you," he whispered, his voice thick with emotion. "But I don't know how to fix what's broken. I don't even know where to start."

Sophia wanted to scream, to shake him, to make him understand that their love wasn't beyond saving. But she had tried that before, and it had only pushed him further away. So instead, she took a deep breath and held his hand tighter, as if that small act could hold the pieces of their shattered connection together.

"I think we both need to start by being honest," she said softly, her voice trembling. "With ourselves. With each other."

For the first time in a long while, she saw a flicker of something—hope, maybe—cross James' face. It was fleeting, but it was there. And for that brief moment, Sophia allowed herself to believe that there might still be a chance. But she knew that the road ahead wouldn't be easy. There were too many secrets buried beneath the surface, too many years of unspoken words and unaddressed wounds.

The question now wasn't whether they could survive the storm that was coming, but whether they could face it together.

2. The Guilt of Choices

SOPHIA SAT BY THE WINDOW, watching the world outside continue as if nothing had changed. The morning sun filtered through the curtains, casting soft light across the room. But inside, everything was different. The guilt weighed heavily on her chest, a constant reminder of the choices she had made, the paths she had chosen, and the family she had neglected in the process.

She thought back to when she had first started climbing the career ladder. It seemed so simple then — a few extra hours at the office, a few missed dinners, a few apologies to the children for not being there. But with each missed moment, the gap between her and her family had grown wider, until it had become a chasm, unbridgeable by mere words.

James had never said anything, not directly. He had always been so understanding, so patient. But Sophia had seen it in his eyes — the quiet resignation. She had seen the way his smiles had become more forced, his laughter less frequent. And she had seen the way he looked at her, like a stranger trying to recall the last time they had truly connected.

The hardest part was the children. Izzy, once so eager to share her day with her mother, had withdrawn into herself. Ethan, sensitive and eager to please, had started to take on responsibilities that should not have been his. He began taking care of things around the house, things that Sophia should have been handling. There was a part of her that admired his maturity, but another part of her — the motherly part — that ached for the innocence he had lost too soon.

And then there was the guilt of the unspoken things. The times she had told herself she would make it up to them, only to be swept away by the next project, the next meeting, the next deadline. Each time, her promises felt empty, like words on paper that couldn't be turned into reality.

It wasn't just about time — it was about priorities. And somewhere along the way, she had allowed her career to become her identity. She had sacrificed the very people who had once meant the world to her, all for the sake of something intangible. Success. Recognition. The feeling of being needed. But in her pursuit of these things, she had lost the one thing she couldn't get back: time with her family.

James had tried to make her see it, but the conversations never went anywhere. The walls they had built between them were too high to climb, too thick to break. She had told herself that she was doing it for them, that a better future would make up for the sacrifices. But now, as she sat in the silence of their home, she couldn't help but wonder if it had been worth it.

And then there were the silent battles, the ones she fought within herself. The guilt wasn't just about the choices she had made, but about the guilt of feeling trapped in them. It was a weight she couldn't shake, a constant presence that lingered in every room, every conversation, every quiet moment.

Sophia had thought that making her family proud meant achieving success, pushing herself to be the best, to be admired. But now, she realized how little that truly mattered. Success had come at a cost she hadn't fully understood until it was too late. And now, as the cracks in her marriage and her family deepened, she found herself asking the one question she had avoided for so long: *Was it worth it?*

Sophia leaned back in her chair, closing her eyes as if she could will herself to find some peace in the chaos of her mind. The guilt was not just a fleeting feeling; it had become part of her, woven into the fabric of her daily life. Each time she looked at her children, she saw the distance between them, a gap that no words could fill.

Ethan had changed the most. He had always been the quiet one, the observer, but now he was different. There was a maturity in him that felt out of place for a boy of his age. He had stopped asking her to help with his homework, stopped showing her his drawings or telling her about his day. He had stopped needing her, or so it seemed. Instead, he had started taking on more responsibilities around the house, as though trying to fill the empty spaces left by her absence.

Izzy, on the other hand, had retreated into herself. The spark in her eyes that had once been so bright was now dimmed, buried under layers of disappointment. She didn't want to share her thoughts with Sophia anymore, didn't want to talk about her school day or her friends. Instead, she spent more time in her room, her door closed, the distance between them growing wider with every day that passed.

It was in these moments, when she saw the effects of her choices reflected in their faces, that the weight of her decisions felt unbearable. The hours she had poured into her work, thinking she was building a future for them all, had instead built a wall. A wall that no longer just separated her from her children, but from the woman she had once been — the mother, the wife, the person who had cared for them with unconditional love.

James, too, had become a stranger in his own right. The easy laughter they once shared had vanished. The conversations that once flowed so effortlessly between them had turned into formal exchanges, filled with polite nods and forced smiles. There was no passion left, no shared dreams. Just the remnants of what once was, lingering in the spaces between them, a quiet reminder of everything they had lost.

It was as though, in her quest for success, she had lost sight of what truly mattered. She had been so consumed with the idea of achievement, of proving herself worthy of respect and admiration, that she had failed to see the needs of the people who mattered most. The people who loved her unconditionally, and who, in turn, needed her love just as much.

The guilt didn't come from any one action. It was the accumulation of small moments, the neglect of what was truly important. The missed soccer games, the forgotten birthday parties, the unreturned phone calls. It was the realization that, in the end, no amount of success or recognition could ever replace the simple, everyday moments she had allowed to slip away.

Sophia stood and walked to the kitchen, her movements slow, deliberate. She poured herself a glass of water, the cool liquid a temporary relief to the tightness in her chest. She wanted to fix it, to make everything right again, but she didn't know how. She didn't know how to turn back the clock, how to undo the choices she had made.

Maybe it wasn't about fixing things. Maybe it was about learning to live with the consequences of those choices, accepting that some things couldn't be undone. Perhaps it was time to stop running from the guilt and face it head-on. To look her family in the eye and tell them that she was sorry, truly sorry, for the time she had stolen from them.

But the thought of those words, of confronting the hurt she had caused, made her heart ache with fear. Fear of rejection, fear of failure. Fear that the damage was irreversible.

She could feel the weight of the choices she had made, but she also felt a flicker of hope — a glimmer that maybe, just maybe, it wasn't too late to begin again. That the guilt, while powerful, didn't have to define her. That there could still be room for redemption, if only she had the courage to take the first step.

3. Shattered Illusions

THE DINNER TABLE WAS set meticulously, the fine china gleaming under the soft, warm glow of the chandelier. Sophia Collins, always the perfectionist, had ensured every detail was in place. The flowers in the vase, a deep shade of violet, matched the tablecloth, and the crystal glasses caught the light just so. Yet, despite the outward appearance of harmony, something in the air felt wrong. There was an underlying tension that neither the polished silverware nor the soft jazz playing in the background could mask.

James sat at the head of the table, his usually confident posture slightly slouched. His eyes flicked over to his wife, but he didn't speak. The silence between them was as thick as the scent of roast lamb that filled the room. For weeks, they had been skirting around the issues that were slowly eroding the foundation of their marriage, both pretending that everything was fine. But the cracks were becoming too noticeable to ignore.

Sophia smiled mechanically as she passed a dish to their daughter, Izzy, who was barely touching her food. The young woman had always been the quiet observer in the family, the one who noticed the subtle shifts in behavior that others overlooked. It was no surprise that she had been the first to see the growing distance between her parents, though she would never admit it aloud. Her eyes met her mother's for a brief second, a silent exchange passing between them, but neither of them said a word.

Ethan, their younger son, was more focused on his phone than the strained family dinner. He wasn't yet old enough to fully understand the gravity of what was happening, but he could sense the tension. He had always been more attuned to his mother's moods than to his father's, and tonight, Sophia seemed different—distant, as though she were miles away even though she sat right across from him.

James cleared his throat, breaking the silence. "We need to talk, Sophia." The words hung in the air like a threat, though they were spoken calmly, even tenderly. It wasn't the first time he had said that, but it was the first time it felt so final. There was a weariness in his voice, a deep exhaustion that came from years of unspoken resentment.

Sophia's hand paused mid-motion, the spoon in her grasp trembling slightly. She had known this conversation was coming, but she had hoped it would stay buried, at least for a little while longer. She had been too focused on her career, too obsessed with the idea of success to acknowledge the cracks in her marriage, in her family. The truth was, she had been living in a bubble, one that had been carefully constructed over the years. But bubbles were fragile, and hers was about to burst.

"I don't know where to start," she said, her voice barely above a whisper. Her words were edged with vulnerability, a rare admission of uncertainty. The woman who had always been so sure of herself, so determined to control every aspect of her life, was now confronted with the reality that she couldn't fix this on her own. "I thought if I just kept pushing, kept working harder, everything would fall into place. But it hasn't. It hasn't at all."

James didn't respond immediately, his gaze fixed on the table in front of him. He could hear the pain in her voice, and it cut him deeper than he expected. They had both been guilty of living in denial, of pretending that the pieces of their life fit together perfectly when they so clearly did not. But for James, the biggest illusion had been his belief that his silence, his passivity, had kept everything intact. He had fooled himself into thinking that as long as he kept his head down and his family financially secure, everything else would work itself out.

"We've both been pretending, haven't we?" James said finally, lifting his eyes to meet hers. His words were sharp, but there was no anger in them, just the raw, aching truth.

Sophia nodded slowly, her eyes filled with tears that she refused to let fall. "I thought I was doing the right thing," she whispered. "But now... I don't know. I don't know if it was worth it."

The illusion of the perfect family, the ideal life they had once envisioned, had shattered. What remained was a painful, raw reality that neither of them was prepared to face. But they had no choice. The cracks had grown too wide, the lies too many to ignore any longer. The dinner, once meant to be a moment of connection, had become the stage for an unavoidable reckoning.

The family was no longer the united front they had once been, and the road ahead was uncertain. But in the silence that followed, there was an understanding: the first step toward healing was admitting the truth, no matter how much it hurt.

Sophia's fingers clenched around the edge of her glass, the cool surface offering a fleeting comfort. Her mind raced, replaying the years of choices that had led to this moment, the quiet compromises she had made in pursuit of success and recognition. How had she let her family slip through her fingers like this? The guilt weighed heavily on her chest, suffocating her in ways she hadn't imagined. But there was no turning back now. The illusion of perfection had crumbled, and in its place was a painful, humbling reality.

Izzy's gaze had been fixed on her mother the entire time, but she remained silent. It wasn't because she lacked the words; rather, it was because she had already said too much. Her rebellious teenage years had been spent watching her mother chase dreams that seemed to grow farther out of reach with each passing year. She had seen the hollow eyes, the distracted smiles, the absence at important moments. Yet, what could she say now? The chasm between her parents had long since widened beyond her ability to fix.

Ethan, on the other hand, seemed to sense that something was shifting, though his understanding was still clouded by childhood simplicity. He picked at his food, his expression pensive, before blurting out, "Why don't we just talk about it, then? Like, really talk. Why do we always have to pretend things are fine?" His words were unexpectedly mature, a piercing observation that seemed to hang in the air long after he had spoken.

Sophia's eyes welled up. She had tried so hard to protect her children from the mess she had created. But in doing so, she had built a wall between them, one she wasn't sure could be torn down. Ethan's innocence, his simplicity, stung her deeply. In trying to shelter him, she had deprived him of the truth, and now she was paying the price.

"We've been hiding from the truth for so long," Sophia said, her voice breaking, her mask of control finally cracking. "But the truth doesn't stay hidden forever. I've been too focused on my career, on being... on being someone who mattered outside of this family." She took a breath, wiping away a tear that threatened to fall. "I thought I could juggle it all. I thought if I could just... succeed, everything else would fall into place. But I've been lying to myself. And now it's too late."

James watched her, his expression softening. He could see the vulnerability in her eyes, the raw honesty that had always been buried beneath her carefully constructed façade. He had spent years resenting her for her ambition, for what he perceived as her neglect. But now, seeing her like this, he realized how far they had drifted apart. The resentment, the anger—those emotions, too, had been a form of self-deception, a shield to protect him from confronting the truth of their failing marriage.

He reached across the table, his hand resting on hers, a silent gesture of understanding. "You're not alone in this, Sophia," he said quietly. "I've been blind too, and I've been holding on to things that should have been let go a long time ago."

There was a long pause, as if both of them were waiting for the other to speak, to offer some sort of resolution, a way forward. But no words came. The weight of their shared history was too heavy to be lifted in a single conversation. It would take time—time to heal, to rebuild what had been shattered.

Izzy finally spoke, her voice hesitant but resolute. "Maybe it's time for us to stop pretending, too. We're not kids anymore, Mom. We can handle the truth. We can help you, and we can help each other. But only if we stop hiding from it." Her words were blunt, but there was a strength in them that made Sophia pause. It was as though her daughter had grown into the person she had always hoped she would be—someone who saw through the lies and had the courage to confront the truth.

Ethan looked up at her, his face earnest. "Yeah, we're a family. We should be talking, not just hiding behind... all this." He gestured vaguely to the pristine table, the perfect meal that was now an ironic symbol of their fractured lives. "The house, the career, the stuff—it's not enough if we're all just pretending."

Sophia sat back in her chair, her chest tight with emotion. The truth, though painful, had been spoken. And in that moment, she realized that their family's future didn't have to be defined by the lies and illusions that had once held them together. Perhaps, in some strange way, this brokenness was the beginning of something new. Something real.

"Maybe we do need to start over," she whispered, more to herself than to anyone else. "Maybe the first step is just... being honest."

James gave a small nod, a flicker of hope crossing his face. It wasn't a promise that everything would be easy, nor that all the wounds would heal immediately. But it was a step in the right direction—a step away from the illusion that had defined their lives for so long.

In the silence that followed, the weight of what had been said settled into the room. There were no guarantees, no immediate fixes. But there was something far more important: the willingness to face the truth, together. And for the first time in a long while, there was a glimmer of hope that, even in the midst of shattered illusions, they could find a way back to each other.

The conversation lingered in the air, the unspoken words hanging like a fog. As the evening wore on, the reality of their shared truths began to sink in, heavier than any storm they had weathered. Each of them retreated into their own thoughts, unsure of how to bridge the gap between what had been said and what still needed to be understood.

Sophia stood, excusing herself with a quiet murmur, her steps slow and deliberate as she made her way to the kitchen. She needed space, a moment to process the gravity of the situation. The kitchen was where she had always found solace, even if it had been an illusion of control—cooking, cleaning, managing the chaos of the family. But now, as she stood by the sink, the familiar hum of the refrigerator and the soft clink of dishes felt strangely alien. The scent of garlic and herbs, once comforting, now seemed to mock her. Had she been so consumed by her desire to be successful that she had lost touch with the very people she had been striving to provide for?

She closed her eyes, pressing her fingers to her temples, trying to stave off the overwhelming wave of guilt. Could she really repair this? Could she fix the fractures in her family that had deepened over time?

James appeared in the doorway, his presence unannounced, but not unwelcome. "You okay?" His voice was quiet, hesitant, as though he wasn't sure if he had the right to ask. They hadn't spoken like this in years—truly spoken, not just exchanged pleasantries or avoided conflict.

Sophia met his gaze, her breath shaky as she exhaled. "I don't know, James. I don't know if I can fix this."

James stepped forward, his hand reaching out to touch her shoulder gently. "I don't know if we can either, but maybe we don't need to fix it all at once. Maybe we just need to start. Together."

His words were simple, but there was an honesty in them that disarmed her, stripping away the defenses she had so carefully constructed. He wasn't offering grand solutions or empty promises. He was acknowledging the brokenness, and, for the first time, it didn't feel like a defeat. It felt like a possibility.

"I've been holding on to the idea of what we should have been," she admitted, her voice barely above a whisper. "I've been chasing something I thought would make us whole. But I don't even know if I remember how to be the kind of person I used to be, the kind of mother you needed me to be. I don't know if I even remember how to be... us."

James looked at her, his face softening. "We're still here. We're still trying. That's something, right?"

Sophia nodded, her throat tight. It wasn't much, but it was a start. The weight of their years of distance couldn't be erased in a single conversation, but it was a crack in the wall they had built between them. A crack that, with time and effort, could widen enough to let light in.

Back at the table, Izzy and Ethan exchanged looks, sensing the shift in the air. Ethan, ever the optimist, broke the silence with a question that seemed almost too innocent for the gravity of the situation. "So, does this mean we don't have to pretend anymore?"

Izzy smiled faintly, her eyes betraying the deep well of emotion she usually kept buried. "Yeah," she said softly, her voice tinged with a sadness that wasn't there before. "Maybe it's time we stop pretending everything's perfect. Because it's not. And that's okay."

Sophia returned to the table, her eyes red from the brief breakdown in the kitchen. She looked at her children, the faces she had neglected but never stopped loving, and felt something stir inside her—a desire to rebuild, not from the illusion of perfection, but from the raw truth of who they were now.

James reached for her hand as she sat down, his grip steady, a silent promise that they would move forward, one step at a time. "We'll get through this," he said quietly, though the weight of their history hung between them.

Izzy and Ethan nodded, their expressions softening as they, too, grasped the reality of the moment. They didn't have all the answers, and they didn't know what the future held. But they had each other, and that, for now, was enough.

The evening stretched on, the silence no longer heavy with unspoken resentments, but filled with the tentative hope of a family learning to rediscover each other. As the hours passed, they spoke more freely, not yet entirely free of the discomfort that clung to them but moving toward a place of honesty—a place where the illusion of perfection no longer had to be their shield.

It would take time, no doubt. There would be moments of doubt, moments where old habits resurfaced, where the weight of their past would feel insurmountable. But for the first time in a long while, Sophia felt something shift within her—a willingness to face the truth, however uncomfortable, and to embrace the messiness of life and love.

The illusion of what their family should have been had crumbled, yes. But in its place, perhaps, there was the beginning of something truer. Something real.

And that was enough for now.

As the days passed, the conversation from that night lingered in Sophia's mind. It wasn't a magical fix, nor was it the end of their troubles, but it had been a step—small, tentative, but a step nonetheless. She had spent years holding onto an ideal, a dream of how life should be, but now she was learning that it was okay to let go of that dream and accept the truth of who they were, as imperfect as it was.

One evening, a week after the conversation at the table, Sophia found herself sitting alone in the living room, the quiet hum of the house wrapping around her. The children were upstairs—Izzy, still lost in her world of art, and Ethan, buried in his books. James was working late again, lost in the demands of his career, but that night, it wasn't his absence that troubled her. It was her own sense of disconnection, a feeling she hadn't realized was so deep until now.

She glanced at the photographs on the wall, capturing moments of a family that once felt whole—before the cracks started to show. Before the illusions of success and perfection had overshadowed the small, intimate moments they had once shared. Sophia reached for one of the frames, the image of her and James on their wedding day, their smiles so genuine, so full of hope.

It felt like a lifetime ago.

Her hand trembled slightly as she set the picture back down. Had she ever really known who she was, apart from the roles she played? A wife. A mother. A career woman. Each one had defined her, but none of them had truly captured the essence of who she was at her core. Somewhere along the way, she had gotten lost in trying to meet expectations—her own, society's, and, most painfully, her family's. She had convinced herself that perfection was the goal, that if everything was just right, the cracks wouldn't show, and maybe, just maybe, they would all be happy.

But it wasn't true. It never had been.

Sophia's thoughts were interrupted by the sound of footsteps on the stairs. She looked up, her eyes meeting Izzy's, who stood in the doorway with an unreadable expression.

"Izzy..." Sophia began, her voice soft. "You okay?"

Izzy nodded, but her eyes held something deeper, something Sophia couldn't quite place. "I'm fine, Mom. Just wanted to talk."

Sophia gestured to the seat beside her. "Come sit. I'm here."

Izzy hesitated for a moment before slowly walking over and sitting down. The silence stretched between them, but it wasn't uncomfortable this time. It was the kind of silence that came with understanding, the kind that only existed when two people had shared something real, even if it was just an unspoken acknowledgment of their struggles.

"I've been thinking," Izzy began, her voice quieter than usual. "About everything. About you... and Dad... and me."

Sophia turned her body slightly, giving Izzy her full attention. "What about it?"

Izzy shifted in her seat, clearly grappling with something she hadn't yet put into words. "I think I understand now. Why you've been so distant. I've always thought it was because of... of your work, or because you didn't care, but now, I think I get it. You were just trying to be something... someone that you thought we needed you to be."

Sophia's heart clenched. She had always tried to be the perfect mother, the perfect wife, the perfect everything—but in doing so, she had created distance, not just from her family, but from herself. "I'm sorry, Izzy," she whispered. "I didn't mean to hurt you."

Izzy's eyes softened, her tone gentle. "You didn't hurt me. You were just... lost. Like the rest of us."

Sophia let out a long, shaky breath. She had been so consumed by her need to prove something—to herself, to James, to everyone—that she hadn't noticed how much her family had been unraveling until it was too late. "I've spent so much time trying to be perfect, trying to be what I thought you needed me to be, that I lost sight of everything that really mattered. I lost sight of *you*, Izzy."

For a moment, Izzy didn't say anything, just stared at her mother, as if processing everything she had just heard. Then, finally, she spoke. "Maybe we just need to stop pretending, Mom. Stop pretending we have it all together, because none of us do. But we're still here. Together."

Sophia smiled softly, a tear escaping down her cheek. "Together," she echoed, the word tasting like a promise. "Yeah, maybe that's all we really need."

James arrived home late that night, as usual, but something was different about the atmosphere in the house. The tension that had once filled the air seemed to have lifted, replaced by a quiet, tentative hope. Sophia stood in the kitchen when he entered, her back to him as she stirred a pot on the stove. She didn't say anything at first, but he knew her well enough to sense the change. He knew something had shifted, though he didn't yet understand what.

"Izzy and I talked," she said after a moment, her voice low but steady. "About everything."

James nodded, leaning against the doorframe. "I know. She came to me, too."

Sophia looked over her shoulder at him, surprised. "She did?"

James smiled faintly, though there was a sadness behind his eyes. "Yeah. She's growing up, Sophia. We both are."

The weight of his words settled over her like a heavy quilt. They were both growing up—learning, evolving, but not necessarily in the ways they had expected. Their lives had been defined by the roles they had played, but perhaps now, in the wreckage of their illusions, they were beginning to see the possibility of something more genuine.

Sophia turned back to the stove, stirring absentmindedly. "I don't know if we can fix everything, James. But maybe that's okay."

"I don't think we need to fix everything," James replied. "We just need to start over. Together. For real this time."

Sophia let out a quiet laugh, a sound that surprised both of them. "Together," she repeated. "Yeah. That sounds good."

It wasn't a perfect ending, and it wouldn't be an easy road. But for the first time in a long time, Sophia felt as though she was ready to walk it—not as a perfect mother, a perfect wife, or a perfect woman, but simply as herself. And maybe, just maybe, that was enough.

4. Reaching Out

THE TENSION IN THE house had been building for weeks. Sophia could feel it, the way the air felt heavier, how the silence between her and James stretched longer than it ever had before. Every evening, they sat across from each other at the dinner table, the weight of unspoken words making the food taste bland. It wasn't that they didn't love each other anymore—it was that they didn't know how to love each other anymore.

Sophia had always been the one to hold everything together. She had been the glue that kept their family from falling apart, the one who made sure everyone's needs were met, even at the cost of her own. But now, she felt as though she was falling through the cracks. Her dreams of a successful career, of something more than just being a wife and mother, had started to take root, and yet, she couldn't shake the feeling that in reaching for more, she was losing everything she already had.

James, on the other hand, had always been the steady one. The dependable one. But beneath his calm exterior, there was a growing sense of frustration. He had spent so many years focusing on his job, on providing for the family, that he hadn't noticed how far apart he and Sophia had drifted. She had changed, he had changed, and the house that had once been filled with laughter now echoed with silence. He wanted to reach out to her, to bridge the gap between them, but every time he tried, he felt as if he was only making things worse.

It was their daughter, Izzy, who first noticed. She had grown up seeing her parents as the perfect pair, the two of them seemingly invincible in their love for one another. But recently, she had watched them withdraw into themselves. She had overheard their arguments, seen the way they avoided each other, and it scared her. For the first time, she realized that the love she had always taken for granted wasn't as certain as she had once believed.

"I don't think we can just pretend everything is fine anymore," she said one evening after dinner. She had been quiet for most of the meal, but now, her voice was firm, filled with a maturity beyond her years. "You both have to talk to each other. You can't just let it go on like this."

Sophia looked at her daughter, the concern in Izzy's eyes mirroring her own. She had always been proud of Izzy's strength, but now, she felt a pang of guilt. She had tried to shield her children from the strain between her and James, but Izzy was no fool. She could see it all too clearly.

James cleared his throat, breaking the silence that had settled over the table. "We're trying, Izzy. We're both trying."

But were they really? Or were they just existing beside each other, too afraid to confront the truth?

That night, after the kids had gone to bed, Sophia sat on the edge of their bed, staring at the wall. She could hear the soft sound of James's breathing beside her, but she didn't feel any closer to him. The distance between them felt infinite, and for the first time, she wasn't sure if they could bridge it.

"Sophia..." James's voice broke through her thoughts, hesitant, unsure. "We can't keep doing this. We can't keep pretending everything is fine."

Sophia turned to him, meeting his eyes for the first time in days. There was a vulnerability in his gaze that she hadn't seen in years. It was a small crack, but it was enough to let a glimmer of hope through.

"I don't know where to start," she admitted, her voice barely above a whisper.

"You don't have to know right now," James said softly. "But we need to start somewhere. We need to reach out to each other, before it's too late."

In that moment, Sophia realized that reaching out didn't mean they had to have all the answers. It didn't mean they had to fix everything overnight. It meant taking the first step, even if it was small, even if it was uncertain. It meant trying, together, to find their way back to each other.

And so, as the night stretched on and the house grew quiet, they both took that first step. They reached out—not with answers, but with a willingness to try. It was the beginning of something, maybe even the beginning of healing, and that was enough for now.

Chapter 5: The Burden of Choices

1. The Path Not Taken

Sophia stood at the window, the faint glow of the evening sun casting a warm hue over the garden below. It was one of those rare moments when the world felt still, untouched by the constant motion of her everyday life. Her gaze wandered over the familiar scene—the flowers she had planted with her own hands, the sprawling oak tree that had witnessed so many changes in the years she had lived here. Yet, despite the beauty of it all, a sense of restlessness stirred within her, like a quiet whisper that she could never quite silence.

It had been a long time since she had truly asked herself whether she was happy. And even longer since she had wondered what her life would have been like if she had chosen a different path, one where she had prioritized her dreams over the expectations of others.

Her mind drifted back to those early days, before marriage, before children, when she had been a young woman full of ambition and excitement. She had wanted to conquer the world, to build a career that would make her feel alive, to create something of her own. She had imagined herself in boardrooms, making decisions that shaped the future, traveling to foreign cities, living a life full of adventure and purpose. But somewhere along the way, she had set those dreams aside. She had made sacrifices, for her family, for James, for the children.

At first, it hadn't been a difficult decision. Sophia had always been someone who valued loyalty and duty, someone who believed that family came first. But as the years passed, she began to question whether that decision had been the right one. Had she given up too much of herself? Had she settled for a life that wasn't truly hers, just to meet the expectations of others?

James had always been supportive, in his own way, but she had never felt that he truly understood the depth of her inner conflict. He was content with the life they had built together, content with the roles they had taken on. But Sophia could no longer ignore the feeling that something was missing. She was stuck in a life that wasn't bad, but it wasn't the life she had dreamed of either.

The familiar knock on the door brought her back to reality. Ethan's voice echoed from the other side, calling out to her as he always did. It was a simple request, a reminder of her role as a mother, the one she had embraced so willingly in the beginning. Yet now, each call, each demand, felt like a chain that bound her to a future she hadn't chosen.

For a brief moment, she considered walking away. Leaving everything behind and finding the path she had left behind. But even as the thought crossed her mind, she knew it was not a possibility. Family, duty, love—these things held her in place, even when she longed for more.

As she opened the door to greet her son, a small part of her wondered what it would feel like to walk away from it all, to step into a life where the only expectations were her own. The life she could have had, the life she had once dreamed of. Would she feel fulfilled? Would she be happier? Or would she only find that the sacrifices she had made had been worth it after all?

Her heart ached with the question, and yet, she knew that no answer would come easily. There was no right or wrong path, only the one she had walked, with all its joys and regrets. And as she bent down to listen to Ethan's excited chatter, Sophia understood that the choice she had made, even with all its imperfections, had shaped her into the woman she was today.

It was the path she had taken—perhaps not the one she had always envisioned, but the one that had led her here, to this moment. And for better or worse, it was hers to own.

2. Rising Tensions

THE AIR IN THE HOUSE seemed thicker than usual, a silent pressure that hung over everyone. It wasn't loud or dramatic, but the tension was unmistakable. It wasn't the kind of tension that comes with raised voices or slammed doors, but the kind that comes from the quiet awareness that something was deeply wrong. No one had to say it, but everyone felt it—like a storm cloud that hadn't yet broken, but hovered ominously above.

Sophia stood by the window, staring out at the garden, but her mind was miles away. Her fingers absentmindedly traced the cold glass, as though trying to connect to something real, something solid in a world that had become increasingly slippery. She had been running on empty for months now, juggling the responsibilities of work, motherhood, and a marriage that was more of a fragile truce than a partnership. She'd always told herself that it would get easier, that things would settle down, but they never did. And now, standing there, she couldn't shake the feeling that the balance she had worked so hard to maintain was finally tipping.

Across the room, James sat in his usual chair, the one by the fireplace. He stared into the flames, but his thoughts weren't on the dancing embers. His mind, like Sophia's, was consumed by the growing distance between them. There was a time when he would have done anything to bridge that gap, when he would have reached out, tried to fix things. But lately, it felt like every attempt had only pushed them further apart. It wasn't just the little misunderstandings anymore. It was something deeper, something unspoken but undeniable.

Their children weren't immune to the tension either. Izzy, who had once been the family's brightest spark, now wandered the halls like a ghost, her once vibrant energy replaced by a quiet reserve. She had always been the one to speak her mind, to call things as they were, but lately, even she had grown distant. The teenage rebellion had given way to something more complicated—something that made Sophia and James both ache with a mixture of frustration and guilt. They wanted to fix it, to know what was wrong, but they were afraid to ask. What if the answers were things they weren't ready to hear?

And then there was Ethan. The youngest, the sensitive one. He had always been the glue that kept them together, his soft smiles and thoughtful gestures a balm for the cracks in their lives. But now, he was withdrawing too, spending more time alone in his room, avoiding the family dinners, retreating into his world where the weight of their unspoken issues couldn't reach him. It was as if he, too, knew that the foundation they had built together was starting to crumble.

The tension wasn't loud. It didn't shout. But it was there, woven into the fabric of their every interaction. A misplaced word, a lingering look, a silence that lasted just a little too long. It was the things left unsaid that spoke the loudest. And each of them felt it in their own way, each of them carrying a burden that they were unwilling—or perhaps unable—to share.

The dinner table, once a place of laughter and conversation, had become a battleground of sorts. No one wanted to be the first to acknowledge the elephant in the room, to speak the words that everyone was thinking. And yet, in the silence, the tension only grew, building in the corners of their home, growing heavier with every passing day.

Sophia thought back to when things had been easier. When their family had been more than just a group of people living under one roof. There had been a time when they had laughed together, when their bond felt unbreakable. But now? Now, it seemed like the more they tried to hold on, the further they drifted from one another.

She closed her eyes for a moment, inhaling deeply, as though she could breathe away the weight of it all. But when she opened them again, nothing had changed. The distance was still there. The storm was still coming. And she had no idea how to stop it.

Sophia took a few more steps back from the window, her gaze now shifting toward the hallway. James was still sitting there, unmoving, like he was waiting for something—or maybe waiting for everything to change without him having to take the first step. He had always been the quieter one, more reserved, his emotions hidden beneath layers of calm. But tonight, there was something in his posture that was different. Tired. Resigned. She knew him well enough to see the weight he carried, even if he never spoke of it.

She walked over to him, her steps tentative, as though she were walking on fragile ground. The closer she got, the more the space between them seemed to grow, until it felt like there was an ocean between them, vast and unbridgeable.

"James," she finally said, her voice softer than she intended. "We need to talk."

He didn't respond immediately. His eyes remained fixed on the fire, his face unreadable. She waited, hoping that he would meet her halfway, but the minutes stretched on in silence. It was as if he were processing something too difficult to express, or maybe he was afraid that speaking would make everything worse.

Finally, he spoke. "What is there to talk about, Sophia?" His voice was low, almost indifferent, and the words felt like a weight in the room. "We both know where this is heading."

She felt a chill in her bones, a quiet dread creeping in. She had expected a conversation, an exchange of words, but this... this felt like resignation. A finality she wasn't ready for.

"You can't just give up on us," she said, her voice trembling, a hint of desperation slipping through. "I know things haven't been perfect. But we've always made it through before."

James let out a bitter laugh, the sound sharp and cutting. "Have we? Or have we just been pretending?"

His words stung more than she wanted to admit. Pretending. Was that what they had been doing all this time? Putting on a façade of happiness, a mask to hide the cracks in their marriage? Had they really been fooling themselves, or had they just been too afraid to face the truth?

Sophia took a deep breath, trying to steady herself, but the weight of it all—the years, the lies, the unspoken frustrations—pressed on her chest, making it harder to breathe. "What do you want me to say, James?" she asked quietly. "I don't want to pretend anymore. I want to fix this. I want to know what's going on with you, with us."

James finally turned his head, meeting her eyes for the first time in what felt like an eternity. His gaze was hard, guarded, as though he were measuring her words, deciding whether or not to let her in. For a brief moment, she saw the pain there, the raw vulnerability that he had kept hidden for so long. But it was quickly replaced by the familiar mask of indifference.

"I don't know if it can be fixed," he said, his voice rough. "Maybe we've reached the point where we've already lost too much."

The silence that followed his words was suffocating, each of them lost in their own thoughts, their own fears. The weight of unspoken words filled the room, heavier than anything they could have said aloud. Sophia's heart ached, her mind racing with what-ifs and maybes, but deep down, she knew he was right. They had been slipping for a long time. And now, they were standing on the edge of something that neither of them was sure they could return from.

But even as the tension between them thickened, there was a flicker of something. A small, almost imperceptible spark of hope. Maybe it wasn't too late. Maybe, just maybe, they could still find their way back.

As if on cue, a soft knock on the door broke the stillness. Ethan's voice came from the other side, his tone hesitant. "Mom, Dad, can we talk?"

The interruption felt like a lifeline, a small moment of distraction from the storm that was brewing between them. But it also reminded them of something more important—something that neither of them could ignore. Their children, their family. Despite the growing distance between them, they were still a part of this. They still mattered. And maybe, just maybe, they could all find a way to weather the storm together.

Sophia glanced at James one last time, her expression softening. She didn't know what the future held, or whether things could ever truly go back to the way they were. But for the first time in a long while, she felt a flicker of hope. Not for perfection, but for possibility.

She took a deep breath and opened the door.

The door creaked as it swung open, and Ethan stood there, his small figure framed in the doorway. His eyes were wide, a mixture of uncertainty and concern etched across his face. The sight of him, standing there in the dimly lit hallway, made the weight of the moment feel even more pressing. He had always been the sensitive one, the one who seemed to sense when something was off, even if no one had said a word.

"Is everything okay?" Ethan asked softly, his gaze flicking between his parents. It wasn't a question that needed an answer.

THE SHIFTING BALANCE 131

He already knew the tension between them, the distance that had grown over time. The question was just his way of trying to make sense of it, trying to understand a world that was suddenly filled with cracks and sharp edges.

Sophia gave him a tight smile, one that didn't quite reach her eyes. She wanted to reassure him, tell him that everything would be okay, but the truth was, she wasn't sure anymore. "We're fine, sweetheart," she said, her voice steadier than she felt. "Just having a conversation."

Ethan didn't look convinced. His brow furrowed as he stepped into the room, glancing at both of them. He was quiet for a long moment, as if considering his next words carefully. The tension in the air was palpable, but he wasn't ready to let it go.

"You've been having a lot of those lately," he said finally, his voice just above a whisper, but the weight of his words hung in the space between them. "And every time, it feels like... like you're farther apart."

Sophia's heart tightened at his words. Ethan had always been perceptive, but hearing him speak so plainly about their struggles stung. She had tried so hard to keep the family together, to make sure the cracks didn't show, but here was her son, pointing them out in the clearest terms. He had been paying attention, and she couldn't hide from that truth.

James didn't respond immediately, but his jaw tightened, and Sophia could see the conflict in his eyes. He wasn't angry—not at Ethan—but the frustration was there, buried deep beneath the surface. "We're doing our best, Ethan," he said, his voice softer now, as if trying to reassure not just his son, but himself as well. "It's just... not always easy, you know?"

Ethan nodded, but the doubt was still there, hanging in his eyes. "I know," he said, his voice small. "But I don't want it to keep going like this. I don't want it to get worse."

The words landed in the room like a soft blow, and for a moment, everything felt unbearably heavy. They were all carrying their own weight, their own unspoken fears, and Ethan's words brought them all crashing to the forefront. Sophia looked at her son, his young face a mixture of worry and quiet wisdom, and she knew she couldn't keep pretending anymore. She couldn't hide from the truth, not with him, not with anyone.

She glanced at James, meeting his eyes for the first time in what felt like ages. There was a silent understanding between them now, an unspoken agreement that things couldn't stay the way they were. No more pretending. No more silence. They had to face it, even if it was hard.

Sophia took a deep breath, her hands trembling slightly as she reached for Ethan, pulling him into an embrace. For a moment, they stood there, her son's small frame pressed against hers, his arms wrapped around her tightly as if trying to hold everything together, just for a little while longer. She felt the weight of his love, his concern, and the way he still believed, despite everything, that things could be okay. It was that belief, that hope, that kept her going.

"We're going to work on it," she said quietly, her voice thick with emotion. "All of us. Together."

James nodded slowly, his own hand resting on Ethan's shoulder. It wasn't much, but it was a start. It was the first step toward something that, though uncertain, felt more real than anything they'd said in a long time.

For the first time in what felt like forever, the tension in the room began to ease, just a little. There were still so many unanswered questions, so many cracks to repair, but in that moment, with Ethan between them, they didn't need all the answers. They just needed to be there—for each other, and for themselves. They didn't know what the future would hold, but for the first time in a long while, they were willing to find out together.

As the evening settled in around them, the warmth of the fire flickered gently in the hearth, casting long shadows on the walls. The air was thick with unspoken thoughts, yet there was a subtle shift between the three of them, as if they had taken a step toward something that had been long overdue. Sophia held Ethan close for a moment longer before letting him pull away, his small hands still gripping her tightly, as if afraid that if he let go, things would fall apart.

James had retreated into the chair, his face shadowed by a mix of exhaustion and quiet contemplation. There was something different about him now, as though the weight of his unspoken thoughts was becoming too heavy to carry in silence. Sophia could feel his gaze on her, but she didn't look at him yet. She wasn't ready to face what was unsaid. Not just yet.

Ethan, sensing the shift in the room, quietly made his way to the kitchen. He had always been the one to break the silence, but tonight, he seemed to understand that there was nothing left to fix with words. Not right now. He needed space, and so did they. As the door to the kitchen creaked closed behind him, a hush fell over the room.

Sophia took a seat across from James, her hands resting on her lap as she tried to steady her breathing. The silence between them stretched on, neither of them willing to speak first. It wasn't out of avoidance, but more out of a shared recognition that whatever was going to happen next, they would have to face it together. The time for pretending was over.

Finally, James broke the silence. His voice was low, almost hesitant. "I never meant for things to get like this, Sophia."

Sophia met his eyes then, her heart aching at the vulnerability she saw there. It wasn't something he showed often—this side of him that was unsure, searching for answers in the same way she was. She had spent so much time wondering if he still cared, if they could still salvage whatever was left between them. And now, sitting here with him, she realized that maybe they had both been too afraid to admit how much they had been hurting.

"I know," she said softly, her voice catching in her throat. "I didn't either. But we've both been so focused on everything else, we forgot about each other. About us."

James ran a hand through his hair, his expression filled with regret. "I thought if I just kept doing what I thought was right—working hard, providing—I could fix everything. But I didn't stop to ask if it was what you needed. What we needed." He paused, the weight of his words sinking in. "I didn't realize how much I had been shutting you out. And in the process, I shut myself out, too."

Sophia felt a lump form in her throat at his confession. The truth of it hit her harder than she expected. She had always known that James was a man of action, someone who believed in doing what needed to be done, even if it meant sacrificing pieces of himself. But hearing him admit it, hearing him finally acknowledge the pain they had both been carrying, made her realize just how deep the wounds went.

"We both made mistakes," she said, her voice steadying. "I was so caught up in trying to keep everything together, trying to hold onto something that was slipping away, that I stopped seeing you. I stopped seeing the man I fell in love with."

James looked at her then, his eyes softening, and for a moment, it felt as if the years of tension, of distance, were melting away. It wasn't a magic fix—it couldn't be. But it was a beginning. The first real conversation they'd had in what felt like forever. The first step toward something that might be worth fighting for.

He reached across the space between them, his hand resting gently on hers. The touch was tentative at first, as if both of them were unsure of what it meant, but it was enough to bridge the gap, even if just for a moment.

"We're not perfect, Sophia," James said quietly, his voice filled with something raw, something real. "But I want to try. I don't want to lose us."

Sophia squeezed his hand, her heart beating in time with his. There were no guarantees, no promises that things would magically fix themselves overnight. But she wasn't alone in this anymore. And maybe, just maybe, that was enough.

"Neither do I," she whispered.

Outside, the wind howled through the trees, the storm still raging, but inside the house, there was a quiet calm that had settled between them. The storm outside didn't matter. What mattered was that they had found a moment of peace, a fragile truce amidst the chaos. And for now, that was all they needed.

As the night wore on, they sat in silence, the fire crackling softly in the background. They didn't need to say anything more. They had said enough. The rest, the healing, would come in time.

For the first time in a long time, Sophia allowed herself to believe that there was still hope. And that hope, however small, was enough to carry them through the rising tensions of tomorrow.

The days that followed were filled with an awkward, tentative peace. It wasn't as though everything had been solved with one conversation—far from it. But there was a shift, a subtle change in the way they moved through their daily lives. The silence between James and Sophia wasn't as heavy, though it was still there, lingering like the remnants of a storm.

Ethan seemed to sense the shift too. He was quieter, more observant, as if he was watching his parents carefully, waiting to see if the fragile thread of connection between them would hold.

Sophia noticed how he clung to little routines that gave him comfort, like drawing at the kitchen table or reading quietly by the window. The normalcy of his actions brought a kind of solace to the house, a reminder that, despite everything, life continued.

But there were moments—brief, fleeting—when Sophia would catch James looking at her in a way he hadn't in years. A look that was both questioning and searching, as if trying to understand how to rebuild what had been broken without fully knowing where to start. His gestures, too, had softened. He no longer retreated to his work so quickly after dinner, and on the weekends, he would sometimes join her and Ethan for walks in the park. It wasn't much, but it was something.

Still, the tension was never far from the surface. It hovered in their interactions, present even in the quietest of moments. They were navigating through uncharted territory, unsure of which steps would lead them back to the closeness they had once shared. The distance between them wasn't just emotional—it was physical too. The brief touches, the shared glances, had not yet translated into the ease of familiarity they had once taken for granted. Every moment of connection felt like a fragile truce, like something they were still learning to negotiate.

Sophia found herself thinking more often about the past, about the times when their life had seemed simpler, more certain. Before the weight of unspoken words had built a wall between them. But she knew that those days were gone. The person she was now was different, shaped by everything that had happened, just as the man James had become was a reflection of the struggles he had faced. They were both standing at the edge of something—neither fully knowing what the future would bring, but both afraid to step back into the chaos they had known before.

One afternoon, as the sun began to set, casting a golden glow across the living room, James asked her to sit with him. The invitation was simple, but there was an earnestness in his voice that made her pause.

"Can we talk?" he asked, his hands clasped together in his lap.

Sophia hesitated. The last few weeks had been filled with conversations, but they had all been small, tentative exchanges, never venturing too deep. She knew that this was different—that this was a conversation that would require more than just words. It would require honesty, vulnerability, and perhaps even forgiveness.

"About what?" she asked, sitting down across from him.

"About us," he said quietly. "About what we're doing, where we're going."

Sophia exhaled slowly, her gaze drifting to the window where the last rays of sunlight were disappearing behind the trees. She had been dreading this moment, but she also knew it was inevitable. They couldn't keep pretending everything was fine when it wasn't. She met his eyes, and in that brief moment, she saw the same uncertainty reflected in his gaze that she had been carrying within herself.

"I don't know what's going to happen, James," she said, her voice thick with emotion. "I don't know if we can fix this. But I do know that I can't keep living like this. We've both been carrying so much weight, and I don't want to carry it anymore."

James nodded slowly, as if understanding. "Neither do I," he replied. "But I don't want to lose you. I don't want to lose what we had."

They sat there for a long time, the silence between them not as uncomfortable as it had been before. It wasn't filled with anger or resentment—it was just the silence of two people who were trying to figure out how to move forward, one step at a time.

And then, in a quiet voice, James spoke again. "I know I've hurt you. I know I've failed you in so many ways, but I want to try. I want to find a way back to each other, if you'll let me."

Sophia looked at him, really looked at him, and saw the man who had once been her everything. The man she had loved, the man who had stood by her through the hardest of times. There was still something there, something worth fighting for. She wasn't sure what the future would hold, but in that moment, she felt the weight of his words settle in her chest.

"I'm scared, James," she said softly. "I'm scared that we've already lost too much. That we've gone too far to fix this."

"I'm scared too," he admitted, his voice low. "But I don't want to give up without trying."

Sophia felt a flicker of hope stir inside her, though she was reluctant to fully embrace it. She didn't know what it would take to repair the damage, to rebuild the trust that had been broken. But she knew one thing: they couldn't keep going in circles, pretending everything was okay when it wasn't.

"Let's try," she said, her voice steady now. "Let's try together."

The resolve in her words surprised even her, but it was the truth. They had been through too much, and they had spent too many years in silence, not speaking the things that mattered. Now, it was time to confront the pain, to face the hard truths, and see if there was still a way forward.

As the evening light faded into night, they sat in silence again, but this time, it wasn't the same kind of silence. This time, it felt like a beginning.

And in the quiet, there was hope.

The next few days passed in a haze of tentative steps, each one moving them closer to something neither of them was fully ready to embrace. But the silence between them had shifted, and with it came the possibility of something new. Sophia could feel the weight of each moment, each word, each glance. They were both trying, in their own way, to rebuild what had once been.

The mornings were the hardest. There was always that moment when they would wake up—each of them unsure how to approach the other. Sometimes, James would make an effort to linger a little longer at the breakfast table, and Sophia would make small talk, even though the tension between them still made her throat tight. Ethan, ever the observant child, seemed to sense their unease but said nothing. His silence was a constant reminder that he, too, was affected by what was happening between his parents.

It wasn't until one rainy evening, when the world outside seemed to blur into a wash of grey, that the walls they had been building around themselves finally began to crumble. They had spent the day in the same quiet manner they had been keeping up for weeks, each of them avoiding the deeper conversations they knew they had to have. But that night, as they sat in the dimly lit living room, something shifted.

Sophia was sitting on the couch, a book open in her hands, though her eyes weren't really on the pages. Her mind was elsewhere—on James, on Ethan, on the weight of the past and the uncertainty of the future. James was across the room, staring out the window, lost in his thoughts. It was in those moments of stillness that the truth of their situation became undeniable.

"I've been thinking," James began, his voice low, but steady. Sophia's heart skipped a beat. She put the book down and looked up at him, waiting for him to continue.

"I've been thinking about how much time we've lost," he said, turning toward her. "How much I've lost, and how much you've lost. And I can't help but feel like I've failed you... failed us."

Sophia's breath caught in her throat, but she didn't look away. She knew the truth of his words, and they echoed the feelings she had been holding in for so long. She had thought about it, too—about how the years had slipped by unnoticed, how the love they had once shared had withered under the weight of unspoken grievances, of neglect, of misunderstandings.

"I've failed too," she said softly, her voice catching as she spoke. "I've been so caught up in what we lost, I didn't realize how much we still had. And I'm sorry for that."

There was a long pause. James crossed the room and sat down beside her, his presence both comforting and painful. He reached for her hand, and for the first time in what felt like forever, she didn't pull away. Their fingers brushed, tentative at first, but then, with a quiet sense of mutual understanding, they intertwined.

"I don't know how we fix this," James whispered, his forehead resting against hers. "But I know that I want to try. I want to find a way back."

Sophia closed her eyes, letting his words settle over her. She wasn't sure what the path forward looked like. She wasn't sure if they could ever get back to what they had before. But there was something in his voice, in the way he held her hand, that made her believe they could start again.

"I want that too," she whispered. "I don't want to lose us. Not completely."

In that moment, as the rain pattered against the windows and the world outside seemed to fall away, they shared a silent agreement. They didn't have all the answers, and the road ahead was still uncertain. But for the first time in a long time, they felt a flicker of hope.

As the night deepened and the storm outside grew stronger, they stayed there, together, not speaking anymore but simply being. The weight of the past was still there, but for the first time, it didn't feel like a burden. It felt like the beginning of something new.

And in the quiet of that moment, something shifted within them both. The cracks that had run deep between them began to heal, not because they had all the answers, but because they were willing to find them together.

The days that followed were neither easy nor perfect, but they were different. There was a tentative understanding between them, an unspoken promise to try, to rebuild what had once felt unshakable. James and Sophia began to find new ways to communicate, exploring the delicate art of vulnerability and honesty that had been so absent in the past.

It was a slow process. They didn't rush things, and they didn't try to force a resolution. The emotional terrain they were walking on was fragile, and they knew better than to expect immediate changes. But the small moments mattered—the shared glances over coffee, the quiet talks late at night when Ethan was asleep, the gentle touches that began to replace the coldness that had settled between them for so long.

One evening, as they sat together in the kitchen after dinner, James spoke again. This time, there was a sense of clarity in his voice, an openness that had been missing for so long.

"I've been thinking about what you said," he began, breaking the comfortable silence between them. "About not wanting to lose us completely. And I realize... I've been afraid too. Afraid of failing you, of failing Ethan, of not being enough."

Sophia's eyes softened as she looked at him. She could see the weight of his words, the vulnerability he was offering. It reminded her of why she had loved him in the first place—the raw honesty, the willingness to confront his own flaws, and the hope that they could still find their way back to each other.

"You're not alone in that fear," she said, her voice steady but full of emotion. "I've been afraid too. Afraid that we wouldn't find our way back, that we'd be too far gone. But I'm willing to try. I want us to try. For Ethan, for us."

A brief silence hung between them as they both considered what they had said. It was clear that they were still treading carefully, still testing the waters of trust and connection. But the foundation was beginning to be rebuilt, piece by piece.

In the weeks that followed, they made small changes. James took on more responsibility at home, helping with dinner and making an effort to be more present with Ethan. Sophia, in turn, began to open up more about her own needs and desires, no longer burying them in the name of preserving peace. The small acts of kindness and compromise began to stack up, and slowly, the cracks between them began to heal.

But there was still a long road ahead. They both knew that. Their past would not be erased overnight, and the scars that lingered would take time to fade. There were days when the old tensions resurfaced, when old habits threatened to pull them back into the darkness they had worked so hard to escape. But with each passing day, they grew stronger, more aware of the delicate balance they were trying to restore.

Ethan, too, seemed to sense the change. His mood improved, and he began to open up more, sharing his thoughts and feelings with both of them. He was a quiet observer of the world around him, but there was no mistaking the fact that the changes in his parents were making an impact on him. He no longer carried the same heavy silence that had weighed on him in the past. There was hope in his eyes now, a hope that had been missing for so long.

Sophia and James knew that the real work had only just begun. They couldn't afford to slip back into old patterns, to let the comfort of silence or avoidance creep back into their lives. But for the first time in a long while, they were ready to fight for each other. They were ready to rebuild, not just for themselves, but for Ethan, too.

And as the seasons began to change, so too did the rhythms of their lives. There was still work to be done, still moments of doubt and fear, but there was also a sense of possibility—a belief that they could find their way back to something that was worth saving. Together.

As the months passed, the delicate shifts in their relationship continued to evolve. The days that had once been filled with tension and silence were now marked by more open conversations and shared experiences. They began to rediscover the rhythm they had lost, finding a new kind of intimacy that wasn't rooted in old patterns but in mutual respect and understanding.

The changes were small but significant. James, once so consumed by his work, began taking more time off to be present in their home. He would help Ethan with his school projects or take him to the park on weekends, moments that felt precious to Sophia. She, in turn, started to embrace the idea of vulnerability, of speaking her truth even when it was hard. She'd always been the one to carry the weight of their family, and now she was learning to lean on James again, to trust him in ways she hadn't allowed herself to in years.

They spent evenings together, sometimes talking about their past, sometimes simply enjoying the quiet comfort of one another's presence. There were moments of laughter, of lightness, and in those fleeting instances, they could almost forget the darkness that had once threatened to consume them. For a while, it felt like they were on the cusp of something new, something stronger than before.

But as the days grew longer, they realized that their past was not something they could simply leave behind. The shadows of old wounds lingered, and despite their best efforts, there were times when they found themselves circling the same unresolved issues, the same frustrations. It wasn't easy to move forward when the weight of what had happened before still weighed heavily on their hearts.

One evening, as they sat down for dinner, the conversation turned to the future. It had been a quiet day, the kind where the world outside seemed to stand still, allowing space for introspection.

"I've been thinking about what comes next," James said, his tone reflective. "We've made progress, but we both know it's not enough. We still have a long way to go, don't we?"

Sophia paused, her fork halfway to her mouth, as she considered his words. There was a vulnerability in his voice that made her heart ache. He wasn't asking for answers, just acknowledging the uncertainty that still loomed between them.

"We do," she replied softly, setting her fork down. "We've come a long way, but there's still so much we need to work through. And I'm not going to lie—it's scary. The idea of going back to what we were before feels like we'd be trying to force something that's already broken."

James nodded, a somber understanding in his eyes. "I don't want to go back. I don't want to pretend everything is fine when it's not. But I want to be better. For you. For us. For Ethan."

His words hung in the air, heavy with truth. It wasn't enough just to survive anymore. They both needed more than that. They needed to rebuild, not just for their son but for themselves—for the love they had once shared and the future they still hoped to create.

Sophia took a deep breath, feeling the weight of the moment settle in her chest. "I agree," she said, her voice steady. "We can't go back to what we had, but maybe we can build something better. Something new. But it won't happen if we don't keep pushing forward. We have to be honest with each other. Even when it's hard."

For the first time in a long while, Sophia saw a glimmer of hope in James's eyes, the same hope that had once drawn them together. It wasn't a perfect hope—it was fragile, tentative, still in the process of being nurtured—but it was there. And in that moment, it felt like enough.

They both knew that they were at a crossroads. Their past was still a shadow over their future, but the future was not yet written. There were so many questions they didn't have answers to, and so many challenges still ahead of them. But in that moment, as they shared the weight of their truths and their fears, they also shared something more—a quiet understanding that they were no longer alone in this journey.

And perhaps that was enough to begin again.

As the weeks turned into months, the tentative steps forward became more grounded. The progress wasn't always linear, but there was a new sense of intentionality in their actions. James and Sophia found themselves looking at each other with a mix of familiarity and wonder, as if rediscovering the person they had once known so well, yet now seen through the lens of all that they had been through.

Ethan, too, began to reflect the subtle shifts in the atmosphere at home. The quiet, withdrawn boy who once seemed to carry the weight of his parents' struggles now engaged more openly with them. He laughed at their inside jokes, shared his thoughts more freely, and even started bringing home small successes from school to show them. It was clear that, while they were working on their relationship as partners, they were also rebuilding as a family, creating a space where love, even in its brokenness, could still thrive.

But with growth came challenges. There were nights when the weight of their past seemed too heavy to bear, when the fear of failure loomed large. There were moments of doubt, of wondering if they had done enough, if they were truly making progress or merely treading water.

One evening, after a particularly intense conversation about their future, they found themselves sitting in silence. The air between them was thick with unspoken thoughts, a tension that neither of them knew how to alleviate. James, sensing her unease, reached across the table and took her hand in his.

"Sophia," he said quietly, his voice low with sincerity. "I don't know if I can promise you that everything will be perfect. I can't promise that we won't have bad days or that I won't make mistakes. But I can promise that I will keep trying. That I will keep showing up, even on the hardest days."

Sophia's heart softened at his words. She had heard similar promises before, but this time, there was something different in his voice. There was no pretense, no attempt to cover up the complexity of the situation. It was just honesty.

"I believe you," she said, her voice thick with emotion. "I can't expect perfection. But I can expect effort. And that's enough for me."

They sat there for a while, their hands intertwined, allowing the moment to stretch out between them. It wasn't a grand declaration or a sweeping gesture, but it was real. It was a quiet commitment, one built on the understanding that they weren't perfect, but they were willing to work through the imperfections together.

In the days that followed, there was a new sense of calm in their home. Not that everything was easy—far from it—but there was a shared understanding that progress didn't mean perfection. It meant showing up for each other, even when the world around them felt uncertain. It meant holding space for the pain, the fear, and the hope, all at once, without trying to force any one emotion to dominate.

They found ways to laugh together again, to enjoy simple moments without the weight of past arguments or unresolved conflicts hanging over them. They planned small outings, a weekend trip to the coast, or a day at the park, where they could just exist as a family without the pressure of "fixing" anything. These moments, though simple, became the foundation of something deeper—something that couldn't be measured in quick fixes or immediate results, but rather in the slow, steady rhythm of trust being rebuilt.

One evening, as they sat on the couch, watching a movie with Ethan, Sophia realized something. She wasn't waiting for the perfect resolution anymore. She wasn't expecting a sudden shift that would make everything right. Instead, she was learning to appreciate the small victories—the quiet moments of connection, the laughter, the shared understanding.

It was enough to know that, despite all the uncertainties, they were still here, still trying. And that, she thought with a smile, was more than she could have hoped for at the start of their journey.

As the months continued to pass, the rhythm of their lives began to change in ways neither James nor Sophia had fully anticipated. They were no longer two separate entities trying to co-exist in a strained marriage. Slowly but surely, they were becoming a team again, though the path wasn't always smooth. There were still moments of silence, times when they retreated into their own corners of the world to recharge or to think. But there were also moments of connection—moments that felt like the tender beginnings of something new, something they could build together.

James started to take more responsibility in their home life, sharing the mental load that Sophia had shouldered alone for so long. He became more attuned to her needs, recognizing the subtle signs when she was overwhelmed or when she simply needed space to breathe. He didn't always get it right, but the effort was there. And that effort mattered.

Sophia, too, made small but significant changes. She began to let go of the need for everything to be perfect, to constantly control the way things unfolded. She found herself relying more on James, trusting him with more of her fears, her frustrations, and her hopes. The walls she had so carefully built around herself began to erode, bit by bit. For the first time in a long time, she felt as if she wasn't carrying the weight of the world alone. It was a feeling she had almost forgotten.

But even as they found their way back to each other, the past still lingered. The scars were there, hidden beneath the surface, sometimes visible, sometimes not. The betrayals, the unspoken hurts, the long nights of silence—they were all part of their story now. And while they couldn't erase the past, they were learning how to live with it, how to make peace with the shadows that followed them.

There were still moments when the weight of it all became too much. James would retreat into his work, losing himself in his responsibilities, while Sophia would find herself questioning whether they were truly moving forward, or simply moving in circles. The old fears crept back in—the fear of failure, of repeating past mistakes, of falling back into the same patterns that had once nearly destroyed them.

One evening, after a particularly difficult conversation about their future, Sophia found herself standing at the kitchen window, staring out into the night. The quiet of the house felt suffocating, and for a moment, she felt the old pang of loneliness that had so often accompanied her in the past. She was alone with her thoughts, unsure of what the next step was, unsure of what she wanted or needed from James.

James, sensing her distance, entered the room quietly. Without a word, he stepped up behind her and wrapped his arms around her waist, pulling her close. For a moment, neither of them spoke. There was a comfort in the silence, a sense of reassurance in the simple act of being together, even when things were uncertain.

"I'm scared," she whispered after a while, her voice barely audible. "I'm scared that we're still so broken. That no matter how hard we try, it's never going to be enough."

James's grip tightened slightly, as if to reassure her that he was there, that he understood. "I know," he said softly. "I'm scared, too. But we're here. We're still trying. And that's what matters. We can't fix everything, but we can face it together."

Sophia turned in his arms to face him, her eyes searching his for any sign of doubt. She found none. Only sincerity. Only a quiet promise.

"We've been through so much," she said, her voice trembling. "I just don't know if I can keep doing this. I don't know if I can keep hoping."

James cupped her face gently, his thumb brushing the tear that had slipped down her cheek. "You don't have to hope every day. You don't have to carry all of it on your own. But I'll be here. And I'll keep hoping, for both of us."

And for the first time in what felt like a long time, Sophia allowed herself to believe him. She allowed herself to believe that maybe—just maybe—they could rebuild, not perfectly, but steadily, piece by piece. It wouldn't be easy. There would be moments of doubt, moments when they would question whether they were really making progress. But the hope, fragile as it was, had taken root.

As they stood together, the weight of the past still lingering but no longer defining them, they understood that they weren't seeking perfection. They were seeking progress. And progress, they had learned, wasn't always linear. But as long as they continued to move forward, together, that would be enough.

As spring arrived, bringing with it the promise of renewal, so too did their lives begin to take on a new rhythm. There was a lightness in the air that hadn't been there before, as if the weight of the past had lifted, even if only slightly. The days were longer, filled with soft sunlight and the quiet hum of daily life. The house, once filled with tension, now resonated with the sound of laughter, the kind that felt spontaneous, unforced.

James and Sophia had found their footing in a way that felt both familiar and new. Their conversations had shifted from the heavy, introspective discussions about their future to the simple, everyday moments of connection. They no longer felt the need to dissect every argument, every misstep. Instead, they allowed the small victories to carry more weight—the shared cup of coffee in the morning, the quiet moments at night when they sat side by side, just being there for each other.

Ethan, too, had begun to show more of his personality. The walls he had built around himself during the turbulent years of their marriage seemed to be softening. He no longer retreated into the shadows, nor did he carry the burden of the family's troubles on his young shoulders. Instead, he began to engage with his parents in a way that felt natural, a tentative bridge being built between them, as if he were finally allowing them into his world.

One Saturday afternoon, as they all sat in the living room, sharing a pizza, Ethan looked up from his phone and broke the comfortable silence.

"Hey, you guys are going to that wedding next month, right?" he asked, his voice tentative but curious.

James and Sophia exchanged a glance. The wedding in question was an old friend's from college, someone they had both lost touch with over the years. It wasn't a major event, but it had a certain significance—an invitation to re-enter the world outside of their bubble, a symbol of moving forward.

"I think we should go," James said, breaking the quiet.

Sophia nodded, her expression thoughtful. "Yeah. It feels like it's time. We've been hiding out for too long."

Ethan's eyes lit up, and a small smile played at the corner of his lips. "It'll be fun, right? We can all dress up, and you two won't argue over who gets the last piece of cake."

Sophia laughed, the sound light and free. "No promises about the cake."

For the first time in a long while, the future seemed like something to look forward to, not something to fear. They were not fixed—far from it. But they were no longer stuck. They were moving forward, step by tentative step.

The weeks that followed were a series of quiet, incremental changes. They planned the wedding trip, shopped for new clothes, and made small decisions that felt weighty in their simplicity. They didn't talk about their past mistakes as often, but when they did, it was with a sense of understanding, as if they were acknowledging their history without allowing it to define them.

On the day of the wedding, they stood together in the bright light of a spring morning, the world outside filled with the hum of possibility. The church, with its stained-glass windows and echoes of vows exchanged long ago, felt like a place of new beginnings. As they watched the ceremony unfold, surrounded by old friends and new faces, James and Sophia found themselves holding hands, not out of necessity, but because it felt right. There were no grand speeches, no public declarations of change. There was just the quiet certainty of knowing they were still here, together, despite everything they had been through.

Later that evening, as they danced beneath the soft glow of fairy lights, Sophia leaned her head on James's shoulder and whispered, "We've come a long way, haven't we?"

James smiled, a look of contentment crossing his face. "Yeah. We have."

And in that moment, as the music swirled around them and the world seemed to pause for just a heartbeat, they both understood that the journey wasn't over. There would be more hurdles to face, more challenges to overcome. But they had already proven, time and time again, that they could handle them. Together.

In that quiet understanding, they found peace. Not the kind that comes from the absence of conflict, but the kind that comes from knowing, beyond all the noise and uncertainty, that they had made it through. They had chosen each other, not once, but every day. And that, in itself, was enough.

3. The Weight of Regret

SOPHIA STOOD BY THE window, her fingers lightly tracing the cool glass, her gaze fixed on the horizon. It was one of those moments when the weight of time pressed down on her, not from the responsibilities of the day, but from the silent accumulation of years filled with choices, mistakes, and moments lost. She hadn't meant for it to happen this way; she hadn't expected to feel so... distant, so disconnected from the very life she had worked so hard to build. But as the years unfolded, one decision led to another, each one pushing her further from the people she loved most.

Regret had a way of creeping up on you. It was a slow, insidious presence that often arrived unannounced, wrapping itself around your chest until it felt like you couldn't breathe. It wasn't something that screamed at you or demanded your attention. No, regret was quieter than that. It whispered. At first, it felt like a fleeting thought, a passing inconvenience. But over time, it became louder, more persistent, and harder to ignore.

Sophia had thought that sacrificing her time with her children and husband for her career would be worth it. She believed that once she reached a certain point, everything would fall into place. She would have the success she desired, and in return, her family would understand. But now, years later, as she looked at the quiet house, the silence between her and her husband felt like a tangible thing. It hung in the air, thick and heavy, making it impossible for her to ignore the growing distance between them.

James, too, had his share of regret. He had tried to be the supportive husband, the one who stood by while Sophia pursued her dreams. But he couldn't help feeling like a bystander in his own life. His role had always been that of a provider, a protector. But somewhere along the way, he had lost himself. The weight of his own decisions, of always putting the family's needs ahead of his own, had left him feeling like he was drowning in obligations he didn't know how to escape.

The regrets were not just about the big moments—those glaring, obvious choices that seemed to stand out in sharp relief. They were also about the small ones. The times when a quiet conversation was needed, but neither of them knew how to start it. The times when they both ignored the growing tension, hoping it would resolve itself, only to find that it had become too tangled to undo.

Sophia turned away from the window and sighed. She had been so focused on achieving the next goal, the next milestone, that she had failed to notice the cracks that were forming in her relationships. She thought her family would always be there, that the love they shared would be enough to carry them through any storm. But love, like everything else, required nurturing. And now, with time slipping away, it felt like that love was something fragile—something that could break if she didn't act quickly.

Her thoughts drifted to Izzy and Ethan. Her children had grown up with so much love, but also so much silence. What had they seen? What had they felt during those years when she was too busy to notice? She had given them things—material things, things that others might have envied—but had she given them the one thing they needed most: her presence?

It was the kind of realization that made her want to turn back time, to go back to those moments when she could have made a different choice. But time, of course, didn't work that way. It moved forward relentlessly, and all she had now were the consequences of the decisions she had made.

Regret, in its most painful form, was the realization that the time to fix things was running out. Sophia knew that the next few months would be critical. She couldn't undo the past, but she could still change the future. The thought of facing her family—of facing James—was daunting, but the alternative was a life of hollow success, a life where she had everything she had worked for but nothing that truly mattered.

In the silence of the house, she made a promise to herself. She would find a way to bridge the gap. She would face the consequences of her choices, no matter how difficult, and do what was necessary to rebuild what had been broken.

But as she stood there, staring out at the fading light, the weight of regret pressed heavily on her chest, reminding her of just how much had been lost.

Sophia took a deep breath, trying to steady herself as the flood of emotions threatened to overwhelm her. She had always been the one to hold everything together, to push through the pain, to put the family's needs before her own. But now, for the first time in a

THE SHIFTING BALANCE 155

long while, she was facing the reality of her choices, the truth that had been sitting in the corners of her mind all these years.

Her gaze shifted to the photograph on the mantelpiece—the one taken at their family vacation, the last one they had before everything began to unravel. It felt like a lifetime ago. She remembered the way Izzy had laughed, her carefree spirit shining through, and how Ethan, so serious even at a young age, had clung to her side, always wanting to be near. They had been a family then, united in a way that seemed so distant now.

The years of endless deadlines, business trips, and late nights in the office had gradually pulled her away from them. At the time, it had felt like it was all for their future, for their security. But now, with the sharp clarity that only comes in moments of self-reflection, Sophia realized that the future had arrived, and it wasn't the one she had imagined.

Her relationship with James had grown strained under the weight of her absence. She had excused her neglect, telling herself that he understood, that he supported her ambition. But what had he really felt all those years? How many times had he reached out for her attention, only to be met with a distant, preoccupied version of the woman he had married? The guilt gnawed at her, sharp and biting. She had wanted to be everything to everyone, and in the process, had become nothing to herself.

Sophia picked up her phone, her fingers trembling slightly as she scrolled through the contacts. She hesitated for a moment, her thumb hovering over James's name. She wanted to reach out, to open the conversation, but the fear of facing the truth paralyzed her. What if it was too late? What if the space between them had become too wide to bridge?

The thought of talking to him about everything—about her regrets, her desires, and her fears—was terrifying. She had spent so long avoiding the hard conversations, burying her feelings under layers of work and superficial distractions. But now, with regret weighing so heavily on her heart, she knew that avoidance would only make things worse.

She put the phone down, determined to take action. She couldn't keep running from the mess she had created. She needed to confront it, to face her family, to face James. It wouldn't be easy. In fact, it might be the hardest thing she had ever done, but she couldn't keep pretending that everything was fine when it wasn't.

The evening passed in a blur. Dinner was a quiet affair, with everyone eating in separate corners of the house, each absorbed in their own thoughts. Sophia felt the tension, the unspoken words that hung between her and James, between her and her children. She couldn't avoid it any longer. She had to break the silence.

Later that night, after Izzy and Ethan had gone to bed, Sophia sat down next to James on the couch. He was staring at the television, but his mind seemed far away, as though he was already preparing for the conversation they both knew was coming.

She turned to him, her voice barely a whisper. "James, we need to talk."

He glanced at her, his face unreadable, and then nodded. "I know."

The weight of the moment hung in the air, thick and suffocating. Sophia could feel her heart racing, the regret and fear intertwining into something almost unbearable. But she had made a choice—she was going to face it, no matter how painful it might be.

For the first time in years, they would have to confront the truth.

James turned off the television and set the remote aside, his gaze steady but distant. It was clear he had been waiting for this moment, just as she had. The years of silent distance between them had been building up to this, a moment neither of them had been able to avoid any longer.

Sophia took a deep breath, gathering her courage. "I've been thinking a lot about everything, about us... about the kids. About all the time I lost, and the time I thought I could get back once I reached a certain point." Her voice cracked slightly, the vulnerability unfamiliar and uncomfortable. But it felt necessary, like peeling away layers of something heavy that had been suffocating her for too long.

James didn't interrupt. He just watched her, his eyes searching, as if trying to understand the depth of her words, the weight behind them. There was a part of him, she knew, that had been waiting for her to come to this realization, to finally admit what they had both been avoiding for so long. The quiet desperation in his expression softened, just enough for Sophia to notice.

"I'm sorry," she said, her voice barely above a whisper. "I know I've been absent. I know I've let you down, and I've let them down." She gestured toward the children's rooms, her heart aching. "I thought if I just kept pushing forward, if I could just keep climbing, everything would work out. But I've lost sight of the most important things."

James shifted in his seat, his expression hard to read. "We've both been lost, Soph," he said, his voice low but heavy with emotion. "I've been here, but I haven't been here. You've been in your own world, and I've... I've been avoiding the fact that I wasn't the man I used to be, either. I've kept quiet, kept it all in, thinking it would fix itself."

Sophia nodded slowly, feeling the truth in his words. She hadn't been the only one retreating. She hadn't been the only one neglecting their marriage. They had both, in their own ways, drifted apart, and the silence between them had only grown louder with time.

"I want to change that," she said, her voice stronger now. "I want to rebuild, James. I don't want to keep living like this, in this... this space where we're just going through the motions." She paused, her heart racing as she finally looked him in the eyes. "But I need you to want it too. I need you to be with me, not just physically, but emotionally, mentally. I can't do this alone."

James didn't respond immediately. Instead, he stood up and walked to the window, looking out at the night. For a moment, he was silent, his back to her, as if he were gathering his thoughts, his emotions. Sophia held her breath, unsure of what he was thinking, wondering if he would even want to try. The silence between them felt deafening.

When he finally spoke, his voice was raw, a mixture of frustration and something softer, almost sad. "I've wanted that for years, Soph. I've wanted us to be... to be who we were. But I don't know if I can just turn it back on, just like that. I've been carrying my own regrets, my own burdens. And I don't know if I'm strong enough to just let them go and trust again."

Sophia felt a lump form in her throat. It wasn't the answer she had hoped for, but it was the truth. And for the first time in years, they were both speaking the truth—no pretenses, no distractions. The weight of their regrets hung heavily in the room, but so did the flicker of something else. A hope, however small, that they might still be able to find their way back to each other.

She stood up, slowly, moving toward him, until she was close enough to reach out and touch his arm. "We can't change the past," she said, her voice trembling with the weight of it all. "But we can try to make the future different. I don't want to keep living with these regrets, James. I don't want to keep wondering what might have been."

James turned to face her then, his eyes dark and conflicted. But there was something else in them now—something that had been buried for too long. The smallest glimmer of hope, the possibility of something better.

"I don't know if I can fix everything, Soph," he said quietly. "But I'll try. I'll try if you will."

Sophia nodded, her heart swelling with the quiet relief of knowing they weren't giving up on each other. Not yet. "I will," she whispered, the words carrying more weight than she had expected. "I will try, too."

And in that moment, despite all the years that had passed, despite the pain and the regret, there was something else. A fragile, tentative hope that maybe, just maybe, they could rebuild what had been broken.

But they both knew it wouldn't be easy. It would take time, effort, and the kind of honesty that they had avoided for too long. And yet, as they stood there, facing each other in the quiet darkness, they also knew that it was a chance worth taking.

The next few weeks were a delicate balancing act. Sophia and James didn't expect to solve everything overnight, but they did take the first step toward healing—a step that felt more significant than any grand gesture could ever be. It wasn't the sweeping apology or the dramatic confrontation that might have happened in some movie. It was in the quiet moments: the conversations that went beyond surface-level pleasantries, the shared glances over dinner, the slowly rekindled trust that had once felt irreparably broken.

Sophia made a conscious effort to be present. She left her work behind at the office more often, even if it meant turning down opportunities for career advancement. She began having dinner with the family again, putting aside her phone and making a real effort to engage with Izzy and Ethan, who had grown distant during the years of her absence. They were hesitant at first, but gradually they warmed to her, their trust in her rebuilding, even if it would take time.

James, too, began opening up more. He started coming home earlier, not just physically present but mentally engaged, asking Sophia about her day and sharing small victories from his own. They would sit together on the porch after dinner, drinking tea or wine, talking about things that had been left unsaid for far too long. It was awkward at first—there was no denying that—but it was a start.

One evening, as the sun dipped below the horizon and the last remnants of daylight faded into night, James turned to her, his expression contemplative. "I've been thinking a lot about what you said... about rebuilding. It's not just about the past, is it? It's about what we want in the future. What we want to be for each other and for the kids."

Sophia nodded, her fingers brushing the cool glass of her wine. "Exactly. We can't undo the damage we've done, but we can stop making the same mistakes. We can do better."

There was a silence between them, but it wasn't uncomfortable. It was the kind of quiet that comes with understanding. A shared acknowledgment that they were on the same path now, even if they didn't know where it would lead.

"I've missed us," James said, his voice low. "I've missed... who we were before everything got so complicated."

Sophia's heart squeezed at the honesty in his words. "I've missed us too," she admitted. "But maybe it's not about going back to who we were. Maybe it's about figuring out who we are now, in this moment, and building from there."

James smiled slightly, the weight of years of resentment lifting just a little. "You're right. We have to create something new, something that works for both of us... something that doesn't repeat the same mistakes."

They sat in silence for a moment, watching the stars emerge one by one in the evening sky. Sophia could feel the weight of the past—of her regret, of the things they had both failed to say and do—but it wasn't as oppressive as it had been. There was room now, in the space between them, for something else: hope, perhaps, or even love, redefined.

The next day, as she walked into the kitchen to prepare breakfast, Sophia noticed something small but significant. James had left a note on the counter—a simple phrase written in his familiar handwriting: *I'm here. Let's figure this out together.*

Sophia's breath caught in her throat as she picked up the note. It wasn't grand or poetic, but it was everything she needed to hear. It was the acknowledgment that they were still in this, still willing to try.

For the first time in a long time, she allowed herself to believe in the possibility of change, of transformation. The weight of regret was still there, a constant reminder of what had been lost, but it didn't define them anymore. They were both determined to rebuild, step by step, knowing that the road ahead would be difficult, but not impossible.

As the days turned into weeks and then months, their relationship began to shift. They learned to forgive—not just each other, but themselves as well. The guilt that had plagued them both began to lose its grip, replaced by a tentative optimism that they might just be able to rewrite their story, together.

It wouldn't be easy. There would be setbacks, missteps, and moments of doubt. But Sophia knew, with a quiet certainty, that as long as they kept trying, as long as they kept talking and rebuilding, they had a chance.

And sometimes, that was enough.

4. Shifting Priorities

SOPHIA HAD ALWAYS BELIEVED in the balance between career and family, or at least she told herself that she did. For years, she had juggled both with meticulous care, making sure that neither side of her life was neglected. But lately, something had begun to shift, an undercurrent of tension that she couldn't quite identify. It was subtle at first, a quiet whisper in the back of her mind that told her she wasn't quite where she was supposed to be.

Her career had flourished in ways she had never expected, each promotion a victory she had worked for and earned. But with each new achievement came more demands, more travel, more time away from home. It had started with late nights at the office, and then, it was business trips that stretched for days, sometimes weeks. Slowly, imperceptibly at first, the time she spent with her family began to dwindle.

James, her husband, never said anything at first. He was always the quiet one, content to let her lead when it came to decisions about their life together. But Sophia could feel the distance growing between them, like an invisible thread slowly unraveling. The small things began to matter more—the long silences after dinner, the way he would retreat into his books or his work when she came home exhausted.

Izzy, their daughter, had always been independent, always eager to carve out her own space in the world. But recently, Sophia had noticed the subtle changes in her too. The quick glances, the barely concealed impatience when Sophia tried to give advice, the way her daughter seemed to drift further away from her with every passing day. It was as if Sophia had become a stranger in her own home, a figure who came and went, leaving behind a trail of apologies and promises she could never fully keep.

Ethan, their youngest, was different. He clung to her in the way he always had, his bright eyes searching for her whenever she was around. But even he was beginning to notice the shift, the way his mother was always busy, always distracted. He would ask her, sometimes with a quiet voice full of uncertainty, when she was coming home for good, or if she could stay for dinner, just this once. Each time, Sophia's heart would break a little more.

She had always prided herself on being able to handle it all, to keep the delicate balance between her ambition and her family. But now, standing in the kitchen one quiet evening, she couldn't help but wonder how long she could keep up the charade. Was this really the life she had dreamed of, or had she simply been chasing something she could never fully grasp?

Her priorities had always seemed so clear—work hard, provide for her family, create a life that was comfortable and secure. But as the years passed, those priorities began to shift, imperceptibly at first, until she found herself standing at a crossroads. The questions that had been lingering in the back of her mind for so long were finally demanding an answer. What was the point of all the success if it came at the cost of everything she held dear? And could she ever find a way to reconcile the two worlds that seemed to be pulling her in opposite directions?

As the days went on, Sophia felt the weight of her choices more and more. Every email, every phone call, every meeting was another thread pulling her away from the life she had once known. And yet, she couldn't stop. She couldn't turn back, not now, not when everything seemed so close to falling into place. The tension between her desires, her obligations, and her family was growing unbearable, a constant pressure that threatened to crack her wide open.

And yet, there was something inside her, some quiet whisper, that told her it wasn't too late. That maybe, just maybe, she could find a way to shift the balance once again. But it would take courage, the kind she hadn't felt in years. It would take a willingness to face the reality of what she had lost and what she still had left to gain.

The question now was whether she was willing to make the sacrifices necessary to restore that balance, to reclaim the life she had almost forgotten. And if she could, would it be enough to heal the wounds that had been created in her absence?

Chapter 6: In the Shadow of Lies

1. Webs of Deceit

The quiet hum of the evening was broken only by the soft ticking of the clock on the wall. Sophia sat at the kitchen table, staring at the steaming cup of tea before her, the words she had overheard earlier replaying in her mind. Her thoughts spiraled, tangled in a web she hadn't realized had been woven so carefully around her.

Her life, once straightforward and predictable, now felt like a labyrinth. James, her husband, had always been the silent protector, the rock she could lean on. But lately, something had shifted. She could feel it in the way he looked at her sometimes, like he was searching for something in her that wasn't there. The way he'd pull away, retreating into himself, as though there was a part of him she could no longer reach. His words no longer carried the weight they once did, and every conversation felt like a performance—one they both played, but neither believed.

Sophia couldn't remember the last time they had shared an honest conversation. Everything seemed scripted, a polite dance around the truth. But tonight, she had heard it—just a slip, a fleeting moment, but it was enough to make her question everything. A phone call she hadn't meant to overhear, a whispered promise, the sound of a name that wasn't hers.

She hadn't confronted him yet. Part of her still wanted to believe that she had misunderstood. But another part, the part that had been quietly watching, knew better. She had known, deep down, that something had changed. The quiet nights spent alone in their bedroom, the missed calls, the sudden trips—each piece of the puzzle had fallen into place. And now, this. A revelation, hidden in plain sight.

As she stood up, the cup of tea forgotten, a rush of emotion hit her all at once. Anger. Hurt. Betrayal. But it was the fear that gripped her the hardest. What would happen now? What would she do with the truth once she had it? Would she confront him, demand an explanation? Or would she simply let it unfold, piece by painful piece, as the lies continued to unravel?

The thought of it left her paralyzed. How had they gotten here? How had the web of deceit become so intricate, so suffocating, that she could no longer see where the truth ended and the lies began?

Her reflection in the dark window caught her attention. The woman she saw there was familiar, yet foreign—someone who had been both complicit and unaware. She had played her part, kept up the facade, all the while oblivious to the growing cracks in her world.

The silence in the house felt heavier now, as though the walls themselves were aware of the secrets being kept. Sophia knew that once she pulled at the thread, there would be no going back. The lies would either be exposed, or they would consume her entirely.

She took a deep breath, feeling the weight of the decision settle on her chest. The truth was coming, whether she was ready or not. And when it did, there would be no turning away from the consequences.

Sophia's thoughts were interrupted by the sound of footsteps in the hallway. She froze, her pulse quickening as James appeared in the doorway. He looked at her with his usual quiet expression, his eyes soft but guarded.

"I thought I heard you up," he said, his voice low, almost casual. "Everything okay?"

Sophia forced a smile, though it felt more like a mask than anything genuine. She nodded, though her mind was far from calm. "Yeah, just thinking."

James didn't press further, as he usually didn't. He had mastered the art of evading uncomfortable conversations, of shifting the focus away from things that mattered. The perfect defense against questions she wasn't sure she wanted to ask. He walked over to the counter, pouring himself a glass of water, completely unaware—or perhaps pretending not to be—of the storm brewing in the room.

But Sophia's eyes never left him. She studied his every movement, the small things that had once been reassuring now feeling foreign, even suspicious. The way his fingers lingered on the rim of the glass for just a second too long, the almost imperceptible hesitation before he spoke. All the things she had ignored in the past, convinced they were nothing but her overactive imagination. Now, they felt like pieces of a puzzle that didn't quite fit.

Her mind screamed at her to confront him, to tear down the walls between them. But what would she say? How would she even begin to approach the truth she now knew was hidden in plain sight? The questions were overwhelming, like a wave building on the horizon, threatening to crash down at any moment.

James set the glass down with a soft clink, his gaze finally meeting hers. He raised an eyebrow, his lips curling into a faint smile. "You're awfully quiet tonight. What's on your mind?"

Sophia opened her mouth, but no words came. She felt the weight of his gaze like a physical pressure on her chest. Her body was telling her to speak, to expose everything, but the fear of the unknown, the fear of what would happen once the lies came to light, kept her paralyzed.

"I'm fine," she said at last, her voice barely above a whisper.

James nodded, but there was a flicker of something in his eyes—a flicker she hadn't seen before. A warning? Guilt? Or was it just her mind playing tricks on her? She couldn't be sure anymore.

He turned away, moving toward the living room, his footsteps retreating into the distance. But the silence he left behind was suffocating. It was a silence filled with unsaid words, with the weight of all that had been concealed.

Sophia stood still for a moment, her breath shallow, her thoughts in turmoil. She had been living in a world of illusions for so long, wrapped in the comfort of the lies that had kept her safe. But now, the truth was creeping in, demanding to be heard.

The hardest part wasn't the truth itself—it was what it would mean for everything she thought she knew about herself, about James, about their life together. The lies had become a comfort, a protective layer. But now, they felt like chains, holding her in place, keeping her from moving forward.

She closed her eyes and took a deep breath, trying to steady her racing thoughts. The truth had a way of clawing its way to the surface, no matter how deeply it was buried. She couldn't hide from it forever.

But when it came, she knew, there would be no turning back.

The hours passed in a blur, the weight of the evening's revelations lingering like a shadow that refused to dissipate. Sophia sat in the dimly lit kitchen, staring at her phone, wondering if she should make the call. The call that would expose everything—the call that might tear apart the fragile veneer of her life.

But what if she was wrong? What if she had misinterpreted everything? It was a dangerous thought, one that clung to her like a lifeline, keeping her from plunging into the unknown. The fear of being wrong, of confronting a reality she wasn't ready for, held her in place, paralyzed in indecision.

Her fingers hovered over the screen, just inches away from dialing the number she had never thought she would need to call. The number that belonged to Sarah, James's old friend—someone he had reconnected with recently. Someone who had been a fixture in their lives, until recently, when she had disappeared for weeks on end, only to return with vague excuses and mysterious stories.

Sophia had always brushed it off, but now the pieces were starting to form a picture, and she couldn't ignore it any longer.

The phone buzzed in her hand, and she startled, dropping it onto the table. She looked down, her heart skipping a beat as she saw James's name on the screen.

"I'm sorry, I didn't mean to startle you," he said softly when she answered. "I was just wondering if you were ready to talk about... whatever's been on your mind."

Sophia's heart pounded in her chest, the knot in her throat tightening. His voice was calm, but she could hear the undercurrent of something she couldn't place. Was it guilt? Or just the same practiced detachment that had always been there?

"James, I..." she began, her voice faltering as she tried to find the words. She knew she needed to confront him, but a part of her was still holding on to the small, fragile thread of hope that everything would somehow return to normal, that the lies would prove to be just misunderstandings.

But the truth was already there, swirling in the back of her mind, waiting to be acknowledged. The lies, the secrets, the evasions—they were all part of something much larger than she had initially realized. And now, as the pieces fell into place, she couldn't deny it any longer.

"You've been distant," she said, the words coming out almost mechanically, though every syllable felt like a weight pressing down on her. "I've seen the way you've been acting lately. I've heard things."

The silence on the other end of the line stretched, and for a moment, Sophia wondered if he would simply hang up. But then, he spoke, his voice low, almost too controlled.

"Don't do this," he said, his tone warning, but there was an edge of something else there—something that Sophia couldn't name.

"I have to do this," she replied, her own voice steadying as the resolve she hadn't known she had began to build. "I have to know the truth, James."

Another long pause. The tension in the air was thick, palpable. Sophia could hear the faint rustle of papers in the background, the soft clicking of a pen on a hard surface. It was all too ordinary, too normal, for a conversation that felt like it was about to shatter everything they had built.

And then, finally, the words came.

"I didn't mean for it to go this far," James said, his voice almost a whisper now, the vulnerability in it so raw that it took her by surprise. "But you deserve to know. I've been trying to protect you from it... from the truth."

The room seemed to close in around Sophia, and for the first time, she felt the full weight of the situation—the weight of the truth that had been hidden from her for so long. She wasn't ready for it. She wasn't prepared for the unraveling that would follow.

But there was no turning back now. The web of deceit had already ensnared them both, and no matter how much she wished it were different, the only choice left was to face it head-on.

Sophia's voice was barely a whisper when she spoke again.

"Tell me everything."

There was a brief silence on the other end of the line before James spoke again, his voice barely audible. "It wasn't supposed to be like this," he said. "I never meant for it to hurt you."

Sophia could hear the regret in his voice, but it wasn't enough to soothe the storm that was growing inside her. The weight of his confession, of the things he was about to say, pressed down on her chest like a heavy hand.

She closed her eyes for a moment, trying to steady herself. "What do you mean? What are you talking about, James?"

The silence stretched again, but this time it wasn't empty. It was heavy with the weight of secrets long buried, the kind of secrets that, once revealed, could not be undone. Sophia held her breath, knowing that the moment of truth was finally upon her.

"It's Sarah," James said, his voice still shaky. "I... I never stopped seeing her. After all these years, we reconnected, and it just... it happened. I didn't know how to tell you. I thought it was just a phase, something that would pass."

Sophia felt the blood drain from her face. Her grip on the phone tightened as the truth hit her, crashing over her like a wave. It was all true—everything she had feared, everything she had sensed but refused to acknowledge.

"So, it's true then," she whispered, more to herself than to him. "You've been seeing her behind my back."

"I never meant for it to be like this," James repeated, his words desperate now, almost pleading. "I thought it was just a mistake. I thought I could stop it before it went too far. But I couldn't."

The bitterness in Sophia's chest began to bubble up, filling her throat, making it hard to breathe. She had been living in a lie, a perfect illusion of love and trust, and now that illusion was shattered. Her mind raced, trying to make sense of the pieces, trying to find a way to hold on to the man she thought she knew.

But he was no longer the person she had married. The man she had trusted had turned out to be someone else entirely.

"Why?" she asked, her voice shaking with a mix of anger and disbelief. "Why did you do it, James? Why her?"

"I don't know," he said, his voice strained. "I don't have an answer. I wish I could explain it, but I can't. I just... I didn't know how to stop."

Sophia felt a wave of nausea wash over her. She wanted to scream, to lash out, to make him understand the depth of the betrayal. But the anger was swallowed up by something darker—something deeper. She had always believed that they had something special, something unbreakable. Now, it felt like everything she had built her life around was nothing more than a facade.

"I don't know if I can forgive you for this," she said, the words coming out in a whisper, but they cut through the silence like a knife.

"I don't expect you to," James replied, his voice thick with emotion. "I just... I need you to know the truth. I owe you that much."

The truth. It was more than she could bear, more than she had ever imagined. The weight of it felt suffocating. But even as the truth settled in, Sophia knew one thing for sure: this was the moment everything changed. There would be no going back.

She closed her eyes, trying to find some semblance of peace amidst the chaos swirling inside her. But there was no peace to be found—not in this, not in the lies, not in the brokenness that now defined her world.

"Goodbye, James," she said quietly, her voice barely above a whisper.

And with that, she ended the call.

Sophia sat in the silence that followed, the weight of the phone still heavy in her hand. The room around her felt colder, the light from the kitchen dimmer, as though everything in her world had shifted, leaving her suspended in a place she couldn't recognize. She had hoped for closure, for some sense of resolution, but all she felt was emptiness.

The conversation with James had been everything she feared and more. She had wanted the truth, and now she had it. But the truth didn't bring peace—it only brought more questions. How had she missed the signs? How had she been so blind to the cracks forming in their life together?

She thought of Sarah, the woman who had once been nothing more than a distant name, an old friend of James's. Now, she was the embodiment of everything that had gone wrong. Sophia's mind raced, replaying every interaction, every time Sarah had come over for coffee or they'd run into her in passing, each moment now tainted by the weight of what had been happening behind the scenes.

As she sat there, lost in thought, a sudden noise broke her reverie—the unmistakable sound of the front door opening. Her heart skipped in her chest. James was home. It had only been minutes since their call, yet he was already back, no doubt hoping for some kind of explanation, some way to salvage whatever was left of their relationship.

But there was no salvaging this. Not now.

Sophia stood up from the kitchen table, her legs unsteady, and walked slowly to the door. She could hear his footsteps in the hallway, his presence filling the space with a sense of urgency she couldn't ignore. He was trying to find her, trying to talk to her. But there was nothing left to say.

As she opened the door, her eyes met his, but they no longer saw the man she had once trusted. There was no familiarity, no warmth. Only a stranger staring back at her, someone she no longer recognized.

James opened his mouth as if to speak, but Sophia raised her hand, cutting him off. She didn't need to hear his excuses, his apologies. The truth had already been laid bare. The lies were no longer hidden. And in that moment, she knew exactly what she had to do.

"I don't want to hear it, James," she said, her voice steady, though inside, she felt like she was falling apart. "I've heard enough."

His face twisted in confusion and pain, but she couldn't bring herself to care anymore. The man she had loved was gone, replaced by someone she didn't know, someone who had betrayed her in ways she could never have imagined.

"I'm not asking for forgiveness," James said, his voice raw, almost pleading. "I just wanted to explain. I wanted you to understand why it happened."

Sophia shook her head, her eyes hardening. "I don't need to understand. I don't need any explanations. I just need you to leave. This... this is over."

She stepped back, making space between them, her heart breaking with each word. This wasn't the life she had planned. This wasn't the future she had imagined. But it was the one she had been forced into, whether she was ready or not.

James stood there for a moment longer, his face pale and stricken, as if he couldn't quite grasp what was happening. But Sophia didn't wait for him to come to terms with it. She couldn't. Her heart was already broken, and there was no point in prolonging the inevitable.

"Goodbye, James," she whispered, and with that, she closed the door.

2. The Unraveling Thread

IT BEGAN WITH A SIMPLE tug, barely noticeable, like a loose thread in the fabric of their lives. But soon, it grew—slowly at first, like the faintest whisper of a storm. The quiet tension between Sophia and James had always been there, an unspoken undercurrent in their relationship, but it had been manageable. They had learned to live with it, to ignore it, to push it to the corners of their minds where it wouldn't disturb the illusion of harmony they had so carefully constructed.

THE SHIFTING BALANCE

But now, that thread was unraveling. The fabric of their family, so meticulously woven over the years, was starting to show its seams. The cracks were no longer hidden by the layers of routine and expectation. The smiles that had once seemed genuine now felt forced, the conversations increasingly punctuated by silence. **Sophia**, who had once believed that work and family could be balanced with enough determination, now found herself questioning whether she had sacrificed too much. The late nights at the office, the missed birthdays, the hours spent away from home—had they been worth it? Could she go back, undo the damage, and still find the love and connection she had once shared with James?

James, on the other hand, had always been the quiet provider, the one who kept things steady, even when his own desires and feelings were ignored. He had never been the one to speak out, to demand more. But now, as he watched Sophia's increasing distance and her obsession with her career, he couldn't help but feel a deep, aching resentment. His own dreams had been put on hold for years to support hers, to make sure the family had what it needed. And yet, it felt like she was slipping further away, as if the distance between them was not just physical, but emotional as well. He wanted to scream, to lash out, to make her see what he was going through. But all that came out were sighs, each one heavier than the last.

In the silence that had begun to fill their home, their children—**Izzy** and **Ethan**—could feel the shift. They may not have fully understood the depth of the problems between their parents, but they sensed the tension in the air. **Izzy**, the older daughter, had become more distant, retreating into her own world of rebellion and confusion. She had always admired her mother's strength, her ambition, but now, she felt abandoned. **Ethan**, younger and more sensitive, tried to hold everything together. He would ask his parents if they were okay, but they would only smile and reassure him that everything was fine, even though they both knew it wasn't.

The unraveling thread was no longer just a symbol of their personal struggles—it had become a reality they could no longer ignore. Every word that went unsaid, every moment of silence, added another tug, another twist, until the thread itself was at the breaking point. And when it finally snapped, everything they had taken for granted—everything they thought they knew about love, about family, about each other—would be tested.

But even as the thread unraveled, there was still hope. There was still the possibility of mending, of rebuilding what had been lost. It wouldn't be easy. It might not even be possible. But for Sophia, for James, and for their children, it was the only chance they had left to salvage what was once whole. The unraveling had begun, but how it would end was still to be determined.

As the days passed, the unraveling thread continued to stretch, its tension becoming unbearable with each new incident. **Sophia** found herself caught between guilt and frustration, constantly balancing her responsibilities at work with her failing connection to her family. Her career, once a source of pride, had become the very thing that pulled her further away from the people she loved most. She had always believed in the importance of providing, of achieving, but now she questioned the cost. Was it worth sacrificing the intimacy, the closeness, the moments that truly mattered?

James, meanwhile, felt like he was losing his grip on everything he had worked so hard to build. Every conversation with Sophia felt like a battle, with words that once flowed easily now heavy with the weight of unspoken truths. He loved her—he always had—but that love was being suffocated, not by distance, but by the invisible walls they had both erected over time. He had always been the stable one, the anchor, but lately, he felt himself slipping, losing his sense of who he was in the process. His frustration began to show in ways it hadn't before—sharp words, bitter silences, moments of sudden outbursts when the pressure became too much to bear.

Izzy, caught in the crossfire of her parents' unraveling bond, struggled with her own sense of identity. She had always been the perfect child, the one who followed the rules, who excelled in school, who kept her emotions in check. But now, the facade was beginning to crack. Her relationship with her mother, once one of admiration and respect, had become strained. She resented the distance, the absence, and she resented the way her mother seemed to prioritize everything else over their relationship. Yet, at the same time, she feared the idea of confronting her mother, of forcing her to see the hurt that had been building up inside for so long.

Ethan, ever the peacemaker, sensed the discord more acutely than anyone realized. He still tried to hold onto the hope that things would return to normal, that the tension would somehow disappear. He tried to fill the silence with his laughter, with his innocent attempts at making everyone happy, but no amount of pretending could mask the truth. He knew something was wrong. And that knowledge, heavy for someone so young, became his own silent burden. He began retreating into his room more often, his quiet nature becoming more pronounced as he tried to make sense of the storm raging just beyond his door.

But the true breaking point came one evening when the family gathered for dinner. It was supposed to be a simple meal, a moment of reconnection, but the weight of everything that had been unsaid finally erupted. **Sophia** had come home late from work again, exhausted, her mind consumed with a project that seemed never-ending. **James**, who had been waiting, had prepared the meal, but his patience was wearing thin. The conversation, once casual, turned sharp, the words cutting deeper than they had in years. The small issues, the little irritations, the long-held frustrations—everything came pouring out. And with each word, the thread continued to unravel, faster now, as if time itself was speeding up.

"Why can't you just be here, Sophia?" James' voice cracked, a rare break in his usually calm demeanor. "We're falling apart, and you're not even noticing."

Sophia, stung by the accusation, tried to explain herself, but the words felt hollow, rehearsed. She had excuses—always excuses. She had work to do. She had deadlines. She had responsibilities. But as she looked at James, at the hurt in his eyes, she realized that the excuses no longer mattered. She was losing him.

"I'm trying, James," she said, her voice barely above a whisper. "But I don't know how to fix this."

For a moment, the room fell silent. It wasn't the kind of silence that held comfort or understanding—it was heavy, suffocating. Izzy and Ethan sat at the table, their plates untouched, their eyes flicking nervously between their parents. The air was thick with tension, thick with all the things they were afraid to say. And for the first time in a long time, they all felt the weight of what was happening—not just between Sophia and James, but within themselves.

The unraveling thread was no longer something that could be ignored, something that could be hidden behind a smile or a busy schedule. It had reached its breaking point, and now, they all had to face the truth.

What came next was uncertain. The road to repair, to healing, seemed distant, and the fear of losing everything was too real to ignore. But as the evening wore on, and the family sat in the ruins of what had once been their sanctuary, one thing became clear: nothing would be the same again. And perhaps, that was the first step toward something new.

The days following that dinner were filled with a strange kind of quiet. The anger had dissipated, but it had left behind an emptiness that was even more unsettling. **Sophia** spent hours staring at her reflection in the mirror, trying to reconcile the person she had become with the woman she had once dreamed of being. Her career had consumed her, and in doing so, it had quietly stripped her of the very thing she had worked so hard to build: her family. But as much as she regretted the missed moments, the lost time, she felt trapped in a cycle that she couldn't seem to break. The demands of her job, the pressure to succeed—it had all become so overwhelming, and she didn't know how to get off the treadmill that was taking her further away from the people she loved.

James, too, was struggling. The hurt from their argument still lingered, but it was no longer just the words that stung—it was the realization that their relationship had slowly eroded without either of them noticing. He had always been the steady one, the one who kept things together, but now he was uncertain. Every time he looked at Sophia, he saw a woman he no longer recognized. The warmth that once filled their home had turned cold, and no amount of patience or silence seemed to mend the distance between them. He had tried to be understanding, tried to make space for her, but now he wasn't sure if it was too late.

Izzy became more withdrawn as the days wore on. The conflict between her parents had created a rift within her as well, and she found herself pulling away from both of them. She had always been the one to keep the peace, the one to protect her younger brother from the harsh realities of adult life, but she couldn't protect herself from the growing turmoil inside her. The resentment she felt toward her mother was growing, and at the same time, she hated herself for feeling it. She missed the woman who had once been her role model, the mother who had encouraged her to chase her dreams. But now, all she saw was someone who had abandoned them for the sake of success. It was a feeling that left her torn, unsure of where to direct her anger, her pain.

Ethan, ever the silent observer, had begun to retreat even further. His once bright eyes, full of innocence and hope, were now clouded with confusion. He could no longer pretend that everything was okay. The truth, however unspoken, hung in the air like a weight he couldn't escape. He didn't fully understand the complexities of relationships, the reasons why people fell apart, but he understood that something was broken. And like Izzy, he didn't know how to fix it.

One evening, after a particularly long day for Sophia, she found herself in the living room, staring out the window, as if looking for answers in the dark. Her mind raced with a thousand thoughts, none of them providing any clarity. As she sat there, she heard the sound of footsteps behind her. It was James, who had quietly entered the room without her noticing. He didn't speak at first—he simply stood there, as if waiting for her to say something.

Finally, Sophia spoke, her voice small but filled with emotion. "James... I don't know how we got here. How did we let it go this far?"

James let out a heavy sigh, his voice strained but calm. "We were both so caught up in our own worlds, Sophia. You with your career, me with trying to hold everything together. But somewhere along the way, we stopped seeing each other. And now... I'm not sure how to find my way back."

Sophia turned to face him, her eyes filled with regret. "I never meant to lose you. I thought I could do it all, but I can't. I don't know how to make it right."

James stepped closer, his presence offering some comfort, but there was no magic solution. "Maybe we don't need to make it all right overnight. Maybe we just need to start with being honest with each other. No more pretending."

For the first time in weeks, there was a flicker of hope. The unraveling thread hadn't fully snapped, and though it was frayed and torn, there was still a chance to repair it. They both knew it wouldn't be easy, that the road ahead was uncertain, but it was the first step toward reclaiming something they had almost lost.

As they sat in silence, each lost in their own thoughts, they realized that they had a choice to make. They could continue down the path they were on, allowing the unraveling to take its course, or they could begin the slow, painful process of reweaving the strands of their broken relationship. It wasn't an easy choice, but it was the only one that mattered now.

And as the night wore on, they knew one thing for certain: the journey ahead would be long and difficult, but it would be theirs to walk together.

The days following that conversation felt like a fragile truce. **Sophia** and **James** tried to reclaim some semblance of normalcy, but the air between them remained thick with unspoken words. They were each taking tentative steps, testing the waters, unsure of how much they could trust the other to truly understand. But as much as the distance between them had grown, there was something within both of them that refused to let go completely. Maybe it was love, or maybe it was fear of truly facing the consequences of what they might lose, but they both clung to the idea of trying, even if only for a little longer.

At the dinner table, the atmosphere had shifted. It was no longer filled with easy laughter or shared stories, but a quiet tension that had become their new normal. **Izzy** no longer tried to hide the frustration she felt; it was etched on her face in the way she avoided eye contact with her parents. She didn't have the words to explain what she felt, but the silence between them said it all. It was as if the family they once were had been replaced by something unrecognizable. The weight of the tension was too much for her to bear, and it showed in her increasingly distant behavior. She would disappear into her room for hours, retreating into her books or scrolling mindlessly through her phone, unable to face the reality unfolding around her.

Ethan, in contrast, seemed to have taken the family's disintegration the hardest. The little boy who once bubbled with excitement and mischief now kept to himself, his quiet nature deepening into something more reflective. He still tried to make his parents smile—he would draw pictures for them, make little jokes, attempt to create moments of lightness—but it felt hollow. His efforts were increasingly met with distracted nods or absent-minded smiles. He could feel the change, even if he couldn't articulate it. It wasn't just that their marriage was on the rocks; it was that something was fundamentally wrong with the fabric of their lives.

One evening, Sophia returned home early, something rare in recent weeks. Her office had let out earlier than expected, and for the first time in a while, she found herself with a few hours of precious time. She walked through the door, expecting the usual quiet, but instead, she was met with an odd stillness. There was no sound of the television, no distant murmur of voices—just silence.

She moved cautiously through the house, her footsteps echoing on the hardwood floors. She found **Izzy** sitting on the couch, her eyes downcast, a book in her lap that she wasn't reading. Sophia opened her mouth to say something, but hesitated. She didn't know what to say anymore. Words had become fragile things between them, easily broken.

Instead, Sophia sat down beside her daughter, just close enough to offer comfort without crowding her. The silence stretched between them before Izzy finally spoke, her voice softer than Sophia had ever heard it.

"Why don't you ever have time for us anymore?" Izzy's words felt like a slap, though she had meant them to be nothing more than an honest question. Sophia flinched, but there was no avoiding it.

"I'm sorry," Sophia said, her voice cracking slightly. "I don't know how things got so out of control. I thought I could handle it all, but... I've been failing you."

Izzy didn't respond immediately. Instead, she closed her eyes for a moment, her expression unreadable. "I just don't get it, Mom. You used to say family was the most important thing. But now it feels like... we're just in the way."

Sophia felt a pang of guilt stab her chest. Izzy was right, and hearing it out loud was like a harsh wake-up call. She had lost sight of what truly mattered. The familiar ache of regret settled in her stomach, but she didn't know how to fix it.

Before she could say anything else, **Ethan** walked in, holding a drawing in his small hands. "Mom, look!" he said, his voice bright despite the heaviness in the air. He handed her the picture, and Sophia smiled weakly, trying to force some normalcy back into their world.

It was a simple drawing of their family, with stick figures of herself, James, Izzy, and Ethan, all holding hands under a large tree. The innocence of it made her heart ache. She wondered if Ethan truly understood the implications of their fractured family. The love he had for them, the hope he placed in that small sketch, felt like a reminder of what they were all losing.

Sophia crouched down to Ethan's level, pressing the drawing to her chest. "Thank you, Ethan," she said softly, her voice thick with emotion. "This is beautiful."

Ethan beamed, seemingly unaware of the weight of his gesture. "I want us to be happy again, Mommy."

Tears welled up in Sophia's eyes as she hugged her son tightly. "Me too," she whispered, her voice barely audible.

At that moment, **James** entered the room, looking at the family with a quiet sadness in his eyes. His earlier resolve to not talk about the situation seemed to crumble in the face of his children's vulnerability. He knew the road ahead was uncertain, and the idea of repairing what had been broken felt impossible, but seeing Sophia with their children, the raw emotion in her eyes, gave him a sliver of hope.

The unraveling thread had taken so much from them, and yet, as fragile as their bond seemed, there was still a thread of connection, a thread of hope that neither of them was ready to let go of.

Sophia took a deep breath and turned to James. "Maybe it's time we really start trying. No more pretending. No more excuses. We need to rebuild this—together."

James nodded slowly, a quiet understanding passing between them. It wouldn't be easy, but for the first time in what felt like a long time, they both knew that they were ready to face the future, whatever it held. Together.

The days that followed were an uneasy mixture of hope and hesitation. They both knew that words were not enough to repair the damage that had been done, but there was a fragile sense of resolve growing between them. It was as though they were walking on a tightrope, unsure of when the balance would shift and send them tumbling back into old habits, but they were determined to try.

Sophia took a week off from work, something she had never done in years. She told herself it was a necessary break, but deep down, she knew it was to focus on what really mattered—her family. She spent time with **Ethan**, doing the little things she had missed: making pancakes together in the morning, playing in the backyard, reading stories before bed. With **Izzy**, it was more difficult. The silence between them felt heavy, laden with unspoken words. But Sophia was patient, respecting her daughter's space while still making small attempts to bridge the gap.

That night, as the family sat around the dinner table, there was a subtle shift in the air. It wasn't dramatic; there were no grand declarations or sweeping gestures. It was just a moment of quiet, shared understanding. **James** had put down his phone—something he rarely did these days—and was actually looking at his children, engaging with them in a way that felt like it had been lost for far too long.

Izzy, still somewhat distant, picked at her food but eventually made eye contact with her father. "You're really here, aren't you?" she asked, her voice carrying a mix of disbelief and longing.

James paused, his fork halfway to his mouth. "I am," he said, and for the first time in a long while, there was a sincerity in his voice. "I've been too caught up in... other things. But I'm here now. For you. For all of us."

Sophia's heart swelled with something fragile—hope, maybe, or a sense of cautious optimism. She knew they weren't out of the woods yet. She could feel the weight of the years that had been lost, the years when they had simply existed in the same house without truly being a family. But there was a glimmer of something—something they hadn't had in a long time. A spark of possibility.

Later that evening, as the children went to bed, **James** and **Sophia** sat in the living room, the faint glow of the fireplace casting long shadows on the walls. The quiet between them was no longer uncomfortable; it felt like a space where they could finally begin to talk, really talk, for the first time in ages.

James leaned forward, his elbows on his knees, his gaze fixed on the flames. "Sophia," he started, his voice quieter than usual, "I've been thinking a lot about us. About how we got here." He looked at her, his eyes filled with an emotion she couldn't quite place. "I don't want to keep pretending anymore. I don't want to lose what we have left. I know I've been distant, but I want to change. For you, for me, for all of us."

Sophia felt a knot in her chest loosen, though the weight of his words still hung in the air. "I don't want to lose us either, James," she said softly. "But we can't go on like this, pretending everything's okay when it's not. We've both made mistakes, but I think we can still fix this—if we're willing to put in the work."

James nodded, though the burden of their history was heavy between them. "We have a lot to fix, but I'm ready to try. I don't want to wake up one day and realize we've missed our chance."

Sophia reached over, taking his hand in hers. It was a small gesture, but it felt like the first real connection they'd had in a long time. "Me neither," she said quietly.

In the days that followed, they both took small steps toward rebuilding. It wasn't easy. There were moments of frustration, moments when old habits crept back in, but there were also moments of genuine connection—shared laughter over a meal, a quiet moment of understanding between them when neither knew what to say. These small acts of rebuilding, though fragile, became the foundation they began to rely on.

Izzy, though still distant, began to open up little by little. One afternoon, she and Sophia went for a walk in the park, something they used to do often before life got too complicated. As they walked, Izzy spoke more than she had in weeks, revealing her fears and frustrations. "I don't know if things can ever go back to the way they were," she admitted, her voice low. "But... I guess it's better to try than just keep pretending."

THE SHIFTING BALANCE

Sophia listened, her heart aching for her daughter. "We'll never go back to the way things were, Izzy," she said softly. "But maybe we don't need to. We can make something new. Something better."

And for the first time in a long time, **Izzy** smiled, though it was small, fleeting. But it was a start.

By the time the weekend came, the family found themselves in a strange, almost peaceful routine. They still had their moments of tension, but the sense of disconnect was starting to fade, replaced by tentative steps toward healing. The path ahead was uncertain, filled with both hope and doubt, but they were walking it together—slowly, cautiously, but together nonetheless.

Sophia had come to realize something in the quiet of those moments: the unraveling thread of their family was not beyond repair. It would take time, patience, and a willingness to face the brokenness head-on, but it was not lost. The thread, though frayed and fragile, could still be mended, and perhaps in the process, they could find something stronger than they had before.

The next few weeks passed in a blur of small victories and setbacks. It wasn't the smooth recovery they had hoped for, but it was progress. The family's rhythm, once disrupted, was gradually finding its pace again.

James had taken to attending therapy sessions with Sophia, something he had resisted for months. At first, it had felt like a chore—a formality, even—but slowly, he began to see it differently. The sessions weren't just about fixing what had been broken, but about understanding the dynamics that had led to their distance in the first place. It was painful, but the honesty was something he hadn't expected to feel. Each session revealed more about his own fears, his self-imposed isolation, and his regret for the years he had let slip by without truly being present.

One afternoon, as they sat together after a particularly intense session, James finally voiced something that had been haunting him. "I didn't just disconnect from you, Sophia," he said, his voice tight, as though admitting it caused physical pain. "I shut down everything. I stopped trying to fix things because... because I didn't think I was worth fixing. I thought maybe I didn't deserve it."

Sophia was quiet for a long moment, her heart aching for the man who had once been her partner, the one who had shared her dreams and fears. The one who, in his own way, had tried so hard to protect their family—even if he had done it in all the wrong ways. "James," she finally said, her voice soft, but steady, "you do deserve to be fixed. We all do. We've all made mistakes. But that doesn't mean we have to give up on each other. And it doesn't mean we're broken beyond repair."

He looked at her, and for the first time in a long time, she saw the flicker of hope in his eyes. It was small, fragile, but it was there. "I want to believe that," he said quietly. "I really do."

Sophia reached out, placing her hand on his. It wasn't a grand gesture, but it was enough for that moment. It was a reminder that they were still here, still trying, still choosing to fight for what mattered.

Later that evening, they sat down with **Izzy** to talk. The tension was still there between them, unspoken but palpable. Izzy had withdrawn further over the past week, and Sophia couldn't help but feel a rising sense of dread. She was afraid of pushing too hard, of forcing a conversation that might drive her daughter further away. But she knew that silence wouldn't heal anything—it would only make the rift wider.

"Izzy," Sophia began gently, "I know things have been hard between us, and I don't want to rush anything. But I want you to know that we're here. We're really here. And we're trying."

Izzy looked up, her expression guarded, but there was something softer in her eyes. She didn't respond immediately, but after a long silence, she spoke. "I don't know how to do this," she admitted, her voice trembling slightly. "I don't know how to go back to being a family. It feels like too much has happened, like we can never fix it."

Sophia felt her heart twist at the vulnerability in her daughter's voice. "We don't have to go back to what we were," she said softly. "We just need to figure out what we want to be now. It's going to take time, but I'm willing to wait. I'll do whatever it takes."

Izzy met her gaze, the walls around her slowly starting to crumble. "I just don't want to keep pretending everything's okay when it's not," she said quietly.

"And you don't have to," Sophia reassured her. "You never have to pretend with me, Izzy. I'll always be here, no matter what. We're going to figure this out together."

For the first time in what felt like forever, Izzy offered a small smile. It was tentative, fragile, but it was a start. They weren't fixed, not yet, but maybe they could begin to rebuild.

As the days passed, the weight of the past slowly began to lift. They still had their struggles, of course. There were moments of miscommunication, moments where the old patterns threatened to resurface. But with each step, each small conversation, they were beginning to reforge their connections.

In the evenings, they would sit together on the porch, talking about their day, about everything and nothing. The laughter was starting to return, hesitant but genuine. And when the silence did come, it was no longer uncomfortable. It was the quiet of shared understanding, a peace that had been absent for far too long.

Sophia had learned something in the weeks since they had begun this journey: rebuilding a family wasn't about perfection. It wasn't about erasing the mistakes of the past, but about acknowledging them and moving forward, one step at a time. It was about the willingness to keep showing up, even when it was hard, even when the road ahead seemed uncertain.

And though they weren't there yet, though the journey ahead was still long and fraught with challenges, she knew one thing for certain: they were no longer unraveling. They were beginning to weave something new, something stronger, and in that, there was hope.

The weeks that followed became a series of quiet breakthroughs. James continued with his therapy sessions, each one peeling back more layers of his past, forcing him to confront long-buried fears. His relationship with Sophia was still fragile, but the cracks in the foundation began to close, even if just a little. They spent time together, not always talking, but simply being, reconnecting with the part of each other they had lost over the years.

Izzy, too, began to open up in her own way. It wasn't easy—teens, especially ones who had been through as much as she had, rarely had simple solutions for their pain. But little by little, she began to trust them again, sharing her thoughts, her fears, her frustrations. It wasn't that she had forgotten what had happened, but she started to see that maybe, just maybe, she could find her place in this fractured family again.

One evening, as the sun dipped below the horizon, James and Sophia sat on the couch, each lost in their own thoughts. They had talked about everything and nothing, as they often did now. It was in these small moments that they were rediscovering each other—the quiet comfort of just being together, not needing to fill every second with words.

"I'm sorry," James said, breaking the silence that had stretched on for several minutes.

Sophia turned toward him, her heart beating a little faster at the sincerity in his voice. "For what?"

"For not being here when you needed me," he said, the words coming slowly, as if they had weight he hadn't fully understood until now. "For shutting you out when you needed me the most. I thought... I thought I was protecting you, but I see now I was just hiding."

Sophia didn't know how to respond at first. The apology felt long overdue, but it also felt like the first step toward something deeper. "I don't blame you for being lost, James," she said quietly. "I was lost too. We both were. But it's not about the past anymore. It's about what we're willing to do now. And I'm willing to fight for us—for our family."

The vulnerability in her words hit him harder than any argument or confrontation ever could. He reached for her hand, his grip firm but gentle. "I'm willing to fight too," he said. "I know I have a lot to make up for. But I'll keep trying. I promise you that."

They sat in silence for a while, but it wasn't an uncomfortable silence. It was one of those rare, fleeting moments of peace that seemed to hang in the air, full of the unspoken understanding that sometimes, words weren't necessary.

The next morning, as they sat around the breakfast table, the air felt different—lighter, somehow. The tension of the past had not disappeared entirely, but it was no longer the dominant force in their home. The routine of their day-to-day life had returned, but now there was an undercurrent of connection, a quiet bond that they hadn't shared in years.

Izzy, who had been mostly silent during the morning, suddenly broke in with a soft question. "Do you think we'll ever be the same?" she asked, her voice barely above a whisper.

Sophia paused, unsure of the right answer. Would they ever be the same? The question was complicated. The wounds they had carried for so long had changed them all, but that didn't mean they couldn't heal, or even rebuild.

"We might not ever be exactly the same," Sophia said, her voice steady, "but we can be something new. Something better. We just have to keep working at it, one day at a time."

Izzy looked down at her cereal, her fingers tracing the rim of her bowl. "I think I can live with that," she said quietly.

And for the first time in what felt like an eternity, Sophia allowed herself to believe it too. They weren't the same family they had been before, but they didn't need to be. They were becoming something stronger, something more resilient. A family rebuilt, not on perfection, but on the willingness to try, to change, and to love.

As the day wore on, and life continued with its usual mix of ordinary moments, Sophia found herself holding onto this new sense of hope. It wasn't just about fixing the past—it was about building something from the ground up. And that, she realized, was where the real healing began.

The days that followed felt like the slow unfurling of a long-forgotten melody. There were moments of doubt, of course—those silent exchanges when the weight of unspoken words felt too heavy to bear. But there were also moments of breakthrough, small victories that chipped away at the walls they had all built around themselves. James and Sophia spent more time together, rediscovering the quiet magic of shared mornings, of discussing everything and nothing in the stillness of their home. Izzy, too, seemed to soften, her walls slowly coming down as she realized her parents weren't giving up on her.

One afternoon, as Sophia cleaned the kitchen, she noticed James standing in the doorway, his gaze distant but thoughtful. She dried her hands on a towel and crossed the room to him, her heart already beating a little faster.

"Something on your mind?" she asked, her voice calm but curious.

He sighed deeply, the lines of worry creasing his forehead. "I've been thinking about how we got here. About everything we've been through. And I can't help but wonder... how much of it was because I couldn't face my own fears. My own guilt."

Sophia's heart clenched at his words, knowing exactly what he meant. She had lived with the same guilt, the same feeling of failure. But now, standing before him, she saw the difference—the rawness in his eyes, the vulnerability that he had kept hidden for so long. He wasn't the same man who had withdrawn into himself, the one who thought he had to carry everything alone.

"I think we both had our share of fears, James," she said softly, placing a hand on his arm. "But we're here now. And that counts for something."

He looked at her then, really looked at her, as if seeing her for the first time in a long while. His lips parted as if to say something more, but he didn't. Instead, he took her hand in his, holding it tightly, and in that simple gesture, there was more than words could ever convey.

Later that evening, when they sat down for dinner, there was a new lightness in the air. Even Izzy, who had been quiet all week, seemed to be in a better mood. Her shoulders weren't as tense, her face not as guarded. She looked up from her plate, meeting her mother's gaze for a moment before speaking.

"Mom, Dad... I've been thinking," she said, her voice tentative but growing stronger. "Maybe... maybe we could start over. Like, actually start over. Not just pretend everything's fine, but really try. Together."

Sophia's breath caught in her throat. She had been waiting for this moment, but she hadn't known when it would come. Izzy had been so distant for so long that she hadn't dared to hope for a real conversation. But here it was—this tiny spark of hope, of possibility.

"That's exactly what we're doing, Izzy," Sophia said, her voice filled with quiet emotion. "We're trying. Every single day. And we'll keep trying, no matter how hard it gets. Because you're worth it. All of you are."

Izzy nodded, her eyes glistening with something that resembled hope. "I think I can live with that," she said, echoing the words from that morning.

The rest of the meal passed in an easy silence, the kind that didn't need to be filled with constant conversation. The unspoken understanding that they were moving forward together, not as they once were, but as they could be, was enough. There were still difficult days ahead, still moments of doubt and uncertainty, but for the first time in years, they were walking the same path. Together.

As night fell and the house quieted, Sophia sat in the living room, her mind wandering over the events of the past few months. They hadn't come out of their struggles unscathed. The wounds were still there, raw and tender. But somehow, they were healing. Slowly, steadily, with each passing day.

And that was all she could ask for.

The weeks continued to pass, and with each one, the family took small but significant steps forward. The air in the house was different now—softer, less heavy with unspoken resentment. They still had their moments of tension, but those moments no longer felt insurmountable. Instead of running from their issues, they began to face them together, and it made all the difference.

One evening, James and Sophia sat on the porch as the sun dipped below the horizon, casting long shadows across the yard. The world around them seemed peaceful, but both of them knew that peace didn't always come easily. It was something that had to be worked for, earned through patience and understanding. And in that moment, sitting side by side, they felt the weight of what they had been through—and what they had yet to face—but it didn't scare them anymore.

"I've been thinking a lot about the past," James said quietly, his eyes fixed on the fading light. "About all the mistakes I made. I've spent so much time regretting what I didn't do. But I'm starting to realize that regret won't help me fix anything. It's not about what I missed or didn't do right—it's about what I'm willing to do now."

Sophia turned toward him, her heart swelling with emotion. "You're right. We can't change what happened. But we can choose what happens next. And I believe we're making the right choices. We're here. We're still fighting for this."

His hand found hers, and for a moment, they sat in silence, simply being together. There was no rush, no urgency. Just the steady, comforting presence of the person who had been by their side through it all.

As the days turned into weeks, Izzy continued to surprise them. There were still moments when she pulled away, retreating into her shell, but more and more often, she would reach out, a small but significant gesture that spoke volumes. She had started to share more about her own struggles, her own fears, and it was clear that she was beginning to trust them again. Not completely, not yet, but the cracks in her walls were becoming harder to ignore.

One afternoon, after a long day of school, Izzy sat at the kitchen table, scribbling something in her notebook. Sophia noticed the furrowed brow, the intense concentration on her daughter's face. She had learned not to interrupt, but her curiosity got the best of her.

"What are you writing?" Sophia asked, leaning against the counter.

Izzy hesitated for a moment before looking up, her eyes soft but unsure. "Just... a story," she said. "About everything that's been happening. About us."

Sophia's heart skipped a beat. "You're writing about us?"

Izzy nodded. "Yeah. I guess I'm trying to make sense of it all. Everything that's changed. Everything that's still broken."

Sophia walked over to her, sitting down beside her at the table. "You know, you don't have to make sense of it all right now. It's okay to not have all the answers."

"I know," Izzy replied, her voice barely above a whisper. "But... writing helps. It's the only way I can understand it. And maybe... maybe it'll help me understand myself too."

Sophia smiled softly, her hand brushing against her daughter's. "I think that's a beautiful way to heal. And I'm proud of you for doing it, Izzy. For facing your pain, even if it's hard."

Izzy didn't say anything, but she didn't need to. Her soft smile was all the confirmation Sophia needed. They didn't have it all figured out yet, but they were finding their way. And that was enough for now.

As time went on, the family began to move forward with more confidence. The scars from the past would always be a part of them, but they were learning to live with them, to allow them to shape who they were becoming, rather than defining them. James, Sophia, and Izzy were no longer just a broken family—they were a family healing, rebuilding, and forging a future that was theirs to shape.

And for the first time in years, there was a sense of calm that settled over their home. It wasn't perfect. It wasn't always easy. But it was real. And it was enough.

As the seasons began to change, so did the rhythm of their lives. The early days of their reconciliation had been filled with tension and uncertainty, but now, those moments of doubt seemed to fade into the background, replaced by something stronger. There was a quiet resilience in their home now—a sense of purpose, a desire to move forward without looking back.

THE SHIFTING BALANCE

James found himself spending more time with Izzy. They had always been close, but their bond had been strained by years of unspoken resentment. Now, however, there was a new openness between them. Their conversations, once guarded and brief, were longer, more meaningful. James would ask her about school, about her friends, and she would answer with a newfound honesty, her walls slowly crumbling away.

One afternoon, as they sat together in the living room, Izzy looked at him with a seriousness that made James pause.

"Dad, I know we've been through a lot," she said quietly. "But... I think I'm starting to understand. That maybe it wasn't just you who was broken. Maybe we all were. And I know that sounds weird, but I think I've been too focused on myself, on my own pain, to see how much you've been hurting too."

James swallowed hard, surprised by her words. He had never heard her speak so openly, so empathetically. It was as if the veil that had kept them apart for so long was finally lifting. He felt a lump rise in his throat, but he fought it back, not wanting to show weakness.

"I'm sorry, Izzy," he said, his voice thick with emotion. "I've let my mistakes define me for too long. And I didn't give you enough credit for the pain you were carrying. But I'm here now. I want to make it right. I want to be here for you, no matter what."

Izzy reached out, her hand resting gently on his. "I know you do, Dad. And I think... I think I'm ready to let you in. To trust you again."

That moment, simple as it was, marked a turning point in their relationship. It was the kind of breakthrough they both needed, the kind that would allow them to move forward without the weight of the past constantly looming over them.

Sophia, too, had found herself growing. She had always been the caretaker, the one who held everything together. But now, she was learning to care for herself as well. She had begun taking up activities she had once enjoyed, things she had set aside in the chaos of family life—painting, writing, even just spending time alone in the garden. For the first time in years, she was reconnecting with parts of herself she had lost along the way.

One evening, as she stood in front of her easel, brush in hand, she reflected on how far they had all come. There were still days when the weight of their struggles threatened to drag them down, but there were fewer of those days now. And each time they managed to rise above, each time they fought for one another instead of falling apart, she felt a little more hopeful.

That night, after dinner, the family sat together in the living room. It was a quiet evening—no grand gestures, no deep revelations—but there was a comfort in the ordinary. Izzy was curled up on the couch, a book in her lap, while James and Sophia sat side by side, their hands touching, not needing words to convey the strength of their bond.

Izzy broke the silence, her voice soft but steady. "You know, I was thinking today... that maybe we don't have to have everything figured out. Maybe we don't have to be perfect. But as long as we're together, trying, that's enough."

Sophia's heart swelled with pride at her daughter's words. She knew that the road ahead wouldn't always be smooth—that there would be moments of doubt, of frustration, even setbacks. But she also knew, in her bones, that they had found something real. They had found a way to move forward, together.

"I couldn't agree more," Sophia said, her voice warm with conviction. "We may not have all the answers, but we have each other. And that's everything."

James nodded in agreement, squeezing Sophia's hand. "That's all we need."

And for the first time in a long time, they truly believed it.

The following weeks passed in a gentle, unhurried manner, each day unfolding with a quiet promise of progress. The change in their dynamic was subtle but undeniable—there was an underlying sense of peace that had settled in their home. No longer were they weighed down by the constant tension of unspoken resentments or regrets. Now, they were simply trying, each in their own way, to build something that was theirs, something real.

Izzy's progress continued. While she hadn't fully opened up about all of her feelings, there were more moments when she allowed herself to be vulnerable. She began spending more time with Sophia in the kitchen, talking about her day, about school, about everything and nothing. Sophia cherished these moments, even when they were just small, fleeting conversations. It was a sign of trust, a sign of healing.

One Saturday afternoon, as Sophia was putting together a pot of soup in the kitchen, Izzy came in with her notebook, a thoughtful expression on her face. She had been working on her writing for weeks, and though she had never shown anyone her stories before, something about the way she held her notebook made it clear that she wanted to share.

"Mom, I... I wrote something," Izzy said, her voice tentative.

Sophia wiped her hands on a dish towel and turned to her, her heart skipping a beat. She had known Izzy had been writing, but hearing that she wanted to share it was a big step. "I'd love to hear it," she said gently.

Izzy took a deep breath and began to read, her voice soft but steady. The story was a reflection of her own journey—the confusion, the pain, the moments of hope and the long stretches of doubt. But there was also strength in it, a quiet resilience that Sophia hadn't fully seen in her daughter until now. It was as if Izzy had poured all of her frustrations and fears into the words, letting them spill out in a way that she couldn't do in person.

When Izzy finished reading, there was a brief silence between them. Sophia's eyes welled up with tears, not out of sorrow, but out of pride and relief. Her daughter had found her voice. She had found a way to express herself, to make sense of everything that had been weighing her down.

"That was beautiful, Izzy," Sophia said, her voice thick with emotion. "I'm so proud of you."

Izzy looked up, a small smile tugging at the corners of her lips. "You really think so?"

"I do," Sophia replied, her heart swelling. "You've come so far. And this... this is just the beginning."

James, who had been standing in the doorway, watching quietly, stepped forward. "I couldn't agree more," he said, his voice low but full of sincerity. "You've got a gift, Izzy. And I'm proud of you too."

Izzy's cheeks flushed, and for a moment, she seemed almost embarrassed by the praise. But then she smiled, a genuine smile that reached her eyes, and for the first time in a long time, the three of them were truly, completely present with each other.

Later that evening, as they sat down to dinner, the conversation turned to the future. There were no grand plans, no promises of perfection, but there was a quiet sense of optimism in the air. They all knew that the road ahead would not always be easy—that there would be bumps along the way, moments when they'd stumble and fall. But they also knew that they had something strong to hold on to: each other.

As they shared a simple meal, there was a sense of contentment, not born from the absence of challenges, but from the acceptance of them. They were no longer pretending that everything was perfect. They were just being—being together, supporting each other, and finding strength in the journey, however imperfect it may be.

Sophia looked at James, her eyes filled with a quiet gratitude. "We've come a long way, haven't we?"

He nodded, his hand reaching across the table to take hers. "We have. And we'll keep moving forward, no matter what."

Izzy looked up from her plate, her eyes bright with something new—hope. "Yeah, we will. Together."

And in that moment, the thread that had once unraveled now seemed to weave itself back together, stronger than before. They didn't have all the answers. They didn't need to. What mattered was that they were finding their way forward, one step at a time.

The past would always be a part of them, but it no longer defined them. What they had now was something they had earned through their struggles, their pain, and their willingness to face it all together.

And as they sat there, side by side, there was an unspoken understanding between them: whatever came next, they would face it as a family. Stronger, more united than ever.

The days continued to pass, each one reinforcing the quiet strength that had taken root in their home. The familiar rhythm of life—work, school, meals together—seemed less monotonous now, filled with a new kind of warmth. It wasn't the kind of warmth that came from grand gestures or dramatic changes; rather, it was the kind that grew slowly, quietly, from the shared moments of honesty and connection.

Izzy's writing began to flourish. What had started as a quiet hobby was now becoming a way for her to process her thoughts, her emotions, her experiences. She spent hours lost in her stories, pouring her soul into every word. Sophia, ever the supportive mother, encouraged her every step of the way, offering gentle suggestions when asked and providing her daughter with the space she needed to grow.

One evening, as they sat in the living room, Izzy's notebook resting open on her lap, she turned to her mother with a thoughtful expression.

"Mom," she said hesitantly, "I think I want to try sharing my stories with people. I don't know how, but... I think I'm ready."

Sophia looked at her daughter, her heart swelling with pride. It wasn't just the courage to share her work—it was the bravery to step outside of her comfort zone, to expose a part of herself that had been hidden for so long.

"That's a big step, Izzy," Sophia said softly. "But I think it's a good one. You've got so much to share with the world."

James, who had been reading a book on the couch, glanced up and smiled. "We'll help you, no matter what. You're not alone in this."

Izzy's eyes brightened, her uncertainty fading a little. For the first time, she felt like the fear that had once held her back—fear of judgment, of failure—wasn't as overpowering. She had her family by her side, and that made all the difference.

As the days turned into weeks, the family continued to navigate their new reality. The tension that had once defined their household now seemed like a distant memory. There were still challenges, of course—life was never without its struggles—but the way they faced those challenges had changed. They didn't face them alone anymore. They faced them together.

James had found his own path to healing. He had always been the quiet one, the one who buried his emotions under layers of stoicism. But the openness of his family had pushed him to confront his own pain, to let go of the walls he had built around himself for so long. He started attending therapy, something he had resisted for years, and slowly, he began to open up about his past—his regrets, his fears, his dreams. It wasn't easy, and there were days when he felt like he was taking one step forward only to fall

THE SHIFTING BALANCE

two steps back. But with Sophia's unwavering support, and Izzy's quiet understanding, he found the strength to keep going.

There were still moments of tension—moments when old wounds resurfaced, when the past threatened to undo everything they had worked for. But each time, they found a way to come back to one another, to remind themselves that healing was a journey, not a destination.

One evening, as the family sat together on the porch, watching the sun dip below the horizon, they reflected on how far they had come.

"I never thought we'd be here," Sophia said, her voice barely above a whisper.

James turned to her, his hand finding hers. "Neither did I," he admitted. "But I'm glad we are."

Izzy, who had been staring out at the fading light, turned to them and smiled. "We're stronger than we were before. All of us."

And in that moment, the truth of her words settled in. They had been through so much—the hurt, the anger, the secrets—but they had made it to the other side. And though they didn't have all the answers, they had something that mattered far more: each other.

It was a quiet kind of strength—one that didn't rely on perfection or certainty—but on love, resilience, and the willingness to keep moving forward, together.

As the last light of the day disappeared, the family sat in silence, the peaceful hum of the evening wrapping around them. They didn't need to say anything more. They knew, deep in their hearts, that the road ahead would still have its twists and turns, its moments of doubt and fear. But they also knew that they would face it, whatever it was, together. And that, in itself, was enough.

As the days grew warmer, the pace of life continued its steady rhythm, the familiar comfort of routine settling deeper into their lives. It was an odd thing, really—the way normalcy had become a refuge. A few months ago, they had all been tangled in the uncertainty of their own private battles. Now, there was a kind of peace that hung in the air between them, fragile but real.

Izzy's confidence continued to bloom. She shared her stories online, cautiously at first, unsure of how they would be received. But as the comments and messages from strangers began to pour in, she felt a strange mix of exhilaration and relief. People were reading her words, engaging with them, and, more importantly, they were relating to the emotions she poured onto the page. It wasn't fame she sought, but connection—a bridge between her inner world and the world outside her home.

One afternoon, as she sat at her desk, typing the final words of a new story, Sophia knocked gently on the door before entering, carrying two mugs of tea. Her smile was warm, her eyes proud.

"Hard at work, I see," she said, setting the mugs down on the desk.

Izzy looked up, her face lighting up. "I think I finally finished it," she said, her voice laced with a mixture of excitement and disbelief. "It feels... right. Like I've finally found my voice."

Sophia sat beside her, her heart swelling with pride. "You've always had it, Izzy. You just needed to trust it."

Izzy smiled, a quiet relief spreading through her chest. It wasn't just about the writing. It was about the space she had found within herself to embrace who she was, to accept the parts of herself that had once felt broken or incomplete. She was no longer just the quiet girl who had buried herself in books; she was a storyteller, a creator, someone who had something meaningful to say.

Later that evening, as the family gathered around the dinner table, Izzy shared her latest achievement. "I sent my latest story to a few online publications," she announced, her voice a little unsure but filled with determination. "I'm ready to take the next step."

James, who had been quiet for most of the evening, looked up from his plate. His face was softened by a sense of pride that had become more evident as the months passed. "That's amazing, Izzy," he said, his voice steady but filled with genuine admiration. "You've worked hard for this."

Sophia reached across the table, placing her hand over Izzy's. "And you're going to go far. I believe in you."

Izzy's chest tightened with emotion, the weight of her parents' support washing over her. She had never expected this kind of unwavering encouragement. It was as if the walls that had once kept her in silence had finally crumbled, replaced by an unspoken bond of trust and love.

The next few days were a whirlwind of anticipation. Izzy had received a response from one of the publications she had submitted her story to. They wanted to publish it.

She could hardly believe it when the email came through, her hands trembling as she clicked open the message. They had accepted her story. Her first step into the world of publishing was now a reality.

She ran downstairs, holding the phone in her hand, her voice barely audible with excitement. "Mom! Dad! They accepted it! My story's going to be published!"

Sophia and James exchanged a glance before enveloping their daughter in a tight hug. It was a moment of shared joy, a moment that marked not just a personal victory for Izzy, but a collective one for the entire family.

"I knew you could do it," Sophia whispered.

James nodded, his pride evident in his eyes. "We're so proud of you."

Izzy smiled through the tears that had welled up in her eyes. It wasn't just about the story—it was about what it represented. It was proof that she had fought through her own doubts, that she had found her place in the world, and that the love and support of her family had given her the strength to keep moving forward.

As the days passed, life in their home felt a little lighter, a little brighter. They were no longer simply surviving, caught in the weight of their past struggles. They were thriving, growing, and learning to trust in each other and themselves. It wasn't perfect, but it was real, and it was enough.

They had each other. And, in the end, that was the most important thing.

The weeks slipped by in a haze of subtle changes, each one a small shift, a gentle step forward. The warmth of summer began to linger longer in the air, and with it, a new sense of possibility seemed to settle over the family. Izzy's writing continued to take center stage in her life. With each new story she wrote, each piece she shared, she became more confident in her voice, more certain of her place in the world.

Sophia, too, found herself growing in ways she hadn't expected. Watching her daughter chase her dreams, seeing the quiet strength in the way James had started to open up, had begun to transform her. She found herself thinking more about her own path—what she wanted for herself beyond being a wife and mother. For so long, she had been defined by her roles in the family, but now, she realized, she had the space to explore her own desires, her own aspirations.

One evening, as the family sat together on the porch, enjoying the cool breeze of early autumn, Sophia turned to James. She noticed how he had changed. His stoicism, the layers of quiet distance he had kept for so long, seemed to have loosened. The man sitting beside her was more present, more connected—both to her and to Izzy. There was a newfound vulnerability in his eyes that she had not seen in years.

"I've been thinking," Sophia said quietly, her voice almost swallowed by the sound of crickets in the distance. "Maybe it's time I start looking into something of my own. A project, or a job, or—" she hesitated, unsure how to put the words into the air, "maybe something I've always wanted to do but never thought I could."

James looked at her, his gaze thoughtful. "What do you have in mind?" he asked, his tone soft but encouraging.

Sophia smiled, though it was a little unsure. "I don't know yet. But I think it's time to figure it out. I want to build something for myself—something that's not just about the family, but about me."

James nodded, the corners of his mouth curving up in the faintest smile. "You've always put us first. You deserve to have something that's just for you."

Izzy, overhearing the conversation, looked up from the book she was reading and smiled to herself. It was strange to see her mother so... unsure of herself, but it was also encouraging. She had always admired her mother's strength, but this new layer of vulnerability, of self-awareness, felt like the missing piece that Sophia had kept hidden for so long. Maybe it was a sign for all of them—an invitation to keep evolving, to keep pushing beyond the confines of the roles they had once accepted without question.

Izzy's own journey, of course, was far from over. Though she had found success with her writing, she knew that the road ahead would not always be easy. The pressure to keep creating, to keep producing, sometimes felt like a weight on her shoulders. She feared that one day she would wake up and find that she had exhausted her ideas, that the stories would dry up and leave her with nothing. It was a terrifying thought—the fear of failure, of not being able to live up to the expectations she had set for herself.

But she had learned to silence those fears. She had learned, through the support of her family, that failure wasn't something to be feared. It was just a part of the process, an inevitable part of growth. As long as she kept writing, kept pushing through the doubts, she would find her way.

One morning, after a long night of writing, Izzy woke up early to the sound of her mother's voice. Sophia was on the phone in the kitchen, her words laced with excitement. Izzy stretched and padded quietly into the room, catching the tail end of the conversation.

"I think this could be a really great opportunity," Sophia was saying, her voice full of anticipation. "I'll call them back and let them know I'm interested."

Izzy's heart skipped a beat. She had never heard her mother speak this way—so confident, so eager. She felt a quiet thrill of excitement for her mother, a reflection of her own growing sense of possibility.

Sophia hung up the phone and turned, noticing Izzy standing in the doorway. "Good morning, sweetheart," she said, her eyes sparkling. "I think I've just taken my first step toward something new. I'll have to see where it leads, but it feels like the right move."

Izzy grinned. "That's amazing, Mom. I'm so proud of you."

Sophia smiled back, her heart swelling. "Thank you, Izzy. You know, I think this is what we all need. To keep taking steps forward, even if they're small ones. It's how we grow."

And grow they did. Each day, each conversation, each new discovery about themselves brought them closer—not just as a family, but as individuals who were no longer afraid to pursue their own paths, to embrace their own passions and dreams.

They had learned, together, that love wasn't just about protecting each other from pain; it was about supporting each other's growth. It wasn't about holding on too tightly; it was about letting go when the time was right, trusting that the bonds they shared would only grow stronger for it.

As the sun set on another day, casting a golden light over the world outside, they sat together—each of them quietly reflecting on how far they had come and how much further they had yet to go. They had survived the unraveling threads of their past, and now, they were beginning to weave something new.

And for the first time in a long time, they felt ready.

As the days continued to unfold, the sense of change that had taken root in the family's life blossomed into something more profound. Each of them—Izzy, Sophia, and James—felt the pull of new possibilities, though the paths they each walked were still uncertain. They knew that transformation was never a simple or linear journey. The choices they made now, small as they seemed, would ripple through their lives in ways they couldn't yet predict. But for the first time in years, they were all moving forward, together and apart, toward something that felt more authentic, more real.

Izzy's writing had begun to gain more traction, her stories reaching a wider audience, though she still struggled with the weight of self-doubt. The emails from readers who found her words meaningful brought her a quiet sense of satisfaction, but the fear of it all slipping away still lingered at the edges of her mind.

Late one evening, as she sat at her desk, staring at the blinking cursor on her screen, she couldn't help but feel overwhelmed. The silence of the room seemed to press down on her, amplifying her inner turmoil. What if the next book wasn't as well received? What if she couldn't keep writing the way she had?

Her phone buzzed, interrupting her thoughts. It was a message from her mother.

"You're doing great, Izzy. Don't doubt yourself. You're growing every day. Keep going. We all have your back."

Izzy smiled, the warmth of her mother's words washing over her. She took a deep breath, letting go of some of the tension that had built up inside. She wasn't alone in this. She had her family, and they had her.

The next morning, she sat down at her desk with a renewed sense of purpose, the blank page no longer an enemy, but a challenge she was ready to face.

Sophia, on the other hand, was navigating a new chapter in her life. After her phone call with the company, she had decided to pursue a consulting position that would allow her to use her skills in ways she had never imagined. It was a decision that felt both exhilarating and terrifying—stepping out of her comfort zone after so many years of focusing solely on her family.

But the more she thought about it, the more she realized that this was not just about her career. This was about reclaiming a part of herself that she had neglected for too long. It wasn't about being a perfect mother or wife—it was about being a whole person, someone who had desires, dreams, and ambitions outside of the roles she had played for years.

One evening, after dinner, she sat down with James to discuss her decision. He listened attentively, his expression thoughtful, but there was a flicker of something in his eyes—an emotion she couldn't quite place.

"You're sure about this?" he asked, his voice low.

Sophia nodded, her confidence growing as she spoke. "I'm sure. It's time to do something for me, James. I've always put everyone else first, but I think it's time to take a step toward what I want."

James leaned back in his chair, his fingers drumming lightly on the table. For a moment, he said nothing, his mind clearly turning over her words. Finally, he spoke, his voice filled with quiet understanding.

"I think that's good. You deserve it. We all do."

Sophia's heart swelled with gratitude. It wasn't the grand, sweeping affirmation she had hoped for, but it was enough. His support, even in its understated way, meant the world to her. She had often felt alone in her desire for something more, but hearing his words gave her the validation she needed to continue.

In the days that followed, she dove into the work, using the quiet moments at home to prepare for her new role. The balance she had once struggled to maintain—between being a mother, wife, and individual—was slowly starting to shift into something more harmonious. There were days of doubt, days when she wondered if she was making the right choice, but each time, she reminded herself that growth wasn't always comfortable. It wasn't about having everything figured out. It was about taking the next step, no matter how small, and trusting that it would lead her to where she needed to be.

James, too, was going through his own transformation, though his journey was less visible to those around him. His walls, which had once been so firmly in place, had begun to crumble. The conversations with Sophia and Izzy, the quiet moments of reflection, had allowed him to connect with the deeper parts of himself—the parts that had been buried for years beneath layers of guilt, grief, and fear.

One evening, after a long day at work, James found himself sitting alone in the living room, a glass of whiskey in hand. He wasn't particularly fond of the drink, but it had become a familiar comfort in his moments of solitude. As he sat there, staring into the amber liquid, he thought about the choices he had made—both the ones that had led him to where he was now and the ones that had held him back. The guilt was still there, but it was softer now, less consuming. He had started to understand that forgiveness, both from others and from himself, wasn't something that happened overnight. It was a process, a journey that had no clear end.

He set the glass down on the table, feeling the weight of the moment settle over him. It was strange, this feeling of peace mixed with uncertainty. He wasn't sure where this road would take him, but for the first time in years, he wasn't afraid to walk it.

James sat in the quiet of the living room, the faint hum of the city beyond the windows almost like a reminder of the life he was slowly but surely reconnecting to. The walls that had once kept his emotions locked away were beginning to break down, piece by piece, though it wasn't without effort. His reflections had led him to realize that perhaps he wasn't as stuck as he had once believed. He wasn't perfect, but he didn't have to be.

For so long, he had clung to the notion that the mistakes of his past defined him. The guilt of not being there for Sophia in ways she had needed, of not being the father he envisioned himself to be for Izzy, had weighed heavily on him. But now, sitting here with that quiet realization—his past didn't have to be his future—he found a semblance of peace. It was a hard-earned lesson, one that had cost him much, but it was his to learn.

He stood up, stretching his legs and looking at the picture on the mantle: Sophia and Izzy at the beach, laughing, their faces radiant with the joy of simple moments. It was a snapshot of a family he was still part of, a family he had almost lost.

For the first time in a long while, he felt the stirring of hope. Hope for himself. Hope for his relationship with Sophia. Hope for the family they were all learning to rebuild.

The next day, as the sun began to dip below the horizon, Izzy found herself sitting at her desk again, her fingers hovering over the keyboard. There was a quiet urgency in her heart. She knew that she needed to finish the story she had started, not just for her readers, but for herself.

The words had come more easily in recent weeks, flowing from her fingers like an unspoken truth. She no longer worried about whether it would be good enough. The voice that had once felt so foreign to her now felt natural, almost like it had always been there, waiting to emerge. The path she had set herself on was no longer clouded by doubt; she was walking it with purpose.

Her phone buzzed, pulling her from her thoughts. It was a message from Sophia, one she hadn't expected:

"I'm proud of you, Izzy. You're doing amazing things, and I just wanted you to know."

Izzy smiled as she read the words. It was simple, but it meant the world to her. There was so much that had been unsaid between them over the years, but moments like this made it clear that they were starting to bridge the distance that had grown between them.

She sat back in her chair, the weight of her decision to keep writing settling in. She was doing it—she was truly pursuing her dream, and it felt like a victory, even on the small days.

Sophia, too, was finding peace in her own way. The consulting role she had taken on was proving to be a challenge, but it was one that pushed her to grow. At times, she found herself overwhelmed, missing the comfort of her routine, but she knew that this was what she needed to do. It wasn't about abandoning her family; it was about finding a way to balance it all, to not lose herself in the roles she had played for so long.

As the weeks passed, she found herself drawn more and more to the feeling of independence that came with her new job. She had always been the nurturer, the one who held everything together, but now she was beginning to learn that she could be more than that. She could be her own person—ambitious, driven, and capable of achieving her own goals.

The transition wasn't easy, and there were days when she felt guilty for taking time for herself, but she also recognized that this was something she needed. For the first time in a long time, Sophia felt like she was living for herself, not just for others. It wasn't selfish; it was necessary.

And as she sat with James that evening, sharing a quiet dinner after a long day, she could see the change in him too. The walls around him had begun to crumble, his support more tangible, his presence more solid. They weren't perfect—no one was—but they were slowly learning to understand one another in ways they hadn't before.

"We're doing okay, aren't we?" she asked, her voice soft.

James looked up from his plate, his gaze meeting hers. "I think we are," he replied, his voice steady. "We're not there yet, but we're getting there. Together."

For the first time in a long time, Sophia believed him. It wasn't just words. It was real, and that feeling of connection—the deep, unspoken bond they shared—felt stronger than ever.

Izzy's book had found a readership, and though it wasn't a bestseller, it was enough. The reviews were kind, the messages from readers more than she had ever expected. They resonated with her story, with the voice she had struggled to find. It wasn't about the fame or the success. It was about creating something that mattered, something that felt like it was worth the risk.

Sophia had found her balance. James, too, was rediscovering parts of himself that had been dormant for far too long. The family, fractured yet whole, was learning to come together in a way that felt real and honest.

The unraveling thread, which had seemed to pull them all apart, had instead woven them closer, each of them learning to stand on their own while still holding tight to each other. They weren't perfect, but they were real—and that, they all agreed, was enough.

3. Caught in the Lie

SOPHIA STOOD MOTIONLESS in the living room, the letter clutched tightly in her hands. It was an ordinary piece of paper, the kind you'd expect to find in any office, but the weight of it in her grip was anything but ordinary. It had started like any other day. The sun had risen, casting a soft glow through the blinds, and for a moment, everything seemed normal. But this letter — this unexpected, anonymous letter — had shattered the fragile peace she'd worked so hard to maintain.

The words on the page were clear, too clear. They outlined the details of a conversation she'd had months ago, a conversation that was supposed to be private, hidden beneath layers of carefully curated lies. And yet, here it was, staring her in the face, exposing everything she'd kept buried. The lie she thought she had buried so deeply was now standing at the forefront of her life, demanding attention.

She had built her world on stories, on the facade that everything was perfect. For years, she'd played the part of the successful career woman, the dedicated wife, the mother who balanced it all. But the truth was never as tidy as it seemed. There were moments, too many moments, when the weight of her choices had been too much to bear. She had told herself that it was all for the greater good, that her sacrifices were justified, but the nagging doubt had always lingered.

Sophia's mind raced as she remembered the conversation the letter referred to. It had been late one night, long after James had fallen asleep, when the truth had come pouring out. She had confided in a colleague, someone she trusted, someone who had promised to keep her secret safe. But somehow, that trust had been betrayed. The letter was proof of that betrayal, evidence that her carefully constructed life was now crumbling before her eyes.

Her fingers trembled as she tried to steady her breathing. How had this happened? How had everything she'd worked for, everything she had carefully controlled, slipped through her fingers so easily?

The house felt colder now. The walls, once so familiar, seemed to close in on her as if they were privy to the secret she had tried so hard to keep hidden. She glanced at the clock on the wall, the hands ticking relentlessly forward, each second a reminder that time was slipping away. The lie she had lived with for so long was no longer something she could ignore. It was here, in front of her, demanding to be dealt with.

James would be home soon. She could already hear the sound of his car pulling into the driveway, the creak of the front door as it opened. Would he notice? Would he know? The thought of telling him terrified her, but even more terrifying was the idea of continuing to live with the lie, of pretending that everything was fine when it was anything but.

As she stood there, frozen in her own thoughts, she realized the truth: There was no escaping this. The lie had caught up with her, and now she had to face the consequences. There was no going back.

But how would she explain it? Would he understand? Would he ever look at her the same way again? Would their family, their carefully crafted image of the perfect life, survive the truth?

Sophia sank onto the couch, the weight of it all pressing down on her chest. She wanted to scream, to release the tension that had been building for years, but no sound came. All she could do was sit there, with the letter in her hands, and wait for the inevitable.

The truth had a way of catching up with you. No matter how well you thought you had hidden it, no matter how carefully you tried to weave your web of lies, eventually, it all came undone.

And now, Sophia was standing in the ruins of everything she had worked so hard to protect.

Her mind flashed to her children, to Ethan and Izzy. What would they think? Could they ever forgive her? Or had she already lost them too, in the process of trying to keep everything together?

The front door clicked open. James was home.

And so, the moment she had been dreading had arrived.

James stepped into the house, his footsteps echoing softly in the hallway. Sophia could hear him hang up his coat, the rustling of his briefcase as it hit the table. He didn't notice her at first, his mind already shifting gears from the outside world to the quiet of their home. It had been a long day for him too. She could hear the fatigue in his movements, the slow, deliberate way he moved through the house. He was tired, but then again, so was she.

Her throat tightened. This was it. There was no more pretending, no more avoiding the truth. The lie had already taken root, and now it was time to face it head-on.

"Hey," he called out, his voice soft but warm. "You okay? You look... off."

Sophia couldn't bring herself to respond immediately. She just stared at the letter in her hands, unable to hide the tremble in her fingers. She hadn't even realized she was gripping it so tightly.

"Yeah," she finally said, her voice betraying her, thin and distant. "Just a lot on my mind."

James appeared in the doorway, his brow furrowing as he studied her, his tired eyes scanning the room before landing on her face. He seemed to know something was wrong. He always had a way of sensing when something wasn't right. He had always been attuned to her moods, her silences, and this time, it seemed like he could feel the weight of the moment before she even spoke.

He sat beside her on the couch, the cushion dipping slightly under his weight. The room was heavy with an unsaid tension. He reached for her hand, his touch gentle but questioning.

"What's going on, Soph?" he asked softly. "You've been quiet all evening. Is something bothering you?"

Her chest tightened, and for a moment, she couldn't speak. The truth hovered between them, hanging in the air like a storm cloud. She wanted to reach out, to tell him everything, but how could she? How could she explain the unexplainable, the part of herself that had been hidden for so long?

She took a shaky breath and finally spoke, the words tumbling out in a rush. "I... I've been lying to you, James. For a long time."

His eyes widened slightly, and for the briefest moment, she thought she saw a flicker of hurt, quickly masked by concern. But before he could say anything, she continued, the words coming faster now, as if once the dam had broken, it couldn't be stopped.

"It's not what you think," she said, her voice trembling. "I've been keeping something from you—something I should have told you a long time ago. I've been trying to protect you, protect us. But I see now that I was just... running from the truth."

She could see him processing her words, his eyes searching her face as if trying to make sense of the chaos she was revealing. There was silence, an uncomfortable stillness that filled the space between them. He didn't interrupt, didn't demand an explanation right away. He just sat there, waiting for her to continue, as if he knew this wasn't something she could say all at once.

Finally, he spoke, his voice steady but edged with uncertainty. "What are you talking about, Sophia? What have you been hiding from me?"

Sophia's mind raced. She wanted to tell him everything, to lay it all out in the open, but the words felt too heavy, too complicated.

The lie was tangled up with guilt, with fear, and with the consequences of everything that had led her here.

"I... I had an affair," she whispered, the words hanging in the air, thick and suffocating. "A long time ago. And I never told you. I thought if I just buried it, if I pretended it never happened, it would go away. But it didn't. And now... now, it's all coming out."

The room felt like it had been drained of all oxygen. James didn't react immediately. He just stared at her, his expression unreadable. For a moment, she thought he hadn't heard her, that maybe he was in shock. But then, slowly, he spoke.

"I... I don't even know what to say," he said quietly, his voice thick with emotion. "Why didn't you tell me? Why didn't you trust me enough to be honest?"

Sophia's heart ached. She could feel the weight of his disappointment, the hurt in his voice, and it tore at her. This was the moment she had feared, the moment she had hoped would never come. She had hurt him in the worst way possible, and now she had to face the consequences.

"I was afraid," she said softly, her eyes filling with tears. "I was afraid that if I told you, it would destroy everything we've built. I was afraid you wouldn't forgive me. And I couldn't bear the thought of losing you."

James stood up abruptly, pacing across the room, his hands running through his hair in frustration. He turned to face her, his face pale, his jaw clenched tight. She could see the storm brewing in his eyes, the anger and the confusion swirling beneath the surface.

"You should have trusted me, Sophia," he said, his voice tight with emotion. "We've always been able to talk about anything. I thought we were past the point of secrets. And now... now you've shattered that."

Tears streamed down Sophia's face. She wanted to reach out, to make him understand, but she knew that there was nothing she could say to undo the damage. She had made her bed, and now she had to lie in it.

James turned away, his back to her, his shoulders stiff with tension. "I need some time," he said, his voice barely a whisper. "I don't know what to think right now."

Sophia sat there in the silence, the weight of his words sinking in. She had hoped for understanding, for a chance to make things right, but deep down, she knew that what she had done couldn't be fixed so easily. The lie had been too big, too deep. And now, there was no turning back.

Sophia sat in the heavy silence, the distance between them widening with every passing second. James's words echoed in her mind—*I need some time*. She knew that he was right to ask for it. What had she expected? That everything could be fixed with a simple confession, that the lie would somehow unravel without consequence? She had been foolish to think that, and now she had to live with the fallout.

She watched as James walked to the window, his back still turned to her. The soft glow of the streetlights outside cast long shadows across the room, as if the very walls were closing in on her. The atmosphere felt suffocating, thick with regret and unanswered questions. She had ruined everything, and there was no quick fix. The damage was done.

"James," she whispered, her voice raw. "Please... I'm so sorry. I never meant to hurt you."

He didn't turn around. His hands were shoved deep into his pockets, his gaze fixed on the night outside. She could see the tension in his shoulders, the tightness in his posture, and it broke her heart all over again.

"I don't know what to say," he replied quietly, his voice steady but heavy with emotion. "I need to figure out how to process this, how to deal with it. You... you should have trusted me enough to tell me the truth, Sophia. Instead, you've kept it buried, hidden, and now I don't even know who you are anymore."

Her chest constricted, her breath catching in her throat. She had always prided herself on their relationship—the way they had been able to talk about anything, the way they had built a life together based on honesty and trust. And now, that foundation was cracked, broken by her own hands.

"I'm sorry," she repeated, her voice shaking. "I should have told you. I should have trusted you. But I was scared, James. Scared of losing you. And now, look what I've done."

A long pause hung between them, the air thick with the weight of his silence. Sophia could feel her heart pounding in her chest, each beat louder than the last. It was as though time had stopped, and in that moment, all that existed was the space between her and the man she loved.

Finally, James turned to face her. His eyes were tired, bloodshot from the strain of holding back everything he felt. But there was something else there too—something harder, colder. The vulnerability in his expression was gone, replaced by a guarded mask, as if he had already begun to shut himself off from her.

"I need to think," he said, his voice quiet but firm. "And right now, I can't be around you. I need space, Sophia."

She wanted to reach out, to beg him to stay, but she knew that it wouldn't change anything. He was right. He needed space, time to process the betrayal she had handed him. The lie was too big, too deep to just sweep away with apologies. She had done something unforgivable, and now she had to live with the consequences.

"Okay," she said softly, her voice breaking. "I understand."

James gave her one last look—one that was filled with sorrow and disappointment—and then he turned away, heading for the door. Before he left, he paused, his hand resting on the doorknob. He didn't look back, but his words were heavy, like a final blow.

"I don't know what's going to happen, Sophia. But right now, I need to be alone."

And with that, he was gone. The door clicked shut behind him, and the house seemed to fall into an eerie silence. Sophia remained on the couch, staring at the empty doorway, feeling the weight of the lie crush her chest.

The lie that had started as a secret, buried deep within her, had now torn apart everything she held dear. She had lost his trust, and she wasn't sure if she could ever get it back. The guilt and the pain were overwhelming, but beneath it all, a sinking feeling settled deep in her gut. She had made a choice, and now she would have to face the consequences.

And as the night stretched on, Sophia sat alone in the dim light of the living room, unsure of what the future held. She had no answers, no solutions—only the lingering, suffocating weight of the lie that had shattered her world.

Hours passed, and the stillness of the house became suffocating. Sophia sat on the couch, her eyes fixed on the empty space where James had stood just hours before. The silence was unbearable, each minute dragging on like a relentless echo of everything that had gone wrong.

She thought back to their earlier years, to when things had felt so simple, when their love had been a source of strength, not division. How had it all gotten so complicated? The lies, the secrets, the betrayal—how had it all grown so large that she couldn't even see the person she used to be? She felt like a stranger to herself, consumed by the weight of her own actions.

The clock on the wall ticked loudly, a constant reminder of the time slipping away. She reached for her phone, the screen lighting up in her hands. There was a message from her sister, Anna. A simple, innocent text that read: *"Hey, just checking in. How's everything?"*

Sophia stared at the message, her thumb hovering over the keyboard. Should she tell Anna the truth? Could she even bring herself to speak the words aloud, let alone share them with someone else? She had always been able to confide in her sister, but now, after everything that had happened, she wasn't sure she could. Not about this.

She let out a slow breath, shaking her head as if trying to shake off the weight that had settled deep inside her. But no matter how hard she tried, the guilt wouldn't lift. The thought of facing anyone—her sister, her friends, her family—felt impossible. How could she explain what she had done? How could she ever face James again, knowing that she had broken something irreparable between them?

As she set the phone back down, a thought crossed her mind. *Maybe I don't deserve him.*

It was a thought she hadn't allowed herself to consider before, but now, in the quiet aftermath of her lies, it felt undeniable. She had betrayed James's trust, shattered their connection, and left him with nothing but questions and hurt. She didn't know how to fix it, or even if it was fixable. The idea of walking away from everything they had built together felt impossible, but perhaps it was the only choice left.

Her mind kept circling back to the same question: *What now?*

It felt like a lifetime ago that she had been caught up in the lie, telling herself that it was harmless, that it was just one more secret buried deep within her. But now, looking at the pieces of her life scattered around her, she realized how wrong she had been. A lie, no matter how small or seemingly insignificant, always has a way of coming to the surface, of unraveling everything you've tried to keep hidden.

Sophia didn't know how much time passed before she heard the familiar sound of the front door creaking open. Her heart leapt in her chest, and she held her breath, half hoping, half dreading what would happen next.

James's voice echoed through the hallway, low and tense. "Sophia?"

She didn't move at first. The idea of facing him again, of speaking after everything that had happened, seemed impossible. But she couldn't stay hidden forever, and the sound of his voice, full of uncertainty and pain, broke her resolve. She stood, her legs shaky, and slowly walked toward the door.

When she stepped into the hallway, she saw him standing there, just inside the threshold. His eyes were tired, his face drawn with exhaustion, but there was something else there—something that made her heart ache. He was still here. He hadn't left. Not yet.

"I don't know what to say, Sophia," he said, his voice barely above a whisper. He didn't look at her directly, his gaze falling to the floor, as if he couldn't bear to meet her eyes. "But I'm here. I'm still here."

The relief that washed over her was immediate and overwhelming, but it didn't erase the guilt, the fear, the uncertainty. There was still so much that needed to be said, so much that needed to be repaired. But for now, in this moment, the fact that he was still there was a small, fragile hope.

Sophia stepped forward, her hands trembling as she reached out to him. "I know I don't deserve this. But please... please give me a chance to make it right."

James took a step back, his eyes meeting hers, searching for something—some sign that she was truly remorseful, that she understood the gravity of what she had done. He didn't say anything at first, his lips pressed tightly together as if he were weighing his options.

For a long moment, they just stood there, the weight of everything that had happened between them pressing down on both of them. The silence stretched on, heavy and uncomfortable, before James finally spoke.

"I need time," he said, his voice steady but filled with a depth of emotion. "Time to figure this out. Time to see if I can trust you again."

The words hit her like a punch, and she swallowed hard, nodding slowly. She hadn't expected him to forgive her right away. But the pain in his eyes, the hurt that was still so raw, was a reminder of how much damage she had caused. She had broken his trust, and now she had to prove that she was worthy of it again.

"I'll wait," she whispered, her voice thick with emotion. "I'll wait, James. For as long as it takes."

And with that, they stood there in the quiet hallway, both of them lost in their own thoughts, unsure of what the future would bring. But for the first time in a long time, there was a flicker of hope—a tiny, fragile thread that might just pull them back together, if they were both willing to hold on.

The days that followed were an uneasy truce. Sophia moved through the motions of life, doing everything in her power to keep up appearances, but the weight of her betrayal hung over her like a dark cloud. James had withdrawn into himself, no longer the open, easygoing man she had once known. He was still there physically, but emotionally, he seemed a world away.

The small, everyday things that had once brought them joy—cooking together, watching their favorite shows, talking about their dreams—had all become distant memories, like an old song they could no longer remember the lyrics to. They both existed in the same space, but they were no longer connected by the same love that had once seemed unbreakable.

Sophia tried to bridge the gap between them, but every attempt felt like it fell short. She knew James needed time, but time felt like a thief, stealing what little they had left. She spent hours staring at her reflection, wondering who she had become. The woman who had once been confident and sure of herself now felt like a stranger in her own skin.

One evening, as the golden glow of sunset filtered through the windows, Sophia found herself sitting on the edge of the bed, her fingers tracing the edge of the photo frame that held a picture of their wedding day. It felt like a lifetime ago that they had stood there, smiling at the world, full of hope and promise. She ran her thumb over the glass, wishing she could turn back time, erase the lies, and make everything right again.

A soft knock on the door pulled her from her thoughts.

"Yeah?" she called, her voice barely above a whisper.

The door creaked open, and there stood James, his expression unreadable. He had changed so much, and yet, in this moment, he seemed almost the same as before. The familiar spark of warmth that had once defined their relationship was now dimmed, but it was still there—buried beneath the hurt and the mistrust.

"I've been thinking," James said, his voice steady but tinged with uncertainty. "About us. About what comes next."

Sophia's heart pounded in her chest as she stood, her hands trembling slightly. "What do you mean?"

James hesitated, his gaze dropping to the floor for a moment before meeting her eyes. "I can't pretend everything is fine," he said softly. "But I also can't keep living like this, in this... limbo."

Sophia's stomach churned, a knot forming in her chest. She wanted to say something, anything to make him understand, but the words wouldn't come. It felt like they were both on the edge of something—something they couldn't see, but that they both knew was coming.

"I think we need to figure out if this—" He motioned between them, his hand sweeping through the air to encompass the space between them. "—is something worth saving."

The words hit her like a punch. She had known this was coming, had felt the distance growing wider with every passing day, but hearing him say it out loud made it so much more real, so much more final.

Sophia swallowed hard, her throat tight with emotion. "I'm so sorry, James," she said, her voice barely above a whisper. "I never meant to hurt you. I... I just didn't know how to fix it."

"I know," James replied, his voice softening just a fraction. "But it's not just about fixing it. It's about whether we can rebuild what we had. Whether we can trust each other again."

Sophia nodded, the tears welling up in her eyes. "I'll do whatever it takes. I'll work at it every day. I don't want to lose you."

James didn't answer right away. He took a step toward her, his eyes searching hers, looking for any sign that she was truly remorseful, that she was willing to make the effort to rebuild the trust that had been broken.

After what felt like an eternity, he spoke again. "I'm not sure I can forgive you just yet," he said, his voice strained. "But I'm willing to try. I'm willing to give this a chance. For us."

A wave of relief flooded over Sophia, but it was tempered by the reality of what was ahead. Rebuilding trust wouldn't be easy. It would take time—more time than either of them could predict. But for the first time in weeks, she saw a glimmer of hope, a possibility that they could find their way back to each other.

"I won't let you down," she said, her voice firm with determination. "I promise."

James gave her a long look, as if weighing her words, before nodding slowly. "We'll take it one step at a time," he said, his voice steady but full of the uncertainty that still lingered between them.

And with that, he turned to leave, but not without one final glance back at her. The unspoken words hung between them, and for a moment, they both stood there in the quiet of the room, unsure of what the future held, but willing to face it together, however uncertain that might be.

Sophia stood there, watching him walk away, a mix of emotions swirling inside her. She didn't know if they could fix what had been broken. But she was willing to try. She had to try.

And so, with a quiet breath, she wiped away the tears that had gathered in her eyes and turned back to the bed. There was still so much to be done, so much to work through. But in that moment, she knew that the battle wasn't over. It had only just begun.

Sophia sat quietly on the edge of the bed, the weight of her emotions pulling her down like an anchor. She had hoped, even prayed, for this moment—the chance to make things right, to rebuild the trust she had shattered. But now that it was here, the task ahead seemed daunting, perhaps even impossible. How could they go back to who they were before? How could she ever prove to James that she was worthy of his forgiveness?

Her mind replayed the events that had led them to this point, the lies, the deceit, and the moments of weakness that had started this downward spiral. It had been easy at first, slipping into the comfort of a lie. But once it had taken root, it had grown, twisted into something unrecognizable. And now, here they were, on the brink of something neither of them fully understood, yet both feared deeply.

It wasn't just about the betrayal anymore. It was about who they had become in the wake of it. They had both changed, and not necessarily for the better. James, once full of laughter and light, had become quiet, withdrawn. Sophia, who had once felt so confident in their love, was now filled with self-doubt and shame. Could they truly find their way back to each other, or had the damage been too great?

Sophia looked out the window, the setting sun casting a soft glow over the city below. The light was fading, just as her hope had. But even in the darkness, there was still a glimmer of something—something that felt like a second chance, fragile but real. She couldn't give up. Not yet.

The next few days passed in a blur. Sophia and James barely spoke, both lost in their own thoughts. It was as if they were waiting for the other to take the first step, but neither of them knew where to begin. They lived in the same space but felt miles apart. The silence between them was deafening.

One evening, after another day of avoiding each other, Sophia decided it was time. She couldn't wait for James to make the first move. She needed to show him that she was ready to face the consequences of her actions, to prove that she was committed to fixing what she had broken.

She found him sitting on the couch, his eyes focused on the television but clearly not watching. He looked tired, worn down by the weight of everything between them.

"James," she said softly, her voice trembling slightly. He turned to look at her, his expression unreadable. There was no anger in his eyes, no resentment—just a quiet, painful resignation.

"I know I can't undo what I've done," Sophia continued, stepping closer to him. "But I can make it right. I can try to rebuild what we had. I know it won't be easy, but I'm willing to fight for us. For you. If you'll give me the chance."

For a long moment, James didn't say anything. He just stared at her, his gaze searching, as if he was trying to gauge whether her words were sincere or just another empty promise. Sophia held her breath, waiting for him to say something, anything.

Finally, he spoke, his voice quiet but firm. "I don't know if I can trust you again, Sophia. I don't know if I can believe anything you say."

Sophia's heart sank at the words, but she didn't flinch. "I understand," she said softly. "I don't expect you to trust me right away. I don't deserve that. But I'll prove it to you. I'll show you every day that I can be the person you thought I was. The person you deserve."

James looked down at his hands for a moment, his fingers clenching into fists before releasing again. The tension in the room was palpable, thick enough to cut through.

"You've hurt me, Sophia," he said, his voice low. "And I don't know if I can just forget that. But... maybe we can try. Maybe we can start over, from this point, and see where it takes us."

Sophia nodded, a sense of relief flooding through her, even though she knew that this was only the beginning. There were no guarantees, no promises that this would work. But it was a start. And for now, that was enough.

"I'll take whatever you're willing to give," she said, her voice steady now. "I'll wait as long as it takes. But I'm here. And I want this. I want us."

James didn't reply immediately. He simply stood up, his movements slow, as if he was still processing everything. Then, without a word, he took a step toward her, closing the distance between them. He didn't say anything, but for the first time in weeks, Sophia saw a flicker of something—something that resembled hope, even if it was faint.

James reached out, his hand brushing hers gently, and for a moment, it felt like everything might be okay again. The weight of the world wasn't gone, but the silence between them had shifted. It was no longer an impassable chasm. There was space for healing, for rebuilding.

As the days went on, things didn't magically improve. There were still awkward silences, still moments of tension, but there were also small, tentative steps forward. James began to open up again, sharing his thoughts and frustrations with her. Sophia listened, and for the first time in a long while, they spoke openly about

THE SHIFTING BALANCE

their feelings—about the betrayal, the hurt, and the fear that had gripped them both.

It wasn't easy. It was a slow, painful process, and there were moments when Sophia wondered if it was even worth it. But every time she saw James make an effort, every time he took a small step toward forgiveness, she felt a renewed sense of hope.

In the end, they both knew it wouldn't be a smooth ride. There would be more obstacles, more challenges to face, but they were both committed now. They were both willing to try. And that, for now, was enough.

As the weeks passed, their relationship, while still fragile, began to shift in unexpected ways. The trust that had been shattered slowly began to mend, thread by delicate thread. James was cautious, always keeping a small distance, as if testing the waters before diving back in fully. But each time Sophia showed her sincerity, each time she proved that her intentions were true, he allowed a little more room for healing.

Sophia, on the other hand, wrestled with her own internal battles. She had to constantly remind herself of the reasons behind her actions, the motivations that had led her to betray the man she loved. It was not just guilt she felt, but also a deep-seated shame—a feeling that she would have to carry for a long time. She knew she couldn't undo what she had done, but she could try to be better, to be someone worthy of his love again. The road to redemption was long, but she was willing to walk it.

One evening, after another quiet dinner at home, Sophia found herself sitting alone in the living room. The room was dimly lit, the soft glow of the lamp casting long shadows across the walls. James had retreated to his study, his usual refuge when things felt too heavy between them. She could feel the weight of the silence pressing down on her again.

She thought about the future. What would it look like if they were to rebuild their lives together? Could they ever return to what they had before? Or was the damage irreparable, a permanent stain on their shared history?

The sound of footsteps broke her from her thoughts. She looked up to see James standing in the doorway, his eyes searching hers. He hadn't said much lately, but tonight, there was something different in the way he looked at her—a mix of longing and caution, a silent question hanging in the air.

"Sophia," he said softly, his voice steady but laced with something vulnerable. "I've been thinking... about us. About what comes next."

Sophia's heart skipped a beat. She hadn't expected this conversation tonight, but she was ready for it. She had to be. "What do you mean?" she asked, her voice barely above a whisper.

James hesitated for a moment before stepping into the room, sitting down beside her on the couch. He reached out, his hand brushing against hers, tentative but gentle. "I don't know if I can ever fully forget what happened, but... I'm willing to try. I want to give us another chance. But it has to be different this time. We both have to change, Sophia. Not just for the relationship, but for ourselves."

Sophia felt a surge of emotion rise within her, and for a brief moment, her throat tightened with tears. She had been so afraid that this was the end, that they would never find their way back to each other. But now, with James's words hanging in the air, she realized that there was still hope, still a possibility for something better.

"I'm willing to change, James," she said, her voice steady despite the emotions swirling inside her. "I don't expect it to happen overnight, but I'm ready to do whatever it takes to earn back your trust. And to be the person I should have been all along."

James nodded, his eyes never leaving hers. "We both need to heal. And we need to do it together. But first, we need to start being honest with ourselves. About everything."

The honesty between them had always been their foundation, and now, it seemed like they were finally starting to rebuild that foundation, brick by brick. It wouldn't be easy, and there would be moments of doubt, but they were both willing to fight for it. For their love. For the life they had once dreamed of.

Over the next few months, Sophia and James worked tirelessly to rebuild their relationship. They attended therapy together, spoke openly about their fears, their hopes, and their insecurities. They both put in the effort, no longer taking the other for granted. The road to healing was far from smooth, but with each passing day, they learned to trust each other again.

There were setbacks, of course. Old wounds would occasionally resurface, causing moments of tension and conflict. But they had learned to face those moments together, to communicate and work through them instead of letting them tear them apart.

One evening, as they sat together in the living room, the air between them felt lighter. They had come a long way from where they started, and while the scars of the past still lingered, they no longer defined their relationship. They had created something new, something stronger, built on the foundation of trust and mutual respect.

James turned to Sophia, his eyes filled with quiet admiration. "You've come a long way," he said, his voice soft but genuine. "I didn't think we'd make it through, but I'm glad we did. I'm glad we gave this a chance."

Sophia smiled, a small but heartfelt smile. "Me too. I didn't know if I could ever make it right, but I'm starting to believe that we can."

They sat there in silence for a moment, the weight of the past no longer pressing down on them as it once had. There was still work to be done, still challenges to face, but for the first time in a long while, they both felt a sense of peace. It was the beginning of something new, a new chapter in their lives.

And as they both looked toward the future, they realized that the most important thing was not whether they had survived the storm, but how they had emerged from it. They had faced the lies, the betrayal, and the hurt. But now, they were standing on the other side, stronger and more united than ever before.

It wasn't the perfect ending, but it was real. And that was enough.

4. Facing the Consequences

THE AIR IN THE HOUSE felt heavier now, as if the walls themselves were pressing in, holding secrets they weren't meant to bear. Sophia sat at the kitchen table, staring at her coffee cup, though she hadn't taken a sip. Her mind raced, trying to piece together the consequences of everything that had led to this moment. Every decision, every small lie, every ignored whisper from her heart had brought her here. And now, there was no avoiding it.

James walked in, his footsteps soft against the tile, but there was an edge to his presence. He knew. Of course, he knew. How could he not? The tension between them had been building for months, stretching thin like a taut wire ready to snap. Their eyes met, and for a moment, neither of them spoke. What could they say?

"I never thought it would come to this," James finally said, his voice low, tired. There was no anger in his words—just exhaustion, resignation. "We both knew something was wrong, Sophia. We just kept pretending it wasn't."

She swallowed hard, the lump in her throat a physical manifestation of the guilt that had been eating away at her for so long. She wanted to reach out, to apologize, to make it right. But the words felt too heavy, too fragile. What could she say to make up for the years she had spent chasing something outside of herself, leaving her family to deal with the consequences of her absence?

"I thought I was doing the right thing," she whispered, almost as if trying to convince herself. "I thought if I could just make something of myself—something bigger—then maybe we'd all be happier. I thought if I succeeded, it would make everything else work. But now... now I see how wrong I was."

James took a deep breath, rubbing his eyes as if the weight of it all was finally catching up with him. "It's not just about what you did, Sophia. It's about what we both failed to do. We failed to communicate, to listen to each other. We got so caught up in our own lives, we forgot about the one we were supposed to be building together. And now the kids—"

"They feel it too," she interrupted, her voice barely above a whisper. The thought of their children, caught in the middle of their fractured relationship, twisted something deep inside her. "Izzy doesn't talk to me anymore. And Ethan... I can see how lost he feels. He's trying to fix things, but he doesn't know how. None of us do."

James exhaled sharply, the sound almost like a laugh, but it wasn't funny. "We all have our own version of what we think is right, Sophia. But in the end, we're all facing the same truth: the damage has been done. The trust is broken."

She nodded, feeling the weight of his words settle like a stone in her chest. There was no escaping it now. The foundation they had built, all the years of shared history, had been cracked, perhaps beyond repair. And it wasn't just the lies they had told each other—it was the silence, the unspoken resentments that had been allowed to fester. It was the absence of everything they had once shared. It was the emptiness that now filled every room.

"We can try to fix it," she said, more to herself than to him. "We can rebuild. It won't be easy, but we can try."

James met her gaze, his eyes filled with a weariness that mirrored her own. "I don't know if we can. But we have to try, don't we? For the kids... for us."

For a long moment, neither of them spoke. The room was filled with the quiet sound of their breathing, the weight of unspoken questions hanging in the air. Could they truly rebuild what had been broken? Could they face the consequences of their actions and still find their way back to each other?

Sophia didn't have the answer. But for the first time in a long time, she felt the faintest flicker of hope. It wasn't much, but it was something.

Sophia stood up, the chair scraping against the floor as she pushed it back. She paced across the room, feeling the need to move, to do something, anything, to escape the crushing weight of her thoughts. She wanted to fix things now, to reach into the broken parts and pull them together. But how could she? The years of neglect, of silence, couldn't be undone in a moment, in a single conversation.

She stopped near the window, looking out at the garden. It was a cold morning, the sky overcast, the trees swaying gently in the breeze. There was something about the way nature seemed to continue without regard for human turmoil that unsettled her. The world moved on, indifferent to their pain.

James joined her at the window, standing just behind her, but they didn't speak. The distance between them was palpable, like an invisible wall that neither knew how to break. It was easier to stay silent, to let the weight of their unspoken words fill the space between them, than to confront the raw truth of their situation.

"I never wanted this," she finally said, the words catching in her throat. "I never wanted us to fall apart. But somewhere along the way, I stopped seeing you. I stopped seeing us."

James nodded slowly, his expression unreadable. "I know. I did too. We both became strangers to each other. We let everything else take precedence. The work, the expectations, the... everything else. But we didn't protect what really mattered."

The truth of his words stung. She had been so wrapped up in proving herself, in achieving something outside of the home, that she hadn't realized how much she was neglecting the very thing she had once held most dear. Her family. Her children. James. The small moments they once shared, the quiet conversations, the laughter, the bond they had once built—all of it had been lost somewhere along the way.

"I thought I was doing it for us," she continued, her voice soft but resolute. "I thought if I could just make something of myself, if I could show you that I could contribute, I could be more than just a wife, more than just a mother... But it was never enough, was it?"

James turned toward her, his face softening. "You were always enough, Sophia. You just couldn't see it. I couldn't see it either. We were too busy chasing something that didn't matter. We let the world tell us who we were supposed to be, instead of defining it for ourselves."

A heavy silence settled between them again, but this time it wasn't as suffocating. There was something tentative in their words, something fragile that might, with time, grow into something more.

Sophia looked at him, really looked at him, for the first time in what felt like years. He was the same man she had married, but there was a weariness in his eyes now, a burden he carried that mirrored her own. She wondered if they could ever truly bridge the gap that had formed between them, if the love they once had could be salvaged from the wreckage of their mistakes.

"We can start over, right?" she asked, the uncertainty in her voice betraying the desperation she felt inside. "It doesn't have to end like this."

James didn't answer immediately. Instead, he reached out and took her hand, his grip warm but uncertain. "I don't know. But we have to try. We can't keep pretending nothing's wrong. We need to face it, together. Whatever happens after that, at least we'll know we did everything we could."

Sophia squeezed his hand, a fragile promise passing between them. She didn't know what the future held, but she knew one thing for sure: they had to face it, no matter how painful. The consequences were real, and they couldn't be ignored anymore. The weight of their past was heavy, but perhaps, just perhaps, they could find a way to carry it together.

As she stood there, with James by her side, the first light of dawn broke through the clouds, spilling across the room. It was a small thing, a flicker of hope in an otherwise bleak moment. But for the first time in a long time, it was enough.

The days that followed were filled with a quiet tension, a sort of limbo where everything seemed both fragile and uncertain. Sophia found herself caught between the weight of the past and the hope for something better. She couldn't shake the feeling that they were standing at the edge of something vast and unknown, with no clear path ahead. But for the first time in years, there was a glimmer of resolve in her heart. She had to face it. They both did.

At dinner that night, the house felt different. It wasn't the silence that hung heavy in the air, but something more subtle—an awareness that they were all carrying something inside, something that had yet to be fully acknowledged. Izzy and Ethan sat at the table, picking at their food, their eyes avoiding theirs. Sophia could feel the distance, like an invisible chasm between them, and it hurt more than she had anticipated.

"How was school today?" she asked, her voice tentative, as if testing the waters.

Izzy looked up briefly, then quickly looked away. "Fine."

Sophia glanced at James, who was stirring his food absently. He hadn't been much of a presence at the table lately, and it seemed like their children were retreating into their own worlds. She knew they were all affected by the tension, but none of them had the words to bridge the gap.

Ethan, usually so quick to talk, stayed silent, his gaze fixed on his plate. The quiet was deafening.

"Sophia," James spoke softly, breaking the silence. "We need to have a family meeting tomorrow. It's time to be honest with them. They deserve to know what's going on."

She nodded, her throat tight. She knew this moment was inevitable, but it didn't make it any easier. The thought of revealing everything—the truths they had both tried to hide, the mess they had created—seemed almost too much to bear. But they couldn't keep pretending. Their children deserved more than half-hearted attempts at normalcy.

"I'll talk to them," she said, her voice firm but filled with uncertainty. "We have to start somewhere."

Later that night, as they all gathered in the living room, the weight of what was about to unfold settled over them like a storm cloud. Sophia sat on the edge of the couch, feeling the weight of the moment pressing on her chest. Izzy was sitting with her arms crossed, her face a mask of defiance, while Ethan fidgeted with his phone, avoiding eye contact.

James cleared his throat, his voice heavy with the burden of the conversation they had to have. "Kids... we need to talk about what's been happening. Things haven't been right between your mother and me for a while, and we need to be honest with you about it."

Izzy's eyes flicked up sharply, her expression a mix of confusion and suspicion. "What do you mean? Is this about you two?"

Ethan looked up as well, his eyes wide, his youthful innocence fading into a more mature awareness. "Is everything okay?" he asked, the question both innocent and loaded with unspoken fears.

Sophia's heart clenched. How had they come to this point? How had their family become a place of uncertainty and fear instead of comfort and trust? She looked at James, who gave her a small nod, and she knew they had no choice but to be honest.

"We've made mistakes," Sophia began, her voice shaking slightly. "We've both made mistakes. And we haven't been honest with each other, or with you. I... I thought that if I focused on my career, everything else would fall into place. But I was wrong. I neglected the things that matter most."

James spoke then, his voice steady but raw. "We've both been distant, and that's affected you. We should have been more present, more open. And now, we're trying to fix things. It's going to take time, but we're going to do everything we can to make things right."

For a moment, there was only silence. The weight of their confessions hung in the air, the words still settling in the hearts of their children. Sophia could see the uncertainty in Izzy's eyes, the hurt in Ethan's. They were too young to carry such burdens, yet here they were, forced to confront the cracks in the family they once thought was unbreakable.

Izzy was the first to speak, her voice quiet but filled with emotion. "I just want things to be normal again. I want to feel like we're... okay."

Ethan, ever the more sensitive one, nodded. "Me too. But I don't want things to keep being like this. If you guys are gonna fix it, then... do it."

Sophia's heart swelled with a mixture of relief and sorrow. They weren't angry. They weren't blaming them—not yet, at least. But the fear in their eyes was clear. They didn't know what the future held either.

"We will," James said, his voice firm now, a promise in his words. "We're going to make it right. Together."

The conversation was far from over, but for the first time, there was a sense of hope. It was fragile, uncertain, but it was there. And for the first time in a long while, Sophia felt like maybe, just maybe, they could face the consequences of their actions and still find a way to heal.

In the days following their family conversation, the air in the house felt different—not lighter, exactly, but clearer, as though the tension that had been building for months had finally found a place to settle. Sophia and James began to make small, deliberate changes. They were careful not to overpromise, knowing that rebuilding trust would take more than just words. It would take consistency, effort, and time.

Sophia started by simply being present. She made it a point to sit with Ethan during his homework sessions, even if it meant just listening to him talk about his favorite video games. She cooked dinner with Izzy, trying to bridge the gap that had grown between them through shared tasks, even if the conversations were halting and awkward at first.

One evening, as they chopped vegetables side by side, Sophia ventured cautiously into the territory she had avoided for so long. "You know, Izzy, when I was your age, I felt like no one understood me either. I didn't always get along with Grandma and Grandpa."

Izzy rolled her eyes but didn't stop slicing the carrot in front of her. "Yeah, but you had it easy. You didn't have to deal with all this stuff. Social media, school pressure, parents fighting..."

The comment stung, but Sophia knew better than to react defensively. "You're right. Things are different now. And I've been so caught up in my own world that I haven't made enough time to really understand yours. I'm sorry for that."

Izzy hesitated, her hands pausing over the cutting board. "It's not just about time," she said quietly. "It's about feeling like you care. Like what I say matters."

Sophia felt a lump rise in her throat. "It does matter. You matter. I just... I need to do a better job of showing you that. I know I've been failing at it, but I want to change. Will you give me the chance to try?"

Izzy glanced at her, and for the first time in weeks, Sophia saw a flicker of something that wasn't anger or frustration. It was cautious, tentative, but it was a start. "I guess," Izzy mumbled, and Sophia took it as a small victory.

James, meanwhile, worked on finding his own way back into their children's lives. He had always been more of a background figure—supportive but distant, present but not deeply engaged. Now, he made an effort to step forward. He attended Ethan's soccer practice and cheered from the sidelines, even when he didn't fully understand the game. He helped Izzy with her science project, spending hours trying to build a model of the solar system that didn't collapse under its own weight.

One night, after Ethan's game, James sat with him on the couch, flipping through a photo album they hadn't looked at in years. Ethan pointed to a picture of James in his twenties, standing beside an old car with a broad grin. "You look so different here. Like... happier," Ethan said, his tone more curious than accusatory.

James sighed, running a hand through his hair. "That was a good time in my life. But happiness isn't just about moments like that, Ethan. It's about the people you share those moments with.

And I've realized I've been too caught up in the wrong things lately. I've missed out on sharing those moments with you and your sister."

Ethan studied the photo for a moment longer before closing the album. "I don't care about that stuff, Dad. I just want you to be here. Like, really here."

James nodded, the words striking him harder than he expected. "I'm trying, buddy. I promise I'm trying."

The slow but steady changes didn't erase the pain or the mistakes of the past, but they planted seeds of something new: connection, understanding, and a fragile hope that things could be better. Sophia and James began to confront their own fears and failures as well, attending counseling sessions together to address the deeper fractures in their relationship.

In those sessions, they spoke truths they had long buried. Sophia admitted her fear of inadequacy, her struggle to reconcile her ambitions with her role as a mother and wife. James confessed his feelings of invisibility, his resentment at being sidelined in his own family. They cried, argued, and, slowly, began to see each other not as adversaries but as partners who had lost their way.

One evening, as they sat together on the back porch, watching the sun dip below the horizon, James reached for Sophia's hand. "Do you think we can really fix this?" he asked, his voice low but steady.

"I think we can try," Sophia replied, her fingers tightening around his. "And maybe that's enough for now."

The journey ahead was still uncertain, and the road was bound to be fraught with challenges. But for the first time, they weren't facing it alone. Together, they were learning to face the consequences of their past and to take the first tentative steps toward building a future worth fighting for.

Chapter 7: The Breaking Point

1. When Everything Falls Apart

When everything fell apart, the silence was deafening. The kind of silence that didn't just fill the room but seemed to press down on the very fabric of the air. Sophia sat on the edge of the couch, her hands clasped tightly together, her knuckles white with tension. Across from her, James leaned against the kitchen counter, his arms folded, his expression a mix of anger and exhaustion. The house that once echoed with laughter now felt cold, as if the warmth of their family had been drained away.

It had started with something small. It always did. A forgotten appointment. A sharp word spoken too quickly. But over time, these small moments had grown, building on top of each other until they formed a wall that neither Sophia nor James could climb. The arguments had become louder, the silences longer, and the distance between them had stretched into a chasm neither was sure how to cross.

"Do you even hear yourself?" James's voice cut through the quiet, sharp and bitter. "You're always so quick to point fingers, but you never stop to think about what you've done."

Sophia's gaze snapped to him, her eyes flashing with anger. "What I've done? Are you serious? I've been trying to hold this family together while you—" Her voice broke, the weight of unspoken words choking her. She looked away, biting her lip to keep from crying.

The sound of footsteps on the stairs interrupted them. Izzy appeared, her face pale, her arms crossed tightly over her chest. She didn't say anything, but the look in her eyes was enough to make both parents fall silent. Behind her, Ethan lingered in the shadows, his small frame barely visible. He was clutching a book to his chest, his expression confused and frightened.

Sophia felt a pang of guilt as she looked at her children. She had promised herself she would never let things get this bad, that she would protect them from the kind of pain she had known growing up. But here they were, caught in the crossfire of her and James's crumbling relationship.

"Izzy, Ethan," James said, his voice softening. "Go back to your rooms. We'll talk later."

Izzy didn't move. "Later? That's all you ever say. When are you going to stop pretending this is fine? We're not fine. None of us are."

Her words hung in the air, raw and honest. Sophia felt her chest tighten, the weight of her daughter's pain adding to her own. She wanted to say something, to comfort her, but no words came.

James ran a hand through his hair, his frustration evident. "This isn't the time, Izzy."

"It's never the time," Izzy shot back before turning on her heel and storming upstairs. Ethan hesitated, his wide eyes darting between his parents, before he followed her.

When the sound of their footsteps faded, Sophia let out a shaky breath. "We can't keep doing this, James. We're tearing them apart."

James didn't respond immediately. Instead, he stared out the window, his jaw tight. "I know," he said finally, his voice barely above a whisper. "But I don't know how to fix it."

The admission startled her. James was always so sure of himself, so in control. Hearing him admit his uncertainty was both unsettling and strangely comforting. It reminded her that he was human too, that he was struggling just as much as she was.

Sophia stood, crossing the room to stand beside him. For a moment, neither of them spoke. They simply stood there, side by side, looking out at the darkening sky. It wasn't a solution, but it was a start. A fragile thread connecting them, reminding them that they were still in this together, even if everything else was falling apart.

That night, the house remained eerily quiet. Sophia lay awake, staring at the ceiling, her mind replaying the events of the evening. The hurt in Izzy's voice, the fear in Ethan's eyes, and the despair etched into James's face were like echoes she couldn't escape. She turned over, her hand brushing the empty space where James used to sleep. He hadn't come to bed.

Slipping out from under the covers, she padded down the hallway. The soft glow of a lamp spilled from James's office. She hesitated at the door, listening to the faint clink of a glass against the wooden desk. Taking a deep breath, she stepped inside.

James sat hunched over, a tumbler of whiskey in his hand, the bottle half-empty beside him. Papers were scattered across the desk—bills, legal documents, and the remnants of a life they'd once built together.

"You're not sleeping either," she said softly, breaking the silence.

He looked up, his eyes bloodshot and tired. "Didn't seem much point."

Sophia leaned against the doorway, crossing her arms. "This isn't like you."

James let out a bitter laugh. "What is like me anymore, Sophia? Because I don't even know. I'm not the man I was when we started this, and maybe that's the problem."

His words struck her harder than she expected. She stepped closer, pulling out a chair and sitting across from him. "We're both different. Life changes people, James. But it doesn't mean we can't find a way forward."

He shook his head, staring into his glass. "And what does that way forward look like? More arguments? More damage to the kids? I can't keep pretending that we're okay."

Her heart ached at his honesty. "I'm not asking you to pretend. I'm asking you to try. For them. For us."

James looked at her, really looked at her, as if seeing her for the first time in months. "Do you still believe in us, Sophia? After everything?"

She didn't answer immediately. The truth was, she wasn't sure. But she also knew that giving up without trying would haunt her. "I believe we owe it to ourselves to find out."

His eyes softened, the tension in his shoulders easing slightly. "I don't know where to start."

Sophia reached across the desk, her fingers brushing his. "We start by being honest. No more avoiding, no more pretending. Just... honesty."

James nodded, his gaze dropping to their intertwined hands. It was a small gesture, but it felt monumental. "I can do that," he said quietly.

For the first time in weeks, Sophia felt a glimmer of hope. It wasn't a solution, but it was a step—a small, tentative step toward rebuilding what had been lost.

Upstairs, Izzy sat on her bed, headphones clamped over her ears, but no music played. She stared at the ceiling, her mind racing. Ethan was curled up on the floor by her feet, clutching a blanket. They often sought each other out during these nights, finding comfort in the shared silence.

"Do you think they'll ever stop fighting?" Ethan's voice was barely a whisper.

Izzy hesitated. She wanted to reassure him, to tell him everything would be fine, but she couldn't lie to him. "I don't know," she said finally. "But they're still here. That has to mean something."

Ethan nodded, his small face shadowed with worry. "I just want us to be a family again."

Izzy reached down, smoothing his hair. "Me too, Ethan. Me too."

As the night deepened, the family drifted into a restless sleep, each of them grappling with their own fears and hopes. And though the cracks remained, there was an unspoken understanding that they were not ready to give up—not yet.

2. The Distance Between Us

THE ROOM FELT SMALLER with every passing moment, though neither Sophia nor James had moved from their respective corners. The once-vibrant kitchen, the heart of their home, now seemed like a cold, lifeless space. The distance between them was not marked in feet or inches but in silence—a suffocating, deafening silence that no words could bridge.

Sophia's eyes lingered on the half-filled cup of coffee in front of her. The steam had long since vanished, much like the warmth in their conversations. She toyed with the handle, her fingers tracing the smooth ceramic as if searching for some kind of solace in its simplicity. Across the table, James sat rigid, his hands clasped tightly together, knuckles white from the pressure. His gaze was fixed on the window, though it was clear he wasn't looking at anything in particular.

It had been weeks since their last real conversation, and even then, it had ended in frustration and words neither could take back. Their lives had become a careful dance of avoidance, each step taken to ensure they didn't collide. And yet, the space between them felt like an impassable chasm.

"Do you want more coffee?" Sophia finally broke the silence, her voice cautious, almost brittle.

James didn't look at her. "No, I'm fine." His response was curt, devoid of emotion. It was a reply to the question but not an invitation for more.

Sophia bit her lip, fighting the urge to say something—anything—that might spark even the smallest flicker of connection. But the words felt stuck, weighed down by years of resentment and unspoken disappointments.

The truth was, neither knew when the distance had begun to grow. Perhaps it had started with James working late nights, his job demanding more and more of his time. Or maybe it was Sophia's constant push for perfection, her need to maintain a façade of control over a life that often felt like it was slipping through her fingers. Whatever the reason, it had crept into their lives quietly, like a shadow at dusk, until one day, it was all they could see.

James shifted in his seat, the scrape of the chair legs against the floor breaking the tension momentarily. He turned to face her, his expression unreadable. "We can't keep doing this," he said, his voice low but firm.

Sophia looked up, startled by his words but also relieved. Finally, someone had said it. "I know," she admitted, her voice softer than she intended. "But I don't know where to start."

James exhaled sharply, running a hand through his hair. "I don't either," he confessed. "But this...this isn't working."

The honesty hung in the air between them, raw and unfiltered. It wasn't a solution, but it was something—a crack in the wall they'd both built.

Sophia nodded, her fingers still clutching the cup as if it were an anchor. "Maybe we just...talk?" she suggested, the word feeling foreign on her tongue.

James gave a faint, almost imperceptible nod. "Yeah. Maybe we should."

It was a fragile beginning, like the first tentative steps onto a frozen lake. The ice beneath them could shatter at any moment, plunging them into icy depths they weren't sure they could survive. But for now, they both sat there, looking at each other not as adversaries but as two people who once shared something worth saving.

The distance between them wasn't gone. Not yet. But for the first time in a long time, it didn't feel insurmountable.

3. The Fear of Losing Control

SOPHIA SAT AT THE EDGE of the dining table, her fingers tracing absent patterns on the cold glass surface. The room was silent, save for the faint hum of the refrigerator in the corner. It was the kind of silence that pressed against her chest, making it harder to breathe. She stared at the untouched cup of tea in front of her, the steam long gone, leaving only a tepid reminder of her neglected solace.

The day had spiraled out of her grasp before it even began. First, it was the last-minute work email that demanded her immediate attention. Then, the kids—Izzy, with her biting teenage defiance, and Ethan, with his quiet but unsettling rebellion—seemed determined to test every ounce of patience she had left. James, ever stoic, had left for work without so much as a goodbye, his silence feeling more like an accusation than indifference.

Sophia had always prided herself on her ability to manage it all: the deadlines, the dinners, the demands of motherhood. But lately, everything felt like sand slipping through her fingers, faster than she could grasp. And now, as she sat there, the weight of her crumbling control bore down on her like a relentless tide.

Across town, James parked his car in the company lot and sat there for a moment, gripping the steering wheel. His temples throbbed from the argument he and Sophia had the night before—a clash of words sharp enough to leave wounds neither was ready to address. He hated that he couldn't fix things, that he couldn't protect his family from the slow unraveling he felt in every interaction. But more than that, he hated feeling powerless.

James had built his life around being the steady one—the anchor. It was what drew Sophia to him in the first place, or so she had said years ago when their love was fresh and unburdened. But now, that same steadiness felt like a trap. He couldn't let go, couldn't falter, because if he did, the fragile balance of their lives might collapse altogether.

Izzy, meanwhile, sat on her bed with headphones clamped over her ears, drowning out the noise of the world with a playlist she knew by heart. She scrolled through her phone, her thumb hovering over a text from a friend she no longer trusted. The fear of making the wrong move, of saying something that could spread like wildfire through her social circle, kept her frozen.

Ethan peeked through the crack of her door, hesitant to knock. He could sense the tension radiating from his sister's room. It mirrored the same tension he felt whenever he walked into the kitchen and saw their parents avoiding each other's eyes. He didn't understand everything that was happening, but he understood enough to know that something was wrong. And like his father, Ethan felt powerless to change it.

The fear of losing control was not confined to Sophia alone. It seeped into every corner of their home, infecting James's resolve, Izzy's choices, and Ethan's fragile sense of security. It was a silent predator, lurking behind their words and actions, turning even the simplest moments into battles against unseen forces.

Sophia pushed the teacup away and stood, her hands gripping the back of the chair as if to steady herself. She didn't know how to fix this. She didn't know how to be the mother, the wife, the woman she was expected to be when she could barely keep herself from breaking.

But somewhere deep inside, a voice whispered that maybe control wasn't the answer. Maybe the tighter she gripped, the faster everything slipped away.

Sophia took a deep breath and stepped away from the table. The house, though still and quiet, seemed to echo with the weight of everything left unsaid. Her footsteps carried her to the living room, where the family photo wall loomed—each frame a reminder of happier times. She paused before one picture: a family trip to the beach, the sun painting their smiles in golden hues.

She studied her own face in the photo, carefree and radiant, and felt a pang of longing. Where had that version of herself gone? Was she buried under the layers of responsibility and compromise, or had she simply faded over time? Her fingers brushed the frame, and for a fleeting moment, she thought about taking it down. But she didn't.

Upstairs, Izzy finally removed her headphones, the silence almost startling. She flopped back on her bed, staring at the ceiling. Her parents had been fighting more often, and though they tried to keep their voices down, the tension was palpable. It was in the way her mom gripped the steering wheel during school drop-offs, in the way her dad's jokes had grown fewer and farther between. Izzy didn't know what to do with it. She didn't even know how to talk about it.

Ethan, still lingering by her door, decided against knocking. Instead, he retreated to his room, where his action figures were neatly lined up on the shelf. He pulled one down—a superhero with a tattered cape—and held it tightly. He didn't play with them much anymore, but holding them made him feel safer, like there was still someone out there who could fix things.

James sat at his desk at work, but his mind wasn't on the reports in front of him. He stared at the screen, the numbers blurring together. He thought about calling Sophia, about apologizing, though he wasn't even sure what for. For being distant? For not being able to solve everything? For feeling like he was losing her, inch by inch?

Instead, he opened his desk drawer and pulled out the small box he'd bought weeks ago. Inside was a bracelet, delicate and understated, something he thought Sophia might like. But every time he planned to give it to her, the moment never felt right. Now it felt like a cruel joke, this tiny gesture in the face of everything crumbling between them.

The house was still when James returned that evening. The kids were upstairs, and Sophia was in the kitchen, her back turned to him as she chopped vegetables. He paused in the doorway, the smell of garlic and onions filling the air.

"Hey," he said softly.

She turned, her eyes tired but wary. "Hey."

For a moment, neither spoke. The weight of the day hung between them, heavy and oppressive. James wanted to reach for her, to tell her he was sorry, but the words caught in his throat. Sophia wanted to ask him why he seemed so far away, but her pride wouldn't let her.

Instead, they moved around each other in the small kitchen, their movements careful and choreographed, like dancers afraid of stepping on each other's toes.

Later that night, as the house settled into an uneasy quiet, Sophia lay in bed, staring at the ceiling. James was beside her, his breathing slow and even. She turned her head to look at him, studying the lines etched into his face—the ones that hadn't been there when they first met. She wondered if he ever looked at her and thought the same.

As she closed her eyes, one thought circled in her mind: How did we get here?

James stirred in his sleep, his hand brushing hers for just a moment. And though it was fleeting, it was enough to remind her of something she'd nearly forgotten—there was still something worth fighting for.

4. A Silent Cry for Help

THE WALLS OF THE CARTER household were thick with unspoken words, the silence stretching like a taut string ready to snap. James sat at the kitchen table, staring blankly at his coffee cup. The liquid inside had long gone cold, much like the warmth in his relationship with Sophia. She moved about the room, her heels clicking softly against the tiled floor, the sound a sharp contrast to the void between them.

James opened his mouth to speak but stopped. What could he say that wouldn't lead to another argument? His thoughts were a tangled web of frustration and guilt. He couldn't pinpoint when they had drifted apart, only that the gap now felt insurmountable.

Sophia glanced at him briefly, her expression unreadable. "I'll be late tonight," she said, her voice clipped. "Another client dinner."

James nodded. "Sure." It was all he could manage.

Across the hallway, their son Ethan lingered by the staircase, clutching his sketchpad. He had drawn another picture—this time of a family sitting together under a tree, their faces smiling. But the figures in the drawing seemed distant, their outlines blurred, as if even on paper they couldn't fully connect. Ethan sighed, folding the page shut. He couldn't remember the last time his family had sat together like that.

Upstairs, Isabella shut her bedroom door, leaning against it with a heavy sigh. Her music played softly in the background, but it did little to drown out the tension that seeped through the house. She had started spending more time in her room, retreating from the charged atmosphere. The arguments, the silences—they weighed on her in ways she couldn't explain, even to herself.

Sophia paused on her way to the front door. She turned back toward James, her hand lingering on the doorknob. For a moment, something flickered in her eyes—hesitation, perhaps—but then it was gone. "Don't wait up," she said, stepping outside.

James watched her leave, a hollow ache settling in his chest. He glanced at the clock on the wall, its rhythmic ticking a cruel reminder of the time slipping away. He wanted to fix things, to bridge the chasm between them, but where would he even begin? Every attempt to reach her felt like screaming into a void.

"Dad?" Ethan's voice was small but clear, cutting through the quiet. James turned to see his son standing in the doorway, his sketchpad clutched tightly to his chest.

"What is it, buddy?" James asked, his voice softer than he intended.

Ethan hesitated, then held up the drawing. "I made this for you and Mom."

James took the sketch and studied it. The crude lines and bright colors carried a kind of innocence that made his throat tighten. "This is… really good," he said. "Thanks, Ethan."

"Do you think we could do this? Like in the picture?" Ethan's eyes were wide, his tone pleading. "Sit together and talk? Like we used to?"

James struggled for words, his heart heavy. "I'll try, Ethan," he said at last. "I'll try."

The boy nodded, his disappointment barely concealed as he shuffled back to his room. James placed the drawing on the table, its cheerful depiction mocking the reality of their lives.

That night, James sat alone in the living room, the house eerily quiet. He thought of Sophia, of Ethan, of Isabella. They were all crying out in their own ways—silent pleas for connection, for love, for understanding. And he realized, perhaps for the first time, that he wasn't just a bystander in their shared struggle. If he wanted to mend the broken pieces, he had to find his voice and act.

For now, though, he sat there, paralyzed by the enormity of what lay ahead. The silence was deafening, but in its depths, James heard the faintest echo of hope—a whisper urging him not to give up.

Chapter 8: A New Beginning

1. The Journey Within

It began with a silence too loud to ignore. Sophia sat alone in the dim glow of the living room lamp, the soft hum of the refrigerator in the kitchen her only companion. The house, once filled with laughter and chaos, now felt like a stranger to her. The children were asleep, and James had retreated to his study, the door firmly shut. This was the space she feared most—not the physical solitude, but the chasm that had grown between her and the people she loved most.

She leaned back, closed her eyes, and let the day replay itself. The terse exchanges with James at breakfast. The rushed goodbyes with Ethan as he ran out the door, his headphones in, already disconnected from the world around him. The hesitant glance Izzy gave her over dinner, a silent plea for something—what, exactly, Sophia couldn't pinpoint. These moments, once small and easily dismissed, now weighed heavy on her chest.

Sophia thought she had it all figured out once. Her life was a carefully constructed masterpiece, every piece meticulously placed to create the illusion of perfection. A thriving career, a beautiful family, a home that seemed to glow with warmth and success. But perfection, she realized, was a fragile thing. It demanded sacrifices, and over the years, she had sacrificed more than she intended.

She reached for her notebook—her safe space. On its pages, she had written dreams and doubts, fleeting joys, and deep regrets. Tonight, the pen lingered in her hand, hovering over the blank page. Words failed her. How do you begin to unravel a knot you've spent years tightening?

Sophia stared at the notebook, feeling a pang of guilt. She had always believed she was doing the right thing—pushing herself to be everything for everyone. A successful professional for her colleagues, a loving mother for her children, a supportive wife for James. But somewhere along the way, she had lost herself.

Her phone buzzed, breaking the silence. A message from an old college friend, someone who had once been a confidant before life pulled them in separate directions. The text was simple: *"How are you, really?"* The question struck her harder than she expected. How was she? She didn't know anymore.

Sophia stood and walked to the mirror in the hallway. The face staring back at her was familiar but distant. Lines she hadn't noticed before traced the edges of her eyes. Her hair, neatly styled, looked lifeless in the dim light. Was this who she had become?

She thought about James. They used to talk for hours, sharing their dreams, their fears, their everything. Now, their conversations felt more like transactions—functional and void of emotion. Was he feeling the same distance? Did he, too, yearn for the connection they once shared, or had he accepted their new normal?

Sophia knew the answers wouldn't come easily. The journey within, she realized, wasn't about finding quick fixes or blaming others. It was about confronting her own choices, her own fears, and the walls she had built around herself. And it terrified her.

She sank back into the couch, the notebook still in her hands. This time, she wrote a single sentence: *"What if it's not too late?"*

2. The Courage to Change

SOPHIA STOOD BY THE kitchen window, watching the rain trace unpredictable patterns on the glass. Each droplet seemed like a tiny decision, merging, diverging, and ultimately choosing its path. It was a metaphor for her life—or at least the life she had been living for the past decade. A perfectly constructed façade of stability, love, and fulfillment had shielded her from acknowledging the cracks beneath. Until now.

The argument with James the night before still echoed in her mind. He had accused her of being distant, of caring more about her career than their family. His words had cut deep, not because they were entirely true, but because she knew he wasn't entirely wrong. She had built her identity around her achievements, each promotion a validation of her worth, but it had come at a cost—one she was no longer willing to ignore.

Sophia's gaze shifted to the dining table, where a pile of papers lay untouched. Her resignation letter sat on top, its neat folds a stark contrast to the chaos she felt inside. Quitting her job had seemed unthinkable a month ago, but now it felt like the only way forward. She wasn't sure if it was bravery or desperation driving her decision, but either way, she couldn't deny the need for change.

In the quiet upstairs bedroom, James stared at an old photograph of their family, taken on a summer trip to the mountains. He remembered how Sophia had laughed that day, her carefree spirit infectious. But those moments had grown rare, replaced by clipped conversations and empty smiles. He blamed himself as much as her; he had retreated into his own world, burying his frustrations in long hours at work and half-hearted attempts to connect.

James set the photo down and exhaled slowly. He wanted to believe they could find their way back, but hope felt fragile. Change required action, and he wasn't sure if either of them had the courage to take the first step.

Later that evening, as the rain eased into a gentle drizzle, Sophia found herself standing in the doorway of their bedroom. James looked up from his book, his expression guarded but curious. The silence stretched between them, heavy with unspoken words.

"I've been thinking," she began, her voice trembling slightly. "About us. About everything." She hesitated, searching for the right words. "I can't keep pretending everything is fine. I need to make some changes—real changes."

James set the book aside and nodded, his jaw tightening. "I've been thinking too. And maybe we both need to change. I don't want to lose what we have, Sophia."

Her eyes filled with tears, but she didn't look away. For the first time in months, she felt seen, as if the walls they had built between them were starting to crumble. Change was terrifying, but the alternative—staying trapped in a cycle of resentment and regret—was even worse.

The following weeks brought challenges neither of them had anticipated. Sophia's resignation shocked her colleagues, but the freedom she felt afterward was undeniable. She began to rediscover herself, spending time with the kids, experimenting with painting—a hobby she had abandoned years ago—and finding joy in the simplicity of everyday life.

James, too, made an effort. He cut back on his hours at the firm and started joining family dinners again. There were setbacks, moments when old habits crept in and tempers flared, but they kept pushing forward. Each small victory—a shared laugh, an honest conversation—felt like a step closer to the life they both wanted.

One evening, as they sat on the porch watching the sunset, James reached for her hand. "It's not easy, is it?" he said, a faint smile playing on his lips.

Sophia squeezed his hand gently. "No, but it's worth it."

The courage to change wasn't about erasing the past or becoming someone entirely new. It was about learning to face the truth—about themselves, about each other—and choosing to grow together. For the first time in years, they felt like partners again, ready to embrace whatever came next.

THE SHIFTING BALANCE

The days that followed felt like a delicate balance, a constant push and pull between old patterns and new possibilities. Sophia found herself reflecting more on her past choices, questioning the ambitions that had once defined her. It wasn't that she regretted her career—she had accomplished more than she had ever imagined—but she realized it had become a shield, one she hid behind to avoid confronting the emptiness she sometimes felt. Now, with her time no longer dictated by the clock and the corporate grind, she could breathe. She could hear herself think.

Yet, the uncertainty lingered. Had she made the right choice? What if her decision to leave her job wasn't the cure-all she hoped for? She didn't have all the answers, but the act of trying to live more authentically, even in small ways, felt liberating.

James, on the other hand, struggled to recalibrate his own life. The adjustment was more difficult than he had anticipated. He had spent years building a career that now seemed less important in the face of the shifting dynamics at home. Still, the weight of providing for the family, of maintaining the same image of success he had worked so hard to create, tugged at him. His role as the protector, the reliable provider, had been his identity for so long. Letting go of that felt like losing a part of himself.

One Saturday morning, Sophia decided to take the first step in something she had always wanted to do but never had the courage for: an art exhibit. She had always loved painting, a passion that had been buried beneath the weight of responsibilities. Her small living room studio had become her sanctuary over the past few months, and now it felt like the right time to share it with others.

She invited James, of course, but also her closest friends and a few old colleagues. It was a modest exhibit, more about personal fulfillment than professional acclaim. The morning of the event, she could feel the familiar anxiety creeping in, but this time it was different. She wasn't seeking validation. She was seeking truth.

James, standing beside her as the first guests arrived, couldn't help but notice the sparkle in her eyes. There was a calmness about her, a sense of contentment he hadn't seen in years. He marveled at the vibrant colors she had chosen for her paintings—colors that seemed to reflect her inner transformation. He wasn't sure if he understood all of it, but he could feel it in his bones. This was a woman who had found her way back to herself, and in that, he found a new kind of respect.

As the event unfolded, Sophia felt an unexpected warmth in the atmosphere, a kind of peace that had eluded her for so long. Her friends praised her work, but more than the compliments, it was the simple acknowledgment of her journey that touched her deeply. She had changed, yes, but in the most important ways—she had learned to embrace vulnerability and trust the process.

That night, after the exhibit had ended and the house had quieted down, Sophia and James sat together in the dim light of their living room. They didn't need words to fill the silence. The change between them was palpable, and for the first time in a long while, it felt like they were both exactly where they needed to be.

"I'm proud of you," James said softly, his hand brushing against hers.

Sophia smiled, her heart full. "Thank you. For being here. For being part of this."

For a while, they simply sat, the weight of their past and present resting between them. They had taken a leap into the unknown, uncertain of the outcomes but confident in one thing—the courage to change was theirs to claim. Together, they had taken the first steps toward a new kind of life. And that was enough.

3. Rebuilding Trust

IT HAD BEEN WEEKS SINCE the argument, but Sophia couldn't shake the weight of the silence that had settled between her and James. Every conversation now felt like an echo of what had been—an attempt to rebuild something that had crumbled, piece by fragile piece, over the years. Trust, once the foundation of their relationship, now seemed like a distant memory, a place they could no longer return to without fear of breaking something else in the process.

James, for his part, was doing what he always did when faced with a problem—he withdrew. Not physically, not in the way he might have done in the past, but emotionally. It was his default setting, the place he went to when the weight of everything became too much to bear. His silence was his defense mechanism, but Sophia knew it wasn't helping either of them. The walls between them only grew higher with each passing day.

Sophia had always known that trust wasn't something that could be easily fixed. It was a delicate thing, fragile in its construction and incredibly hard to rebuild once broken. But she had hoped. She had hoped that the years of shared history, the moments of connection, and the love they once felt for each other would be enough to bridge the gap.

But hope, she was learning, wasn't enough. It wasn't enough to simply want things to go back to the way they were. The cracks, the deep wounds, they had to be addressed, slowly and carefully. There was no shortcut to healing, no magic words that would make everything better overnight. It was a process—painful, slow, and sometimes excruciating.

One night, after a quiet dinner that had felt more like two strangers sitting at the same table, Sophia decided to take a step that felt as if she were walking on a precipice. She reached out. It wasn't much—just a hand, resting lightly on his arm. But to her, it was everything. It was the first gesture of vulnerability, of admitting that she was scared, that she didn't know how to fix things, but she wanted to try.

James flinched, just for a moment, before his hand covered hers, the warmth of his palm sending a jolt of recognition through her. It wasn't a solution. It wasn't the end of their struggles. But it was something. It was the beginning of something new, something that couldn't be rushed, but had to be built, one small, honest moment at a time.

The silence stretched between them, but it wasn't as suffocating now. There was a glimmer of possibility, a faint hope that maybe, just maybe, they could find their way back. Not to what they had, but to something different, something that didn't rely on the illusion of perfection, but on the raw, unguarded truth of who they were now, both of them, flawed and broken in their own ways.

But even as she felt a flicker of optimism, a part of Sophia knew that the path ahead would be anything but easy. Trust, once lost, couldn't simply be rebuilt with kind words and gestures. It required time—time to prove, time to understand, and time to heal. The wounds they had inflicted on each other wouldn't vanish overnight, no matter how much they wished it.

James had to show her that he could be open again. That he could share his fears, his mistakes, and his dreams without the layers of defense he had built over the years. Sophia, too, had to learn to trust herself again. To trust that she was worthy of the love she so desperately sought to hold on to. It wasn't just about James. It was about her, too.

The road ahead was uncertain, but for the first time in weeks, they both seemed willing to take the first step. They didn't know where it would lead, or if they would ever find their way back to the kind of love they had once shared. But they were starting, and sometimes, that was enough.

The days following that quiet moment at dinner were filled with small gestures—slightly more open conversations, a shared laugh, a brief touch when their hands accidentally brushed against one another. These were the fragile beginnings of something that neither of them could fully define yet. Each moment was like a small thread, woven carefully into the fabric of their relationship, trying to patch the holes, to tie things back together.

For James, it was a slow and painful process. The walls he had built around himself weren't just barriers to others; they were walls he had built around his own heart. He was afraid that any crack, any slight opening, would lead to his heart being exposed, vulnerable once again. It was a fear that had always driven him—his need for control, for maintaining an image of strength, had made him retreat inwardly, even as he tried to maintain the façade of a calm, composed partner.

But trust wasn't about control. It wasn't about keeping the world at arm's length. It was about allowing someone to see you—truly see you, in all your imperfection, your fears, your flaws—and still choosing to stay. And James was beginning to realize that. It wasn't an easy realization, and there were days when the fear of being too open, too exposed, made him want to retreat once again. But something about Sophia's quiet patience, her willingness to wait, began to chip away at the armor he had spent so many years constructing.

Sophia, on the other hand, had to navigate the delicate balance of being vulnerable without losing herself. For so long, she had been the one to hold everything together, to make excuses, to push forward with a smile, even when everything inside her was falling apart. Now, as she reached out to James, she found herself questioning her own worth. Was she enough to rebuild what they had lost? Was the love they had once shared worth fighting for? Or had they drifted so far apart that no amount of effort could bring them back together?

Her doubts lingered in the back of her mind, but with each small breakthrough, each moment of connection, they began to lose their grip on her heart. The act of rebuilding trust wasn't just about repairing the rift between her and James—it was about her own self-discovery. It was about learning to trust herself again, to believe that she could stand strong, even if things didn't work out the way she hoped.

There were days when the progress felt like too little, too late. The tension between them would resurface, old wounds threatening to bleed once more. But there were other days, moments of quiet clarity, when they found themselves laughing together, talking about things they hadn't shared in years. It wasn't perfect, but it was real. And that was what mattered.

One afternoon, they found themselves sitting in the small garden in the back of their house, the sun beginning to set in the distance. James, for the first time in a long while, reached over and took Sophia's hand. It wasn't a grand gesture, but in that moment, it felt like everything. They sat together in silence, but it wasn't the same heavy silence that had plagued them for so long. It was a quiet that held promise, a peace that came from simply being there together.

Sophia squeezed his hand, her heart still wary, but opening a little more with each passing day. "We've got a long way to go," she said softly, her voice steady but full of emotion.

James nodded, his grip tightening around her hand, a silent acknowledgment of the road ahead. "I know," he whispered, his voice rough with something unspoken. "But I'm willing to try, Sophia. I am."

For the first time in what felt like forever, they both dared to believe that maybe—just maybe—the trust they had lost could be found again. It wouldn't be easy, and it wouldn't happen overnight. But the first steps had been taken. And sometimes, that was all you needed to start rebuilding.

4. Rediscovering Love

THE SOUND OF FOOTSTEPS echoed through the quiet house, a subtle reminder that time had passed, that things had changed. Sophia stood by the window, looking out at the garden she had once tended with her own hands. The flowers, though still blooming, seemed less vibrant, their colors faded. Much like the love she once shared with James.

For years, they had been a perfect match—two souls intertwined by shared dreams, ambitions, and a deep sense of connection. But somewhere along the way, those dreams had begun to fray at the edges. The conversations had grown sparse, their silences louder than words ever were. And Sophia couldn't help but wonder how they had lost their way. Where had the love gone?

It wasn't as if she didn't care. Far from it. But the demands of life, the constant push to be more, to do more, had worn them both down. Sophia had thrown herself into her career, convinced that success would somehow make everything better, would fill the void she felt inside. But success never came with the satisfaction she'd hoped for. She had gained so much professionally, but in the process, she had lost touch with what truly mattered.

James, too, had changed. He was still the man she had married, but his distance had grown, not just physically, but emotionally. He had always been the steady one, the rock of the family. But now, she saw a man trapped in the weight of his own silence, burdened by expectations—his own and those of the world around him.

Sophia closed her eyes, her mind flashing back to the early days of their marriage. She remembered the laughter they shared, the spontaneous trips they took, the way their fingers would intertwine so effortlessly, as if they were two halves of a whole. There had been a time when their love felt easy, natural, like breathing. But time had worn that away, layer by layer, until only memories remained.

She wasn't sure how to fix it. She wasn't sure if she could. But there was a small, flickering hope within her—a belief that perhaps it wasn't too late, that perhaps there was still something worth fighting for. She just had to find a way back to him, to them, before the space between them became a chasm too wide to bridge.

Her heart ached, but she knew that the first step was to acknowledge the distance. To face the truth of what had happened to their love, no matter how painful it was. Only then could they begin to rebuild what they had lost, piece by piece.

It wasn't going to be easy. Rebuilding love never was. But Sophia believed it was possible. For the first time in a long while, she felt the faintest stir of something familiar inside—an ember of hope that maybe, just maybe, they could rediscover the love that had once seemed so effortless.

The path ahead was uncertain, but she was ready to take the first step. After all, love wasn't just something you found. It was something you fought for. And she was ready to fight.

Chapter 9: Crossroads

1. The Return to Family

The road had been long, winding through countless days filled with half-formed thoughts, arguments, and misunderstandings. For **Sophia**, the idea of returning home had always seemed like a distant dream, one she had pushed aside for the sake of ambition and success. She had built a life for herself outside the walls of the home she once knew, convinced that the pursuit of her own career would fill the void she felt. But as time passed, that void only deepened, and the weight of her choices pressed heavier on her chest with each passing day.

The phone call from her daughter **Izzy** had been the catalyst, the final push that made Sophia realize what she had been running from for so long. "Mom, are you coming home? We need you," Izzy's voice had been strained, a mix of desperation and longing that pierced through the barriers Sophia had carefully constructed around her heart.

It wasn't just the request that unsettled her; it was the truth that lay beneath it. **James**, her husband, had grown silent in his own right, his stoic exterior hiding a maelstrom of emotions. He had always been the strong, silent type, carrying the weight of the family without complaint. But in his silence, something had shifted—something that Sophia couldn't ignore any longer.

She stood by the window, staring out at the world beyond, her thoughts consumed by the faces she had neglected for too long. The familiar warmth of her home seemed distant now, almost like a place she no longer belonged. She had imagined that success would fill the gaps in her life, but it had only created a chasm between her and the people who had once been her world.

Sophia took a deep breath, making her decision. It was time to face the consequences of her absence. It was time to return, not just physically, but emotionally, to the family she had lost touch with.

As she stepped into the house, the familiar scent of old wood and cinnamon filled the air. The house was quieter than she remembered, the silence almost deafening. It had been a long time since she had felt this kind of stillness. **James** was in the kitchen, his back to her, chopping vegetables with the same precise movements he had always used. His hair had grayed at the temples, his face etched with the lines of years lived in patience and solitude.

"Sophia," his voice broke the silence, as if he had known she was there the whole time. He didn't turn around, but the way he said her name was enough. It was a greeting, yes, but it carried with it years of unsaid words.

"I'm home," she said quietly, stepping into the kitchen. The weight of the words felt heavier than she had anticipated. She wanted to reach out to him, to bridge the gap that had grown between them, but she didn't know where to begin.

James finally turned, his eyes meeting hers. There was no anger there, no judgment, just a quiet understanding. "I know," he said simply, his voice calm but firm.

The room seemed to close in around them as they stood there, two people who had once been in sync but now felt like strangers sharing a space.

"How's Izzy?" Sophia asked, breaking the silence again. She hadn't seen her daughter in months, and the thought of the young woman her daughter had become in her absence stirred something deep within her.

"She's... getting by," James replied, his gaze softening. "But she's been asking for you. We both have."

The words hit her harder than she expected. She had been so focused on her own journey that she hadn't realized how much her absence had affected those she loved most. The weight of regret and the ache of missed moments settled into her chest, making it hard to breathe.

Sophia reached for the counter to steady herself, her mind racing with the realization that this was just the beginning of something much bigger than she had ever anticipated. The journey back to her family wouldn't be easy, but for the first time in years, she felt ready to face it.

As she made her way to the living room, she spotted **Ethan**, her son, sitting on the couch, his eyes fixed on the TV. He didn't look up as she entered, but the slight shift in his posture told her everything she needed to know. **Ethan** had always been the quiet one, the sensitive soul who preferred to stay out of the chaos that often engulfed their family. She had missed his subtle ways of showing affection, his quiet presence that was sometimes more comforting than words.

"Ethan," she called softly, unsure of how to approach him after so long. "How are you?"

He glanced up at her, his eyes betraying the uncertainty that lay beneath his calm exterior. "I'm fine," he said, but the distance in his voice was unmistakable. It was as if a wall had been built between them, and Sophia knew it was going to take time to tear it down.

"I'm sorry," she whispered, taking a step closer. "I should have been here."

He didn't answer at first, his gaze returning to the screen, but then he sighed, almost imperceptibly. "I know, Mom," he said quietly. "I know."

The simple acknowledgment stung more than any argument or confrontation could have. It was a silent understanding, a moment of shared pain that neither of them had been able to express before. And for the first time in a long while, Sophia realized that returning to her family wasn't just about fixing the past—it was about rebuilding what had been broken, piece by piece.

As the evening wore on, the house seemed to slowly come back to life around Sophia. The air was filled with the sounds of family—**James** humming a tune as he finished dinner, **Izzy** chatting on the phone with a friend, **Ethan** fidgeting with his phone, his attention half on the conversation, half on the silence that lingered between them. There was an odd comfort in the normalcy of it all, a reminder of the life she had left behind, and yet, it felt foreign. It felt like she was trying to step into a life that had moved on without her.

Dinner was a quiet affair, the usual banter absent, replaced by a tense sort of politeness. They ate, they exchanged pleasantries, but there was a noticeable barrier that none of them seemed willing—or able—to cross. Sophia felt it most keenly, the heavy weight of years lost, the unspoken words hanging in the air like a storm waiting to break.

After the meal, **Izzy** cleared the table in silence, her movements precise but hurried, as if to avoid the awkwardness of sitting with her mother any longer than necessary. **James** and Sophia found themselves alone at the table, the quiet between them stretching out like an old, worn blanket that neither of them knew how to fold anymore.

"Do you think we can fix this?" Sophia asked, her voice soft but trembling with uncertainty.

James didn't answer immediately. Instead, he reached for his glass of wine, took a slow sip, and placed it down with deliberate care. "I don't know," he said finally. "But I think it's worth trying."

There was a long pause as Sophia processed his words. For a moment, she wanted to reach out, to bridge the gap between them with the words she had so long kept locked away. But it was hard.

So hard to find the words that would erase the distance, the silence, the hurt.

"I've missed you," she said, her voice barely above a whisper.

James looked at her then, his gaze steady, yet filled with an emotion Sophia couldn't quite place. It was not anger, nor was it resentment—it was something deeper. Something unspoken.

"You've missed us?" he asked, the question lingering between them like a challenge.

Sophia felt the weight of his words. She had missed them, of course, but it was more than that. She had missed the person she had been when she was with them. She had lost herself in her pursuit of independence, thinking that success could fill the gaps where love and family had once been. She had been wrong.

"I've missed everything," she said, her voice cracking slightly as the tears she had long fought to keep at bay threatened to spill. "I've missed the way we used to laugh, the way we used to talk about everything. I've missed being a part of this family."

James didn't respond right away. Instead, he stood up and walked over to the window, looking out into the darkening evening. When he turned back to face her, there was a quiet resolve in his eyes.

"You can't just walk back into our lives and expect everything to be the same," he said quietly, but with an unmistakable firmness. "You've been gone too long. Things have changed."

Sophia felt the sting of his words, but she didn't argue. He was right, of course. She had been gone too long, and things had changed. It wasn't just her absence that had affected them—it was the way she had left without a word, without a second thought. She had abandoned them in search of something that, in the end, hadn't brought her the peace she had hoped for.

"I know," she said softly, her eyes meeting his. "But I'm here now. And I'm ready to try."

James studied her for a moment, as if weighing her sincerity. Then, with a slow nod, he walked over to the table and sat down across from her.

"We'll see," he said, his voice softer now, the edge of confrontation replaced by something that resembled hope. "We'll see if we can find our way back."

The next few days were a whirlwind of awkward conversations, tentative steps toward reconnection, and the uncomfortable feeling of trying to fit into a life that had moved on without her. **Izzy** was distant at first, her eyes constantly searching for signs of the woman she used to call mother, the woman who had been there for all of her milestones before disappearing into the world beyond their home. But Sophia saw the small glimmers of recognition, the fleeting moments when Izzy's smile reached her eyes, and she knew that the road to healing, though long, was possible.

Ethan remained aloof, the quiet one who hid his feelings behind layers of sarcasm and indifference. But Sophia noticed the small changes—how he no longer retreated into his room after dinner, how he sat with her in the living room, not saying much, but being present. It was a start, and for Sophia, that was all she needed.

It wasn't easy, and there were moments when she felt like giving up, when the weight of her regrets threatened to crush her. But every day, she found herself growing stronger, more determined to rebuild the relationships she had neglected for so long. Every smile from Izzy, every quiet conversation with James, every shared silence with Ethan—it was all a sign that, despite the cracks and the distance, there was still a foundation there worth rebuilding.

In the quiet of the evening, as the house settled into a gentle rhythm, Sophia realized something important—she hadn't come home to fix everything at once. She hadn't come home to erase the past, but to learn how to live with it, how to grow alongside it. The return to family wasn't about grand gestures or promises of change—it was about the small moments, the quiet steps forward, the willingness to try again, no matter how many times it took.

And as she sat with her family, the weight of their shared silence no longer felt like an obstacle, but a beginning.

Days passed, and with each one, the family adjusted to the delicate new rhythm they were learning to create. The house, once a silent reflection of the years that had passed between them, began to hum with the quiet energy of slowly mending relationships. There was no grand gesture, no sudden transformation—only the slow, steady work of rediscovery.

James had always been the pragmatic one, the one who believed that time would heal most wounds, though he wasn't sure how long it would take for the deep ones to fade. He had spent many nights thinking about their past, their choices, the way Sophia had left without a second glance. But when she had returned, he had seen something in her eyes—a glimpse of the woman he had once known, a woman who had struggled but had not forgotten what mattered.

That made it easier to believe in the possibility of something new.

Each evening, they sat down together for dinner, the conversations still tentative but warming. Izzy had become more open, though there was a guarded quality to her responses, a hesitation when speaking of the past. She would ask about Sophia's travels, her life outside of their small world, but the questions were almost always followed by long pauses, like she was unsure of what to expect.

Ethan, on the other hand, had taken to finding ways to avoid the heavy conversations altogether. His sarcasm and humor acted as a shield, a way to keep the vulnerability at bay. But Sophia saw through it. She had always seen through him. She could feel the quiet hurt, the unsaid words that weighed heavily on him, and she knew that while he acted as if nothing had changed, deep down he was struggling to reconcile the mother he remembered with the stranger she had become.

But she also knew something important: all of them were trying, in their own way.

One afternoon, Sophia sat in the living room with **Izzy**, both of them flipping through old photo albums. It was one of those rare moments of quiet connection. The photos, faded with age, captured memories of a simpler time—Izzy's first day of school, family vacations, birthday parties filled with laughter. They were moments frozen in time, reminders of what they had once been.

"I look so young," Izzy said softly, her finger tracing the image of herself on her first day of kindergarten.

"You were," Sophia replied, smiling at the memory. "You were always so excited about everything. Remember how you used to make me take a picture of you before every new adventure?"

Izzy glanced at her mother, her expression unreadable. "You weren't always there to take them," she said quietly, a touch of sadness in her voice.

Sophia's heart tightened at the unspoken truth, but she knew better than to try to defend herself. The years of absence could not be erased with a few words. They had to be earned, through actions, through time.

"I know," she said softly. "I'm sorry, Izzy. I can't change what happened, but I'm here now. I want to be a part of your life, if you'll let me."

Izzy hesitated, her fingers still on the photo, before she let out a small sigh. "I don't know if I can just forget everything," she admitted, her voice barely above a whisper. "But I'm willing to try."

Sophia smiled, her heart swelling with gratitude. "That's all I can ask for."

Evenings passed into nights, and while the road to healing was not always smooth, Sophia found solace in the small steps they were taking. She spent more time with **Ethan**, encouraging him to open up, to share what was on his mind. At first, he resisted, his walls high and unyielding. But slowly, bit by bit, he began to talk more—about his dreams, his frustrations, and his fears.

One evening, after dinner, as they sat in the quiet of the living room, **Ethan** glanced over at his mother. "So... do you think you can really do this?" he asked, his tone skeptical but not unkind.

Sophia turned to him, surprised by the directness of his question. "Do what?" she asked gently.

"Fix everything," he said, his eyes meeting hers with a mixture of curiosity and doubt. "You've been gone for so long. How do you expect us to just pick up where we left off?"

Sophia paused, considering his words. "I don't know if I can fix everything," she admitted. "But I can try. I want to be here for you, for both of you. I don't want to keep running from the past. I'm not asking for us to go back to what we were. I just want to build something new, something better."

Ethan regarded her for a long moment, his expression unreadable. Then, after what felt like an eternity, he shrugged. "I guess that's all we can do, huh?"

Sophia smiled softly, feeling a small weight lift from her shoulders. "Yeah. All we can do is try."

The weeks that followed were filled with moments of quiet rebuilding. There were still challenges, still times when old wounds flared up and the silence between them felt heavier than before. But through it all, Sophia learned something important: healing wasn't a linear process. It was messy, uncertain, and slow, but it was still possible.

And every time she felt like giving up, she looked at **James**, **Izzy**, and **Ethan**, and she realized that she was already part of something again. The pieces might not fit together perfectly, but they were beginning to take shape. And that was enough for now.

As the sun set over the horizon one evening, casting a warm golden light through the windows of the house, Sophia sat with her family, quietly content. They weren't whole yet, but they were together—and for the first time in a long time, that felt like enough.

The next few months came and went in a blur of mundane moments that carried an unexpected weight. With each passing day, the house became more like a home again, not in the sense of perfection, but in the small, simple ways that signaled progress. They no longer sat in the same silence, or tiptoed around each other, afraid to speak of the past. Instead, they started to find their rhythm again—awkward at first, but steady, like a broken instrument learning to play a new tune.

Sophia's role in their lives had shifted. She wasn't just the absent mother trying to find her place back in their world; she was also someone who had to confront the choices she made, the way her absence had shaped them all. It wasn't always easy. There were days when it felt like everything was falling apart, and she wasn't sure if she had the strength to hold it all together.

Yet, there was something about the quiet support they gave each other that made her believe they could rebuild, even if it was one step at a time. **Izzy** had her moments of coldness, her shields built high whenever they ventured into the more personal territory. But there were other times, in the late hours of the evening, when she would sit with her mother, sharing small, but telling glances that carried a warmth Sophia had longed for.

Ethan's humor, once his armor, began to soften. He still made light of difficult conversations, but there were moments when his eyes softened, his voice quieter as he asked questions about the years she had spent away from them. He didn't press her for details—he didn't need to. It was as if he was testing the waters, letting her come to him at her own pace.

One evening, as the family gathered around the dinner table, something changed. **James** spoke more than he usually did, his words flowing easily, comfortable in the familiarity of family that had been so elusive for so long. He asked about Sophia's plans for the future, and for the first time, Sophia felt a glimmer of hope.

"I've been thinking a lot about what comes next," she said, pushing her food around her plate as she gathered her thoughts. "Not just for me, but for all of us. There's so much I missed, so many moments I can never get back. But I want to create new ones with you. I want us to have something different, something that's ours."

James looked at her, his expression unreadable. "What does that look like?" he asked, his voice steady.

Sophia thought for a moment, her fingers tapping the edge of her glass. "I'm not sure yet. But I know it's not about erasing the past. It's about taking the lessons we've learned and building on them."

Izzy, who had been quiet throughout the conversation, suddenly spoke up. "Does that mean you're going to stay?" she asked, her voice barely above a whisper. The question hung in the air, heavy and full of unspoken weight.

Sophia's heart tightened, but she nodded. "Yes. I'm here, Izzy. And I'm not going anywhere."

It wasn't a promise to fix everything. It wasn't a guarantee that things would be perfect, or even easy. But it was a start—a foundation upon which they could build. Sophia looked around the table at her family, each of them carrying their own scars, their own fears, but also a quiet hope that maybe—just maybe—they could make it work.

The rest of the evening passed in a quiet, almost comfortable silence. They finished their meal and talked about small, insignificant things—work, school, the weather—but for Sophia, it was a step forward. She could feel the distance between them closing, even if it was imperceptible.

As the night drew to a close, Sophia retired to her room, her mind racing with thoughts of the future. She had come back to them with a heavy heart, but also a willingness to change, to heal. And now, as she sat on the edge of her bed, she realized that it wasn't just her family who needed to change—it was her too. She needed to rediscover herself, to find the woman she had once been and the woman she had yet to become.

Tomorrow would be another day. Another chance to try again. But tonight, she allowed herself a moment of peace, the first real peace she had felt in years.

The days that followed were filled with small, yet significant moments. Sophia's return to family life was a quiet, ongoing process. Every morning, as the sunlight filtered through the curtains, she felt a new sense of belonging, but it wasn't easy. There were moments of doubt—times when she wondered if she could ever fully atone for the years she had missed, or if her efforts were enough to mend the wounds that had festered for so long.

But then there were the quiet victories—the evenings when the family gathered on the couch, watching a movie together, without the sharp edges of tension. Or the weekends when Sophia and Izzy would sit in the kitchen, baking together, the faint smell of vanilla and cinnamon filling the air. It was in these simple moments that Sophia saw the possibility of a future with them—one that wasn't defined by past mistakes, but by a shared commitment to rebuild.

One evening, as they all sat at the dinner table, **Ethan** brought up something unexpected. He hadn't spoken much about the past, but tonight there was a quiet urgency in his voice.

"You ever think about how things would have been if you'd stayed?" he asked, his fork paused midair, as if weighing his own words.

Sophia felt a knot form in her chest. She had spent so much time trying to move forward that she hadn't considered looking back. But now, as she sat at the table with her children—her family—she realized how much she had missed. Not just the years, but the moments that could have shaped them into something stronger. Something closer.

"I think about it a lot," she admitted softly, her voice betraying the vulnerability she often tried to hide. "But the truth is, we can't change what happened. All I can do is try to make things better now."

Ethan nodded, his expression serious. "I get that. I just don't want you to feel like you have to prove anything. I know it's hard, but we're not asking for perfection. We're asking for you to be here, now."

Sophia looked at him, her eyes searching his face for any sign of doubt. But all she saw was sincerity. For the first time in a long time, she felt a deep sense of relief. Maybe it wasn't about fixing everything. Maybe it was about being present, truly present, in the moment.

The conversation shifted after that, from the past to the present. They talked about their plans for the future, about the small dreams they hadn't yet shared. Izzy, who had always kept her thoughts close to her chest, spoke up about her ambitions. She wanted to travel, to see the world beyond their small town. Ethan spoke about his hopes for his career, and James, ever the stoic, shared a quiet desire to make their family stronger, to create something lasting.

As the evening drew to a close, Sophia felt a warmth spread through her chest. This was what she had longed for—the sense of connection that had once been so elusive. It was imperfect, messy even, but it was real. And it was hers.

She sat alone in the living room later that night, the soft hum of the refrigerator the only sound breaking the silence. The family had dispersed to their rooms, and she was left with her thoughts. She allowed herself to breathe, to reflect on how far they had come, and how far they still had to go.

But in that moment, she knew something. No matter the challenges ahead, no matter the doubts that would come, she was no longer an outsider. She had found her way back to them. And in doing so, she had started to find herself again too.

Tomorrow would bring its own struggles, of that she was certain. But tonight, there was peace. And for the first time in a long while, Sophia felt like she was exactly where she was meant to be.

The following weeks unfolded with a new sense of normalcy. While the shadow of the past never quite disappeared, it no longer defined the present. They learned to navigate their fractured relationships, step by step, taking each day as it came. It wasn't perfect, and there were days when the weight of everything felt overwhelming, but there was progress—small moments of connection that slowly stitched the fabric of their family back together.

Sophia spent her days trying to make up for the years she had lost, not just in grand gestures, but in the quieter acts of being there. She was present for the school events, the family dinners, and the late-night talks that stretched into the early hours. The children, especially Izzy, began to open up in their own time. It was as though they were slowly peeling back layers of old wounds, revealing the parts of themselves they had kept hidden for so long.

One evening, after a long day, Sophia found herself sitting on the porch with James. The sun was setting, casting a soft glow over the yard, and the air was cool and refreshing.

"You've changed," he said, breaking the silence. It wasn't accusatory, nor was it a compliment. It was a statement of fact.

Sophia looked over at him, surprised by his sudden words. "What do you mean?"

James shifted in his seat, his gaze lingering on the horizon. "When you first came back, you were... different. More guarded. Like you were afraid of what we'd say or think. But now? Now it's like you're actually here. Like you're finally letting us in."

Sophia let his words sink in. It was true. At first, she had been afraid—afraid of rejection, of not being able to repair the damage she had caused. But somewhere along the way, she had stopped holding back. Maybe it was the acceptance from Ethan, or the quiet understanding from Izzy. Maybe it was just the sheer weight of time that had forced her to let go of the past.

"I guess I had to learn how to trust again," she said softly, her voice almost a whisper in the fading light. "Not just you or the kids, but myself too."

James nodded slowly. "It's not easy. But you're doing it. We're doing it."

There was a long pause before Sophia spoke again. "Do you think we'll be okay? Really okay?"

James turned to face her, his eyes steady and sure. "I don't know. But I think we have a better chance now than we did before."

Sophia smiled faintly, the weight of his words grounding her. She didn't know what the future held, but for the first time in a long while, she felt like they could face it together. There were still scars, still unfinished conversations, but there was also the promise of something new—something they had the power to shape.

Later that night, after the house had fallen quiet, Sophia sat in the living room, her mind racing. It was easy to get lost in the uncertainty of what was yet to come, but she refused to let fear control her any longer. She had spent far too many years doing that.

She had made mistakes, yes, but those mistakes didn't have to define her. She had made a promise to herself—to them—that she would try. That she would fight for their family, no matter how difficult it got.

Tomorrow would bring its own challenges, but she was no longer alone in facing them. With each passing day, she felt the bond between them growing stronger, even in the quiet moments. They were learning to trust again, to love again, and in doing so, they were carving out a new future.

As the night deepened and the stars twinkled above, Sophia closed her eyes, letting herself rest for the first time in a long while. The road ahead was uncertain, but she had taken the first steps toward rebuilding everything that truly mattered.

The following month brought a series of changes, some subtle, some more pronounced. The weather turned colder, and with the shift in seasons came a shift in their family dynamic. The days felt shorter, the evenings longer, and the world outside seemed to slow down, as though mirroring their own journey toward healing. Sophia had found a rhythm—one that allowed her to embrace her role without the overwhelming pressure of perfection.

It wasn't easy, and at times, the past would rear its head, sending ripples through their seemingly calm waters. Yet, with each passing challenge, the family grew stronger. They had learned to communicate more openly, even about the difficult things—the things that had been buried under years of unspoken pain. Conversations, once filled with awkward silences, now carried a depth and understanding that surprised even Sophia.

One afternoon, Sophia took a walk with Izzy through the park, the crunch of fallen leaves beneath their feet the only sound in the crisp autumn air. They hadn't spoken much lately, their interactions mostly revolving around schoolwork and daily routines, but today felt different. The silence between them wasn't heavy or uncomfortable. It was simply... peaceful.

Izzy, glancing over at her mother, broke the silence. "I've been thinking about Dad," she said quietly, her voice almost tentative, as though testing the waters.

Sophia's heart skipped a beat, and she glanced over at Izzy. "What about him?"

Izzy looked ahead, her brow furrowed in thought. "I just... I don't know. He's different now, too. He's not as distant, like he used to be. I think he's trying, but I'm not sure how to trust that yet."

Sophia nodded, understanding more than she could express. She had seen the change in James too. He was trying, really trying, to be present in a way he hadn't been before. But like Izzy, there were still reservations—old wounds that had yet to fully heal.

"I think it's going to take time," Sophia said softly. "But we're all here. We're all trying."

Izzy didn't respond immediately, but the way she relaxed in that moment was enough. It was a tentative acceptance, a small step toward rebuilding the trust that had been broken.

That evening, when they all gathered for dinner, the atmosphere was light, though there was an undercurrent of something more—something deeper. They laughed, shared stories, and even argued playfully about who would take out the trash. It wasn't perfect, but it was real. And in its own way, it was everything they had been working toward.

Later, when the kids were in bed, Sophia and James sat on the couch, the glow of the television flickering softly in the background. They hadn't said much during dinner, but there was a quiet understanding between them now.

James shifted, glancing over at Sophia. "I don't know if I've ever really told you this," he began, his voice hesitant, "but I'm proud of you. Of how you've come back. How you've fought to be part of this family again. It's not been easy, and I know it hasn't always been easy for you, but..."

Sophia's breath caught in her throat, the sincerity in his words catching her off guard. She hadn't expected this, not after everything that had happened. She reached over, resting her hand on his. "I'm not perfect," she said quietly, her eyes meeting his. "But I'm here. And I'm trying."

James nodded, his thumb brushing gently over her hand. "That's all we need, Soph. We're all in this together."

The words settled between them, not as a promise of an easy road ahead, but as a commitment to continue moving forward. Together.

The days turned into weeks, and though there were moments of doubt, they were beginning to find their way. Their family, once fractured by years of distance and misunderstanding, was slowly becoming whole again. There were still scars, still silent battles that each of them fought, but there was also love—a love that was starting to grow in ways they hadn't anticipated.

Sophia often thought about how far they had come. In the beginning, it had felt like everything was broken beyond repair. But now, as she watched her children laugh together, as she shared quiet moments with James, she saw the potential for something new. Something stronger.

She had learned, through it all, that the return to family wasn't about erasing the past—it was about moving forward with it. Acknowledging the mistakes, the regrets, and the pain, but also finding space for growth, for healing. The road ahead would continue to be difficult, but now she knew she didn't have to face it alone.

And for the first time in years, she allowed herself to believe that they would be okay.

As the weeks rolled by, a sense of familiarity began to settle into their lives, like a blanket woven from shared moments and quiet understanding. The past, though never far behind, no longer cast its heavy shadow over every decision. There were still awkward silences, still unspoken words, but there was a new kind of hope growing amidst the remnants of old pain.

One particularly rainy afternoon, as the family gathered around the kitchen table, James brought up the idea of a trip. He had been hinting at it for a while now, but the timing had never felt quite right. The last few months had been filled with emotional upheaval and rebuilding, but now, things felt different. He could see that Sophia was ready, that they were all ready, to take a step forward.

"How about we go away for a weekend?" James suggested, his voice casual, but there was a glimmer of excitement in his eyes.

Sophia looked up from the bowl she was stirring, her brow raised in curiosity. "A weekend trip? Where?"

James smiled, leaning back in his chair. "Maybe the coast. We could use a change of scenery. Just the four of us. No distractions."

Izzy, who had been absentmindedly scrolling through her phone, looked up at the mention of the trip. Her eyes lit up with interest. "The coast sounds great. I haven't been to the beach in forever."

Ethan, always the more reserved of the two, glanced at his parents, then nodded slowly. "It could be nice," he said, his voice tinged with uncertainty but not dismissive.

Sophia hesitated for only a moment before agreeing. She knew how important it was for the family to have moments like this, away from the weight of daily responsibilities, where they could simply be together without the expectations and pressures that so often lingered in the background.

"Alright," she said with a soft smile, "let's do it."

The trip was set, and as the days leading up to it passed, there was an undeniable sense of anticipation in the air. It wasn't just about the change of scenery, but the change of pace. The promise of new experiences, shared memories, and the quiet possibility of letting go of the things that had held them back.

On the morning of their departure, the car was packed, and everyone was buzzing with the excitement of the unknown. It wasn't an extravagant vacation, but it was the kind of trip they had been longing for—a chance to reconnect, to share something outside the ordinary confines of their routine.

As they drove through the winding roads, the scenery shifted from the familiar urban sprawl to the rolling hills and stretches of green fields. The air, fresh and earthy, filled their lungs as they ventured further from the city. It wasn't just the landscape that changed; it was as though something inside them was also shifting.

For the first time in a long while, Sophia found herself truly present in the moment. There were no lingering thoughts of the past or worries about the future—just the here and now, surrounded by her family, heading toward something new. It was freeing in a way she hadn't anticipated.

When they finally arrived at the small beach town, the sound of the waves crashing against the shore welcomed them, a soothing melody that filled the air. The town itself was quaint, with little shops lining the cobbled streets and families walking leisurely along the beach.

That evening, as the sun dipped below the horizon, the family gathered on the beach. The sky was painted in shades of orange and pink, and the air was thick with the scent of saltwater. Sophia watched her children as they ran along the shore, their laughter echoing in the evening air. James stood beside her, his arm around her shoulder, and for a moment, she allowed herself to just be.

"I think this is exactly what we needed," Sophia said quietly, her voice soft, almost lost in the sound of the waves.

James nodded, his gaze fixed on the horizon. "Yeah, I think you're right."

They didn't need words to communicate anymore. Their presence, their shared experience, said it all. For the first time in a long time, they weren't just fighting for survival—they were enjoying the simple act of being together.

Later that night, as they sat around a small bonfire on the beach, the flames crackling softly in the cool evening air, Sophia realized how far they had come. The journey wasn't finished, but there was no longer the same sense of urgency. They had learned to take things one step at a time, to appreciate the small victories, and to find joy in the moments between the struggles.

"I don't know what the future holds," she said, her voice carrying the weight of the unspoken fears that still lingered, "but I know we can handle it. Together."

James smiled, his hand resting comfortably in hers. "I've got no doubt about that."

As the fire flickered and the night stretched on, they sat in comfortable silence, each of them quietly acknowledging the strength that had come from facing the past—and the hope that now, the future held something brighter, something worth fighting for.

The next few days were filled with simple pleasures. They spent their mornings walking along the beach, their toes sinking into the soft sand, the rhythm of the waves a constant, calming backdrop to their conversations. The afternoons were for exploring the town, visiting local cafes, and sitting in the sun, allowing time to stretch and expand in ways that had seemed impossible in their normal, busy lives. There was no rush. No deadlines. Just the luxury of being in the moment.

One afternoon, as they sat on a pier overlooking the water, Sophia felt a profound sense of peace. She watched as James and the kids tossed pebbles into the sea, their laughter carrying across the water. It wasn't perfect, but it was real. And for now, it was enough.

"I think this place is magical," she said softly, almost to herself.

James, who had been watching their children, turned to her, a small smile tugging at his lips. "It does feel like that, doesn't it?"

Sophia leaned back, closing her eyes for a moment, letting the cool breeze ruffle her hair. There was something about the ocean—the way it never stopped, the way it always found a way to come back to the shore—that seemed to mirror what she was feeling. After everything that had happened, after all the hurt and distance, they were finding their way back to each other.

"I'm glad we came here," she added, her voice barely above a whisper. "I didn't realize how much we needed this."

James sat down beside her, his presence a quiet strength. "We've been through a lot, Soph," he said. "But I think we're finally starting to understand that we don't have to have everything figured out. We just need to keep moving forward."

Sophia nodded, her eyes fixed on the horizon. "It feels different now, doesn't it? Like we're starting over, but with a new kind of understanding."

He chuckled, a soft, knowing laugh. "Maybe that's all we need—to start over, one step at a time."

As the sun began to set, casting a warm golden hue over the water, the family gathered together, sitting on the pier, taking in the last of the day's light. There was something sacred in this moment, something that felt both familiar and new. For all the chaos they had faced, there was still so much to hold onto.

Later that evening, as they sat around a table at a local seafood restaurant, Sophia looked at each of them—James, Izzy, and Ethan. They weren't perfect, and they still had their moments of doubt and frustration, but they were trying. They were trying, and that was enough.

"To us," she said, raising her glass, "for finding our way back."

James smiled, his eyes meeting hers. "To us."

Izzy clinked her glass with theirs, her usual deflection gone, replaced by something more genuine. "Yeah. To us."

Ethan, ever the quiet one, just nodded, a rare, but sincere smile on his face.

The evening passed in a warm glow, filled with stories and laughter. The world outside may have been uncertain, but here, in this moment, it didn't matter. They had found something far more important than answers—they had found each other.

As they left the restaurant, the town was bathed in the soft glow of streetlights, the night air crisp and refreshing. Sophia felt a deep sense of contentment as they walked back to their rented cottage. They didn't need to talk about the future right now. They didn't need to figure everything out at once. All they needed was to continue walking this path together.

"I'm glad we're here," she said softly as they approached the cottage.

James took her hand, his voice low and steady. "Me too."

And for the first time in a long time, Sophia felt the weight of everything she had been carrying begin to lift. It wasn't gone, and there were still challenges ahead, but the path felt clearer now. The future was still unknown, but they were facing it together.

The following morning, the sun rose over the horizon with a soft glow, casting long shadows across the beach. It was their last day in the small coastal town, and there was an unspoken feeling among them—a quiet understanding that the time they had spent together, free from distractions, had been a gift. It wasn't just the place that had healed them; it was the space they had given each other, the absence of expectation, the ability to just be.

Sophia stood on the porch of their cottage, wrapped in a light sweater, gazing out at the water. The waves rolled in gently, rhythmic and constant. The morning air was cool, and the scent of saltwater hung in the breeze. She could feel it in her chest—the way the weight of the past few years seemed a little lighter, like the ocean had taken some of it away. It wasn't magic, she knew that, but something about being in a place so vast, so unyielding, made her feel that anything was possible.

James joined her a moment later, his footsteps light on the wooden deck. "The kids are still asleep," he said, his voice calm and easy, as if he had shed his own burdens along with the years of stress that had clouded their relationship.

Sophia smiled faintly, turning toward him. "I'm going to miss this place."

He nodded, his expression reflective. "Yeah, it's been good for us. I think we needed it more than we realized."

They stood together in silence for a few moments, both lost in their thoughts, but neither feeling the need to fill the silence. Sometimes, silence between them wasn't uncomfortable. It was peaceful. They had learned how to exist in each other's space without always needing to fill it with words.

Finally, Sophia spoke, her voice quieter now. "Do you think things will stay like this? After we go home?"

James took a deep breath, glancing at her, his expression thoughtful. "I don't know. But I do know that we're stronger than we were before we came here." He paused, the weight of his words sinking in. "We can keep building on that. Together."

Her heart swelled at the simplicity of his answer, but it was also the most honest thing he could have said. It didn't offer false promises, didn't make any grand declarations. It was just the truth—they could keep moving forward, one step at a time, as long as they were together.

Sophia reached out and took his hand, her fingers intertwining with his. "I like that idea," she whispered.

They spent the rest of the morning walking along the beach, watching the sun climb higher in the sky, its warmth spreading across the sand. It felt like a symbol of what they had been through—something that had once been shrouded in darkness, now slowly coming into the light.

Later, after breakfast, they packed up their things, loading the car with the suitcases and bags. It wasn't a grand goodbye, but it didn't need to be. There was a quiet resolution in the way they moved, the way they shared this small task with a sense of unity that hadn't existed before. Even their goodbyes to the cottage were easy—no lingering sadness, no regret. Just a quiet acknowledgment that it had served its purpose, and now it was time to move on.

On the drive back home, the family was quieter than usual, but it wasn't a heavy silence. It was more of a contemplative one, as if they were all processing what the trip had meant to them. The road ahead still seemed long, but the weight of it felt different now, lighter somehow. There was a sense of peace in knowing that they had taken this step, that they had begun to rebuild—not just as a family, but as individuals, too.

The familiar sights of their neighborhood began to appear on the horizon, and as they turned onto their street, Sophia glanced over at James. He gave her a soft, reassuring smile, one that told her everything she needed to know.

"We're home," he said, his voice full of quiet determination.

She nodded, a smile tugging at her lips. "Home," she echoed, knowing that, for the first time in a long time, it truly felt like it.

They pulled into the driveway, and as they unloaded the car, the world seemed a little more manageable, the challenges that had once felt insurmountable now appearing smaller, more conquerable. The house stood before them, the same as it had always been, but somehow different, as if it had absorbed some of the warmth from their time away.

The future, though still uncertain, no longer seemed like an enemy. It was something to be met with cautious optimism, with the understanding that, no matter what came next, they had found a way to move forward—together.

The next few weeks unfolded with a kind of quiet resolution. Life resumed its familiar rhythm, but something had shifted. The small changes they had made—the conversations they'd had, the time they'd spent apart and together—had left an impression that couldn't be undone.

Sophia and James found themselves more attuned to each other, their interactions less weighed down by the misunderstandings and frustrations that had once seemed like permanent obstacles. They didn't need grand gestures to prove they had changed. It was in the small things—James taking a moment to listen, truly listen, when she spoke about her day; Sophia offering him a quiet smile when he needed it most. They were learning how to communicate in ways they hadn't before, not through words alone, but through actions that spoke volumes.

Izzy and Ethan had their moments of typical teenage rebellion, but even their moods seemed to soften. Izzy, who had always kept her emotions locked behind a veil of sarcasm, started to open up more. Her quiet conversations with her mother, late at night when the world was still, became more frequent. Ethan, ever the observer, began to show a side of himself that had been hidden beneath layers of defiance. He began to share more of his thoughts, his fears, his dreams for the future.

It wasn't perfect. They still had their disagreements, their moments of tension, but there was a newfound understanding. There was more room for compassion. The space that had once been filled with unspoken resentment was slowly being replaced with something more forgiving.

One evening, as they sat around the dinner table, the familiar sounds of clinking cutlery and muffled conversation filled the air. It was an ordinary evening, the kind that used to feel heavy with the weight of unspoken words. Now, it felt light.

Izzy, who had been unusually quiet throughout the meal, suddenly looked up from her plate. "I've been thinking," she said, her voice tentative. "Maybe... maybe we could try doing something as a family. Like, together. Not just, you know, dinner, but something more. Something fun."

Sophia raised an eyebrow, a smile tugging at the corners of her mouth. "What did you have in mind?"

Izzy hesitated for a moment, but then a spark of determination appeared in her eyes. "We could go hiking. There's that trail out by the park. I heard it's supposed to be really beautiful, especially at sunset."

James leaned back in his chair, glancing between his wife and daughter, his expression thoughtful. "Hiking, huh?" He raised an eyebrow, a playful glint in his eyes. "I never thought I'd see the day when you'd suggest something like that."

Izzy rolled her eyes, but there was a smile beneath it. "It's not like I'm trying to do something huge. Just... something we can all do together. I think it might be fun."

Sophia's heart swelled with a quiet sense of pride. She had always known that Izzy had a different way of showing affection, but this was something new. It was a step, and it was one that Sophia didn't take for granted.

"Well," Sophia said, setting her fork down, "if Izzy's in, I think we should all give it a try."

Ethan, who had been quiet for most of the conversation, looked up from his phone. "I'm in, I guess," he said, his voice dry but with a hint of interest. "It could be cool, I guess."

James smiled. "Alright then. A family hiking trip. It's a deal."

They finished dinner with a renewed sense of connection, the conversation flowing more easily than it had in a long time. Plans were made, and by the end of the evening, everyone was looking forward to the small adventure that was to come. It wasn't about the hike itself—it was about the effort, the willingness to try something new, something together. It was about showing each other that, no matter how far apart they had been, they were ready to start closing the distance.

The hike, when it came, was simple but meaningful. They made their way up the trail, the sun beginning to dip below the horizon, casting long shadows over the trees. There was a quiet joy in the way they moved together, each step bringing them closer, not just to the summit of the hill, but to each other. At the top, they stood in awe of the view, the sky ablaze with color, the world stretching out before them.

As they stood there, side by side, Sophia realized something important. It wasn't the grand gestures that defined their family. It wasn't the monumental events that made them who they were. It was the small moments—the quiet conversations, the shared experiences, the willingness to keep trying—that would hold them together. And in that moment, as they watched the sun set, Sophia knew that the journey they had started was just the beginning.

The days following their hike felt different, like a subtle shift had occurred that they couldn't quite put into words. The simple act of spending time together—away from the usual distractions—had left a lasting imprint. It wasn't the kind of transformation that could be measured in grand gestures or drastic changes, but in the small, almost imperceptible adjustments in their interactions.

James, who had often been absorbed in his work or distracted by the chaos of everyday life, started showing up more in the small moments. He'd leave his phone on the kitchen counter during dinner, a silent signal that he was present, not just physically but emotionally. He'd make time for the little things, like driving Izzy to school or picking up Ethan from a friend's house. It wasn't about being perfect—no one in the family expected that—but it was about being there. And that mattered more than any words could say.

Sophia noticed it, too. There were times when James would catch her eye across the room, his gaze filled with something softer than usual, something that spoke volumes. He didn't need to say anything. She could tell from the way he looked at her that he understood, that he was no longer just going through the motions but was actively trying to be present in their life together. It wasn't always easy, and there were still moments of frustration, of old habits creeping back, but the effort was real. It was enough.

Izzy, too, seemed more at ease. The tension that had once lingered between them, an unspoken barrier, started to dissipate. Their late-night talks became more frequent, and in those moments, Sophia realized that her daughter wasn't just looking for validation or advice—she was searching for connection. And in those conversations, they were finally starting to bridge the gap that had once felt insurmountable.

Ethan, though quieter, showed his own way of adapting. He wasn't the type to wear his emotions on his sleeve, but Sophia noticed the small gestures—how he'd hang around the kitchen when she was cooking, offering to help even if he didn't really want to. How he'd text her "goodnight" before bed, a habit he'd never had before. His way of showing he cared was different, more subtle, but it was there. And that was enough.

One afternoon, as the family gathered in the living room, Sophia found herself thinking back to the years they had spent apart, the years they had been drifting without even realizing it. She thought of the arguments, the silence, the way they had all retreated into their own worlds, avoiding the messiness of connection. And yet, here they were. No one had been perfect, and there were still plenty of challenges ahead, but for the first time in a long time, Sophia felt the weight of their shared history and the potential of their future.

She turned to James, who was sitting on the couch, idly flipping through a magazine. Their eyes met, and for a moment, neither of them spoke. There was a quiet understanding between them, a silent acknowledgment that they had come a long way.

"I think we're doing okay," Sophia said softly, breaking the silence.

James looked at her, his expression warm. "Yeah. I think we are."

It was a simple answer, but it carried with it the weight of everything they had been through. The journey was far from over, but for the first time, Sophia didn't feel alone in it.

As they sat there, in the quiet comfort of their shared space, Sophia realized that family wasn't about perfection. It wasn't about always getting it right, about never making mistakes. Family was about showing up for each other, about the willingness to try, to learn, and to grow together. It was about acknowledging that the journey wasn't always smooth, but that they would face it side by side.

And as the days went by, they continued to move forward, together. One step at a time.

The weeks that followed were a blend of ordinary moments and small triumphs, each one adding depth to the evolving bond they shared. Sophia noticed how the air between them seemed lighter now, as though the weight of past misunderstandings had begun to lift, inch by inch, like fog slowly dissipating with the dawn. They were still learning, still figuring out how to coexist in a way that respected each other's space while also coming together as a family. It wasn't always easy, and there were moments of tension, but those moments no longer felt insurmountable. They had begun to understand the importance of patience, not just with each other, but with themselves as well.

One evening, after the kids had gone to bed, James and Sophia sat together on the couch, the soft glow of a lamp casting a warm light over the room. It had become their ritual—a moment of quiet at the end of the day, where they could just be. No expectations. No rushing.

"I've been thinking," James said, his voice soft, almost hesitant.

Sophia turned toward him, intrigued by the rare openness in his tone. "What about?"

He shifted slightly, a look of uncertainty crossing his face. "About everything. About us. I know we've been through a lot... and I know I haven't always been the best at showing it, but I want you to know that I'm here. I'm really trying, Sophia. I think I'm starting to understand what it means to be a part of this... of our family."

Sophia's heart skipped a beat. She had heard the words before, of course, but there was something in his voice, something deeper, that made them feel different this time. It wasn't just about the words. It was about the conviction behind them.

"I know," she said, her voice steady. "I've seen it. I've felt it. And I'm trying, too. I think we're both learning how to do this... together. And it's not easy, but it's worth it."

James nodded, a small smile tugging at the corners of his lips. "I think... I think we've been so focused on what was wrong, we forgot to see what was right. We've got a long way to go, but we're moving in the right direction."

Sophia smiled back, her heart warmed by his words. There was truth in them, a truth they hadn't been able to acknowledge before, when everything felt so heavy, so fragile. Now, there was a sense of hope—quiet, steady hope—that they could rebuild, piece by piece. They didn't need to have everything figured out right now. They just needed to keep moving forward, together.

And in that moment, as the weight of the past began to feel lighter, Sophia realized that what mattered most wasn't the destination but the journey itself. They didn't need to be perfect; they just needed to show up. They needed to show up for each other, even when things got tough. And that, in its own way, was enough.

The next weekend, they decided to go on another family outing—a picnic by the lake, a simple way to spend time together without the pressures of daily life. The weather was perfect, the sky a brilliant blue with just a few clouds drifting lazily overhead. As they spread out the blanket and unpacked the food, there was an easy camaraderie between them, a comfort in the quiet rhythms of family life.

Izzy, ever the skeptic, raised an eyebrow as she took a bite of her sandwich. "This is... kind of nice," she said, as though admitting it was a struggle. But there was a glimmer of something in her eyes—something that wasn't there before.

Ethan, who had been uncharacteristically quiet, finally spoke up. "This isn't so bad, I guess." He glanced at his sister, a small smirk on his face. "I mean, I'm not exactly a nature enthusiast, but it's okay."

James chuckled softly. "Hey, you two could have worse hobbies than spending time with your old man in nature."

Sophia watched them all, her heart full as she listened to the banter, the familiar teasing, the ease of it all. It was these moments—these seemingly insignificant moments—that were building the foundation of something stronger, something lasting.

She realized, too, that they weren't just reconnecting as a family—they were rediscovering each other. They were learning how to live with their flaws, how to accept each other's imperfections, and how to be there when it mattered most. They were learning that the process of rebuilding wasn't about erasing the past, but understanding it and using it to create something better. Something real.

As they packed up to leave, their spirits light, there was a feeling of quiet contentment among them. They didn't need grand adventures to feel like a family. It was the small moments, the simple acts of connection, that made all the difference.

And as Sophia looked around at her family, she realized that they were stronger than they had been before. They were not perfect, but they were together. And that, she thought, was all that really mattered.

The following days felt like a continuation of something that had been set in motion long ago, but had only recently begun to take shape. The small, quiet moments of connection began to feel more significant, like the threads of a tapestry being slowly woven together, each piece adding color and depth to the story they were telling.

Sophia noticed a shift in herself too. For so long, she had been focused on what had gone wrong, on the years of frustration and silence that had built walls around her heart. But now, she found herself looking forward to the future with a new sense of optimism. She had learned that it wasn't about waiting for perfection—it was about accepting the imperfections and learning to live with them. It was about finding joy in the everyday, in the laughter shared at the dinner table, in the quiet conversations at night, in the simple presence of those she loved.

One evening, as they sat around the dinner table, James reached across and touched her hand, his fingers warm against her skin. She looked up at him, surprised by the gesture, but in that moment, she saw it—the commitment, the understanding, the desire to move forward together. It wasn't a grand declaration, but it was enough. It spoke volumes more than any words could.

"I'm glad we're doing this," he said quietly, his gaze steady. "This... all of it."

Sophia smiled, her heart full as she squeezed his hand in return. "Me too," she whispered, knowing that this simple acknowledgment of their shared effort was a milestone, a quiet victory.

Days turned into weeks, and the changes, though small, were undeniable. Ethan's reluctance to engage had softened. He was still the quiet one, but there were moments when he would join them without being asked, when he would open up about his day or ask questions about their plans. It wasn't a complete transformation, but it was progress, and that was enough.

Izzy, too, had begun to open up more, her usual guardedness giving way to a vulnerability she had kept hidden for so long. One evening, after dinner, she came to Sophia with something she had written. It was a poem, something she'd composed in one of her quieter moments, and it was full of raw emotion. Sophia could see the effort it took for Izzy to share it, the hesitation in her eyes, but also the trust. She had been so closed off before, but now, there was a crack in the wall that had once surrounded her heart.

"You don't have to share this if you don't want to," Sophia said gently, her voice reassuring. "But I'm proud of you."

Izzy looked at her, her eyes softening. "I know. I just... I wanted you to see it."

And in that moment, Sophia realized that they were all moving in the same direction. Each one of them, in their own way, was learning to trust again, to open up, to share. It wasn't about perfection—it was about being willing to be vulnerable, to take that step toward one another, no matter how difficult it might seem.

One Saturday afternoon, the family decided to take a short trip to the beach. The weather was warm, the sky a clear blue, and the sound of the waves crashing against the shore created a calming backdrop for the day. As they walked along the beach, the sun sinking low in the sky, there was a sense of peace between them. They didn't need to say much; they were just there, in the moment, enjoying each other's company.

Sophia walked beside James, their feet sinking into the sand with each step. She glanced at him, a smile tugging at her lips. "This is nice," she said softly, her words carrying the weight of everything they had been through and everything they had yet to discover.

James nodded, a quiet contentment in his eyes. "Yeah, it really is."

As the day wore on, they found a spot on the sand to sit and watch the sunset. The kids were playing in the distance, their laughter carrying on the breeze, and for the first time in a long while, Sophia felt a deep sense of gratitude. She was surrounded by the people she loved, by the family she had worked so hard to rebuild. They were far from perfect, but they were real. And that, she realized, was more than enough.

As the sun dipped below the horizon, casting a golden glow across the sky, Sophia leaned back, her hand resting in the sand beside her. She didn't need to have all the answers. She didn't need to know exactly what the future held. What mattered was that they were here, together, moving forward.

And that was enough.

The days following their trip to the beach were filled with a quiet sense of fulfillment. There was something about that day—the way the sun had dipped beneath the horizon, the peaceful stillness between them—that seemed to linger. It had been a moment of clarity, where everything seemed to fall into place, even if just for a while.

But life, as always, had a way of introducing new challenges. One morning, as Sophia sat at the kitchen table, sipping her coffee, she noticed the familiar silence in the house. James had left early for work, Ethan was still locked in his room, and Izzy had yet to come downstairs. The routine of their lives had become almost too predictable, and in some ways, it felt like the calm before a storm.

Sophia couldn't shake the feeling that something was brewing—something unsaid, something hidden just beneath the surface. It was as if all the progress they had made was about to be tested.

Later that afternoon, as she made her way to the living room, she found Izzy sitting on the couch, staring out the window. There was a heaviness in the air, a tension that wasn't there before.

"Hey," Sophia said, her voice soft. "What's going on?"

Izzy didn't immediately respond, but after a few moments, she spoke, her voice low. "I don't know. I just... I don't feel like myself lately. I've been thinking a lot about the past... about how much I've changed."

Sophia sat down beside her, her heart aching with understanding. "Change can be hard," she said quietly. "But it's also a part of growing. We can't stay the same forever."

Izzy nodded, but her gaze remained fixed on the view outside. "I know. It's just... there are things I've never really dealt with. Things I've kept buried because I didn't know how to face them."

Sophia's heart skipped a beat. She had always known that Izzy was carrying something heavy, something from the past that had shaped who she was. But hearing her finally say it out loud felt like the first step toward breaking down the walls she had built around herself.

"You don't have to face everything all at once," Sophia said gently. "You can take it one step at a time. And I'll be here, no matter what."

Izzy turned to her then, her eyes brimming with unshed tears. "I don't know where to start. I don't know how to make sense of it all."

Sophia took her hand, squeezing it softly. "You don't have to have all the answers right now. Just take it one day at a time. You don't have to do it alone."

Izzy's shoulders trembled slightly, but she didn't pull away. Instead, she leaned in, resting her head on Sophia's shoulder. And for the first time in a long while, there was a sense of relief in the air—a weight lifting, if only for a moment.

Later that evening, when James came home, he could sense the shift. The air felt lighter somehow, as if something had been spoken, something that had been hanging over them for so long. He wasn't sure what exactly had happened, but he could see it in Sophia's eyes, in the way Izzy carried herself now, as if a part of her had let go.

"How was your day?" James asked, his voice gentle as he approached Sophia in the kitchen.

"It was... good," she replied, offering him a smile. "Izzy opened up a little. It's a start."

James nodded, his gaze thoughtful. "I'm proud of her. And proud of you."

Sophia smiled, the warmth of his words reaching her heart. "It's a step, that's all. But it's a step in the right direction."

As they sat down to dinner that night, the conversation flowed more easily than it had in weeks. There was a sense of familiarity, but also a newness—a sense of discovery that made everything feel fresh. Even Ethan, who had been withdrawn for so long, participated in small exchanges, offering his thoughts on the meal or a story from school.

It wasn't perfect, and it didn't need to be. What mattered was that they were together, and they were learning how to be there for each other in ways they hadn't before.

And so, life continued, day by day, with all its quiet victories and small defeats. Sophia knew that the road ahead wouldn't always be smooth. There would be moments of doubt, moments of fear, and moments of pain. But she also knew that there would be moments of love, of growth, of laughter. And those were the moments that made it all worthwhile.

In the end, that's what family was—a collection of imperfect moments, strung together by love, held together by the unspoken bond that tied them all.

And for the first time in a long while, Sophia was at peace with that.

As the weeks passed, the family found themselves gradually slipping into a new rhythm, one that, while not perfect, felt more genuine than anything they had experienced in a long time. There were still difficult days—moments of tension between Izzy and Ethan, the weight of unspoken words between James and Sophia—but they faced these challenges with a sense of understanding that had been missing before.

Sophia watched as Izzy slowly began to open up more, revealing pieces of herself that had been hidden for so long. It wasn't easy, and there were days when the silence between them was heavy, thick with the weight of emotions neither of them knew how to express. But Sophia was patient. She had learned, over the years, that healing didn't come in neat, predictable steps. Sometimes it came in fits and starts, a few words here, a shared glance there, until finally, the walls began to crumble.

One Saturday afternoon, as they sat together in the living room, Sophia couldn't help but notice the subtle shift in Izzy's demeanor. She wasn't as guarded as before. There was an openness in her eyes, a vulnerability that had been absent for years.

"Mom," Izzy said, her voice hesitant but steady, "I've been thinking about what you said... about not having to face everything at once. And I realized something."

Sophia put down the book she was reading and turned her full attention to her daughter. "What is it, honey?"

Izzy took a deep breath, her fingers fidgeting with the hem of her sleeve. "I think... I think I've been holding on to a lot of things because I didn't want to let go of them. Even though they were hurting me, I thought I needed them to make sense of who I am."

Sophia's heart swelled with pride, and she reached out, placing a hand on Izzy's. "You're so strong, Izzy. It takes a lot of courage to realize that. You don't have to carry that burden anymore."

Izzy nodded, but there was a sadness in her eyes that Sophia couldn't ignore. "I'm still scared, though. I don't know if I can let go completely. What if I forget who I was before? What if I can't find myself again?"

Sophia squeezed her hand gently. "You're not going to forget who you are. You're just going to grow into a new version of yourself. One that's freer, and more at peace."

For the first time in a long while, Izzy smiled. It was a small, fragile thing, but it was real. And in that moment, Sophia knew that they were on the right path. It wouldn't be easy, but they were going to make it through. Together.

Meanwhile, James had been quietly observing these shifts within their family, sensing the change but unsure of how to contribute. He wasn't one to express his feelings easily, but there was a deep love for his family that burned quietly inside him. He knew his role was to support, to be the steady hand when things felt uncertain, and to show up even when he didn't have the words to fix everything.

One evening, as he and Sophia stood in the kitchen, preparing dinner together, he spoke up, his voice soft but serious. "I've been thinking about... everything," he began, stirring a pot of pasta. "About the way we've been handling things lately. I know I haven't been the best at communicating. But I want you to know that I'm here. I'm all in."

Sophia looked at him, her heart filling with warmth. "I know you are, James. I never doubted that."

He met her gaze, his expression earnest. "It's just that sometimes I feel like I don't know how to help. I don't know what you need, what the kids need."

Sophia smiled gently, her eyes filled with understanding. "You don't have to have all the answers. Just being here, showing up, that's what matters. And you've been doing that."

James nodded, his shoulders relaxing a little. "I'm glad. I just want to make sure we're all okay. That we're all moving forward."

Sophia reached out, touching his arm. "We are. Slowly, but we're getting there."

As they sat down to eat, the conversation flowed easily, the tension that had once filled their home now replaced with a sense of comfort. It wasn't perfect, but it was real. And that, in its own way, was enough.

The days continued to pass in this new, fragile peace. There were moments of laughter—simple, easy moments that reminded them of the joy they had once shared. There were moments of quiet reflection, when each of them retreated into themselves for a while, but they always returned, drawn back together by the invisible thread that tied them.

One evening, as they sat on the porch watching the sun dip below the horizon, Sophia felt a deep sense of gratitude. Their family wasn't perfect, and there were still many hurdles to overcome, but there was love. There was understanding. And for the first time in a long while, there was hope.

The days continued to weave together, each moment a mix of progress and setbacks. The family learned to navigate their newly defined relationships, taking small but meaningful steps toward healing and understanding. Izzy's openness was still fragile, but each conversation, each shared moment, strengthened the connection between them. She had become more willing to express her feelings, even when it was uncomfortable. There were still awkward silences, but they were no longer filled with the same oppressive weight they had once carried. Now, they seemed to be an invitation—an invitation to try again, to move forward, no matter how slowly.

James had begun to open up in his own way. Although he wasn't as emotionally expressive as Sophia or the children, he showed his love through action—fixing the leaky faucet without being asked, helping Izzy with her homework without hesitation, and simply being present, even when he had nothing to say. Sophia appreciated this in ways that words couldn't fully express. She had always known that James loved her, that he cared deeply for their family, but there was something special about seeing him act on that love, without needing validation or acknowledgment. His silent dedication spoke volumes.

One afternoon, after a particularly tense conversation between Izzy and Ethan, Sophia decided that it was time to take another step forward. The rift between the two teenagers had grown increasingly noticeable, and Sophia couldn't help but feel the weight of their distance. They were so alike, yet so different, and their inability to connect had created an invisible barrier in the house. Sophia knew that if they were to move forward as a family, they needed to address this tension, to give it a voice.

"James," she said one evening, as they sat together after dinner, "I think it's time we have a family meeting."

He looked at her, his brow furrowed in confusion. "A family meeting?"

"Yes," she said, nodding. "We need to talk. All of us. About where we're going, how we're feeling. It's been a long time since we've done something like that."

James didn't say anything at first. He had never been one for group conversations, preferring instead to deal with things in smaller, more manageable ways. But he saw the determination in Sophia's eyes, and he knew that she was right. They needed to do this.

"Okay," he said quietly. "When?"

"Tomorrow," Sophia replied, already planning the details in her mind. "After dinner. Everyone needs to be there."

The following evening, after they had eaten, the family gathered in the living room. The atmosphere was thick with anticipation, a strange blend of unease and curiosity hanging in the air. No one spoke at first, and the silence stretched long enough that it almost became uncomfortable.

Finally, it was Sophia who broke the silence. "I think it's time we all talked about how we're feeling. About what's been happening. And where we want to go from here."

Izzy shifted in her seat, her arms crossed tightly over her chest, her eyes avoiding everyone's gaze. Ethan sat next to her, fidgeting with his phone, clearly uninterested in the conversation.

Sophia took a deep breath, her voice gentle but firm. "I know that things have been difficult between you two," she said, looking at Izzy and Ethan. "And I know that we've all been struggling to find our way. But I want to remind you both that we're family. And families don't give up on each other. No matter how hard it gets, we need to find a way to understand each other."

Ethan glanced up, his eyes narrowed. "What are we supposed to say, Mom? That everything's fine when it's not?"

Sophia met his gaze with a quiet resolve. "No. I'm not asking for things to be perfect. But I'm asking for honesty. For us to be real with each other. We can't fix what we don't acknowledge."

Izzy finally looked up, her eyes betraying the frustration and sadness she had been holding inside. "I don't know how to fix it," she whispered. "I don't know how to make it all go away."

Sophia's heart ached for her daughter, but she understood. Healing wasn't a quick fix—it was a slow, painful process, and sometimes it felt impossible. But they had to try. "It's not about fixing it all at once, Izzy," she said softly. "It's about being willing to try. And to be honest about what we're feeling."

James, who had been silently observing, finally spoke. "I know it's hard," he said, his voice low. "But we can't keep letting things fester. We need to face them together."

For a long moment, the room was silent again. The weight of their words lingered in the air, and for the first time in a long time, it felt as though they were on the verge of something important.

Finally, Izzy spoke, her voice small but determined. "I'll try," she said. "I'll try to talk. But I don't know if I can fix everything."

"You don't have to fix everything," Sophia replied, her voice filled with understanding. "Just be honest. That's enough."

The meeting didn't solve all of their problems, but it was a start. It was a step toward rebuilding trust, toward opening up the lines of communication that had been shut for so long. It was the first time in a long while that the family had truly acknowledged the tension between them—and the first step toward healing.

As the days passed, they began to make small strides. There were still difficult moments—moments of silence, moments of hurt—but there were also moments of connection, moments of understanding, and slowly, the cracks in their relationships began to heal. It wasn't easy, and it wasn't quick, but they were no longer running from their problems. They were facing them together.

And for the first time in a long while, they were beginning to believe that maybe, just maybe, they could make it through.

The days following the family meeting were marked by small, yet significant shifts. The unease that had previously hung in the air like a constant storm cloud seemed to dissipate just a little. They still had far to go, but there was a noticeable difference in how they interacted with each other. Izzy and Ethan, though not yet fully reconciled, began to share more than they had in weeks. Their conversations were tentative, sometimes awkward, but they were trying. And for Sophia, that was enough for now.

James, too, seemed to be stepping up in his own way. He didn't always know the right words to say, but his actions spoke louder than anything he could have expressed. He took the time to help Ethan with his school project, offering quiet guidance and support. Ethan didn't always accept it right away, but James didn't back down. He knew that sometimes love wasn't about the grand gestures; it was about showing up, day after day, even when the other person didn't seem to want it.

One Saturday afternoon, Sophia suggested that they all take a break from their usual routines. "Let's go to the park," she said, "It's been a while since we did something together, outside of all the stress. Maybe some fresh air will do us good."

At first, there was hesitation. Izzy and Ethan both had other plans—Izzy with her friends and Ethan with his online gaming. But Sophia was persistent. She wanted them to have time away from the distractions, a chance to reconnect. After some convincing, they agreed. They packed a picnic, and the family set off to the park, the air cool and crisp, the autumn leaves swirling around them.

The park was peaceful, a quiet escape from the chaos of everyday life. The trees stood tall, their branches bare, but still full of character. The small lake shimmered under the sun, birds singing from the trees. It was a different world, one that felt distant from the tension and hurt that had plagued them for so long.

Izzy sat on the grass with her phone, scrolling through social media, while Ethan kicked a soccer ball around with James. Sophia found a bench by the lake and sat down, watching her family. For a moment, she let herself relax, to enjoy the beauty of the day. It felt like a fragile peace, but it was peace nonetheless.

Eventually, Izzy put her phone down and joined her father and brother in the game. It was a small step, but Sophia noticed. There was a shift in the air, a subtle but unmistakable change. They weren't fully there yet, not by a long shot, but for the first time in a long time, Sophia could see the possibility of something better on the horizon.

As the day wore on, they shared a simple picnic by the lake, the sound of laughter echoing in the air. Even the small moments—like Ethan teasing Izzy about her soccer skills, or James offering to take the soccer ball home to "practice"—felt significant. It was as if they were finally breaking through the walls they had built around themselves, the ones that had kept them apart for so long.

That evening, as they drove home, Sophia glanced at each of them—James at the wheel, Izzy with her earbuds in, Ethan leaning against the window. It wasn't perfect. There were still moments of tension, still unfinished conversations, but they were together. And for now, that was enough.

Over the next few weeks, they continued to make small steps toward mending their fractured family. Izzy and Ethan began to spend more time together, even if it was just sitting in silence or bickering over trivial matters. But those moments were different now—there was an underlying understanding, a willingness to be present for each other, even when it wasn't easy.

Sophia and James, too, were finding their way back to each other. It wasn't as simple as it once had been, and there were days when the weight of everything seemed almost too much to bear. But they were trying. They were talking more, communicating in ways they hadn't in years. It was a slow and steady rebuilding, one that would take time, but it felt real.

And as for Sophia—she had learned that, while it was important to face the truth and deal with the hard things, it was just as important to give herself grace. She had spent so much of the past year trying to fix everything, trying to be the perfect mother and wife, trying to hold it all together. But she realized now that it wasn't about perfection. It was about being present, being willing to try, and showing up for the people who mattered most, even when the journey was messy.

The road ahead would undoubtedly be filled with challenges. There would be moments of frustration, of doubt, of fear. But for the first time in a long time, Sophia felt hopeful. The path to healing wasn't straight, and it wasn't easy. But they were walking it together. And that, she knew, was enough.

As the weeks passed, the family slowly began to find their rhythm again. It wasn't always smooth—there were arguments, misunderstandings, and moments where old patterns resurfaced, but there was also something new. They were talking more, truly listening, and making space for one another's feelings. The silence that had once been so pervasive was slowly replaced with conversation, and although not everything was healed, there was a sense of progress.

Izzy's relationship with her mother, which had been marked by tension, began to shift. They had shared so many silent dinners, but now they could have conversations, small as they might have been. Izzy still held her distance at times, but Sophia could sense that her daughter was starting to let her guard down. It wasn't the same as before, but it was something.

Ethan, on the other hand, had become more open. He had always been a quiet child, but now he began to share more about his world—his thoughts, his frustrations, even his dreams. James, in particular, had found a new way to connect with him. The father-son relationship, always tenuous, had grown stronger. They spent time together, doing things that allowed Ethan to feel seen and understood, from working on small home projects to playing video games—something they hadn't done together before. Even in the most mundane activities, there was a new kind of closeness.

And then, there was James. Despite the quiet moments, Sophia could see him trying harder than ever to be present. The weight of the past had often kept him withdrawn, but now he was more patient with their children, more present in their lives. There was a tenderness in his actions, a softness in his words. Sophia knew he was struggling with his own doubts and insecurities, but he was showing up in ways that made her believe in their future.

Sophia, too, had changed. The emotional walls she had built around herself started to crumble. The guilt, the responsibility, the overwhelming need to fix everything—she began to let go of it piece by piece. There were days when she still felt the weight of all the things unsaid, but there was also a peace she hadn't known before. She allowed herself to lean on James more, to ask for help, to admit when she didn't have all the answers.

One evening, after a particularly difficult day, the family sat down for dinner. There were no grand gestures, no significant moments—just the quiet hum of ordinary life. Ethan had a funny story from school, and Izzy and James exchanged a teasing remark. For a moment, the family was just that—a family. In that space, Sophia realized something. They would never be perfect, but maybe that was the point. There was beauty in imperfection, in the messy, unrefined nature of love and family.

As the months passed, Sophia and James found their footing once again. They continued to rebuild, brick by brick, their connection strengthened by the shared moments, the quiet understanding that sometimes it was enough to simply be there for each other. They still faced challenges—there were days when the scars from their past felt too heavy to bear—but they faced them together, as a family. And that made all the difference.

For Izzy and Ethan, the road ahead was still uncertain. They would have their ups and downs, moments of distance and conflict. But the foundation had shifted, and Sophia had hope that, in time, they would find their way. After all, family wasn't just about the good moments—it was about sticking together through the hard ones.

Sophia sat in the living room one quiet evening, her family scattered around her. James was reading in his chair, Izzy was on the couch with her phone, and Ethan was tucked into a corner, playing a game. The house was full of life, in its own quiet, imperfect way.

Sophia felt a warmth spread through her—a sense of contentment, of knowing that they were exactly where they needed to be.

The journey ahead would never be simple, but in that moment, Sophia realized that the strength of their family wasn't measured by their perfection. It was measured by their willingness to love, to grow, and to be present for one another, no matter the circumstances.

And as she watched her family, she couldn't help but feel a deep sense of gratitude. They were far from where they once were, and though there was still a long road ahead, they had made it this far—together.

It was enough.

2. New Understandings

THE ROOM WAS QUIET, save for the occasional creak of the floorboards as someone shifted their weight. The tension in the air was palpable, like a storm about to break. Sophia sat across from James, her hands clasped tightly in her lap. The space between them seemed to grow with each passing second, as if the years of silence and misunderstandings had solidified into an unbreachable wall.

"James," she said softly, her voice tentative, as though testing the waters of a conversation that had been a long time coming. "Do you ever wonder where we went wrong?"

He met her gaze, his eyes tired but not unkind. There was something in them, though—an understanding that had been absent for far too long. He had always been the strong, silent type, a man of few words, but something about this moment felt different. It felt as if they were both standing at the edge of something, a precipice that could either lead them to a new chapter or push them into an abyss of regret.

"Every day," James answered quietly. He shifted in his chair, his fingers tapping against the armrest. "But I don't know where to start."

Sophia exhaled slowly, her shoulders slumping slightly. It had been years since they had talked like this, without the layers of anger or resentment clouding their words. Life had always been a series of expectations—his, hers, the world's. They had both played their roles, acting out the script they thought they were supposed to follow. But somewhere along the way, they had lost sight of each other.

"You know," she continued, her voice gaining strength, "we spent so much time chasing what we thought we needed. The career, the house, the perfect life. But we never really stopped to ask if that was what we wanted. What we *needed*."

James looked at her, really looked at her, and for the first time in what felt like forever, he saw her—not as the wife who had pushed him to the brink of exhaustion with her ambition, but as the woman who had once captured his heart with her laughter, her warmth, her dreams.

"I didn't know how to be what you needed," he admitted. "I thought if I just worked hard enough, if I could provide everything, that would be enough. But I was wrong."

Sophia's eyes softened, and for a moment, the years of resentment melted away. She had always known that he loved her in his own way, but love, she had learned, wasn't just about providing—it was about connection, communication, understanding.

"You were never alone in this," she said, her voice barely a whisper. "I wasn't asking you to fix everything. I was asking you to be with me, to be part of this journey with me. I wanted us to be a team. But somewhere along the way, I lost sight of what that meant. I pushed too hard. I... forgot how to *talk* to you."

The vulnerability in her words hit James like a wave, and for the first time in years, he felt a glimmer of something he had long thought lost—hope. Hope that maybe, just maybe, they could rebuild what had been broken.

"I never knew how much I needed you until I was afraid of losing you," he said, his voice thick with emotion. "I always thought I could handle it on my own, that if I did everything right, it would all work out. But I see now that I can't do it alone. I don't want to."

Sophia reached across the table, her fingers brushing against his. The touch was tentative at first, as if testing the waters of a connection that had long been neglected. But when their hands finally met, it was like the first ray of sunlight breaking through a stormy sky—warm, gentle, full of promise.

"I'm sorry," she whispered, her voice thick with emotion. "I should have seen you, too."

And in that moment, everything shifted. The years of silence, the unspoken words, the misunderstandings—they didn't vanish overnight, but they started to lose their power. What was left was a fragile but growing understanding that maybe, just maybe, they could start again. Not as who they had been, but as who they could be—together.

The silence that followed was not uncomfortable, as it once might have been. It was filled with something deeper—something more genuine than the words they had exchanged over the years. James squeezed Sophia's hand, feeling the warmth of the connection between them, a lifeline they hadn't realized they were both desperately searching for.

"I've spent so much time focusing on the wrong things," he confessed, his voice steady but laden with regret. "I thought success, wealth, all that... that was the measure of a man. But none of that means anything if you're not with the right person. If you don't share it with someone who understands you, who sees you, who stands by you when everything else falls apart."

Sophia nodded slowly, her eyes bright but shadowed with the weight of past mistakes. "I understand now," she said, her voice gaining strength. "I thought the same. I thought that if I could prove I was enough, if I could show the world I was strong, then everything else would fall into place. But I lost myself in the process."

They both sat there for a moment, reflecting on the unspoken years, the silence that had grown between them like an insurmountable wall. But it wasn't insurmountable. Not anymore. The understanding they had found in that brief exchange was just the beginning—a fragile bridge they could cross together, if they were willing.

"Do you think we can fix it?" Sophia asked, her voice barely above a whisper. She was afraid to ask, afraid to hope for something that might not be possible. But the question had to be asked.

James looked at her, his gaze soft but resolute. "I don't know," he replied honestly. "But I want to try. I want to rebuild what we had. Not just for the sake of our past, but for the future we can still have. If you're willing."

Sophia's heart gave a small leap, but she knew better than to rush into promises. They had both made mistakes—had both allowed their own insecurities to shape their actions and words. Yet, in this quiet space, there was a possibility. Not a guarantee, but a hope.

"I'm willing," she said, her voice trembling with emotion. "I'm willing to try."

They sat there for a while longer, not needing words to fill the space between them. There was no rush to fix everything at once, no expectation of perfection. They both knew that healing would take time, but for the first time in a long while, they felt like they were heading in the right direction.

"I think," James said after a moment, breaking the silence, "we've both been so busy living the life we thought we were supposed to have that we forgot to live the life we actually wanted."

Sophia looked at him, her heart full. "It's funny how we spend so much time chasing what we think we need, only to realize that it's the simple things we were searching for all along."

James smiled softly, a genuine smile, one that reached his eyes. "Maybe it's not too late to start over."

"Maybe," Sophia echoed. "Maybe it's just the beginning."

And as they sat there, hand in hand, the future no longer seemed so daunting. It was uncertain, yes, but for the first time in a long while, they faced it together—with new eyes, new understanding, and the shared belief that maybe, just maybe, they could find their way back to each other.

3. The Choice That Defines Us

EVERY DECISION WE MAKE, no matter how small it seems, carries the weight of an uncertain future. Some choices are simple, almost instinctual, and others echo in our lives long after we make them. But it is the defining choices, the ones that seem monumental, that carve deep paths in the soil of our existence, paths that we can never quite erase.

For **Sophia Collins**, the choice was made years ago, but she didn't realize it at the time. She thought she was simply doing what was expected of her: building a career, being a mother, a wife, a daughter. But the weight of it all had begun to press down on her, the relentless pressure to be everything to everyone, to uphold an image of a perfect life. Somewhere along the way, she had traded her own desires for the comfort of others' expectations. And now, standing in front of the mirror in her bedroom, the woman who stared back was unfamiliar to her.

James had watched it happen. He had seen his wife slip further and further away, her ambitions growing while her presence in their home shrank. He had made choices of his own—sacrifices for the sake of the family, for the sake of keeping the peace. He believed his work, his role as the provider, was enough. But it wasn't. It hadn't been for years.

Their children, too, stood at the edge of choices that would shape them forever. **Izzy**, the eldest, had always been the one to push against the boundaries, testing the limits of what her parents could accept. As a young adult now, she was becoming more of a stranger to them with each passing day, making decisions that defied everything they had taught her. **Ethan**, the youngest, was quieter, more observant, but no less affected by the cracks in their family. He didn't speak as much, but his silence was loud, a constant reminder of the rift between his parents and their expectations for him.

It was on an ordinary evening, one that began like any other, that the consequences of those choices began to unfold. **Sophia** found herself sitting in the living room, holding a glass of wine, staring at a life she had built with someone she no longer recognized. The phone buzzed in her hand—an invitation to a prestigious gala, the kind that promised further career advancement. But as she read the message, she felt a pang of emptiness. She had been invited to so many such events before, but each one only seemed to widen the gap between her and the life she had once dreamed of.

James walked into the room, his presence a silent weight. He knew she was slipping away, but what could he do? They had been together for so long, yet the connection that once burned so brightly between them now seemed like a fading ember, too delicate to rekindle.

"Do you ever wonder if this is all worth it?" she asked him, her voice barely above a whisper.

James paused, his brow furrowing as he considered the question. He had never thought to ask that himself. His choices, the sacrifices he had made, had always been about providing stability, about doing what he thought was best for their family. But what was best? And for whom?

"I don't know," he finally said, his voice tinged with uncertainty. "I think we're just... living. Getting by."

Izzy, who had been listening from the doorway, stepped into the room, her expression a mixture of frustration and sadness. "It's not enough, is it?" she asked, her voice sharp with the anger of youth. "All these years of pretending everything's fine when none of us are really happy."

Sophia looked at her daughter, her heart heavy with guilt. How had it come to this? She had wanted to protect them, to build a future they could all be proud of. But in doing so, she had failed to see the cracks forming beneath the surface, the quiet rebellion of her children, the silent resignation of her husband.

Izzy's words hung in the air, an unspoken truth that none of them could ignore anymore. The choices they had made—seemingly small and inconsequential at the time—had led them to this point, this moment of reckoning. The question now was not what they could fix, but what they would allow themselves to face.

Ethan, who had remained quiet until now, looked up from his book. "What if we just... stopped pretending?" he said softly, his words carrying the weight of someone who had been watching from the sidelines, waiting for an opening. "What if we started making choices for ourselves, not for anyone else?"

It was the simplest statement, yet it felt like the key to everything. Perhaps it was the key to the family's survival, or perhaps it was the beginning of the end. Only time would tell.

Sophia's hands trembled slightly as she set the glass down. For the first time in years, she felt the possibility of something new, something terrifying yet freeing. She looked at her family, at the people who had once meant everything to her, and wondered: could they, too, stop pretending? Could they each make the choice that defined them—not as a wife, a mother, a daughter, or a son—but as an individual?

In that moment, she understood. The choice was never about what they had done before, but what they were willing to do now. It was the first step toward a life they had all been too afraid to live, a life that would be shaped not by expectations, but by the courage to choose themselves.

Sophia sat there for a moment longer, the weight of the decision pressing on her chest. Could she really walk away from the life she had built? The thought terrified her, but at the same time, it stirred something deep inside—a longing she had buried for too long.

Her eyes flickered toward James, who was still standing by the door, lost in his own thoughts. The silence between them was heavy, thick with unspoken words. She had always believed they could work through anything together. But now, in this fragile moment, she wasn't sure. They had become strangers in their own home, bound by years of unaddressed resentment and unvoiced fears. Their relationship, once built on love and trust, had been eroded by time and circumstance. But was it too late to rebuild?

Izzy, who had crossed her arms tightly across her chest, spoke again, her voice softer this time. "You know, we don't have to keep going down this path. We don't have to keep pretending everything's fine just because we're scared of what might happen if we don't."

Sophia looked at her daughter, truly seeing her for the first time in years. Izzy had always been the rebellious one, the one who questioned everything. But now, there was a maturity in her eyes that hadn't been there before. It was as if she, too, had come to understand that the road they were on wasn't the one they wanted to keep walking.

James finally spoke, his voice tinged with frustration. "But what do you expect us to do? Leave everything behind? Throw away all these years of effort? Do you think it's that simple?"

There it was again—the fear. Fear of loss, fear of change, fear of the unknown. Sophia had heard it in his voice countless times over the years. It wasn't just about their relationship anymore—it was about their whole life, the life they had built around expectations and comfort. But the truth was, that life had never felt real. Not for her, and maybe not for James either.

"Maybe it's not about throwing anything away," Sophia said quietly, her voice surprisingly firm. "Maybe it's about finding something we've lost along the way. I don't want to keep living this life of just existing. We've stopped living, James. And that's what we need to fix."

Izzy nodded in agreement. "It's not just about you two, either. We're all part of this family, and we've all made choices that have led us here. But it's never too late to change, to choose differently."

The words hung in the air like a challenge. Sophia felt the weight of them sink deep into her bones. They were right. It wasn't just about her or James; it was about all of them, each one carrying their own burden of choices, regrets, and hopes for a future they weren't sure they could reach. But wasn't that what life was? A series of choices, each one leading them to a place they never thought they would be.

"I think we need to stop being afraid," Sophia whispered, more to herself than anyone else. "We need to stop fearing what might happen if we choose differently, and start embracing the possibility of something better."

There was a long silence before James finally spoke, his voice rough but sincere. "Maybe we can try. Maybe we can make this work. But it's going to take more than just words. It's going to take everything we've got."

Sophia felt a small spark of hope flicker within her. She wasn't sure if this was the beginning of something new or just another fleeting moment. But it felt different. It felt like the first step toward something real.

Izzy smiled faintly. "I think we're finally talking about what matters. That's a start."

Ethan, who had been watching quietly from the corner of the room, stood up. "We all need to make a choice, right?" he asked softly. "So, what's our next step?"

It was a simple question, but one that felt so important. The answer was unclear, but in that moment, Sophia realized that it didn't matter. What mattered was that they were finally willing to face the truth—the truth about their lives, their choices, and the possibility of change. They had finally stopped pretending.

Sophia looked around at her family, each of them standing in their own space, each with their own doubts and hopes. But for the first time in a long while, she felt the possibility of something real. Something that was no longer defined by the roles they had played for so long, but by the courage to choose for themselves, to choose to face the future together, whatever it might hold.

She stood up, her hands shaking slightly as she walked toward James. She reached for his hand, and this time, he didn't pull away. Instead, he squeezed her hand gently, as if to say that, yes, they were going to try. Together.

For the first time in a long time, Sophia felt like she was making the right choice. The choice that would define her. Define them all.

And as the family stood together, facing the unknown, they understood that the future was not something to fear. It was something to embrace, to shape with their own hands, one choice at a time.

4. Healing Wounds

THE WEIGHT OF THE PAST seemed to hang over their home like a thick fog, obscuring the clarity of their shared future. It wasn't just the silence between them that felt heavy—it was the unspoken truths, the quiet betrayals, the moments where their hearts had once been in sync but had now drifted apart. James sat at the kitchen table, his hands gripping a mug of coffee that had long since gone cold. His eyes were distant, searching for something he could no longer find in the room, in the house, or even in himself.

Sophia, moving through the house like a ghost, tried to focus on the small tasks she had set for herself. The clutter of everyday life had become both a distraction and a comfort—something to keep her mind busy, to avoid the conversation that had been inevitable for weeks. Her heart ached with every movement, each step leading her closer to the realization that their once unbreakable bond had cracked, and the pieces were scattered in places neither of them had dared to look.

The kids, too, felt the shift. Izzy, the older one, had grown quieter, her usual rebellious spirit replaced by a heavy melancholy that Sophia couldn't ignore. Ethan, always more sensitive, seemed to be retreating into himself, holding back the words he longed to say. Neither of them could pretend that the air in the house was the same anymore.

For months, there had been no fight, no loud confrontation. Instead, it had been the slow unraveling, the subtle withdrawal of affection, the avoidance of eye contact that spoke louder than any argument could. James had retreated into his work, buried himself in tasks that demanded his attention but never his heart. Sophia, too, had thrown herself into her career, using it as both a shield and a weapon against the growing chasm between them.

But now, sitting in the quiet of the house, each knew that healing could not happen without facing the pain they had both ignored for so long. They had built their lives on expectations—of success, of love, of what a family should be. But those expectations had proven to be fragile, and they now lay shattered in the wake of their choices.

Sophia turned from the counter and looked at James, her heart heavy with words she had never been able to say. The love they had once shared, the passion that had burned so brightly between them, seemed like a distant memory, something that belonged to a different time. But somewhere beneath the anger and the hurt, she knew that the desire to fix what had been broken still existed. She wasn't sure how, or if it was even possible, but the first step towards healing was acknowledging the wound.

"James," she finally said, her voice softer than she expected, "we need to talk."

He met her gaze, his eyes weary, full of unspoken regrets. "I know," he replied, his voice rough. "I've been avoiding it too long."

It wasn't a promise that things would be easy. It wasn't even a guarantee that they could find their way back to what they once were. But it was a start. And for the first time in a long time, both of them felt the faint stirrings of something resembling hope.

They sat in silence for a long moment, the weight of their shared history hanging between them. It was strange, this space they found themselves in—too familiar to feel new, but too distant to feel like home. For the first time in a long time, James felt the full force of regret. Not just for the arguments they'd never had, the silence that had become their language, but for the things he had taken for granted. The way Sophia's laugh had once filled the house with warmth. The way they used to finish each other's thoughts, their connection so effortless it felt like magic. Now, all of that seemed like another lifetime.

Sophia broke the silence, her voice barely above a whisper. "I don't know when it all started to fall apart. I thought... I thought we could handle anything, but somewhere along the way, we just lost each other." Her words were raw, exposed. She hadn't meant to say them out loud, but they slipped out like air escaping from a balloon, and there was no taking them back.

James nodded slowly, the weight of her confession sinking deep into him. "I've been thinking the same thing. But it's not just one thing. It's a thousand little things that add up over time, until you don't even recognize what you're holding anymore."

Her eyes filled with tears, but she quickly wiped them away, not wanting to appear weak. "I'm not blaming you, James. I just... I don't know how to fix it. I don't even know if I can." Her voice faltered for a moment, but she steadied herself. "I've tried, in my own way. But I don't think I've been honest with myself about what's been happening between us."

James leaned forward, his elbows on his knees, hands clasped together in thought. "I haven't been honest either," he admitted quietly. "I've been avoiding... everything. The truth. You. Me." He let out a deep sigh. "I've been so focused on fixing everything outside of us, that I forgot about what we need. What you need. What *we* need."

The realization hung in the air, as if it was a delicate thread that neither of them wanted to break. The foundation they had built their lives upon had cracked, but perhaps, just perhaps, they could rebuild it—piece by piece, if they were willing to put in the work.

Sophia took a deep breath. "We've hurt each other, James. We've both made mistakes. But that doesn't mean it's over. It doesn't mean we can't try to fix this. To heal." She swallowed hard, the emotion welling up inside of her. "But I need you to want it too. I need you to be here, to truly be here. Not just physically, but emotionally. Mentally."

James looked at her then, really looked at her, seeing her not as the woman who had once been his partner, but as the woman she was now—the woman who had carried the weight of their brokenness, silently, for so long. He saw the pain in her eyes, the weariness in the way she held herself, and it struck him in a way nothing else ever had.

"I'm here, Sophia," he said, his voice firm with a sincerity that he hadn't allowed himself to feel in years. "And I want to be here. Not just for you, but for us. For what we could still be."

She didn't say anything at first, just stared at him, as if searching for any trace of dishonesty, any glimmer of doubt. But all she saw was the rawness of his words, the vulnerability he rarely allowed himself to show. Slowly, a faint smile tugged at the corners of her lips. It wasn't a smile of victory or relief—it was a smile of cautious hope. It was a smile that said, *Maybe we can try again.*

"Okay," she whispered, her voice trembling slightly. "Okay."

And just like that, the first step toward healing had been taken. It wasn't a grand gesture or a dramatic confession. It wasn't even a promise that everything would magically fall into place. But it was a beginning. A chance for them both to confront the wounds they had inflicted on each other, to face the past with honesty and the possibility of forgiveness. For the first time in a long time, they allowed themselves to hope—not for a perfect future, but for one that was built on the truth of who they were and what they had shared.

The days that followed were not easy. Healing, after all, was never a smooth or linear process. There were moments when the silence between them felt too thick to cut through, when old habits crept back in, and they found themselves retreating to the familiar comfort of distance. But they were trying—slowly, cautiously, but they were trying.

Sophia began to notice the small shifts. James was staying at the dinner table longer, engaging in conversations he had once dismissed. He was home more often, not just physically, but emotionally. He asked about her day, really listened when she spoke. It wasn't a grand gesture, but it was progress. The foundation, once cracked beyond recognition, was starting to show signs of repair.

And James—he noticed it, too. He saw how Sophia's eyes softened when she looked at him, how the warmth that had once felt lost began to return in her touch. She no longer wore the walls she had built around herself; instead, she allowed him in again, even when it was painful. Even when the hurt felt like it might overwhelm them both.

But there were still moments, moments when the weight of their past would resurface. Arguments would spark over nothing—little things that had never seemed important, but now, in the rawness of their emotional exposure, felt like they could tear them apart again.

One evening, after a particularly tense discussion about a decision they had to make for their son, Ethan, they found themselves in the same place they had been so many times before—standing at a crossroads, unsure of how to move forward.

Sophia stood in the kitchen, staring out the window, her hands gripping the edge of the counter. The cool breeze from the open window blew gently, but it did little to ease the tension building in her chest. She had wanted so badly for everything to be perfect, for the healing to be quick, for everything to fall back into place as if nothing had ever been broken. But the truth was, healing didn't work like that. It wasn't a simple fix; it was an ongoing process, one that demanded patience and, most of all, time.

James walked in, his steps slow but deliberate. He didn't speak at first, just stood there, watching her. He knew she needed space, but he also knew that silence wasn't the answer. Not this time. Not anymore.

"Sophia," he said softly, his voice carrying the weight of unspoken apologies, "I know I messed up. I know I've hurt you. But I want to be better. For you, for us. I know it won't be easy, but I'm here. I'm really here this time."

Sophia closed her eyes, the words he had just spoken landing with a mixture of relief and sorrow. There was a part of her that wanted to pull away, to protect herself from the pain of more disappointment, but she couldn't. Not this time. She had waited too long for this, for him to truly see her, for him to truly *be* with her.

"I want that too," she whispered, her voice thick with emotion. "I want us to get through this. But we can't just keep pretending that everything is fine when it's not. We need to face everything—the good, the bad, the ugly. We need to be honest with each other. No more hiding. No more silence."

James nodded, stepping closer, his gaze unwavering. "No more silence," he agreed.

For the first time in what felt like years, they truly looked at each other—not as husband and wife merely going through the motions, but as two people standing together at the edge of something new. It wasn't perfect, but it was real. And that was all they had left to build on.

The conversation didn't end with a neat resolution. There were no promises of eternal happiness or guarantees that everything would be fixed by tomorrow. But there was understanding, a quiet recognition that they had both been lost and now, together, they had a chance to find their way back.

As the days passed, they continued to rebuild. They still had their moments of doubt, their flashes of frustration, but there was a subtle shift—a growing awareness that healing was a journey, not a destination. Each small gesture, each difficult conversation, was a step forward.

And slowly, piece by piece, they began to find their way back to each other—not as they once were, but as they had become, shaped by the scars of their past but determined to move forward, hand in hand, into whatever the future held.

The weeks that followed were a delicate dance. James and Sophia had learned to communicate in ways they had never had to before. The simple act of sitting down at the end of the day, sharing a quiet meal together, became a small but significant victory. They weren't perfect, but they were present. And that, for now, was enough.

Ethan, their teenage son, seemed to notice the shift, though he didn't know how to express it. He was quieter than usual, his sharp eyes watching them both with a mixture of curiosity and caution. He had grown used to the tension, to the unspoken distance that had lingered in their house for so long. But now, with his parents finding their way back to each other, there was a strange comfort in the air. It was the kind of comfort that came not from perfection but from the willingness to try, from the understanding that not everything needed to be fixed all at once.

One afternoon, after school, Ethan came home and found his parents sitting together in the living room. They were talking—no arguing, no awkward silences—just talking. Ethan hesitated at the door, unsure if he should interrupt. But there was something in the way they were looking at each other, something unfamiliar and yet so desperately needed, that made him feel like he could breathe a little easier.

"Hey, Ethan," Sophia called, noticing him standing in the doorway. "Come join us. We were just talking about what we can do to make things better around here."

Ethan stood frozen for a moment, his gaze flicking between his parents. He had heard these kinds of conversations before, but there had always been a sense of forced cheerfulness, as if they were pretending things could go back to normal. This time, it felt different. It wasn't forced, it wasn't a lie—it was real.

Slowly, he walked over to the couch and sat down, his eyes still warily observing them both. "So, what's the plan?" he asked, his voice quieter than usual.

Sophia smiled, but it wasn't the kind of smile that came from false hope. It was a smile that said they had no clear answers, but they were willing to figure it out together. "Well, we're not sure yet. But we're going to keep trying. That's the first step, right?"

James nodded, his expression earnest. "We're learning, Ethan. We're learning how to listen to each other. And we're learning how to be a family again. It won't happen overnight, but we're here."

For a moment, there was silence. Ethan shifted in his seat, unsure how to respond to the sincerity in their voices. But then, without thinking, he smiled—just a small, almost imperceptible smile—but it was enough. It was a smile that spoke of hope, of a future where the pieces could finally fall back together.

The evening passed quietly. They all stayed in the living room, talking about small things—school, friends, plans for the weekend. It wasn't the deep conversation that had been missing for so long, but it was a start. It was the kind of connection they hadn't had in ages, and for the first time in a long while, the house didn't feel so heavy.

THE SHIFTING BALANCE

That night, as James lay in bed, his thoughts wandered back to the conversation they had shared earlier. It wasn't easy, admitting the brokenness, facing the truth of how far they had fallen apart. But something in Sophia's eyes had shifted, and something in him had changed, too. They weren't fixed, not by a long shot, but there was a new kind of understanding between them. A new kind of space where forgiveness could live, where love could grow again.

As he drifted off to sleep, he felt a small glimmer of peace. It wasn't a perfect peace, but it was enough. Enough to build on, enough to keep moving forward.

And that, he realized, was the truest form of healing. Not perfection, not even complete restoration—but the willingness to keep trying, the courage to take one more step, no matter how difficult.

The following days brought with them a sense of cautious optimism. James and Sophia found themselves slipping into a new rhythm, one that required patience and understanding rather than quick fixes. There were still moments of tension, still small misunderstandings that sparked frustration. But instead of avoiding the discomfort, they learned to sit with it, to address it as it came rather than letting it fester in the background.

One evening, as they sat together on the porch after dinner, James turned to Sophia, his voice softer than usual. "I've been thinking," he began, his words tentative, "about how we got here. How we let things get so broken. I don't think I realized, at the time, how much I was pulling away. How much I was pushing you out. I'm sorry for that."

Sophia looked at him, her expression unreadable for a moment. She had heard the words before—he had apologized countless times over the years—but this time, it felt different. This time, it felt real. She could see in his eyes that he was not just sorry for what had happened but was acknowledging the pain he had caused.

"I know you are," she said quietly, her voice steady. "But I think, for a long time, I was pulling away too. Not just from you, but from everything. I thought if I built these walls, I'd be safe. But all I did was make it harder for us to reach each other."

James nodded, his gaze dropping to the ground. "I don't want us to stay in that place. I don't want to keep making the same mistakes. We both have our scars, but we don't have to keep reopening them."

Sophia reached out, her hand brushing against his. It was a simple gesture, but it spoke volumes. She was there, not just physically but emotionally, too. "We don't," she agreed. "But it's going to take time. And we can't rush it."

For a moment, they sat in silence, the sound of the evening wind rustling through the trees surrounding their house. The world outside felt calm, almost as if it were giving them permission to heal, to take the time they needed.

The next few days were filled with small, steady steps forward. James and Sophia attended therapy together, something they had avoided for years. At first, the sessions felt awkward—like trying to speak a language they had almost forgotten. But as time went on, they began to find a new way of communicating, a way that didn't rely on anger or defensiveness but on honesty and vulnerability.

Ethan, too, seemed to be adjusting. He still had his moments of resistance, his reluctance to fully engage with the changes happening in their home. But he was starting to open up, slowly but surely. He would talk to his parents more, sharing pieces of his day, his thoughts, his struggles. It wasn't the easy, carefree conversation they had once hoped for, but it was progress.

One evening, after a particularly emotional therapy session, they sat together on the couch, the weight of the day still lingering in the air. Ethan was sitting across from them, his face more relaxed than it had been in months.

"You guys...you really trying to fix things?" he asked, his voice cautious, but not as defensive as it used to be.

Sophia exchanged a glance with James, both of them knowing the answer. "We are," she said, her voice firm yet tender. "It's not going to be easy, Ethan. But we're trying. And we're not giving up."

James nodded in agreement. "No matter what happens, we're here for each other. We're a family."

Ethan looked between them, his expression softening. "I hope so," he muttered, almost to himself. Then, after a beat, he added, "Maybe we can do this. All of us."

It was a small acknowledgment, but for James and Sophia, it felt like a breakthrough. Their son, the one who had grown up watching their struggles from the sidelines, was starting to believe in the possibility of healing too. And that, in its own way, was a victory.

The healing process, they all knew, was far from complete. There would be setbacks, misunderstandings, and challenges ahead. But for the first time in a long while, they were no longer walking that path alone. They were walking together, each step a little easier than the last, each moment a little more filled with hope.

And maybe, just maybe, that was enough.

As the weeks stretched into months, the small victories began to accumulate. James and Sophia found themselves learning to navigate the complexities of their relationship anew. It wasn't always graceful. There were times when the old habits crept back—moments of defensiveness, silence, the familiar tension. But they were catching themselves now, recognizing the signs before they let things spiral out of control. They were choosing, every day, to be better than they had been before.

One weekend, they decided to take a family trip—a chance to reconnect outside the familiar walls of their home. It was an effort to build new memories, to replace the ones that had been marked by hurt and distance. They drove to the mountains, a place they had once loved to visit but had abandoned after years of growing apart. The drive was quiet, the landscape changing as they left behind the bustling city streets and entered the calm serenity of nature.

Sophia glanced at James as they drove, her fingers lightly brushing the edge of his hand. "It feels different, doesn't it?" she asked, her voice soft, almost as if she were speaking to herself.

James nodded, his gaze focused on the road ahead, but there was something in the way he looked at her that made her feel seen—really seen, for the first time in a long time. "Yeah," he said quietly. "It does. It's...like we're not the same people we were."

Sophia smiled, a flicker of something warm in her chest. "That's good, right?"

"Yeah," James replied, his lips curving into a small but genuine smile. "I think it is."

They arrived at the cabin they had rented, and the sense of peace was almost immediate. The air was crisp, the trees towering around them like silent sentinels. The quiet of the mountains settled around them, and for a while, they didn't need words. They simply existed in each other's company, in the stillness of the world.

That evening, they sat around a fire pit outside, roasting marshmallows and talking in the way that only families can—casual, relaxed, without the weight of old arguments or unspoken words. Ethan, despite his usual reluctance to engage, was laughing with them, his eyes twinkling in the firelight.

For a moment, it felt like they were whole again—like they had found their way back to a version of themselves that they had forgotten existed. It wasn't perfect, but it was real. And it was enough.

The night grew colder, and the fire flickered low, but they didn't feel the need to rush back inside. Instead, they sat together, watching the stars begin to emerge in the darkened sky. It was a peaceful kind of silence, one that spoke more than words ever could.

As the evening wore on, James looked up at the sky, his thoughts drifting. "I don't know what the future holds," he said softly, his voice just above a whisper. "But I think I'm ready for whatever comes next."

Sophia turned to him, her eyes meeting his in the dim light. "Me too," she said, her voice steady. "We'll face it together."

And for the first time in a long while, James believed her. He believed that they could face whatever came next, not as individuals struggling to survive but as a family willing to grow, to heal, and to move forward, no matter how uncertain the path ahead might be.

The road to healing was long, and it was still unclear how far they had come or how much further they had to go. But they were no longer walking it alone. And that, in itself, was a victory.

The days that followed their trip in the mountains seemed to carry a quiet momentum. It was as if the time spent away from the pressures of daily life had given them the space to breathe, to reset, and to look at each other through a clearer lens. James and Sophia found themselves rediscovering the simple joy of being in one another's presence without the weight of old wounds hanging over them.

Ethan, too, seemed to be shifting. His attitude had softened, and though there were still moments when he retreated into himself, there was an openness to his conversations that hadn't been there before. He asked more questions, listened with more attentiveness, and—most surprising of all—he started sharing his own struggles, his fears, and his thoughts. It was small progress, but it was progress all the same.

One afternoon, James and Sophia decided to take a walk in the park near their home. It had become a new ritual of sorts—a time for them to be together without distractions. They walked slowly, side by side, the sound of their footsteps muffled by the soft ground beneath them. The air was crisp, a hint of winter hanging in the breeze, and the park was nearly empty, save for a few people enjoying the last days of autumn.

"I've been thinking," James said, his voice carrying just the right weight of seriousness. "About everything that's happened, and everything we've been through."

Sophia looked at him, her gaze steady and curious. "What about it?"

He hesitated for a moment before continuing. "I think we've learned more than we realize. About ourselves, about each other. And about what we're capable of."

Sophia felt a wave of gratitude wash over her, the kind that came from knowing that James was truly seeing her, that he recognized the effort she had put in, the strength it had taken for her to heal alongside him. "It's not easy, is it?" she said softly. "Healing. But... I don't want to go back to where we were."

James nodded. "Neither do I. I don't ever want to forget this. Forget how we're fighting for this."

They paused for a moment, watching a family walk past them, the parents holding hands, their children running ahead. It was a simple sight, but it stirred something deep within both of them—a reminder of what they had, and what they could build again.

"I don't think I ever truly appreciated what we had before," James continued, his voice quieter now. "I was so focused on everything that went wrong that I missed the good things. The things that kept us together, even when it felt like we were falling apart."

Sophia smiled, her eyes softening. "I know. I think I did the same. It's easy to get lost in the mistakes, the regrets, but... it's the moments in between that matter the most. The quiet ones. The ones that say more than words ever could."

James stopped walking for a moment, turning to face her fully. His eyes locked onto hers, filled with sincerity. "I want to make those moments count. I want to be here for you, in the small things, in the quiet moments. I want to keep fighting for us, every day."

Sophia felt a lump form in her throat, her heart swelling with something unspoken. "I'm not perfect, James. And I know neither are you. But I think we can do this. We can keep going, even if it's one small step at a time."

They stood there for a long moment, simply holding each other's gaze, feeling the weight of their words settle between them like a promise. It wasn't a perfect resolution. It wasn't an end to the pain or the difficulties they would still face. But it was a beginning—a renewed sense of hope, a commitment to fight for the things that mattered most.

As they continued their walk, the world around them seemed quieter somehow, as though the universe itself was offering them a brief moment of peace. The path ahead was still uncertain, but for the first time in a long time, they felt ready to face it—together.

The healing process wasn't over, and it wouldn't happen overnight. But they had learned, in the most profound way, that the journey was worth it. That no matter how many wounds they carried, no matter how long it took, they could heal—if they chose to. And if they continued to choose each other, day after day.

The weeks following that quiet afternoon walk were filled with steady progress, though not without their moments of doubt. Healing wasn't linear; it came in waves, some days calmer than others. But each day, they chose to meet those challenges together, not as two people merely surviving, but as a couple actively rebuilding.

James continued to work on his own emotional growth. He spent more time reflecting on the past, not just the mistakes but also the moments when he had felt love—love that was genuine and deep, even in its imperfect forms. There were times when the weight of everything seemed overwhelming, when he doubted whether they could truly move beyond the scars of their past. But then Sophia would say something, or Ethan would share a rare moment of vulnerability, and he'd be reminded of how far they had come.

Sophia, too, was healing. She had moments when the fear of losing everything resurfaced, the memories of the past creeping back like shadows. But the difference now was that she could acknowledge those fears without letting them consume her. She had learned how to express herself more clearly, how to ask for what she needed without the shame that used to accompany such requests. The quiet strength she had always carried within her began to surface in new ways. She found herself taking more chances—opening up more, loving more freely, even when it felt risky.

One evening, as the family gathered for dinner, Ethan unexpectedly spoke up. It wasn't much, just a simple comment, but it marked a shift. "This is... nice," he said, looking around the table at his parents. "It's been a while since we all just sat together like this."

Sophia glanced at James, her heart swelling with emotion. She could see it—the slow, steady change in Ethan. He was opening up, piece by piece, just like they were. And that realization made everything they had fought for worth it.

"We're getting better, aren't we?" James said quietly, almost to himself, as he passed the mashed potatoes to Ethan.

Sophia smiled, her eyes meeting his. "We are. It's not perfect, but it's real. And that's enough."

Later that evening, as they sat together on the couch, the warmth of the room wrapping around them, James reached for Sophia's hand. There was a moment of silence between them, but it wasn't uncomfortable. It was a silence that spoke of understanding, of shared experiences, of love that had been tested and found to be resilient.

"I used to think that love meant never having to go through pain," James said softly, his thumb brushing over her hand. "But now, I think love is about choosing to keep going, even when it's hard."

Sophia nodded, squeezing his hand. "I agree. We're learning that every day. And maybe that's the truest form of love."

James smiled, his gaze soft. "Maybe. But no matter what, I'm here. I'm in this with you."

Sophia felt her heart settle into a quiet peace. She had heard these words before, but now, they didn't just feel like words—they felt like a promise, something deeper than the surface of their conversation.

As they sat in the quiet, the weight of their shared history felt lighter. Not gone, not forgotten, but softened by the work they had put in—by the healing they had chosen. There would be challenges ahead, and there would be moments of doubt, but they had learned how to face them together.

And in that quiet moment, they both understood something that had taken them a long time to grasp: healing wasn't about erasing the past; it was about accepting it, learning from it, and choosing to move forward with hope, even in the face of uncertainty. It was about finding peace within the storm, knowing that as long as they had each other, they could weather anything.

The next few months passed with a sense of newfound calm. The echoes of the past were still there, occasionally whispering in the quiet moments, but they no longer held the same power over them. It was as if the tension that had once gripped their lives had finally begun to loosen, not all at once, but in slow, deliberate threads.

Sophia and James had learned how to speak to each other differently. Their conversations, once tense with unspoken resentments, were now marked by a gentler tone, a willingness to listen and understand. The walls they had built—guarded and fortified—were slowly coming down, one brick at a time. It wasn't perfect, and there were moments when old patterns crept in, but each time they caught themselves, they corrected course. They were, in a sense, relearning how to be together in a way that was healthy and sustainable.

Ethan's progress was just as remarkable. He had always been a quiet soul, reluctant to share his emotions. But over the months, he had begun to open up more, especially with his parents. He still had moments of withdrawal, times when the weight of the past seemed too heavy to carry, but they had learned not to push him. They gave him space when he needed it, but they also made sure he knew they were there when he was ready to talk. Slowly, Ethan began to trust them again.

One afternoon, as the sun was beginning to set, casting a soft orange glow over the neighborhood, Ethan asked James to join him in the garage. It was a simple request, one that might have seemed insignificant to an outsider, but to James, it felt like a step forward.

They worked on the old motorcycle in the corner of the garage, a project that James had started long before Ethan had shown any interest. As they tightened bolts and adjusted gears, the conversation drifted between idle chatter and more meaningful topics. Ethan didn't say much, but James could feel the shift—the unspoken understanding between them that they were no longer just father and son trying to co-exist. They were rebuilding their relationship, piece by piece, in moments like this.

"Hey, Dad," Ethan said suddenly, breaking the silence. "I was thinking... maybe we could take this bike out together sometime. You know, just the two of us."

James looked up, his hands still covered in grease, but his heart swelling with something unexpected. "Yeah? I'd like that, Ethan. I really would."

It wasn't a grand gesture, but it was everything. It was a sign that Ethan was finally willing to engage, to share moments with his father, to bridge the gap that had seemed so insurmountable not so long ago.

That evening, after they had finished working on the bike, the family sat down for dinner together. The atmosphere was different. There was a warmth in the room that had been absent before, a quiet comfort in knowing that they were no longer just co-existing under the same roof, but were actually starting to rebuild what had been broken.

"How was the garage?" Sophia asked, her voice light, but filled with curiosity.

Ethan smiled, something James hadn't seen in a long time. "It was good," he said, his voice steady. "We're making progress on the bike."

Sophia exchanged a look with James, her eyes reflecting the pride and hope they both felt. They had made progress too—together, as a family, in ways that were sometimes hard to put into words. But it was real. It was something they could feel in their bones.

Later that night, as they all settled into bed, James found himself thinking about the journey they had been on. He couldn't help but marvel at how far they had come, at how much healing had taken place, even when it hadn't seemed possible. There was no magical solution, no quick fix for the wounds they had all carried for so long. But there was something far more valuable: time. Time to heal, to grow, and to choose to love each other again.

And that, James realized, was enough.

The road ahead was still uncertain, and the scars of the past would never fully disappear. But as long as they continued to face it together, there was nothing they couldn't overcome.

The days that followed carried with them the promise of a new chapter. There was a subtle but undeniable change in the way they all interacted, like the first warm breeze of spring pushing against the last remnants of winter. They were no longer tiptoeing around each other, afraid to say the wrong thing or provoke the past. The heaviness that had once plagued their conversations had begun to lift, replaced by a cautious optimism.

James and Sophia had begun to carve out time for themselves, too—moments where they could just be with each other, without the weight of everything else pressing down. They would take long walks in the park, or sometimes, just sit together in silence, their hands entwined. It wasn't always perfect, and there were moments when the tension would creep back in, but they had learned to embrace the imperfections. They understood now that healing didn't mean erasing the past; it meant accepting it and choosing to move forward anyway.

Ethan's transformation continued, though in ways that still surprised them. He was more present, more open with his feelings, but he also had moments when he needed solitude. James understood that now, recognizing that his son's silence didn't mean distance—it meant that Ethan was still processing, still working through everything in his own way. He had learned not to take it personally, to give Ethan the space he needed while still remaining steadfast in his presence.

One evening, as James and Sophia were preparing dinner, Ethan came into the kitchen, holding something in his hands. He seemed hesitant at first, but when he saw the curiosity on their faces, he spoke.

"I... uh, I made something," Ethan said, a slight nervousness in his voice. "I thought it might help."

Sophia and James exchanged a glance before looking back at him. Ethan handed them a small, framed picture. It was a drawing of their family, done in soft colors, with each of them smiling and standing together. It wasn't perfect, the lines a little uneven, but it was real. It was a gesture that spoke volumes, more than words ever could.

"This is... beautiful, Ethan," Sophia said, her voice thick with emotion.

James felt something stir in his chest, a mixture of pride and gratitude. "You did this for us?" he asked, his voice softer than usual.

Ethan nodded, looking down at the floor for a moment before meeting their eyes. "I thought it might help... to remind us of what we have. What we're building."

Tears welled in Sophia's eyes, and she pulled Ethan into a tight hug. "Thank you. This means everything to us."

James stood beside them, placing a hand on Ethan's shoulder. "You're a part of this, Ethan. Always."

For the first time in what felt like forever, the air in the room felt light, unburdened. It was a simple moment, but it was one that marked the beginning of something new. They were no longer just surviving the aftermath of their struggles; they were actively creating a new story, one built on understanding, love, and the willingness to rebuild what had been broken.

As the days passed, there were still moments of uncertainty—times when the past would surface, uninvited. But they had learned to face those moments head-on, together. They had learned that healing wasn't a destination, but a journey. And each day, they took one more step forward, hand in hand.

One afternoon, as the family sat on the porch watching the sunset, James turned to Sophia, his eyes filled with something deeper than gratitude. It was a quiet recognition of how far they had come, of the strength it had taken to reach this point.

"We've come a long way, haven't we?" he said softly.

Sophia smiled, her gaze drifting over to Ethan, who was sitting quietly beside them, lost in the fading light. "We have," she agreed. "But I think we're just getting started."

And in that moment, with the warm glow of the setting sun surrounding them, they all knew that the journey they had embarked on was far from over. But they also knew, with a certainty they hadn't felt in a long time, that whatever came next, they would face it together.

Together. It was the word that held them all together now, the word that had been missing for so long, but that now echoed in everything they did. It was a word that spoke of hope, of second chances, and of the strength found in vulnerability and love.

And as the last rays of sunlight faded from the horizon, they were ready. Ready for whatever came next, because they knew that together, they could face anything.

The weeks that followed were filled with small victories, the kind that didn't always make headlines but left a lasting impact. Ethan's laughter came more easily now, the kind of laughter that was free and unguarded, a sound they hadn't heard in a long time. His conversations with James grew deeper, more genuine, as they shared their thoughts on everything from motorcycles to life's bigger questions. It wasn't always easy, but there was something incredibly powerful about the way they both listened to each other, truly listened, without judgment or expectation.

Sophia, too, found herself rediscovering a part of her that had been buried under the weight of their past. There were moments when she caught herself smiling for no reason, feeling a warmth that wasn't just from the sunlight streaming through the windows, but from the way their home had changed. It felt less like a house and more like a place of refuge, a sanctuary built by their collective efforts. And it wasn't just the space around them that had changed. It was the space within them, the way they all began to understand each other's needs, fears, and desires.

One evening, while they were all sitting around the dining table, the conversation turned to plans for the future. James, who had always been the practical one, found himself talking about things that weren't so much about logistics but about dreams.

"What if we take a trip? A real trip," he said, looking at Sophia, then Ethan. "Somewhere far away. Just the three of us."

Sophia raised an eyebrow, the suggestion unexpected, but the idea seemed to take root in her mind. "Where would we go?"

James shrugged, a twinkle in his eye. "It doesn't matter. Somewhere we can just be. Somewhere that doesn't remind us of anything but each other. We've got to make memories that are just ours."

Ethan, who had been quietly eating his dinner, looked up, his interest piqued. "I think I'd like that," he said, surprising both of them. He had always been the one to shy away from change, from anything that felt too unfamiliar. But something had shifted in him, too.

A trip. A new adventure. It was the kind of idea that spoke of rebirth, of moving forward in a way that they hadn't done in years. It was a tangible symbol of the progress they had made, of the possibility that the future held. It was a promise of more healing, of more moments where they could just be—a family, without the weight of old wounds.

The next few days were spent researching destinations, each of them contributing ideas. Ethan suggested a quiet beach town, somewhere they could relax and disconnect from the noise of their daily lives. Sophia, ever the romantic, wanted a place with rich history, something that would feel timeless. James, with his love for adventure, dreamed of a place where they could explore, get lost, and discover something new together.

In the end, they chose a small coastal village in Italy. It wasn't a place known for its grand attractions, but it was beautiful in its simplicity. The kind of place where time seemed to slow down, and the only thing that mattered was the moment you were in.

As they booked their tickets and planned their itinerary, there was a sense of anticipation in the air, a feeling of excitement that hadn't been there before. They were preparing not just for a trip, but for the next phase of their journey—one where they could continue to heal, to grow, and to rediscover each other.

The day they left felt like a quiet milestone. There was no grand farewell, no dramatic departure. It was simply a family taking a step toward something new, something that would forever change the way they saw the world—and themselves.

The trip was everything they had hoped for and more. They spent their days wandering the cobblestone streets, exploring hidden corners of the village, and sitting by the sea, talking for hours as the sun dipped below the horizon. They shared meals in small trattorias, laughed at inside jokes, and found joy in the simplicity of just being together. It was a place that allowed them to leave behind the past and simply exist in the present, a gift they hadn't realized they needed so badly.

But perhaps the most profound moment came on the last night of their trip. They were sitting at a small table by the water, the last of the evening light casting a golden glow over the scene. Ethan, who had once been the quiet observer, spoke up.

"I think... I think I'm starting to understand," he said, his voice soft but certain.

James and Sophia looked at him, both of them sensing the weight of his words. "Understand what?" James asked gently.

Ethan looked out at the water for a moment before meeting their eyes. "What it really means to be a family. To really be together, without all the noise and the distractions. To just... be."

Sophia reached across the table and took his hand, her heart swelling with a mixture of pride and love. "We're glad you're here with us, Ethan," she said, her voice thick with emotion. "We're always here for you."

James nodded, his eyes glistening with unshed tears. "We're a team," he said simply. "Always."

And in that moment, under the vast Italian sky, they understood. They understood that the journey wasn't about perfection. It wasn't about fixing what was broken overnight or pretending that everything was okay. It was about showing up, day after day, even when it was hard. It was about the willingness to continue, to choose each other, to heal together.

The healing wasn't complete—nothing ever truly is—but it was real. And it was enough.

As the flight home drew closer, the family found themselves in a reflective silence, the kind that felt comforting after so much emotional growth. The beauty of the trip lingered with them, and it wasn't just the picturesque views or the rich food that had left an imprint. It was the time spent without distractions, the moments where they were allowed to be just who they were, without the weight of the past or the expectations of the future.

On the flight, they talked little, each of them lost in their own thoughts. Ethan stared out the window, his mind still on the endless horizon they had watched every evening as the sun set. The colors of the sky had reminded him of the way things could change, how even the darkest moments could give way to something more beautiful. The feeling of closure, however incomplete, was something he could hold onto.

Sophia leaned her head against the seat, her thoughts wandering to all the small conversations they'd had. The way she and James had found their rhythm again, the way they could sit quietly without the constant tension that had once defined their relationship. There was a new understanding between them now, one that didn't require words. It was in the way they smiled at each other across the room, in the way they found joy in the simplest of gestures.

James, for his part, had been quiet but thoughtful. The trip had given him a glimpse of what they could be, of the family they could become if they continued on this path of healing. His usual practical mindset had been replaced by something softer, a realization that there was more to life than fixing problems and managing tasks. Sometimes, it was about allowing things to unfold, about being present for the people you loved, even when you didn't have all the answers.

The airport terminal was bustling when they landed, and the familiar chaos of their everyday lives immediately came rushing back. But something was different this time. The noise, the rush, the responsibilities—it all felt distant, almost secondary. They had come home, yes, but they had also returned with a new sense of purpose. They were no longer bound by the old wounds that had kept them from moving forward. The past might still be a part of them, but it no longer defined who they were or what they could become.

As they stepped into the taxi that would take them back home, the city felt less oppressive, less overwhelming. The streets, though familiar, didn't carry the same weight they once did. The traffic wasn't a source of frustration but a reminder that life continued, that there were always new things to discover, new chapters to write.

Back at the house, the walls didn't feel as cold, the silence didn't seem as heavy. There was a sense of quiet peace that settled over the home, and though they knew the healing process wasn't over, it felt like the beginning of something lasting. The journey hadn't been easy, and it wasn't going to be easy in the future either, but they had learned how to walk through the storm together. That, in itself, was a victory.

In the days that followed, they continued their efforts to rebuild. It wasn't always smooth sailing—there were setbacks, moments when old habits crept back in. But now, when tension arose, they knew how to handle it. They talked. They listened. They respected each other's space and emotions. They learned to forgive, not just the other person, but themselves.

Ethan began to open up more, sharing his thoughts with both Sophia and James. He wasn't afraid to show vulnerability anymore, and the trust that had once felt fragile was now something solid, something he could rely on. There were still days when the shadows of the past lingered, but they no longer held him captive.

Sophia and James found themselves having more meaningful conversations, not just about their relationship but about the world around them. They learned to dream together again, to create a vision for their future that wasn't burdened by the past. They were partners, not just in the challenges of life, but in the joy of simply being.

And so, life moved on, with its ups and downs, its victories and defeats. But in the spaces between the chaos, they found something worth holding onto: a sense of peace, a sense of family, and the knowledge that no matter what, they would face it together.

Chapter 10: The Shifting Balance

1. A Family Reborn

The silence that had settled over the Collins-Carter household was heavier than any words left unsaid. It wasn't the quiet of peace, but the kind that comes after a storm—when everything has been uprooted, and there's no certainty about where things will land. Yet, as the dust began to settle, there was a subtle shift in the air. It was as though the family, once so fragmented, was slowly finding its way back to each other—one small gesture at a time.

Sophia sat at the kitchen table, staring out the window at the rain that was beginning to taper off. She hadn't been sure, for the longest time, if they would make it back from the brink. She had been so focused on building her career, on proving to herself and the world that she could do it all, that somewhere along the way, she had lost sight of what truly mattered—her family.

The past months had been a whirlwind. The cracks that had long been hidden beneath the surface of their relationships had deepened, but they hadn't shattered entirely. Not yet. As she ran a hand through her hair, she couldn't help but think about how fragile it all was—the love, the trust, the connection between them. Had they really been close, or had it all been an illusion, a picture-perfect family built on expectations rather than understanding?

"Mom?" came the soft voice of her son, Ethan. He was standing in the doorway, hesitant but determined. His eyes, so much like her own, were filled with something she hadn't seen in a while—hope.

Sophia smiled, the warmth in her chest both a relief and a reminder of how far they still had to go. "Hey, Ethan," she said softly, gesturing for him to join her at the table. "How was your day?"

He sat down, his usual energy replaced by a quiet maturity. The events of the past few months had changed them all, not just in their relationships with each other but in how they saw themselves. Ethan, always the peacemaker, had matured faster than she had anticipated. His once-innocent outlook had been replaced with a quiet wisdom, as though he understood more about the world than anyone could have imagined.

"It was good," he said, offering a small smile. "Izzy called. She said she's coming home for the weekend."

Sophia's heart skipped a beat at the mention of their daughter. Izzy had been away at college, trying to find her place in the world, and had distanced herself from the family in the process. The strain between her and James had been palpable ever since. Sophia wasn't sure what to expect from their reunion—whether it would be a warm embrace or the awkward tension that often lingered after long absences.

"That's wonderful," Sophia said, though her voice betrayed a hint of uncertainty. The last time they had all been together under one roof had felt like a lifetime ago.

As if reading her thoughts, Ethan added, "I think she's been thinking a lot about us. About everything that's happened."

Sophia nodded slowly, the weight of his words sinking in. They had all been living in their own worlds, disconnected from one another in ways they hadn't fully realized. But now, as they all began to come back together, there was a sense of urgency, as though the time for healing was quickly running out.

Later that evening, the sound of the front door opening was followed by the familiar sound of footsteps—a sound that had been missing for too long. Sophia looked up to see Izzy standing in the doorway, her expression guarded, as though she was unsure of how to re-enter this space that had once been hers.

"Izzy," Sophia said softly, her heart swelling with emotion. The girl she had raised, the one who had once clung to her every word, was now a young woman, standing on the threshold of something new. "It's so good to see you."

Izzy's eyes softened, and for a moment, the distance between them seemed to vanish. "I missed you, Mom," she said quietly, stepping into the embrace. The tension that had gripped Sophia's chest for months slowly began to lift, as though the simple act of holding her daughter again was enough to start mending the pieces of their fractured family.

"I missed you too, Izzy," Sophia whispered. The words, long buried under layers of guilt and regret, finally found their way to the surface. "We've all missed you."

This moment, this reunion, felt like the beginning of something new. But they knew it wouldn't be easy. Healing never was. There would be conversations to be had, forgiveness to be sought, and, most of all, a deeper understanding of one another to be built. Yet, despite the uncertainties, there was a quiet optimism that maybe—just maybe—their family could be reborn. It would take time, effort, and a willingness to face the past, but the possibility of a fresh start was enough to keep them moving forward.

Izzy placed her bag down, her eyes scanning the room. The house felt different, quieter, yet there was an undercurrent of something stirring—a new kind of energy, one that felt more genuine than before.

"I don't know how it's going to go, Mom," she said, looking directly at Sophia. "But I want to try. I want to be here again."

Sophia's heart ached as she nodded. "We all do. And we'll figure it out together."

As the night wore on and they all gathered around the table for a meal they hadn't shared in what felt like years, there was an unspoken agreement between them. The road ahead would be difficult. There would be moments of doubt, of pain, and maybe even frustration. But there would also be love—real love, built on honesty and understanding, and the willingness to rebuild what had been broken.

A family reborn, not in perfection, but in the quiet, messy, beautiful way that families truly are.

As the evening unfolded, the familiar warmth of shared meals and quiet conversations filled the room. The table, once a place of tension and silence, now became a sanctuary for laughter, however tentative at first. They hadn't all sat down together like this in months, and each moment felt like a fragile step toward something they weren't sure they could define just yet. But for now, it was enough to simply be in the same space, breathing the same air, surrounded by the presence of each other.

James, who had been quiet since Izzy's arrival, cleared his throat, breaking the comfortable silence. His eyes met Sophia's across the table, and for a moment, the old familiar ache between them resurfaced. Yet, there was something different in his gaze now—something softer, less burdened by the weight of past mistakes.

"Izzy," he began, his voice low but steady, "I'm glad you're here. I... I know things haven't been easy between us." He paused, swallowing hard. "I'm sorry for not being the father you needed. And for not being the husband Sophia needed. I can't change the past, but I'll do whatever it takes to make things right."

Izzy looked at him, her face unreadable. The years of tension between them seemed to stretch into the air, thick and almost tangible. She had never fully understood why things had fallen apart the way they had—why her father, the man who had once been her hero, had become so distant. And then, in turn, why her mother had allowed the distance to grow.

But now, as she looked at him, she saw something different—vulnerability. Not the kind of vulnerability that came from weakness, but the kind that came from facing the truth, however painful it might be. And in that moment, she realized that maybe, just maybe, they were both trying to change, to rebuild the bridges that had been burned.

"I don't know if I can forgive everything," Izzy said softly, her voice thick with emotion. "But I want to try, too. I want to give this a chance. I want to know you again. All of you."

Her words hung in the air, an unspoken promise to start anew. It wasn't a declaration of perfect reconciliation, but rather a fragile beginning, a recognition that healing would require time, patience, and, above all, effort from all sides. And that was something Sophia had come to realize over the past few weeks—healing was never linear. It wasn't about erasing the past; it was about acknowledging it, learning from it, and then moving forward with the strength to face whatever came next.

James nodded, his eyes brimming with gratitude. "Thank you," he said quietly. "That means more than I can say."

As they finished their meal, the conversation shifted, and for the first time in a long while, there were no uncomfortable pauses. They laughed about small things—Ethan's latest antics at school, the ridiculousness of a new family reality show they'd all watched together once upon a time—and slowly, the walls between them began to crumble. The familiar rhythm of their interactions began to resurface, albeit cautiously.

But there were still unsaid things in the room, lingering beneath the surface. Sophia could sense them, feel them in the subtle glances exchanged between her and James, in the way Izzy seemed to watch both of them, as though gauging whether they could truly make this work.

Later, after the dishes were done and the house settled into the quiet hum of the night, Sophia and James found themselves sitting together on the couch, the comfortable space between them no longer filled with unspoken resentments, but with an understanding that had taken years to build.

"I'm scared, James," Sophia admitted, her voice barely above a whisper. "Scared that we're too broken to fix. Scared that we've missed our chance."

James reached over, taking her hand in his. His touch was warm, familiar, yet there was an unfamiliar softness to it—one that felt like the beginning of something new. "We don't have to fix everything overnight," he said, his voice steady but full of emotion. "We just need to keep showing up. For each other. For the kids. We don't have to have all the answers, but if we're both willing to try... maybe that's enough."

Sophia nodded, her chest tight with emotion. "Maybe that's enough."

They sat in the silence that followed, not the uncomfortable kind, but one that was filled with possibilities. It wasn't a promise of instant perfection or a swift resolution to their past. But it was a start—one step forward in the direction of rebuilding something worth saving.

Across the hall, Izzy sat in her room, staring at the photo of their family that had once been a symbol of everything they had been. She reached out, fingers brushing over the edges of the frame, and for the first time in a long while, she felt the faintest stir of hope. Maybe, just maybe, this time, they could all come back together. And maybe, in the end, that would be enough to heal the broken parts they had carried for so long.

In the end, family wasn't about perfection. It was about love, patience, and the willingness to rebuild after everything had been torn apart. And in this quiet, fragile moment, they were reborn—not as the people they once were, but as the people they were becoming.

2. The Ties That Bind

THERE'S A QUIET POWER in family, a connection that threads its way through every moment, every glance, every touch. It's invisible, yet unbreakable—sometimes holding people together, and at other times, pulling them apart. These ties can be the foundation of love and support, or the weight of unspoken expectations, silently suffocating those caught within them.

Sophia Collins stood at the kitchen window, staring out into the sprawling garden that had once been a place of joy for her family. Now, it felt like a silent witness to all the things left unsaid, all the promises broken in the pursuit of something more. Her husband, James, sat at the kitchen table, his fingers wrapped around a mug of coffee, his gaze distant. They had long ago stopped talking about the small things—the things that mattered. Instead, they found themselves circling around the larger questions, the ones that no longer seemed easy to answer.

She thought about the ties that bound them—those vows they'd made all those years ago. At one time, they had meant everything. Now, they felt like a distant memory, a lifetime ago, a string of words that no longer held meaning in the face of their silence. There was love between them, but it had become a quiet, almost passive force. The passion they once shared had dimmed, replaced by something steadier, perhaps safer—but far more fragile.

James watched his wife, his expression unreadable. He could feel the space between them growing, and though he wanted to close the distance, he wasn't sure how. The weight of the years, the mistakes, and the regret weighed heavily on him. He had tried to be the provider, the protector, the man she needed. But somewhere along the way, in his quest to hold everything together, he had forgotten the most important thing: the very essence of what made them a family.

The ties that bound them had become frayed, weakened by time and neglect. Yet, they were still there, barely holding on, threading their way through every awkward silence, every half-hearted gesture of affection.

Sophia turned away from the window, her mind a whirlwind of conflicting emotions. She loved James. She loved their children. But somewhere along the way, she had lost herself. In the pursuit of success, of everything she thought she was supposed to be, she had forgotten the one thing that had once mattered most: the connection that bound them together.

"James," she said quietly, her voice trembling just slightly. "I don't know if we can keep going like this."

He didn't reply immediately, his gaze still fixed on his coffee. He knew the truth, had known it for a long time, but the words were harder to say than she realized. They had tried everything: therapy, late-night talks, weekends away. But nothing seemed to close the gap between them. Nothing could erase the distance they had put between themselves over the years.

"I don't know either," he said finally, his voice barely a whisper. "I don't want to lose you, Sophia, but I don't know how to find my way back."

The truth hung in the air between them, heavy and suffocating. The ties that bound them were tangled now, knotted with regret, with fear, with unanswered questions. And yet, despite everything, they both knew something still lingered in the silence—a spark, however faint, that refused to be extinguished.

The sound of footsteps in the hallway interrupted their moment. Izzy, their daughter, appeared in the doorway, her presence a reminder of everything they had fought for, everything they had built. She was a product of their love, their hopes and dreams, and yet, she too seemed to be drifting, pulling away in search of her own path.

"Mom, Dad, you both okay?" Izzy asked, her voice soft but filled with concern.

Sophia and James exchanged a glance, the briefest flicker of understanding passing between them.

"We're okay," Sophia replied, though the words felt like a lie, a fragile attempt to convince themselves as much as their daughter.

Izzy smiled faintly, though there was a sadness behind her eyes that Sophia couldn't ignore.

"We're not okay, are we?" Izzy said quietly, almost to herself.

The truth was that none of them were okay. But the ties that bound them—the love, the history, the shared memories—still held them together. They were fragile, but they were not yet broken. And as long as they were willing to fight, those ties had the power to heal, to rebuild, to mend the frayed edges of their lives.

But healing wasn't a simple thing. It would take time, effort, and the willingness to confront the unspoken truths that lay beneath the surface. It would require each of them to make a choice: to continue to drift apart or to find their way back to each other, to reclaim what had once been.

As Sophia and James exchanged another look, a silent understanding passing between them, they both knew that the journey ahead wouldn't be easy. But as long as they were willing to fight for it, perhaps the ties that had once seemed so fragile could become strong again. And maybe, just maybe, they could find their way back to the family they had once been.

3. The End of the Beginning

THE MORNING LIGHT CREPT through the curtains, casting soft shadows on the worn wooden floor of the living room. It was a quiet kind of day, the kind that felt like the world was holding its breath. The house, once filled with the bustling energy of family, now seemed distant, as if it too was processing the shifts that had taken place within its walls. Sophia stood by the window, gazing out at the familiar view of their garden, but today, even the roses seemed distant, their beauty muted by the weight of her thoughts.

It had been a long road to get here, and yet, it felt like they had only just begun. The events of the past few months had pulled at the very fabric of their family, revealing both the strength and fragility beneath. There were moments when Sophia had wondered if they would ever come back from the brink, if the fractures that had formed would heal, or if they would remain permanent scars.

James, standing in the doorway, watched her with a quiet intensity. He had always been the steady one, the anchor in their marriage, but even his stability had been tested. He had seen the changes in her, in the children, in the way they had all drifted apart before finding their way back. He knew there was no going back to the way things were, but perhaps that was a good thing. They had been living in a shadow of themselves, haunted by expectations, by the lives they had thought they wanted, and now, they were facing the reality of who they had become and who they still had the potential to be.

"Are you coming to breakfast?" James asked softly, his voice breaking the silence.

Sophia nodded without turning to face him. "In a minute."

He hesitated, but then crossed the room, standing beside her. The space between them felt both distant and intimate at the same time. There were no words for what they had been through, no easy way to sum up the journey they had taken. All they had were the moments between them—the quiet ones, the painful ones, and the ones that still held the promise of something new.

"We can't change what's happened," James said, his voice steady, "but we can change how we move forward."

Sophia's gaze shifted from the garden to him, her eyes reflecting the weight of all the unsaid things between them. "Do you really believe that?" she asked, her voice barely a whisper.

He nodded slowly. "I have to. We both do."

It wasn't just about rebuilding their relationship—it was about understanding that what had come before, the struggles, the secrets, the misunderstandings, were part of their story, but they did not define it. They had been broken, yes, but perhaps they could be something else, something better. It was a quiet realization, but it was the first step toward something different.

For the first time in a long while, there was hope in the air. It wasn't a grand, sweeping promise, but a small, steady flicker that things might be okay, in time. Sophia took a deep breath, letting the air fill her lungs as she turned back to the window. The garden, once muted, seemed to pulse with life once more, as if the world itself was beginning to bloom again.

She knew the road ahead wouldn't be easy. They still had their work cut out for them. But maybe, just maybe, they had reached the end of one chapter and were ready to begin the next.

The end of the beginning.

As Sophia turned away from the window, her gaze lingering on the family photos scattered around the room, a quiet realization settled over her. The journey had been long, and the path they had walked was neither straightforward nor easy. But now, with each passing day, there was a subtle shift—a softening of the edges where once there had been sharpness, where once they had all been so consumed by their own pain and pride that they had forgotten how to truly see each other.

James sat down at the kitchen table, the morning light spilling across the surface, illuminating the coffee mugs, the empty plates, and the scattered newspapers. It was all ordinary, nothing exceptional, and yet there was something deeply profound about the simplicity of it. A sense of normalcy that had been absent for so long.

Sophia joined him, taking her place across from him, her eyes tired but somehow clearer than before. There was no grand revelation or sudden epiphany that had sparked this moment—it had been a slow unraveling, a peeling away of the layers they had so carefully constructed over the years. And now, sitting together in this quiet moment, they both understood that they had reached a crossroads.

"Do you remember the first time we met?" Sophia asked, her voice soft, as if testing the waters of their past.

James smiled faintly, his eyes reflecting a moment of nostalgia. "I do. You were standing at the bus stop, your hair pulled back in that messy bun, wearing a coat that looked a size too big for you. I thought you were the most beautiful woman I'd ever seen."

She laughed lightly, the sound unfamiliar to her own ears. "You always said I looked like I was lost in the world."

"And you were," he said gently, his eyes holding a depth that only time and experience could bring. "But then, so was I."

The truth of it hit her harder than she expected. They had both been lost, each carrying their own burdens, their own dreams and fears, without ever truly understanding each other. They had been so consumed with their own versions of what life should be, they had forgotten to simply live it together.

They had built something, though. Despite the mistakes, the lies, the hidden fears, they had created a life—a family. A foundation that, though cracked and fragile, still held the possibility of becoming something stronger, something more authentic. It wasn't too late. It couldn't be.

"Maybe we've spent so long thinking we had to be perfect," Sophia murmured, looking down at her hands, "that we've forgotten what it means to just be real with each other."

James reached across the table, his hand warm against hers. "We don't have to be perfect, Soph. We just have to be honest. And we have to be willing to try. Together."

And just like that, the final thread of doubt, the last whisper of uncertainty, seemed to dissipate between them. They still had so much to work through, so many things unsaid, so many scars to heal. But for the first time in a long while, the future felt possible again. They weren't standing at the edge of a cliff anymore. They were standing at the edge of something new—a new beginning, built on the lessons of the past.

They weren't just surviving anymore. They were learning how to live again.

The end of the beginning was no longer a moment of closure. It was the opening of a door to everything that lay ahead.

4. What Lies Ahead

THE DAYS FOLLOWING their decision were a whirlwind of emotions, unspoken words, and decisions that seemed too heavy to bear. The road ahead was uncertain, a path veiled in both the promise of renewal and the haunting shadow of unresolved pasts. For Sophia, the uncertainty felt like a constant weight on her chest, pushing her to question everything she thought she knew about love, sacrifice, and the choices that had led her here.

James stood in the doorway, watching as Sophia carefully placed the last of the boxes into the trunk of the car. Her movements were deliberate, each one a reflection of the inner turmoil she had been carrying for so long. He could see it in the stiff set of her shoulders, the way her hands trembled ever so slightly as she closed the lid. There were no more words between them, no more promises. Just the quiet understanding that things had changed—irreparably.

"What happens now?" James asked, his voice quiet, barely a whisper in the heavy silence.

Sophia paused for a moment, her gaze lifting to meet his. There was a time when they would have talked for hours, exchanging thoughts and fears, dreaming of what could be. But now, those moments felt like distant memories, too fragile to hold onto.

"I don't know," she admitted, her voice barely above a breath. "I don't know what happens next, James. I just know that we can't keep pretending that everything is fine."

He nodded, though the motion felt mechanical, like a gesture that was meant to appease both of them, but didn't truly change anything. Neither of them had the answers, and the uncertainty lingered between them like an unspoken truth. They were standing at the edge of something new, something they couldn't yet define.

The drive to the coast was long and silent. The landscape outside the car window blurred into streaks of green and blue, the world around them moving at a pace that felt both too fast and too slow. Sophia couldn't help but feel like they were running, though neither of them had spoken of it. The weight of their past, the lies they had told themselves and each other, still hung heavy in the air. It would take more than just time for those wounds to heal; it would take a reckoning, a confrontation with everything they had avoided.

Sophia stared out the window, watching the horizon stretch out before her, feeling the tension of what lay ahead. There was no way to know if they would find peace, if they would find forgiveness. The path was open, but it was unclear where it would lead.

As they neared the ocean, the sound of waves crashing against the shore filled the silence, a rhythmic lullaby that seemed to echo her own restless thoughts. She had come here to escape, but she knew that no matter how far they drove, no matter how many miles they put between themselves and the life they once knew, they would still have to face the truth. It was waiting for them, just beyond the horizon.

James broke the silence with a question that hung in the air, too big to ignore. "Do you think we can fix this?" He didn't ask for reassurance. He asked because, like her, he was uncertain of everything. He had always been the one to hold things together, to fix what was broken. But this time, he didn't have the answer.

Sophia took a deep breath, letting the sound of the waves fill her senses. For a moment, she allowed herself to hope, to believe that maybe, just maybe, there was a chance for them. But that hope was fragile, like the delicate foam that washed up on the shore. The truth was, she didn't know. And maybe that was the first step—accepting the unknown, embracing the uncertainty.

"I don't know," she said again, her voice quiet but steady. "But I think we're finally ready to find out."

As the car pulled onto the empty beach, the sun dipped low in the sky, casting a warm golden glow across the water. It was the kind of beauty that made everything else seem insignificant, if only for a moment. But even in that brief pause, she could feel the weight of what had been, and the realization that the future was still unwritten. They had a long road ahead of them, but for the first time in a long while, it felt like they were no longer running from their past.

They were walking into the unknown together, side by side, ready to face whatever came next.

• • • •

Afterword

AS THE LAST PAGE TURNS and the final chapter of this journey comes to a close, the questions and emotions that linger are perhaps more telling than any definitive answers could be. Life, like the story we've just followed, is never truly about finding complete resolutions. It's about the journey—the mistakes, the lessons, and the growth that comes with them.

Sophia and James's story is not just a reflection of love, lies, and expectations but of the human experience itself. They found themselves at the intersection of past choices and future possibilities, unsure of where the road ahead would lead. And in that uncertainty, they discovered something profoundly important: the willingness to face what had been, to acknowledge the truths they'd long avoided, and to step into an unknown future, hand in hand.

Love is complicated. It doesn't always fit neatly into the boxes we try to place it in. There are no perfect relationships, no flawless resolutions. And yet, perhaps that's what makes it worth pursuing—the constant ebb and flow of compromise, understanding, and self-discovery. The very act of trying, of navigating through the lies and expectations, is what makes love real. It's in the imperfections where we find our strength.

The central question of the novel—whether it's possible to fix what's broken—remains as complex as the characters who wrestle with it. Can the past ever truly be forgiven? Can trust, once shattered, ever be rebuilt? Perhaps. Or perhaps not. What matters is not the certainty of the answer, but the willingness to move forward regardless.

As we close the book on this story, let us remember that the journey is never truly finished. Sophia and James may have found a new beginning, but their story is part of a larger, ongoing narrative that each of us contributes to in our own way. We, too, must face our truths, take our chances, and navigate the shifting balance of love, lies, and expectations that shape our lives.

In the end, life's most important lessons are not those we learn easily, but those we earn through struggle, growth, and the courage to face what lies ahead.

Milton Keynes UK
Ingram Content Group UK Ltd.
UKHW042034031224
452078UK00001B/136